MY FAMILY MIGHT be able to help me make my choice, if I could talk about my aptitude test results. But I can't. Tori's warning whispers in my memory every time my resolve to keep my mouth shut falters.

Caleb and I climb the stairs and, at the top, when we divide to go to our separate bedrooms, he stops me with a hand on my shoulder.

"Beatrice," he says, looking sternly into my eyes. "We should think of our family." There is an edge to his voice. "But. But we must also think of ourselves."

For a moment I stare at him. I have never seen him think of himself, never heard him insist on anything but selflessness.

I am so startled by his comment that I just say what I am supposed to say: "The tests don't have to change our choices."

He smiles a little. "Don't they, though?"

"Promising author Roth tells the riveting and complex story of a teenage girl forced to choose between her routinized, selfless family and the adventurous, unrestrained future she longs for. A memorable, unpredictable journey from which it is nearly impossible to turn away."

"This is one fast-paced read that sticks in your head for days after you put it down, both because of its video-game-like scenes and its thought-provoking premise."

"This gritty, paranoid world is built with careful details and intriguing scope. The plot clips along at an addictive pace, with steady jolts of brutal violence and swoony romance. Fans snared by the ratcheting suspense will be unable to resist speculating on their own factional allegiance. Guaranteed to fly off the shelves."

"With brisk pacing and lavish flights of imagination, **DIVERGENT** clearly has thrills, but it also movingly explores a more common adolescent anxiety—the painful realization that coming into one's own sometimes means leaving family behind, both ideologically and physically."

—NEW YORK TIMES BOOK REVIEW

"The depth and richness of Beatrice herself make this an accessible option for both sci-fi buffs and realistic fiction fans."

—BCCB

"Roth paints her canvas with the same brush as Suzanne Collins. The plot, scenes, and characters are different but the colors are the same and just as rich. Fans of Collins, dystopias, and strong female characters will love this novel."

—SLJ

"You'll be up all night with **DIVERGENT**, a brainy thrill-ride of a novel."

—BOOKPAGE

DIVERGENT

VERONICA ROTH

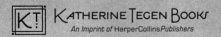

KATHERINE TEGEN BOOKS
An Imprint of HarperCollins Publishers

Katherine Tegen Books is an imprint of HarperCollins Publishers.

Divergent
Copyright © 2011 by Veronica Roth

www.epicreads.com

Library of Congress Cataloging-in-Publication Data
Roth, Veronica.
Divergent / Veronica Roth. — 1st ed.
p. cm.
Summary: In a future Chicago, sixteen-year-old Beatrice Prior must choose among
five predetermined factions to define her identity for the rest of her life, a decision
made more difficult when she discovers that she is an anomaly who does not fit into
any one group, and that the society she lives in is not perfect after all.
ISBN 978-0-06-202403-9 (pbk.) — ISBN 978-0-06-228985-8 (movie tie-in)
[1. Identity—Fiction. 2. Family—Fiction. 3. Courage—Fiction. 4. Social classes—
Fiction. 5. Science fiction.] I. Title.
PZ7.R7375Di 2011   2010040579
[Fic]—dc22   CIP
                                                                AC

Typography by Joel Tippie

14 15 16 17 18 LP/BV 50 49 48 47 46 45
❖
First paperback edition, 2012

To my mother,
who gave me the moment when Beatrice realizes how strong
her mother is and wonders how she missed it for so long

DIVERGENT

CHAPTER ONE

THERE IS ONE mirror in my house. It is behind a sliding panel in the hallway upstairs. Our faction allows me to stand in front of it on the second day of every third month, the day my mother cuts my hair.

I sit on the stool and my mother stands behind me with the scissors, trimming. The strands fall on the floor in a dull, blond ring.

When she finishes, she pulls my hair away from my face and twists it into a knot. I note how calm she looks and how focused she is. She is well-practiced in the art of losing herself. I can't say the same of myself.

I sneak a look at my reflection when she isn't paying attention—not for the sake of vanity, but out of curiosity. A lot can happen to a person's appearance in three months.

In my reflection, I see a narrow face, wide, round eyes, and a long, thin nose—I still look like a little girl, though sometime in the last few months I turned sixteen. The other factions celebrate birthdays, but we don't. It would be self-indulgent.

"There," she says when she pins the knot in place. Her eyes catch mine in the mirror. It is too late to look away, but instead of scolding me, she smiles at our reflection. I frown a little. Why doesn't she reprimand me for staring at myself?

"So today is the day," she says.

"Yes," I reply.

"Are you nervous?"

I stare into my own eyes for a moment. Today is the day of the aptitude test that will show me which of the five factions I belong in. And tomorrow, at the Choosing Ceremony, I will decide on a faction; I will decide the rest of my life; I will decide to stay with my family or abandon them.

"No," I say. "The tests don't have to change our choices."

"Right." She smiles. "Let's go eat breakfast."

"Thank you. For cutting my hair."

She kisses my cheek and slides the panel over the mirror. I think my mother could be beautiful, in a different world. Her body is thin beneath the gray robe. She has high cheekbones and long eyelashes, and when she lets her hair down at night, it hangs in waves over her shoulders. But she must hide that beauty in Abnegation.

We walk together to the kitchen. On these mornings when my brother makes breakfast, and my father's hand skims my hair as he reads the newspaper, and my mother hums as she clears the table—it is on these mornings that I feel guiltiest for wanting to leave them.

+ + +

The bus stinks of exhaust. Every time it hits a patch of uneven pavement, it jostles me from side to side, even though I'm gripping the seat to keep myself still.

My older brother, Caleb, stands in the aisle, holding a railing above his head to keep himself steady. We don't look alike. He has my father's dark hair and hooked nose and my mother's green eyes and dimpled cheeks. When he was younger, that collection of features looked strange, but now it suits him. If he wasn't Abnegation, I'm sure the girls at school would stare at him.

He also inherited my mother's talent for selflessness. He gave his seat to a surly Candor man on the bus without a second thought.

The Candor man wears a black suit with a white tie— Candor standard uniform. Their faction values honesty and sees the truth as black and white, so that is what they wear.

The gaps between the buildings narrow and the roads

are smoother as we near the heart of the city. The building that was once called the Sears Tower—we call it the Hub— emerges from the fog, a black pillar in the skyline. The bus passes under the elevated tracks. I have never been on a train, though they never stop running and there are tracks everywhere. Only the Dauntless ride them.

Five years ago, volunteer construction workers from Abnegation repaved some of the roads. They started in the middle of the city and worked their way outward until they ran out of materials. The roads where I live are still cracked and patchy, and it's not safe to drive on them. We don't have a car anyway.

Caleb's expression is placid as the bus sways and jolts on the road. The gray robe falls from his arm as he clutches a pole for balance. I can tell by the constant shift of his eyes that he is watching the people around us—striving to see only them and to forget himself. Candor values honesty, but our faction, Abnegation, values selflessness.

The bus stops in front of the school and I get up, scooting past the Candor man. I grab Caleb's arm as I stumble over the man's shoes. My slacks are too long, and I've never been that graceful.

The Upper Levels building is the oldest of the three schools in the city: Lower Levels, Mid-Levels, and Upper Levels. Like all the other buildings around it, it is made of glass and steel. In front of it is a large metal sculpture that the Dauntless climb after school, daring each other to go higher and higher. Last year I watched one of them fall and break her leg. I was the one who ran to get the nurse.

"Aptitude tests today," I say. Caleb is not quite a year older than I am, so we are in the same year at school.

He nods as we pass through the front doors. My muscles tighten the second we walk in. The atmosphere feels hungry, like every sixteen-year-old is trying to devour as much as he can get of this last day. It is likely that we will not walk these halls again after the Choosing Ceremony— once we choose, our new factions will be responsible for finishing our education.

Our classes are cut in half today, so we will attend all of them before the aptitude tests, which take place after lunch. My heart rate is already elevated.

"You aren't at all worried about what they'll tell you?" I ask Caleb.

We pause at the split in the hallway where he will go one way, toward Advanced Math, and I will go the other, toward Faction History.

He raises an eyebrow at me. "Are you?"

I could tell him I've been worried for weeks about what the aptitude test will tell me—Abnegation, Candor, Erudite, Amity, or Dauntless?

Instead I smile and say, "Not really."

He smiles back. "Well . . . have a good day."

I walk toward Faction History, chewing on my lower lip. He never answered my question.

The hallways are cramped, though the light coming through the windows creates the illusion of space; they are one of the only places where the factions mix, at our age. Today the crowd has a new kind of energy, a last day mania.

A girl with long curly hair shouts "Hey!" next to my ear, waving at a distant friend. A jacket sleeve smacks me on the cheek. Then an Erudite boy in a blue sweater shoves me. I lose my balance and fall hard on the ground.

"Out of my way, Stiff," he snaps, and continues down the hallway.

My cheeks warm. I get up and dust myself off. A few people stopped when I fell, but none of them offered to help me. Their eyes follow me to the edge of the hallway. This sort of thing has been happening to others in my faction for months now—the Erudite have been releasing antagonistic reports about Abnegation, and it has begun to affect the way we relate at school. The gray clothes, the plain hairstyle, and the unassuming demeanor of my faction are supposed to make it easier for me to forget myself, and easier for everyone else to forget me too. But now they make me a target.

I pause by a window in the E Wing and wait for the Dauntless to arrive. I do this every morning. At exactly 7:25, the Dauntless prove their bravery by jumping from a moving train.

My father calls the Dauntless "hellions." They are pierced, tattooed, and black-clothed. Their primary purpose is to guard the fence that surrounds our city. From what, I don't know.

They should perplex me. I should wonder what courage—which is the virtue they most value—has to do with a metal ring through your nostril. Instead my eyes cling to them wherever they go.

The train whistle blares, the sound resonating in my chest. The light fixed to the front of the train clicks on and off as the train hurtles past the school, squealing on iron rails. And as the last few cars pass, a mass exodus of young men and women in dark clothing hurl themselves from the moving cars, some dropping and rolling, others stumbling a few steps before regaining their balance. One of the boys wraps his arm around a girl's shoulders, laughing.

Watching them is a foolish practice. I turn away from the window and press through the crowd to the Faction History classroom.

CHAPTER
TWO

THE TESTS BEGIN after lunch. We sit at the long tables in the cafeteria, and the test administrators call ten names at a time, one for each testing room. I sit next to Caleb and across from our neighbor Susan.

Susan's father travels throughout the city for his job, so he has a car and drives her to and from school every day. He offered to drive us, too, but as Caleb says, we prefer to leave later and would not want to inconvenience him.

Of course not.

The test administrators are mostly Abnegation volunteers, although there is an Erudite in one of the testing rooms and a Dauntless in another to test those of us from Abnegation, because the rules state that we can't be tested by someone from our own faction. The rules also say that we can't prepare for the test in any way, so I don't know what to expect.

My gaze drifts from Susan to the Dauntless tables across the room. They are laughing and shouting and playing cards. At another set of tables, the Erudite chatter over books and newspapers, in constant pursuit of knowledge.

A group of Amity girls in yellow and red sit in a circle on the cafeteria floor, playing some kind of hand-slapping game involving a rhyming song. Every few minutes I hear a chorus of laughter from them as someone is eliminated and has to sit in the center of the circle. At the table next to them, Candor boys make wide gestures with their hands. They appear to be arguing about something, but it must not be serious, because some of them are still smiling.

At the Abnegation table, we sit quietly and wait. Faction customs dictate even idle behavior and supersede individual preference. I doubt all the Erudite want to study all the time, or that every Candor enjoys a lively debate, but they can't defy the norms of their factions any more than I can.

Caleb's name is called in the next group. He moves confidently toward the exit. I don't need to wish him luck or assure him that he shouldn't be nervous. He knows where he belongs, and as far as I know, he always has. My earliest memory of him is from when we were four years old. He scolded me for not giving my jump rope to a little girl on the playground who didn't have anything to play with. He doesn't lecture me often anymore, but I have his look of disapproval memorized.

I have tried to explain to him that my instincts are not the same as his—it didn't even enter my mind to give my seat to the Candor man on the bus—but he doesn't understand. "Just do what you're supposed to," he always says. It is that easy for him. It should be that easy for me.

My stomach wrenches. I close my eyes and keep them closed until ten minutes later, when Caleb sits down again.

He is plaster-pale. He pushes his palms along his legs like I do when I wipe off sweat, and when he brings them back, his fingers shake. I open my mouth to ask him something, but the words don't come. I am not allowed to ask him about his results, and he is not allowed to tell me.

An Abnegation volunteer speaks the next round of names. Two from Dauntless, two from Erudite, two from Amity, two from Candor, and then: "From Abnegation: Susan Black and Beatrice Prior."

I get up because I'm supposed to, but if it were up to me, I would stay in my seat for the rest of time. I feel like there is a bubble in my chest that expands more by the second, threatening to break me apart from the inside. I follow

Susan to the exit. The people I pass probably can't tell us apart. We wear the same clothes and we wear our blond hair the same way. The only difference is that Susan might not feel like she's going to throw up, and from what I can tell, her hands aren't shaking so hard she has to clutch the hem of her shirt to steady them.

Waiting for us outside the cafeteria is a row of ten rooms. They are used only for the aptitude tests, so I have never been in one before. Unlike the other rooms in the school, they are separated, not by glass, but by mirrors. I watch myself, pale and terrified, walking toward one of the doors. Susan grins nervously at me as she walks into room 5, and I walk into room 6, where a Dauntless woman waits for me.

She is not as severe-looking as the young Dauntless I have seen. She has small, dark, angular eyes and wears a black blazer—like a man's suit—and jeans. It is only when she turns to close the door that I see a tattoo on the back of her neck, a black-and-white hawk with a red eye. If I didn't feel like my heart had migrated to my throat, I would ask her what it signifies. It must signify something.

Mirrors cover the inner walls of the room. I can see my reflection from all angles: the gray fabric obscuring the shape of my back, my long neck, my knobby-knuckled hands, red with a blood blush. The ceiling glows white with light. In the center of the room is a reclined chair, like a dentist's, with a machine next to it. It looks like a place where terrible things happen.

"Don't worry," the woman says, "it doesn't hurt."

Her hair is black and straight, but in the light I see that it is streaked with gray.

"Have a seat and get comfortable," she says. "My name is Tori."

Clumsily I sit in the chair and recline, putting my head on the headrest. The lights hurt my eyes. Tori busies herself with the machine on my right. I try to focus on her and not on the wires in her hands.

"Why the hawk?" I blurt out as she attaches an electrode to my forehead.

"Never met a curious Abnegation before," she says, raising her eyebrows at me.

I shiver, and goose bumps appear on my arms. My curiosity is a mistake, a betrayal of Abnegation values.

Humming a little, she presses another electrode to my forehead and explains, "In some parts of the ancient world, the hawk symbolized the sun. Back when I got this, I figured if I always had the sun on me, I wouldn't be afraid of the dark."

I try to stop myself from asking another question, but I can't help it. "You're afraid of the dark?"

"I *was* afraid of the dark," she corrects me. She presses

the next electrode to her own forehead, and attaches a wire to it. She shrugs. "Now it reminds me of the fear I've overcome."

She stands behind me. I squeeze the armrests so tightly the redness pulls away from my knuckles. She tugs wires toward her, attaching them to me, to her, to the machine behind her. Then she passes me a vial of clear liquid.

"Drink this," she says.

"What is it?" My throat feels swollen. I swallow hard. "What's going to happen?"

"Can't tell you that. Just trust me."

I press air from my lungs and tip the contents of the vial into my mouth. My eyes close.

+ + +

When they open, an instant has passed, but I am somewhere else. I stand in the school cafeteria again, but all the long tables are empty, and I see through the glass walls that it's snowing. On the table in front of me are two baskets. In one is a hunk of cheese, and in the other, a knife the length of my forearm.

Behind me, a woman's voice says, "Choose."

"Why?" I ask.

"Choose," she repeats.

I look over my shoulder, but no one is there. I turn back

to the baskets. "What will I do with them?"

"Choose!" she yells.

When she screams at me, my fear disappears and stubbornness replaces it. I scowl and cross my arms.

"Have it your way," she says.

The baskets disappear. I hear a door squeak and turn to see who it is. I see not a "who" but a "what": A dog with a pointed nose stands a few yards away from me. It crouches low and creeps toward me, its lips peeling back from its white teeth. A growl gurgles from deep in its throat, and I see why the cheese would have come in handy. Or the knife. But it's too late now.

I think about running, but the dog will be faster than me. I can't wrestle it to the ground. My head pounds. I have to make a decision. If I can jump over one of the tables and use it as a shield—no, I am too short to jump over the tables, and not strong enough to tip one over.

The dog snarls, and I can almost feel the sound vibrating in my skull.

My biology textbook said that dogs can smell fear because of a chemical secreted by human glands in a state of duress, the same chemical a dog's prey secretes. Smelling fear leads them to attack. The dog inches toward me, its nails scraping the floor.

I can't run. I can't fight. Instead I breathe in the smell

of the dog's foul breath and try not to think about what it just ate. There are no whites in its eyes, just a black gleam.

What else do I know about dogs? I shouldn't look it in the eye. That's a sign of aggression. I remember asking my father for a pet dog when I was young, and now, staring at the ground in front of the dog's paws, I can't remember why. It comes closer, still growling. If staring into its eyes is a sign of aggression, what's a sign of submission?

My breaths are loud but steady. I sink to my knees. The last thing I want to do is lie down on the ground in front of the dog—making its teeth level with my face—but it's the best option I have. I stretch my legs out behind me and lean on my elbows. The dog creeps closer, and closer, until I feel its warm breath on my face. My arms are shaking.

It barks in my ear, and I clench my teeth to keep from screaming.

Something rough and wet touches my cheek. The dog's growling stops, and when I lift my head to look at it again, it is panting. It licked my face. I frown and sit on my heels. The dog props its paws up on my knees and licks my chin. I cringe, wiping the drool from my skin, and laugh.

"You're not such a vicious beast, huh?"

I get up slowly so I don't startle it, but it seems like a different animal than the one that faced me a few seconds ago. I stretch out a hand, carefully, so I can draw it back if I need to. The dog nudges my hand with its head. I am suddenly glad I didn't pick up the knife.

I blink, and when my eyes open, a child stands across the room wearing a white dress. She stretches out both hands and squeals, "Puppy!"

As she runs toward the dog at my side, I open my mouth to warn her, but I am too late. The dog turns. Instead of growling, it barks and snarls and snaps, and its muscles bunch up like coiled wire. About to pounce. I don't think, I just jump; I hurl my body on top of the dog, wrapping my arms around its thick neck.

My head hits the ground. The dog is gone, and so is the little girl. Instead I am alone—in the testing room, now empty. I turn in a slow circle and can't see myself in any of the mirrors. I push the door open and walk into the hall-way, but it isn't a hallway; it's a bus, and all the seats are taken.

I stand in the aisle and hold on to a pole. Sitting near me is a man with a newspaper. I can't see his face over the top of the paper, but I can see his hands. They are scarred, like he was burned, and they clench around the paper like he wants to crumple it.

"Do you know this guy?" he asks. He taps the picture on the front page of the newspaper. The headline reads: "Brutal Murderer Finally Apprehended!" I stare at the word "murderer." It has been a long time since I last read that word, but even its shape fills me with dread.

In the picture beneath the headline is a young man with a plain face and a beard. I feel like I do know him, though I don't remember how. And at the same time, I feel like it would be a bad idea to tell the man that.

"Well?" I hear anger in his voice. "Do you?"

A bad idea—no, a very bad idea. My heart pounds and I clutch the pole to keep my hands from shaking, from giving me away. If I tell him I know the man from the article, something awful will happen to me. But I can convince him that I don't. I can clear my throat and shrug my shoulders—but that would be a lie.

I clear my throat.

"Do you?" he repeats.

I shrug my shoulders.

"Well?"

A shudder goes through me. My fear is irrational; this is just a test, it isn't real. "Nope," I say, my voice casual. "No idea who he is."

He stands, and finally I see his face. He wears dark sunglasses and his mouth is bent into a snarl. His cheek is rippled with scars, like his hands. He leans close to my face. His breath smells like cigarettes. *Not real*, I remind myself. *Not real.*

"You're lying," he says. "You're *lying*!"

"I am not."

"I can see it in your eyes."

I pull myself up straighter. "You can't."

"If you know him," he says in a low voice, "you could save me. You could *save* me!"

I narrow my eyes. "Well," I say. I set my jaw. "I don't."

CHAPTER
THREE

I WAKE TO sweaty palms and a pang of guilt in my chest. I am lying in the chair in the mirrored room. When I tilt my head back, I see Tori behind me. She pinches her lips together and removes electrodes from our heads. I wait for her to say something about the test—that it's over, or that I did well, although how could I do poorly on a test like this?—but she says nothing, just pulls the wires from my forehead.

I sit forward and wipe my palms off on my slacks. I had to have done something wrong, even if it only happened in my mind. Is that strange look on Tori's face because she doesn't know how to tell me what a terrible person I am? I wish she would just come out with it.

"That," she says, "was perplexing. Excuse me, I'll be right back."

Perplexing?

I bring my knees to my chest and bury my face in them. I wish I felt like crying, because the tears might bring me a sense of release, but I don't. How can you fail a test you aren't allowed to prepare for?

As the moments pass, I get more nervous. I have to wipe off my hands every few seconds as the sweat collects—or maybe I just do it because it helps me feel calmer. What if they tell me that I'm not cut out for any faction? I would have to live on the streets, with the factionless. I can't do that. To live factionless is not just to live in poverty and discomfort; it is to live divorced from society, separated from the most important thing in life: community.

My mother told me once that we can't survive alone, but even if we could, we wouldn't want to. Without a faction, we have no purpose and no reason to live.

I shake my head. I can't think like this. I have to stay calm.

Finally the door opens, and Tori walks back in. I grip the arms of the chair.

"Sorry to worry you," Tori says. She stands by my feet with her hands in her pockets. She looks tense and pale.

"Beatrice, your results were inconclusive," she says. "Typically, each stage of the simulation eliminates one or more of the factions, but in your case, only two have been ruled out."

I stare at her. "Two?" I ask. My throat is so tight it's hard to talk.

"If you had shown an automatic distaste for the knife and selected the cheese, the simulation would have led you to a different scenario that confirmed your aptitude for Amity. That didn't happen, which is why Amity is out." Tori scratches the back of her neck. "Normally, the simulation progresses in a linear fashion, isolating one faction by ruling out the rest. The choices you made didn't even allow Candor, the next possibility, to be ruled out, so I had to alter the simulation to put you on the bus. And there your insistence upon dishonesty ruled out Candor." She half smiles. "Don't worry about that. Only the Candor tell the truth in that one."

One of the knots in my chest loosens. Maybe I'm not an awful person.

"I suppose that's not entirely true. People who tell the truth are the Candor . . . and the Abnegation," she says. "Which gives us a problem."

My mouth falls open.

"On the one hand, you threw yourself on the dog rather than let it attack the little girl, which is an Abnegation-oriented response . . . but on the other, when the man told you that the truth would save him, you still refused to tell it. Not an Abnegation-oriented response." She sighs. "Not running from the dog suggests Dauntless, but so does taking the knife, which you didn't do."

She clears her throat and continues. "Your intelligent response to the dog indicates strong alignment with the Erudite. I have no idea what to make of your indecision in stage one, but—"

"Wait," I interrupt her. "So you have no idea what my aptitude is?"

"Yes and no. My conclusion," she explains, "is that you display equal aptitude for Abnegation, Dauntless, and Erudite. People who get this kind of result are . . ." She looks over her shoulder like she expects someone to appear behind her. ". . . are called . . . *Divergent*." She says the last word so quietly that I almost don't hear it, and her tense, worried look returns. She walks around the side of the chair and leans in close to me.

"Beatrice," she says, "under no circumstances should you share that information with anyone. This is very important."

"We aren't supposed to share our results." I nod. "I know that."

"No." Tori kneels next to the chair now and places her arms on the armrest. Our faces are inches apart. "This is different. I don't mean you shouldn't share them now; I mean you should never share them with anyone, *ever*, no matter what happens. Divergence is extremely dangerous. You understand?"

I don't understand—how could inconclusive test results be dangerous?—but I still nod. I don't want to share my test results with anyone anyway.

"Okay." I peel my hands from the arms of the chair and stand. I feel unsteady.

"I suggest," Tori says, "that you go home. You have a lot of thinking to do, and waiting with the others may not benefit you."

"I have to tell my brother where I'm going."

"I'll let him know."

I touch my forehead and stare at the floor as I walk out of the room. I can't bear to look her in the eye. I can't bear to think about the Choosing Ceremony tomorrow.

It's my choice now, no matter what the test says.

Abnegation. Dauntless. Erudite.

Divergent.

+ + +

I decide not to take the bus. If I get home early, my father will notice when he checks the house log at the end of the day, and I'll have to explain what happened. Instead I walk. I'll have to intercept Caleb before he mentions anything to our parents, but Caleb can keep a secret.

I walk in the middle of the road. The buses tend to hug the curb, so it's safer here. Sometimes, on the streets near my house, I can see places where the yellow lines used to be. We have no use for them now that there are so few cars. We don't need stoplights, either, but in some places they dangle precariously over the road like they might crash down any minute.

Renovation moves slowly through the city, which is a patchwork of new, clean buildings and old, crumbling ones. Most of the new buildings are next to the marsh, which used to be a lake a long time ago. The Abnegation volunteer agency my mother works for is responsible for most of those renovations.

When I look at the Abnegation lifestyle as an outsider, I think it's beautiful. When I watch my family move in harmony; when we go to dinner parties and everyone cleans together afterward without having to be asked; when I see Caleb help strangers carry their groceries, I fall in love with this life all over again. It's only when I try to live it myself that I have trouble. It never feels genuine.

But choosing a different faction means I forsake my family. Permanently.

Just past the Abnegation sector of the city is the stretch of building skeletons and broken sidewalks that I now walk through. There are places where the road has completely collapsed, revealing sewer systems and empty subways that I have to be careful to avoid, and places that stink so powerfully of sewage and trash that I have to plug my nose.

This is where the factionless live. Because they failed to complete initiation into whatever faction they chose, they live in poverty, doing the work no one else wants to do. They are janitors and construction workers and garbage collectors; they make fabric and operate trains and drive buses. In return for their work they get food and clothing, but, as my mother says, not enough of either.

I see a factionless man standing on the corner up ahead. He wears ragged brown clothing and skin sags from his jaw. He stares at me, and I stare back at him, unable to look away.

"Excuse me," he says. His voice is raspy. "Do you have something I can eat?"

I feel a lump in my throat. A stern voice in my head says, *Duck your head and keep walking.*

No. I shake my head. I should not be afraid of this man. He needs help and I am supposed to help him.

"Um . . . yes," I say. I reach into my bag. My father tells me to keep food in my bag at all times for exactly this reason. I offer the man a small bag of dried apple slices.

He reaches for them, but instead of taking the bag, his hand closes around my wrist. He smiles at me. He has a gap between his front teeth.

"My, don't you have pretty eyes," he says. "It's a shame the rest of you is so plain."

My heart pounds. I tug my hand back, but his grip tightens. I smell something acrid and unpleasant on his breath.

"You look a little young to be walking around by yourself, dear," he says.

I stop tugging, and stand up straighter. I know I look young; I don't need to be reminded. "I'm older than I look," I retort. "I'm sixteen."

His lips spread wide, revealing a gray molar with a dark pit in the side. I can't tell if he's smiling or grimacing. "Then isn't today a special day for you? The day before you *choose?*"

"Let go of me," I say. I hear ringing in my ears. My voice sounds clear and stern—not what I expected to hear. I feel like it doesn't belong to me.

I am ready. I know what to do. I picture myself bringing my elbow back and hitting him. I see the bag of apples flying away from me. I hear my running footsteps. I am prepared to act.

But then he releases my wrist, takes the apples, and says, "Choose wisely, little girl."

CHAPTER FOUR

I REACH MY street five minutes before I usually do, according to my watch—which is the only adornment Abnegation allows, and only because it's practical. It has a gray band and a glass face. If I tilt it right, I can almost see my reflection over the hands.

The houses on my street are all the same size and shape. They are made of gray cement, with few windows, in economical, no-nonsense rectangles. Their lawns are crabgrass and their mailboxes are dull metal. To some the sight might be gloomy, but to me their simplicity is comforting.

The reason for the simplicity isn't disdain for uniqueness, as the other factions have sometimes interpreted it. Everything—our houses, our clothes, our hairstyles—is meant to help us forget ourselves and to protect us from vanity, greed, and envy, which are just forms of selfishness. If we have little, and want for little, and we are all equal, we envy no one.

I try to love it.

I sit on the front step and wait for Caleb to arrive. It doesn't take long. After a minute I see gray-robed forms walking down the street. I hear laughter. At school we try not to draw attention to ourselves, but once we're home, the games and jokes start. My natural tendency toward sarcasm is still not appreciated. Sarcasm is always at someone's expense. Maybe it's better that Abnegation wants me to suppress it. Maybe I don't have to leave my family. Maybe if I fight to make Abnegation work, my act will turn into reality.

"Beatrice!" Caleb says. "What happened? Are you all right?"

"I'm fine." He is with Susan and her brother, Robert, and Susan is giving me a strange look, like I am a different person than the one she knew this morning. I shrug. "When the test was over, I got sick. Must have been that liquid they gave us. I feel better now, though."

I try to smile convincingly. I seem to have persuaded Susan and Robert, who no longer look concerned for my mental stability, but Caleb narrows his eyes at me, the way he does when he suspects someone of duplicity.

"Did you two take the bus today?" I ask. I don't care how Susan and Robert got home from school, but I need to change the subject.

"Our father had to work late," Susan says, "and he told us we should spend some time thinking before the ceremony tomorrow."

My heart pounds at the mention of the ceremony.

"You're welcome to come over later, if you'd like," Caleb says politely.

"Thank you." Susan smiles at Caleb.

Robert raises an eyebrow at me. He and I have been exchanging looks for the past year as Susan and Caleb flirt in the tentative way known only to the Abnegation. Caleb's eyes follow Susan down the walk. I have to grab his arm to startle him from his daze. I lead him into the house and close the door behind us.

He turns to me. His dark, straight eyebrows draw together so that a crease appears between them. When he frowns, he looks more like my mother than my father. In an instant I can see him living the same kind of life my father did: staying in Abnegation, learning a trade, marrying Susan, and having a family. It will be wonderful.

I may not see it.

"Are you going to tell me the truth now?" he asks softly.

"The truth is," I say, "I'm not supposed to discuss it. And you're not supposed to ask."

"All those rules you bend, and you can't bend this one? Not even for something this important?" His eyebrows tug together, and he bites the corner of his lip. Though his words are accusatory, it sounds like he is probing me for information—like he actually wants my answer.

I narrow my eyes. "Will you? What happened in *your* test, Caleb?"

Our eyes meet. I hear a train horn, so faint it could easily be wind whistling through an alleyway. But I know it when I hear it. It sounds like the Dauntless, calling me to them.

"Just . . . don't tell our parents what happened, okay?" I say.

His eyes stay on mine for a few seconds, and then he nods.

I want to go upstairs and lie down. The test, the walk, and my encounter with the factionless man exhausted me. But my brother made breakfast this morning, and my mother prepared our lunches, and my father made dinner last night, so it's my turn to cook. I breathe deeply and walk into the kitchen to start cooking.

A minute later, Caleb joins me. I grit my teeth. He helps with everything. What irritates me most about him is his natural goodness, his inborn selflessness.

Caleb and I work together without speaking. I cook peas on the stove. He defrosts four pieces of chicken. Most of what we eat is frozen or canned, because farms these days are far away. My mother told me once that, a long time ago, there were people who wouldn't buy genetically engineered produce because they viewed it as unnatural. Now we have no other option.

By the time my parents get home, dinner is ready and the table is set. My father drops his bag at the door and kisses my head. Other people see him as an opinionated man—too opinionated, maybe—but he's also loving. I try to see only the good in him; I try.

"How did the test go?" he asks me. I pour the peas into a serving bowl.

"Fine," I say. I couldn't be Candor. I lie too easily.

"I heard there was some kind of upset with one of the tests," my mother says. Like my father, she works for the government, but she manages city improvement projects. She recruited volunteers to administer the aptitude tests. Most of the time, though, she organizes workers to help the factionless with food and shelter and job opportunities.

"Really?" says my father. A problem with the aptitude tests is rare.

"I don't know much about it, but my friend Erin told

me that something went wrong with one of the tests, so the results had to be reported verbally." My mother places a napkin next to each plate on the table. "Apparently the student got sick and was sent home early." My mother shrugs. "I hope they're all right. Did you two hear about that?"

"No," Caleb says. He smiles at my mother.

My brother couldn't be Candor either.

We sit at the table. We always pass food to the right, and no one eats until everyone is served. My father extends his hands to my mother and my brother, and they extend their hands to him and me, and my father gives thanks to God for food and work and friends and family. Not every Abnegation family is religious, but my father says we should try not to see those differences because they will only divide us. I am not sure what to make of that.

"So," my mother says to my father. "Tell me."

She takes my father's hand and moves her thumb in a small circle over his knuckles. I stare at their joined hands. My parents love each other, but they rarely show affection like this in front of us. They taught us that physical contact is powerful, so I have been wary of it since I was young.

"Tell me what's bothering you," she adds.

I stare at my plate. My mother's acute senses sometimes

surprise me, but now they chide me. Why was I so focused on myself that I didn't notice his deep frown and his sagging posture?

"I had a difficult day at work," he says. "Well, really, it was Marcus who had the difficult day. I shouldn't lay claim to it."

Marcus is my father's coworker; they are both political leaders. The city is ruled by a council of fifty people, composed entirely of representatives from Abnegation, because our faction is regarded as incorruptible, due to our commitment to selflessness. Our leaders are selected by their peers for their impeccable character, moral fortitude, and leadership skills. Representatives from each of the other factions can speak in the meetings on behalf of a particular issue, but ultimately, the decision is the council's. And while the council technically makes decisions together, Marcus is particularly influential.

It has been this way since the beginning of the great peace, when the factions were formed. I think the system persists because we're afraid of what might happen if it didn't: war.

"Is this about that report Jeanine Matthews released?" my mother says. Jeanine Matthews is Erudite's sole representative, selected based on her IQ score. My father complains about her often.

I look up. "A report?"

Caleb gives me a warning look. We aren't supposed to speak at the dinner table unless our parents ask us a direct question, and they usually don't. Our listening ears are a gift to them, my father says. They give us their listening ears after dinner, in the family room.

"Yes," my father says. His eyes narrow. "Those arrogant, self-righteous—" He stops and clears his throat. "Sorry. But she released a report attacking Marcus's character."

I raise my eyebrows.

"What did it say?" I ask.

"Beatrice," Caleb says quietly.

I duck my head, turning my fork over and over and over until the warmth leaves my cheeks. I don't like to be chastised. Especially by my brother.

"It said," my father says, "that Marcus's violence and cruelty toward his son is the reason his son chose Dauntless instead of Abnegation."

Few people who are born into Abnegation choose to leave it. When they do, we remember. Two years ago, Marcus's son, Tobias, left us for the Dauntless, and Marcus was devastated. Tobias was his only child—and his only family, since his wife died giving birth to their second child. The infant died minutes later.

I never met Tobias. He rarely attended community events and never joined his father at our house for dinner. My father often remarked that it was strange, but now it doesn't matter.

"Cruel? Marcus?" My mother shakes her head. "That poor man. As if he needs to be reminded of his loss."

"Of his son's betrayal, you mean?" my father says coldly. "I shouldn't be surprised at this point. The Erudite have been attacking us with these reports for months. And this isn't the end. There will be more, I guarantee it."

I shouldn't speak again, but I can't help myself. I blurt out, "Why are they doing this?"

"Why don't you take this opportunity to listen to your father, Beatrice?" my mother says gently. It is phrased like a suggestion, not a command. I look across the table at Caleb, who has that look of disapproval in his eyes.

I stare at my peas. I am not sure I can live this life of obligation any longer. I am not good enough.

"You know why," my father says. "Because we have something they want. Valuing knowledge above all else results in a lust for power, and that leads men into dark and empty places. We should be thankful that we know better."

I nod. I know I will not choose Erudite, even though

my test results suggested that I could. I am my father's daughter.

My parents clean up after dinner. They don't even let Caleb help them, because we're supposed to keep to ourselves tonight instead of gathering in the family room, so we can think about our results.

My family might be able to help me choose, if I could talk about my results. But I can't. Tori's warning whispers in my memory every time my resolve to keep my mouth shut falters.

Caleb and I climb the stairs and, at the top, when we divide to go to our separate bedrooms, he stops me with a hand on my shoulder.

"Beatrice," he says, looking sternly into my eyes. "We should think of our family." There is an edge to his voice. "But. But we must also think of ourselves."

For a moment I stare at him. I have never seen him think of himself, never heard him insist on anything but selflessness.

I am so startled by his comment that I just say what I am supposed to say: "The tests don't have to change our choices."

He smiles a little. "Don't they, though?"

He squeezes my shoulder and walks into his bedroom. I peer into his room and see an unmade bed and a stack of books on his desk. He closes the door. I wish I could tell him that we're going through the same thing. I wish I could speak to him like I want to instead of like I'm supposed to. But the idea of admitting that I need help is too much to bear, so I turn away.

I walk into my room, and when I close my door behind me, I realize that the decision might be simple. It will require a great act of selflessness to choose Abnegation, or a great act of courage to choose Dauntless, and maybe just choosing one over the other will prove that I belong. Tomorrow, those two qualities will struggle within me, and only one can win.

CHAPTER
FIVE

THE BUS WE take to get to the Choosing Ceremony is full of
people in gray shirts and gray slacks. A pale ring of sunlight burns into the clouds like the end of a lit cigarette.
I will never smoke one myself—they are closely tied to
vanity—but a crowd of Candor smokes them in front of the
building when we get off the bus.

I have to tilt my head back to see the top of the Hub, and
even then, part of it disappears into the clouds. It is the
tallest building in the city. I can see the lights on the two
prongs on its roof from my bedroom window.

I follow my parents off the bus. Caleb seems calm, but
so would I, if I knew what I was going to do. Instead I get
the distinct impression that my heart will burst out of my
chest any minute now, and I grab his arm to steady myself

as I walk up the front steps.

The elevator is crowded, so my father volunteers to give a cluster of Amity our place. We climb the stairs instead, following him unquestioningly. We set an example for our fellow faction members, and soon the three of us are engulfed in the mass of gray fabric ascending cement stairs in the half light. I settle into their pace. The uniform pounding of feet in my ears and the homogeneity of the people around me makes me believe that I could choose this. I could be subsumed into Abnegation's hive mind, projecting always outward.

But then my legs get sore, and I struggle to breathe, and I am again distracted by myself. We have to climb twenty flights of stairs to get to the Choosing Ceremony.

My father holds the door open on the twentieth floor and stands like a sentry as every Abnegation walks past him. I would wait for him, but the crowd presses me forward, out of the stairwell and into the room where I will decide the rest of my life.

The room is arranged in concentric circles. On the edges stand the sixteen-year-olds of every faction. We are not called members yet; our decisions today will make us initiates, and we will become members if we complete initiation.

We arrange ourselves in alphabetical order, according

to the last names we may leave behind today. I stand between Caleb and Danielle Pohler, an Amity girl with rosy cheeks and a yellow dress.

Rows of chairs for our families make up the next circle. They are arranged in five sections, according to faction. Not everyone in each faction comes to the Choosing Ceremony, but enough of them come that the crowd looks huge.

The responsibility to conduct the ceremony rotates from faction to faction each year, and this year is Abnegation's. Marcus will give the opening address and read the names in reverse alphabetical order. Caleb will choose before me.

In the last circle are five metal bowls so large they could hold my entire body, if I curled up. Each one contains a substance that represents each faction: gray stones for Abnegation, water for Erudite, earth for Amity, lit coals for Dauntless, and glass for Candor.

When Marcus calls my name, I will walk to the center of the three circles. I will not speak. He will offer me a knife. I will cut into my hand and sprinkle my blood into the bowl of the faction I choose.

My blood on the stones. My blood sizzling on the coals.

Before my parents sit down, they stand in front of Caleb and me. My father kisses my forehead and claps

Caleb on the shoulder, grinning.

"See you soon," he says. Without a trace of doubt.

My mother hugs me, and what little resolve I have left almost breaks. I clench my jaw and stare up at the ceiling, where globe lanterns hang and fill the room with blue light. She holds me for what feels like a long time, even after I let my hands fall. Before she pulls away, she turns her head and whispers in my ear, "I love you. No matter what."

I frown at her back as she walks away. She knows what I might do. She must know, or she wouldn't feel the need to say that.

Caleb grabs my hand, squeezing my palm so tightly it hurts, but I don't let go. The last time we held hands was at my uncle's funeral, as my father cried. We need each other's strength now, just as we did then.

The room slowly comes to order. I should be observing the Dauntless; I should be taking in as much information as I can, but I can only stare at the lanterns across the room. I try to lose myself in the blue glow.

Marcus stands at the podium between the Erudite and the Dauntless and clears his throat into the microphone. "Welcome," he says. "Welcome to the Choosing Ceremony. Welcome to the day we honor the democratic philosophy of our ancestors, which tells us that every man has the right to choose his own way in this world."

Or, it occurs to me, one of five predetermined ways. I squeeze Caleb's fingers as hard as he is squeezing mine.

"Our dependents are now sixteen. They stand on the precipice of adulthood, and it is now up to them to decide what kind of people they will be." Marcus's voice is solemn and gives equal weight to each word. "Decades ago our ancestors realized that it is not political ideology, religious belief, race, or nationalism that is to blame for a warring world. Rather, they determined that it was the fault of human personality—of humankind's inclination toward evil, in whatever form that is. They divided into factions that sought to eradicate those qualities they believed responsible for the world's disarray."

My eyes shift to the bowls in the center of the room. What do I believe? I do not know; I do not know; I do not know.

"Those who blamed aggression formed Amity."

The Amity exchange smiles. They are dressed comfortably, in red or yellow. Every time I see them, they seem kind, loving, free. But joining them has never been an option for me.

"Those who blamed ignorance became the Erudite."

Ruling out Erudite was the only part of my choice that was easy.

"Those who blamed duplicity created Candor."

I have never liked Candor.

"Those who blamed selfishness made Abnegation."

I blame selfishness; I do.

"And those who blamed cowardice were the Dauntless."

But I am not selfless enough. Sixteen years of trying and I am not enough.

My legs go numb, like all the life has gone out of them, and I wonder how I will walk when my name is called.

"Working together, these five factions have lived in peace for many years, each contributing to a different sector of society. Abnegation has fulfilled our need for selfless leaders in government; Candor has provided us with trustworthy and sound leaders in law; Erudite has supplied us with intelligent teachers and researchers; Amity has given us understanding counselors and caretakers; and Dauntless provides us with protection from threats both within and without. But the reach of each faction is not limited to these areas. We give one another far more than can be adequately summarized. In our factions, we find meaning, we find purpose, we find life."

I think of the motto I read in my Faction History textbook: *Faction before blood.* More than family, our factions are where we belong. Can that possibly be right?

Marcus adds, "Apart from them, we would not survive."

The silence that follows his words is heavier than other silences. It is heavy with our worst fear, greater even than the fear of death: to be factionless.

Marcus continues, "Therefore this day marks a happy occasion—the day on which we receive our new initiates, who will work with us toward a better society and a better world."

A round of applause. It sounds muffled. I try to stand completely still, because if my knees are locked and my body is stiff, I don't shake. Marcus reads the first names, but I can't tell one syllable from the other. How will I know when he calls my name?

One by one, each sixteen-year-old steps out of line and walks to the middle of the room. The first girl to choose decides on Amity, the same faction from which she came. I watch her blood droplets fall on soil, and she stands behind their seats alone.

The room is constantly moving, a new name and a new person choosing, a new knife and a new choice. I recognize most of them, but I doubt they know me.

"James Tucker," Marcus says.

James Tucker of the Dauntless is the first person to stumble on his way to the bowls. He throws his arms out and regains his balance before hitting the floor. His face turns red and he walks fast to the middle of the room. When he stands in the center, he looks from the Dauntless bowl to the Candor bowl—the orange flames that rise higher each moment, and the glass reflecting blue light.

Marcus offers him the knife. He breathes deeply—I watch his chest rise—and, as he exhales, accepts the knife. Then he drags it across his palm with a jerk and holds his arm out to the side. His blood falls onto glass, and he is the first of us to switch factions. The first faction transfer. A mutter rises from the Dauntless section, and I stare at the floor.

They will see him as a traitor from now on. His Dauntless family will have the option of visiting him in his new faction, a week and a half from now on Visiting Day, but they won't, because he left them. His absence will haunt their hallways, and he will be a space they can't fill. And then time will pass, and the hole will be gone, like when an organ is removed and the body's fluids flow into the space it leaves. Humans can't tolerate emptiness for long.

"Caleb Prior," says Marcus.

Caleb squeezes my hand one last time, and as he walks away, casts a long look at me over his shoulder. I watch his feet move to the center of the room, and his hands, steady as they accept the knife from Marcus, are deft as one presses the knife into the other. Then he stands with blood pooling in his palm, and his lip snags on his teeth.

He breathes out. And then in. And then he holds his hand over the Erudite bowl, and his blood drips into the water, turning it a deeper shade of red.

I hear mutters that lift into outraged cries. I can barely think straight. My brother, my selfless brother, a faction transfer? My brother, born for Abnegation, *Erudite*?

When I close my eyes, I see the stack of books on Caleb's desk, and his shaking hands sliding along his legs after the aptitude test. Why didn't I realize that when he told me to think of myself yesterday, he was also giving that advice to himself?

I scan the crowd of the Erudite—they wear smug smiles and nudge each other. The Abnegation, normally so placid, speak to one another in tense whispers and glare across the room at the faction that has become our enemy.

"Excuse me," says Marcus, but the crowd doesn't hear him. He shouts, "Quiet, please!"

The room goes silent. Except for a ringing sound.

I hear my name and a shudder propels me forward. Halfway to the bowls, I am sure that I will choose Abnegation. I can see it now. I watch myself grow into a woman in Abnegation robes, marrying Susan's brother, Robert, volunteering on the weekends, the peace of routine, the quiet nights spent in front of the fireplace, the certainty that I will be safe, and if not good enough, better than I am now.

The ringing, I realize, is in my ears.

I look at Caleb, who now stands behind the Erudite. He stares back at me and nods a little, like he knows what I'm thinking, and agrees. My footsteps falter. If Caleb wasn't fit for Abnegation, how can I be? But what choice do I have, now that he left us and I'm the only one who remains? He left me no other option.

I set my jaw. I will be the child that stays; I have to do this for my parents. I have to.

Marcus offers me my knife. I look into his eyes—they are dark blue, a strange color—and take it. He nods, and I turn toward the bowls. Dauntless fire and Abnegation stones are both on my left, one in front of my shoulder and one behind. I hold the knife in my right hand and touch the blade to my palm. Gritting my teeth, I drag the blade down. It stings, but I barely notice. I hold both hands to my chest, and my next breath shudders on the way out.

I open my eyes and thrust my arm out. My blood drips onto the carpet between the two bowls. Then, with a gasp I can't contain, I shift my hand forward, and my blood sizzles on the coals.

I am selfish. I am brave.

CHAPTER SIX

I TRAIN MY eyes on the floor and stand behind the Dauntless-born initiates who chose to return to their own faction. They are all taller than I am, so even when I lift my head, I see only black-clothed shoulders. When the last girl makes her choice—Amity—it's time to leave. The Dauntless exit first. I walk past the gray-clothed men and women who were my faction, staring determinedly at the back of someone's head.

But I have to see my parents one more time. I look over my shoulder at the last second before I pass them, and immediately wish I hadn't. My father's eyes burn into mine with a look of accusation. At first, when I feel the heat behind my eyes, I think he's found a way to set me on fire, to punish me for what I've done, but no—I'm about to cry.

Beside him, my mother is smiling.

The people behind me press me forward, away from my family, who will be the last ones to leave. They may even stay to stack the chairs and clean the bowls. I twist my head around to find Caleb in the crowd of Erudite behind me. He stands among the other initiates, shaking hands with a faction transfer, a boy who was Candor. The easy smile he wears is an act of betrayal. My stomach wrenches and I turn away. If it's so easy for him, maybe it should be easy for me, too.

I glance at the boy to my left, who was Erudite and now looks as pale and nervous as I should feel. I spent all my time worrying about which faction I would choose and never considered what would happen if I chose Dauntless. What waits for me at Dauntless headquarters?

The crowd of Dauntless leading us go to the stairs instead of the elevators. I thought only the Abnegation used the stairs.

Then everyone starts running. I hear whoops and shouts and laughter all around me, and dozens of thundering feet moving at different rhythms. It is not a selfless act for the Dauntless to take the stairs; it is a wild act.

"What the hell is going on?" the boy next to me shouts.

I just shake my head and keep running. I am breathless when we reach the first floor, and the Dauntless burst through the exit. Outside, the air is crisp and cold and the sky is orange from the setting sun. It reflects off the black glass of the Hub.

The Dauntless sprawl across the street, blocking the path of a bus, and I sprint to catch up to the back of the crowd. My confusion dissipates as I run. I have not run anywhere in a long time. Abnegation discourages anything done strictly for my own enjoyment, and that is what this is: my lungs burning, my muscles aching, the fierce pleasure of a flat-out sprint. I follow the Dauntless down the street and around the corner and hear a familiar sound: the train horn.

"Oh no," mumbles the Erudite boy. "Are we supposed to hop on that thing?"

"Yes," I say, breathless.

It is good that I spent so much time watching the Dauntless arrive at school. The crowd spreads out in a long line. The train glides toward us on steel rails, its light flashing, its horn blaring. The door of each car is open, waiting for the Dauntless to pile in, and they do, group by group, until only the new initiates are left. The Dauntless-born initiates are used to doing this by now, so in a second it's just faction transfers left.

I step forward with a few others and start jogging. We run with the car for a few steps and then throw ourselves sideways. I'm not as tall or as strong as some of them, so I can't pull myself into the car. I cling to a handle next to the doorway, my shoulder slamming into the car. My arms shake, and finally a Candor girl grabs me and pulls me in. Gasping, I thank her.

I hear a shout and look over my shoulder. A short Erudite boy with red hair pumps his arms as he tries to catch up to the train. An Erudite girl by the door reaches out to grab the boy's hand, straining, but he is too far behind. He falls to his knees next to the tracks as we sail away, and puts his head in his hands.

I feel uneasy. He just failed Dauntless initiation. He is factionless now. It could happen at any moment.

"You all right?" the Candor girl who helped me asks briskly. She is tall, with dark brown skin and short hair. Pretty.

I nod.

"I'm Christina," she says, offering me her hand.

I haven't shaken a hand in a long time either. The Abnegation greeted one another by bowing heads, a sign of respect. I take her hand, uncertainly, and shake it twice, hoping I didn't squeeze too hard or not hard enough.

"Beatrice," I say.

"Do you know where we're going?" She has to shout over the wind, which blows harder through the open doors by the second. The train is picking up speed. I sit down. It will be easier to keep my balance if I'm low to the ground. She raises an eyebrow at me.

"A fast train means wind," I say. "Wind means falling out. Get down."

Christina sits next to me, inching back to lean against the wall.

"I guess we're going to Dauntless headquarters," I say, "but I don't know where that is."

"Does anyone?" She shakes her head, grinning. "It's like they just popped out of a hole in the ground or something."

Then the wind rushes through the car, and the other faction transfers, hit with bursts of air, fall on top of one another. I watch Christina laugh without hearing her and manage a smile.

Over my left shoulder, orange light from the setting sun reflects off the glass buildings, and I can faintly see the rows of gray houses that used to be my home.

It's Caleb's turn to make dinner tonight. Who will take his place—my mother or my father? And when they clear out his room, what will they discover? I imagine books jammed between the dresser and the wall, books under his mattress. The Erudite thirst for knowledge filling all the hidden places in his room. Did he always know that he would choose Erudite? And if he did, how did I not notice?

What a good actor he was. The thought makes me sick to my stomach, because even though I left them too, at least I was no good at pretending. At least they all knew that I wasn't selfless.

I close my eyes and picture my mother and father sitting at the dinner table in silence. Is it a lingering hint of selflessness that makes my throat tighten at the thought of them, or is it selfishness, because I know I will never be their daughter again?

+ + +

"They're jumping off!"

I lift my head. My neck aches. I have been curled up with my back against the wall for at least a half hour, listening to the roaring wind and watching the city smear past us. I sit forward. The train has slowed down in the past few minutes, and I see that the boy who shouted is right: The Dauntless in the cars ahead of us are jumping out as the train passes a rooftop. The tracks are seven stories up.

The idea of leaping out of a moving train onto a rooftop, knowing there is a gap between the edge of the roof and the edge of the track, makes me want to throw up. I push myself up and stumble to the opposite side of the car, where the other faction transfers stand in a line.

"We have to jump off too, then," a Candor girl says. She has a large nose and crooked teeth.

"Great," a Candor boy replies, "because that makes perfect sense, Molly. Leap off a train onto a roof."

"This is kind of what we signed up for, Peter," the girl points out.

"Well, I'm not doing it," says an Amity boy behind me. He has olive skin and wears a brown shirt—he is the *only* transfer from Amity. His cheeks shine with tears.

"You've got to," Christina says, "or you fail. Come on, it'll be all right."

"No, it won't! I'd rather be factionless than dead!" The Amity boy shakes his head. He sounds panicky. He keeps shaking his head and staring at the rooftop, which is getting closer by the second.

I don't agree with him. I would rather be dead than empty, like the factionless.

"You can't force him," I say, glancing at Christina. Her brown eyes are wide, and she presses her lips together so hard they change color. She offers me her hand.

"Here," she says. I raise an eyebrow at her hand, about to say that I don't need help, but she adds, "I just . . . can't do it unless someone drags me."

I take her hand and we stand at the edge of the car. As it passes the roof, I count, "One . . . two . . . *three!*"

On three we launch off the train car. A weightless moment, and then my feet slam into solid ground and pain prickles through my shins. The jarring landing sends me sprawling on the rooftop, gravel under my cheek. I release Christina's hand. She's laughing.

"That was fun," she says.

Christina will fit in with Dauntless thrill seekers. I brush grains of rock from my cheek. All the initiates except the Amity boy made it onto the roof, with varying levels of success. The Candor girl with crooked teeth, Molly, holds her ankle, wincing, and Peter, the Candor boy with shiny hair, grins proudly—he must have landed on his feet.

Then I hear a wail. I turn my head, searching for the source of the sound. A Dauntless girl stands at the edge of the roof, staring at the ground below, screaming. Behind her a Dauntless boy holds her at the waist to keep her from falling off.

"Rita," he says. "Rita, calm down. Rita—"

I stand and look over the edge. There is a body on the pavement below us; a girl, her arms and legs bent at awkward angles, her hair spread in a fan around her head. My stomach sinks and I stare at the railroad tracks. Not everyone made it. And even the Dauntless aren't safe.

Rita sinks to her knees, sobbing. I turn away. The

longer I watch her, the more likely I am to cry, and I can't cry in front of these people.

I tell myself, as sternly as possible, *that is how things work here*. We do dangerous things and people die. People die, and we move on to the next dangerous thing. The sooner that lesson sinks in, the better chance I have at surviving initiation.

I'm no longer sure that I will survive initiation.

I tell myself I will count to three, and when I'm done, I will move on. *One.* I picture the girl's body on the pavement, and a shudder goes through me. *Two.* I hear Rita's sobs and the murmured reassurance of the boy behind her. *Three.*

My lips pursed, I walk away from Rita and the roof's edge.

My elbow stings. I pull my sleeve up to examine it, my hand shaking. Some of the skin is peeling off, but it isn't bleeding.

"Ooh. *Scandalous!* A Stiff's flashing some skin!"

I lift my head. "Stiff" is slang for Abnegation, and I'm the only one here. Peter points at me, smirking. I hear laughter. My cheeks heat up, and I let my sleeve fall.

"Listen up! My name is Max! I am one of the leaders of your new faction!" shouts a man at the other end of the roof. He is older than the others, with deep creases in his dark skin and gray hair at his temples, and he stands on the ledge like it's a sidewalk. Like someone didn't just fall to her death from it. "Several stories below us is the members' entrance to our compound. If you can't muster the will to jump off, you don't belong here. Our initiates have the privilege of going first."

"You want us to jump off a *ledge*?" asks an Erudite girl. She is a few inches taller than I am, with mousy brown hair and big lips. Her mouth hangs open.

I don't know why it shocks her.

"Yes," Max says. He looks amused.

"Is there water at the bottom or something?"

"Who knows?" He raises his eyebrows.

The crowd in front of the initiates splits in half, making a wide path for us. I look around. No one looks eager to leap off the building—their eyes are everywhere but on Max. Some of them nurse minor wounds or brush gravel from their clothes. I glance at Peter. He is picking at one of his cuticles. Trying to act casual.

I am proud. It will get me into trouble someday, but today it makes me brave. I walk toward the ledge and hear snickers behind me.

Max steps aside, leaving my way clear. I walk up to the edge and look down. Wind whips through my clothes, making the fabric snap. The building I'm on forms one side of a square with three other buildings. In the center of the square is a huge hole in the concrete. I can't see what's at the bottom of it.

This is a scare tactic. I will land safely at the bottom. That knowledge is the only thing that helps me step onto the ledge. My teeth chatter. I can't back down now. Not with all the people betting I'll fail behind me. My hands fumble along the collar of my shirt and find the button that secures it shut. After a few tries, I undo the hooks from collar to hem, and pull it off my shoulders.

Beneath it, I wear a gray T-shirt. It is tighter than any other clothes I own, and no one has ever seen me in it before. I ball up my outer shirt and look over my shoulder, at Peter. I throw the ball of fabric at him as hard as I can, my jaw clenched. It hits him in the chest. He stares at me. I hear catcalls and shouts behind me.

I look at the hole again. Goose bumps rise on my pale arms, and my stomach lurches. If I don't do it now, I won't be able to do it at all. I swallow hard.

I don't think. I just bend my knees and jump.

The air howls in my ears as the ground surges toward me, growing and expanding, or I surge toward the ground, my heart pounding so fast it hurts, every muscle in my body tensing as the falling sensation drags at my stomach. The hole surrounds me and I drop into darkness.

I hit something hard. It gives way beneath me and cradles my body. The impact knocks the wind out of me and I wheeze, struggling to breathe again. My arms and legs sting.

A net. There is a net at the bottom of the hole. I look up at the building and laugh, half relieved and half hysterical. My body shakes and I cover my face with my hands. I just jumped off a roof.

I have to stand on solid ground again. I see a few hands stretching out to me at the edge of the net, so I grab the first one I can reach and pull myself across. I roll off, and I would have fallen face-first onto a wood floor if he had not caught me.

"He" is the young man attached to the hand I grabbed. He has a spare upper lip and a full lower lip. His eyes are so deep-set that his eyelashes touch the skin under his eyebrows, and they are dark blue, a dreaming, sleeping, waiting color.

His hands grip my arms, but he releases me a moment after I stand upright again.

"Thank you," I say.

We stand on a platform ten feet above the ground. Around us is an open cavern.

"Can't believe it," a voice says from behind him. It belongs to a dark-haired girl with three silver rings through her right eyebrow. She smirks at me. "A Stiff, the first to jump? Unheard of."

"There's a reason why she left them, Lauren," he says. His voice is deep, and it rumbles. "What's your name?"

"Um . . ." I don't know why I hesitate. But "Beatrice" just doesn't sound right anymore.

"Think about it," he says, a faint smile curling his lips. "You don't get to pick again."

A new place, a new name. I can be remade here.

"Tris," I say firmly.

"Tris," Lauren repeats, grinning. "Make the announcement, Four."

The boy—Four—looks over his shoulder and shouts, "First jumper—Tris!"

A crowd materializes from the darkness as my eyes adjust. They cheer and pump their fists, and then another person drops into the net. Her screams follow her down. Christina. Everyone laughs, but they follow their laughter with more cheering.

Four sets his hand on my back and says, "Welcome to Dauntless."

CHAPTER SEVEN

WHEN ALL THE initiates stand on solid ground again, Lauren and Four lead us down a narrow tunnel. The walls are made of stone, and the ceiling slopes, so I feel like I am descending deep into the heart of the earth. The tunnel is lit at long intervals, so in the dark space between each dim lamp, I fear that I am lost until a shoulder bumps mine. In the circles of light I am safe again.

The Erudite boy in front of me stops abruptly, and I smack into him, hitting my nose on his shoulder. I stumble back and rub my nose as I recover my senses. The whole crowd has stopped, and our three leaders stand in front of us, arms folded.

"This is where we divide," Lauren says. "The Dauntless-born initiates are with me. I assume *you* don't need a tour of the place."

She smiles and beckons toward the Dauntless-born initiates. They break away from the group and dissolve into the shadows. I watch the last heel pass out of the light and look at those of us who are left. Most of the initiates were from Dauntless, so only nine people remain. Of those, I am the only Abnegation transfer, and there are no Amity transfers. The rest are from Erudite and, surprisingly, Candor. It must require bravery to be honest all the time. I wouldn't know.

Four addresses us next. "Most of the time I work in the control room, but for the next few weeks, I am your instructor," he says. "My name is Four."

Christina asks, "Four? Like the number?"

"Yes," Four says. "Is there a problem?"

"No."

"Good. We're about to go into the Pit, which you will someday learn to love. It—"

Christina snickers. "The Pit? Clever name."

Four walks up to Christina and leans his face close to hers. His eyes narrow, and for a second he just stares at her.

"What's your name?" he asks quietly.

"Christina," she squeaks.

"Well, Christina, if I wanted to put up with Candor smart-mouths, I would have joined their faction," he hisses. "The first lesson you will learn from me is to keep your mouth shut. Got that?"

She nods.

Four starts toward the shadow at the end of the tunnel. The crowd of initiates moves on in silence.

"What a jerk," she mumbles.

"I guess he doesn't like to be laughed at," I reply.

It would probably be wise to be careful around Four, I realize. He seemed placid to me on the platform, but something about that stillness makes me wary now.

Four pushes a set of double doors open, and we walk into the place he called "the Pit."

"Oh," whispers Christina. "I get it."

"Pit" is the best word for it. It is an underground cavern so huge I can't see the other end of it from where I stand, at the bottom. Uneven rock walls rise several stories above my head. Built into the stone walls are places for food, clothing, supplies, leisure activities. Narrow paths and steps carved from rock connect them. There are no barriers to keep people from falling over the side.

A slant of orange light stretches across one of the rock walls. Forming the roof of the Pit are panes of glass and, above them, a building that lets in sunlight. It must have looked like just another city building when we passed it on the train.

Blue lanterns dangle at random intervals above the stone paths, similar to the ones that lit the Choosing room. They grow brighter as the sunlight dies.

People are everywhere, all dressed in black, all shouting and talking, expressive, gesturing. I don't see any elderly people in the crowd. Are there any old Dauntless? Do they not last that long, or are they just sent away when they can't jump off moving trains anymore?

A group of children run down a narrow path with no railing, so fast my heart pounds, and I want to scream at them to slow down before they get hurt. A memory of the orderly Abnegation streets appears in my mind: a line of people on the right passing a line of people on the left, small smiles and inclined heads and silence. My stomach squeezes. But there is something wonderful about Dauntless chaos.

"If you follow me," says Four, "I'll show you the chasm."

He waves us forward. Four's appearance seems tame from the front, by Dauntless standards, but when he turns around, I see a tattoo peeking out from the collar of his T-shirt. He leads us to the right side of the Pit, which is conspicuously dark. I squint and see that the floor I stand on now ends at an iron barrier. As we approach the railing, I hear a roar—water, fast-moving water, crashing against rocks.

I look over the side. The floor drops off at a sharp angle, and several stories below us is a river. Gushing water strikes the wall beneath me and sprays upward. To my left, the water is calmer, but to my right, it is white, battling with rock.

"The chasm reminds us that there is a fine line between bravery and idiocy!" Four shouts. "A daredevil jump off this ledge will end your life. It has happened before and it will happen again. You've been warned."

"This is incredible," says Christina, as we all move away from the railing.

"Incredible is the word," I say, nodding.

Four leads the group of initiates across the Pit toward a gaping hole in the wall. The room beyond is well-lit enough that I can see where we're going: a dining hall full of people and clattering silverware. When we walk in, the Dauntless inside stand. They applaud. They stamp their feet. They shout. The noise surrounds me and fills me. Christina smiles, and a second later, so do I.

We look for empty seats. Christina and I discover a mostly empty table at the side of the room, and I find myself sitting between her and Four. In the center of the table is a platter of food I don't recognize: circular pieces of meat wedged between round bread slices. I pinch one between my fingers, unsure what to make of it.

Four nudges me with his elbow.

"It's beef," he says. "Put this on it." He passes me a

small bowl full of red sauce.

"You've never had a hamburger before?" asks Christina, her eyes wide.

"No," I say. "Is that what it's called?"

"Stiffs eat plain food," Four says, nodding at Christina.

"Why?" she asks.

I shrug. "Extravagance is considered self-indulgent and unnecessary."

She smirks. "No wonder you left."

"Yeah," I say, rolling my eyes. "It was just because of the food."

The corner of Four's mouth twitches.

The doors to the cafeteria open, and a hush falls over the room. I look over my shoulder. A young man walks in, and it is quiet enough that I can hear his footsteps. His face is pierced in so many places I lose count, and his hair is long, dark, and greasy. But that isn't what makes him look menacing. It is the coldness of his eyes as they sweep across the room.

"Who's that?" hisses Christina.

"His name is Eric," says Four. "He's a Dauntless leader."

"Seriously? But he's so young."

Four gives her a grave look. "Age doesn't matter here."

I can tell she's about to ask what I want to ask: *Then what does matter?* But Eric's eyes stop scanning the room, and he starts toward a table. He starts toward *our* table and drops into the seat next to Four. He offers no greeting, so neither do we.

"Well, aren't you going to introduce me?" he asks, nodding to Christina and me.

Four says, "This is Tris and Christina."

"Ooh, a Stiff," says Eric, smirking at me. His smile pulls at the piercings in his lips, making the holes they occupy wider, and I wince. "We'll see how long you last."

I mean to say something—to assure him that I *will* last, maybe—but words fail me. I don't understand why, but I don't want Eric to look at me any longer than he already has. I don't want him to look at me ever again.

He taps his fingers against the table. His knuckles are scabbed over, right where they would split if he punched something too hard.

"What have you been doing lately, Four?" he asks.

Four lifts a shoulder. "Nothing, really," he says.

Are they friends? My eyes flick between Eric and Four. Everything Eric did—sitting here, asking about Four—suggests that they are, but the way Four sits, tense as pulled wire, suggests they are something else. Rivals, maybe, but how could that be, if Eric is a leader and Four is not?

"Max tells me he keeps trying to meet with you, and you don't show up," Eric says. "He requested that I find out what's going on with you."

Four looks at Eric for a few seconds before saying, "Tell him that I am satisfied with the position I currently hold."

"So he wants to give you a job."

The rings in Eric's eyebrow catch the light. Maybe Eric perceives Four as a potential threat to his position. My father says that those who want power and get it live in terror of losing it. That's why we have to give power to those who do not want it.

"So it would seem," Four says.

"And you aren't interested."

"I haven't been interested for two years."

"Well," says Eric. "Let's hope he gets the point, then."

He claps Four on the shoulder, a little too hard, and gets up. When he walks away, I slouch immediately. I had not realized that I was so tense.

"Are you two . . . friends?" I say, unable to contain my curiosity.

"We were in the same initiate class," he says. "He transferred from Erudite."

All thoughts of being careful around Four leave me. "Were you a transfer too?"

"I thought I would only have trouble with the Candor asking too many questions," he says coldly. "Now I've got Stiffs, too?"

"It must be because you're so approachable," I say

flatly. "You know. Like a bed of nails."

He stares at me, and I don't look away. He isn't a dog, but the same rules apply. Looking away is submissive. Looking him in the eye is a challenge. It's my choice.

Heat rushes into my cheeks. What will happen when this tension breaks?

But he just says, "Careful, Tris."

My stomach drops like I just swallowed a stone. A Dauntless member at another table calls out Four's name, and I turn to Christina. She raises both eyebrows.

"What?" I ask.

"I'm developing a theory."

"And it is?"

She picks up her hamburger, grins, and says, "That you have a death wish."

+ + +

After dinner, Four disappears without a word. Eric leads us down a series of hallways without telling us where we're going. I don't know why a Dauntless leader would be responsible for a group of initiates, but maybe it is just for tonight.

At the end of each hallway is a blue lamp, but between them it's dark, and I have to be careful not to stumble over uneven ground. Christina walks beside me in silence. No one told us to be quiet, but none of us speak.

Eric stops in front of a wooden door and folds his arms. We gather around him.

"For those of you who don't know, my name is Eric," he says. "I am one of five leaders of the Dauntless. We take the initiation process very seriously here, so I volunteered to oversee most of your training."

The thought makes me nauseous. The idea that a Dauntless leader will oversee our initiation is bad enough, but the fact that it's Eric makes it seem even worse.

"Some ground rules," he says. "You have to be in the training room by eight o'clock every day. Training takes place every day from eight to six, with a break for lunch. You are free to do whatever you like after six. You will also get some time off between each stage of initiation."

The phrase "do whatever you like" sticks in my mind. At home, I could never do what I wanted, not even for an evening. I had to think of other people's needs first. I don't even know what I like to do.

"You are only permitted to leave the compound when accompanied by a Dauntless," Eric adds. "Behind this door is the room where you will be sleeping for the next few weeks. You will notice that there are ten beds and only nine of you. We anticipated that a higher proportion of you would make it this far."

"But we started with twelve," protests Christina. I close my eyes and wait for the reprimand. She needs to learn to stay quiet.

"There is always at least one transfer who doesn't make it to the compound," says Eric, picking at his cuticles. He shrugs. "Anyway, in the first stage of initiation, we keep transfers and Dauntless-born initiates separate, but that doesn't mean you are evaluated separately. At the end of initiation, your rankings will be determined in comparison with the Dauntless-born initiates. And they are better than you are already. So I expect—"

"Rankings?" asks the mousy-haired Erudite girl to my right. "Why are we ranked?"

Eric smiles, and in the blue light, his smile looks wicked, like it was cut into his face with a knife.

"Your ranking serves two purposes," he says. "The first is that it determines the order in which you will select a job after initiation. There are only a few *desirable* positions available."

My stomach tightens. I know by looking at his smile, like I knew the second I entered the aptitude test room, that something bad is about to happen.

"The second purpose," he says, "is that only the top ten initiates are made members."

Pain stabs my stomach. We all stand still as statues.

And then Christina says, *"What?"*

"There are eleven Dauntless-borns, and nine of you," Eric continues. "Four initiates will be cut at the end of stage one. The remainder will be cut after the final test."

That means that even if we make it through each stage of initiation, six initiates will not be members. I see Christina look at me from the corner of my eye, but I can't look back at her. My eyes are fixed on Eric and will not move.

My odds, as the smallest initiate, as the only Abnegation transfer, are not good.

"What do we do if we're cut?" Peter says.

"You leave the Dauntless compound," says Eric indifferently, "and live factionless."

The mousy-haired girl clamps her hand over her mouth and stifles a sob. I remember the factionless man with the gray teeth, snatching the bag of apples from my hands. His dull, staring eyes. But instead of crying, like the Erudite girl, I feel colder. Harder.

I will be a member. I will.

"But that's . . . . not fair!" the broad-shouldered Candor girl, Molly, says. Even though she sounds angry, she looks terrified. "If we had *known*—"

"Are you saying that if you had known this before the Choosing Ceremony, you wouldn't have chosen Dauntless?" Eric snaps. "Because if that's the case, you should get out now. If you are really one of us, it won't matter to you that you might fail. And if it does, you are a coward."

Eric pushes the door to the dormitory open.

"You chose us," he says. "Now we have to choose you."

+ + +

I lie in bed and listen to nine people breathing.

I have never slept in the same room as a boy before, but here I have no other option, unless I want to sleep in the hallway. Everyone else changed into the clothes the Dauntless provided for us, but I sleep in my Abnegation clothes, which still smell like soap and fresh air, like home.

I used to have my own room. I could see the front lawn from the window, and beyond it, the foggy skyline. I am used to sleeping in silence.

Heat swells behind my eyes as I think of home, and when I blink, a tear slips out. I cover my mouth to stifle a sob.

I can't cry, not here. I have to calm down.

It will be all right here. I can look at my reflection whenever I want. I can befriend Christina, and cut my hair short, and let other people clean up their own messes.

My hands shake and the tears come faster now, blurring my vision.

It doesn't matter that the next time I see my parents, on

Visiting Day, they will barely recognize me—if they come at all. It doesn't matter that I ache at even a split-second memory of their faces. Even Caleb's, despite how much his secrets hurt me. I match my inhales to the inhales of the other initiates, and my exhales to their exhales. It doesn't matter.

A strangled sound interrupts the breathing, followed by a heavy sob. Bed springs squeal as a large body turns, and a pillow muffles the sobs, but not enough. They come from the bunk next to mine—they belong to a Candor boy, Al, the largest and broadest of all the initiates. He is the last person I expected to break down.

His feet are just inches from my head. I should comfort him—I should *want* to comfort him, because I was raised that way. Instead I feel disgust. Someone who looks so strong shouldn't act so weak. Why can't he just keep his crying quiet like the rest of us?

I swallow hard.

If my mother knew what I was thinking, I know what look she would give me. The corners of her mouth turned down. Her eyebrows set low over her eyes—not scowling, almost tired. I drag the heel of my hand over my cheeks.

Al sobs again. I almost feel the sound grate in my own throat. He is just inches away from me—I should touch him.

No. I put my hand down and roll onto my side, facing

the wall. No one has to know that I don't want to help him. I can keep that secret buried. My eyes shut and I feel the pull of sleep, but every time I come close, I hear Al again.

Maybe my problem isn't that I can't go home. I will miss my mother and father and Caleb and evening fire-light and the clack of my mother's knitting needles, but that is not the only reason for this hollow feeling in my stomach.

My problem might be that even if I did go home, I wouldn't belong there, among people who give without thinking and care without trying.

The thought makes me grit my teeth. I gather the pillow around my ears to block out Al's crying, and fall asleep with a circle of moisture pressed to my cheek.

CHAPTER EIGHT

"THE FIRST THING you will learn today is how to shoot a gun. The second thing is how to win a fight." Four presses a gun into my palm without looking at me and keeps walking. "Thankfully, if you are here, you already know how to get on and off a moving train, so I don't need to teach you that."

I shouldn't be surprised that the Dauntless expect us to hit the ground running, but I anticipated more than six hours of rest before the running began. My body is still heavy from sleep.

"Initiation is divided into three stages. We will measure your progress and rank you according to your performance in each stage. The stages are not weighed equally in determining your final rank, so it is possible, though difficult, to drastically improve your rank over time."

I stare at the weapon in my hand. Never in my life did I expect to hold a gun, let alone fire one. It feels dangerous to me, as if just by touching it, I could hurt someone.

"We believe that preparation eradicates cowardice, which we define as the failure to act in the midst of fear," says Four. "Therefore each stage of initiation is intended to prepare you in a different way. The first stage is primarily physical; the second, primarily emotional; the third, primarily mental."

"But what . . ." Peter yawns through his words. "What does firing a gun have to do with . . . bravery?"

Four flips the gun in his hand, presses the barrel to Peter's forehead, and clicks a bullet into place. Peter freezes with his lips parted, the yawn dead in his mouth.

"Wake. Up," Four snaps. "You are holding a loaded gun, you idiot. Act like it."

He lowers the gun. Once the immediate threat is gone, Peter's green eyes harden. I'm surprised he can stop himself from responding, after speaking his mind all his life in Candor, but he does, his cheeks red.

"And to answer your question . . . you are far less likely to soil your pants and cry for your mother if you're prepared to defend yourself." Four stops walking at the end of the row and turns on his heel. "This is also information you may need later in stage one. So, watch me."

He faces the wall with the targets on it—one square of plywood with three red circles on it for each of us. He stands with his feet apart, holds the gun in both hands, and fires. The bang is so loud it hurts my ears. I crane my neck to look at the target. The bullet went through the middle circle.

I turn to my own target. My family would never approve of me firing a gun. They would say that guns are used for self-defense, if not violence, and therefore they are self-serving.

I push my family from my mind, set my feet shoulder-width apart, and delicately wrap both hands around the handle of the gun. It's heavy and hard to lift away from my body, but I want it to be as far from my face as possible. I squeeze the trigger, hesitantly at first and then harder, cringing away from the gun. The sound hurts my ears and the recoil sends my hands back, toward my nose. I stumble, pressing my hand to the wall behind me for balance. I don't know where my bullet went, but I know it's not near the target.

I fire again and again and again, and none of the bullets come close.

"Statistically speaking," the Erudite boy next to me—his name is Will—says, grinning at me, "you should have

hit the target at least *once* by now, even by accident."
He is blond, with shaggy hair and a crease between his
eyebrows.

"Is that so," I say without inflection.

"Yeah," he says. "I think you're actually defying nature."

I grit my teeth and turn toward the target, resolving to
at least stand still. If I can't master the first task they give
us, how will I ever make it through stage one?

I squeeze the trigger, hard, and this time I'm ready for
the recoil. It makes my hands jump back, but my feet stay
planted. A bullet hole appears at the edge of the target,
and I raise an eyebrow at Will.

"So you see, I'm right. The stats don't lie," he says.

I smile a little.

It takes me five rounds to hit the middle of the target,
and when I do, a rush of energy goes through me. I am
awake, my eyes wide open, my hands warm. I lower the
gun. There is power in controlling something that can do
so much damage—in controlling something, period.

Maybe I do belong here.

+ + +

By the time we break for lunch, my arms throb from holding up the gun and my fingers are hard to straighten. I
massage them on my way to the dining hall. Christina

invites Al to sit with us. Every time I look at him, I hear his sobs again, so I try not to look at him.

I move my peas around with my fork, and my thoughts drift back to the aptitude tests. When Tori warned me that being Divergent was dangerous, I felt like it was branded on my face, and if I so much as turned the wrong way, someone would see it. So far it hasn't been a problem, but that doesn't make me feel safe. What if I let my guard down and something terrible happens?

"Oh, come on. You don't remember me?" Christina asks Al as she makes a sandwich. "We were in Math together just a few *days* ago. And I am *not* a quiet person."

"I slept through Math most of the time," Al replies. "It was first hour!"

What if the danger doesn't come soon—what if it strikes years from now and I never see it coming?

"Tris," says Christina. She snaps her fingers in front of my face. "You in there?"

"What? What is it?"

"I asked if you remember ever taking a class with me," she says. "I mean, no offense, but I probably wouldn't remember if you did. All the Abnegation looked the same to me. I mean, they still do, but now you're not one of them."

I stare at her. As if I need her to remind me.

"Sorry, am I being rude?" she asks. "I'm used to just saying whatever is on my mind. Mom used to say that politeness is deception in pretty packaging."

"I think that's why our factions don't usually associate with each other," I say, with a short laugh. Candor and Abnegation don't hate each other the way Erudite and Abnegation do, but they avoid each other. Candor's real problem is with Amity. Those who seek peace above all else, they say, will always deceive to keep the water calm.

"Can I sit here?" says Will, tapping the table with his finger.

"What, you don't want to hang out with your Erudite buddies?" says Christina.

"They aren't my buddies," says Will, setting his plate down. "Just because we were in the same faction doesn't mean we get along. Plus, Edward and Myra are dating, and I would rather not be the third wheel."

Edward and Myra, the other Erudite transfers, sit two tables away, so close they bump elbows as they cut their food. Myra pauses to kiss Edward. I watch them carefully. I've only seen a few kisses in my life.

Edward turns his head and presses his lips to Myra's. Air hisses between my teeth, and I look away. Part of me waits for them to be scolded. Another part wonders, with a touch of desperation, what it would feel like to have someone's lips against mine.

"Do they have to be so *public*?" I say.

"She just kissed him." Al frowns at me. When he frowns, his thick eyebrows touch his eyelashes. "It's not like they're stripping naked."

"A kiss is not something you do in public."

Al, Will, and Christina all give me the same knowing smile.

"What?" I say.

"Your Abnegation is showing," says Christina. "The rest of us are all right with a little affection in public."

"Oh." I shrug. "Well . . . I guess I'll have to get over it, then."

"Or you can stay frigid," says Will, his green eyes glinting with mischief. "You know. If you want."

Christina throws a roll at him. He catches it and bites it.

"Don't be mean to her," she says. "Frigidity is in her nature. Sort of like being a know-it-all is in yours."

"I am not *frigid*!" I exclaim.

"Don't worry about it," says Will. "It's endearing. Look, you're all red."

The comment only makes my face hotter. Everyone else chuckles. I force a laugh and, after a few seconds, it comes naturally.

It feels good to laugh again.

After lunch, Four leads us to a new room. It's huge, with a wood floor that is cracked and creaky and has a large circle painted in the middle. On the left wall is a green board—a chalkboard. My Lower Levels teacher used one, but I haven't seen one since then. Maybe it has something to do with Dauntless priorities: training comes first, technology comes second.

Our names are written on the board in alphabetical order. Hanging at three-foot intervals along one end of the room are faded black punching bags.

We line up behind them and Four stands in the middle, where we can all see him.

"As I said this morning," says Four, "next you will learn how to fight. The purpose of this is to prepare you to act; to prepare your body to respond to threats and challenges—which you will need, if you intend to survive life as a Dauntless."

I can't even think of life as a Dauntless. All I can think about is making it through initiation.

"We will go over technique today, and tomorrow you will start to fight each other," says Four. "So I recommend that you pay attention. Those who don't learn fast will get hurt."

Four names a few different punches, demonstrating

each one as he does, first against the air and then against the punching bag.

I catch on as we practice. Like with the gun, I need a few tries to figure out how to hold myself and how to move my body to make it look like his. The kicks are more difficult, though he only teaches us the basics. The punching bag stings my hands and feet, turning my skin red, and barely moves no matter how hard I hit it. All around me is the sound of skin hitting tough fabric.

Four wanders through the crowd of initiates, watching us as we go through the movements again. When he stops in front of me, my insides twist like someone's stirring them with a fork. He stares at me, his eyes following my body from my head to my feet, not lingering anywhere—a practical, scientific gaze.

"You don't have much muscle," he says, "which means you're better off using your knees and elbows. You can put more power behind them."

Suddenly he presses a hand to my stomach. His fingers are so long that, though the heel of his hand touches one side of my rib cage, his fingertips still touch the other side. My heart pounds so hard my chest hurts, and I stare at him, wide-eyed.

"Never forget to keep tension here," he says in a quiet voice.

Four lifts his hand and keeps walking. I feel the pressure

of his palm even after he's gone. It's strange, but I have to stop and breathe for a few seconds before I can keep practicing again.

When Four dismisses us for dinner, Christina nudges me with her elbow.

"I'm surprised he didn't break you in half," she says. She wrinkles her nose. "He scares the hell out of me. It's that quiet voice he uses."

"Yeah. He's . . ." I look over my shoulder at him. He is quiet, and remarkably self-possessed. But I wasn't afraid that he would hurt me. ". . . definitely intimidating," I finally say.

Al, who was in front of us, turns around once we reach the Pit and announces, "I want to get a tattoo."

From behind us, Will asks, "A tattoo of what?"

"I don't know." Al laughs. "I just want to feel like I've actually left the old faction. Stop crying about it." When we don't respond, he adds, "I know you've heard me."

"Yeah, learn to quiet down, will you?" Christina pokes Al's thick arm. "I think you're right. We're half in, half out right now. If we want all the way in, we should look the part."

She gives me a look.

"No. I will not cut my hair," I say, "or dye it a strange color. Or pierce my face."

"How about your bellybutton?" she says.

"Or your nipple?" Will says with a snort.

I groan.

Now that training is done for the day, we can do whatever we want until it's time to sleep. The idea makes me feel almost giddy, although that might be from fatigue.

The Pit is swarming with people. Christina announces that she and I will meet Al and Will at the tattoo parlor and drags me toward the clothing place. We stumble up the path, climbing higher above the Pit floor, scattering stones with our shoes.

"What is wrong with my clothes?" I say. "I'm not wearing gray anymore."

"They're ugly and gigantic." She sighs. "Will you just let me help you? If you don't like what I put you in, you never have to wear it again, I promise."

Ten minutes later I stand in front of a mirror in the clothing place wearing a knee-length black dress. The skirt isn't full, but it isn't stuck to my thighs, either—unlike the first one she picked out, which I refused. Goose bumps appear on my bare arms. She slips the tie from my hair and I shake it out of its braid so it hangs wavy over my shoulders.

Then she holds up a black pencil.

"Eyeliner," she says.

"You aren't going to be able to make me pretty, you

know." I close my eyes and hold still. She runs the tip of the pencil along the line of my eyelashes. I imagine standing before my family in these clothes, and my stomach twists like I might be sick.

"Who cares about pretty? I'm going for noticeable."

I open my eyes and for the first time stare openly at my own reflection. My heart rate picks up as I do, like I am breaking the rules and will be scolded for it. It will be difficult to break the habits of thinking Abnegation instilled in me, like tugging a single thread from a complex work of embroidery. But I will find new habits, new thoughts, new rules. I will become something else.

My eyes were blue before, but a dull, grayish blue—the eyeliner makes them piercing. With my hair framing my face, my features look softer and fuller. I am not pretty—my eyes are too big and my nose is too long—but I can see that Christina is right. My face is noticeable.

Looking at myself now isn't like seeing myself for the first time; it's like seeing someone else for the first time. Beatrice was a girl I saw in stolen moments at the mirror, who kept quiet at the dinner table. This is someone whose eyes claim mine and don't release me; this is Tris.

"See?" she says. "You're . . . striking."

Under the circumstances, it's the best compliment she could have given me. I smile at her in the mirror.

"You like it?" she says.

"Yeah." I nod. "I look like . . . a different person."

She laughs. "That a good thing or a bad thing?"

I look at myself head-on again. For the first time, the idea of leaving my Abnegation identity behind doesn't make me nervous; it gives me hope.

"A good thing." I shake my head. "Sorry, I've just never been allowed to stare at my reflection for this long."

"Really?" Christina shakes her head. "Abnegation is a strange faction, I have to tell you."

"Let's go watch Al get tattooed," I say. Despite the fact that I have left my old faction behind, I don't want to criticize it yet.

At home, my mother and I picked up nearly identical stacks of clothing every six months or so. It's easy to allocate resources when everyone gets the same thing, but everything is more varied at the Dauntless compound. Every Dauntless gets a certain amount of points to spend per month, and the dress costs one of them.

Christina and I race down the narrow path to the tattoo place. When we get there, Al is sitting in the chair already, and a small, narrow man with more ink than bare skin is drawing a spider on his arm.

Will and Christina flip through books of pictures, elbowing each other when they find a good one. When they sit next to each other, I notice how opposite they are,

Christina dark and lean, Will pale and solid, but alike in their easy smiles.

I wander around the room, looking at the artwork on the walls. These days, the only artists are in Amity. Abnegation sees art as impractical, and its appreciation as time that could be spent serving others, so though I have seen works of art in textbooks, I have never been in a decorated room before. It makes the air feel close and warm, and I could get lost here for hours without noticing. I skim the wall with my fingertips. A picture of a hawk on one wall reminds me of Tori's tattoo. Beneath it is a sketch of a bird in flight.

"It's a raven," a voice behind me says. "Pretty, right?"

I turn to see Tori standing there. I feel like I am back in the aptitude test room, with the mirrors all around me and the wires connected to my forehead. I didn't expect to see her again.

"Well, hello there." She smiles. "Never thought I would see you again. Beatrice, is it?"

"Tris, actually," I say. "Do you work here?"

"I do. I just took a break to administer the tests. Most of the time I'm here." She taps her chin. "I recognize that name. You were the first jumper, weren't you?"

"Yes, I was."

"Well done."

"Thanks." I touch the sketch of the bird. "Listen—I need

to talk to you about . . ." I glance over at Will and Christina. I can't corner Tori now; they'll ask questions. ". . . something. Sometime."

"I am not sure that would be wise," she says quietly. "I helped you as much as I could, and now you will have to go it alone."

I purse my lips. She has answers; I know she does. If she won't give them to me now, I will have to find a way to make her tell me some other time.

"Want a tattoo?" she says.

The bird sketch holds my attention. I never intended to get pierced or tattooed when I came here. I know that if I do, it will place another wedge between me and my family that I can never remove. And if my life here continues as it has been, it may soon be the least of the wedges between us.

But I understand now what Tori said about her tattoo representing a fear she overcame—a reminder of where she was, as well as a reminder of where she is now. Maybe there is a way to honor my old life as I embrace my new one.

"Yes," I say. "Three of these flying birds."

I touch my collarbone, marking the path of their flight—toward my heart. One for each member of the family I left behind.

CHAPTER NINE

"SINCE THERE ARE an odd number of you, one of you won't be fighting today," says Four, stepping away from the board in the training room. He gives me a look. The space next to my name is blank.

The knot in my stomach unravels. A reprieve.

"This isn't good," says Christina, nudging me with her elbow. Her elbow prods one of my sore muscles—I have more sore muscles than not-sore muscles, this morning—and I wince.

"Ow."

"Sorry," she says. "But look. I'm up against the Tank."

Christina and I sat together at breakfast, and earlier she shielded me from the rest of the dormitory as I changed. I haven't had a friend like her before. Susan was better friends with Caleb than with me, and Robert only went where Susan went.

I guess I haven't really had a friend, period. It's impossible to have real friendship when no one feels like they can accept help or even talk about themselves. That won't happen here. I already know more about Christina than I ever knew about Susan, and it's only been two days.

"The Tank?" I find Christina's name on the board. Written next to it is "Molly."

"Yeah, Peter's slightly more feminine-looking minion," she says, nodding toward the cluster of people on the other side of the room. Molly is tall like Christina, but that's where the similarities end. She has broad shoulders, bronze skin, and a bulbous nose.

"Those three"—Christina points at Peter, Drew, and Molly in turn—"have been inseparable since they crawled out of the womb, practically. I hate them."

Will and Al stand across from each other in the arena. They put their hands up by their faces to protect themselves, as Four taught us, and shuffle in a circle around each other. Al is half a foot taller than Will, and twice as broad. As I stare at him, I realize that even his facial features are big—big nose, big lips, big eyes. This fight won't last long.

I glance at Peter and his friends. Drew is shorter than

both Peter and Molly, but he's built like a boulder, and his shoulders are always hunched. His hair is orange-red, the color of an old carrot.

"What's wrong with them?" I say.

"Peter is pure evil. When we were kids, he would pick fights with people from other factions and then, when an adult came to break it up, he'd cry and make up some story about how the other kid started it. And of course, they believed him, because we were Candor and we couldn't lie. Ha ha."

Christina wrinkles her nose and adds, "Drew is just his sidekick. I doubt he has an independent thought in his brain. And Molly . . . she's the kind of person who fries ants with a magnifying glass just to watch them flail around."

In the arena, Al punches Will hard in the jaw. I wince. Across the room, Eric smirks at Al, and turns one of the rings in his eyebrow.

Will stumbles to the side, one hand pressed to his face, and blocks Al's next punch with his free hand. Judging by his grimace, blocking the punch is as painful as a blow would have been. Al is slow, but powerful.

Peter, Drew, and Molly cast furtive looks in our direction and then pull their heads together, whispering.

"I think they know we're talking about them," I say.

"So? They already know I hate them."

"They do? How?"

Christina fakes a smile at them and waves. I look down, my cheeks warm. I shouldn't be gossiping anyway. Gossiping is self-indulgent.

Will hooks a foot around one of Al's legs and yanks back, knocking Al to the ground. Al scrambles to his feet.

"Because I've told them," she says, through the gritted teeth of her smile. Her teeth are straight on top and crooked on the bottom. She looks at me. "We try to be pretty honest about our feelings in Candor. Plenty of people have told me that they don't like me. And plenty of people haven't. Who cares?"

"We just . . . weren't supposed to hurt people," I say.

"I like to think I'm helping them by hating them," she says. "I'm reminding them that they aren't God's gift to humankind."

I laugh a little at that and focus on the arena again. Will and Al face each other for a few more seconds, more hesitant than they were before. Will flicks his pale hair from his eyes. They glance at Four like they're waiting for him to call the fight off, but he stands with his arms folded, giving no response. A few feet away from him, Eric checks his watch.

After a few seconds of circling, Eric shouts, "Do you

think this is a leisure activity? Should we break for nap-
time? Fight each other!"

"But . . ." Al straightens, letting his hands down, and
says, "Is it scored or something? When does the fight end?"

"It ends when one of you is unable to continue," says
Eric.

"According to Dauntless rules," Four says, "one of you
could also concede."

Eric narrows his eyes at Four. "According to the *old*
rules," he says. "In the *new* rules, no one concedes."

"A brave man acknowledges the strength of others,"
Four replies.

"A brave man never surrenders."

Four and Eric stare at each other for a few seconds. I
feel like I am looking at two different kinds of Dauntless—
the honorable kind, and the ruthless kind. But even I
know that in this room, it's Eric, the youngest leader of
the Dauntless, who has the authority.

Beads of sweat dot Al's forehead; he wipes them with
the back of his hand.

"This is ridiculous," Al says, shaking his head. "What's
the point of beating him up? We're in the same faction!"

"Oh, you think it's going to be that easy?" Will asks,
grinning. "Go on. Try to hit me, slowpoke."

Will puts his hands up again. I see determination in

Will's eyes that wasn't there before. Does he really believe he can win? One hard shot to the head and Al will knock him out cold.

That is, if he can actually hit Will. Al tries a punch, and Will ducks, the back of his neck shining with sweat. He dodges another punch, slipping around Al and kicking him hard in the back. Al lurches forward and turns.

When I was younger, I read a book about grizzly bears. There was a picture of one standing on its hind legs with its paws outstretched, roaring. That is how Al looks now. He charges at Will, grabbing his arm so he can't slip away, and punches him hard in the jaw.

I watch the light leave Will's eyes, which are pale green, like celery. They roll back into his head, and all the tension falls from his body. He slips from Al's grasp, dead weight, and crumples to the floor. Cold rushes down my back and fills my chest.

Al's eyes widen, and he crouches next to Will, tapping his cheek with one hand. The room falls silent as we wait for Will to respond. For a few seconds, he doesn't, just lies on the ground with an arm bent beneath him. Then he blinks, clearly dazed.

"Get him up," Eric says. He stares with greedy eyes at Will's fallen body, like the sight is a meal and he hasn't eaten in weeks. The curl of his lip is cruel.

Four turns to the chalkboard and circles Al's name. Victory.

"Next up—Molly and Christina!" shouts Eric. Al pulls Will's arm across his shoulders and drags him out of the arena.

Christina cracks her knuckles. I would wish her luck, but I don't know what good that would do. Christina isn't weak, but she's much narrower than Molly. Hopefully her height will help her.

Across the room, Four supports Will from the waist and leads him out. Al stands for a moment by the door, watching them go.

Four leaving makes me nervous. Leaving us with Eric is like hiring a babysitter who spends his time sharpening knives.

Christina tucks her hair behind her ears. It is chin-length, black, and pinned back with silver clips. She cracks another knuckle. She looks nervous, and no wonder—who wouldn't be nervous after watching Will collapse like a rag doll?

If conflict in Dauntless ends with only one person standing, I am unsure of what this part of initiation will do to me. Will I be Al, standing over a man's body, knowing I'm the one who put him on the ground, or will I be Will, lying in a helpless heap? And is it selfish of me to crave victory, or is it brave? I wipe my sweaty palms on my pants.

I snap to attention when Christina kicks Molly in the side. Molly gasps and grits her teeth like she's about to growl through them. A lock of stringy black hair falls across her face, but she doesn't brush it away.

Al stands next to me, but I'm too focused on the new fight to look at him, or congratulate him on winning, assuming that's what he wants. I am not sure.

Molly smirks at Christina, and without warning, dives, hands outstretched, at Christina's midsection. She hits her hard, knocking her down, and pins her to the ground. Christina thrashes, but Molly is heavy and doesn't budge.

She punches, and Christina moves her head out of the way, but Molly just punches again, and again, until her fist hits Christina's jaw, her nose, her mouth. Without thinking, I grab Al's arm and squeeze it as tightly as I can. I just need something to hold on to. Blood runs down the side of Christina's face and splatters on the ground next to her cheek. This is the first time I have ever prayed for someone to fall unconscious.

But she doesn't. Christina screams and drags one of her arms free. She punches Molly in the ear, knocking her off-balance, and wriggles free. She comes to her knees, holding her face with one hand. The blood streaming from her nose is thick and dark and covers her fingers in seconds. She screams again and crawls away from Molly. I can tell by the heaving of her shoulders that she's sobbing, but I can barely hear her over the throbbing in my ears.

Please go unconscious.

Molly kicks Christina's side, sending her sprawling on her back. Al frees his hand and pulls me tight to his side. I clench my teeth to keep from crying out. I had no sympathy for Al the first night, but I am not cruel yet; the sight of Christina clutching her rib cage makes me want to stand between her and Molly.

"Stop!" wails Christina as Molly pulls her foot back to kick again. She holds out a hand. "Stop! I'm . . ." She coughs. "I'm done."

Molly smiles, and I sigh with relief. Al sighs too, his rib cage lifting and falling against my shoulder.

Eric walks toward the center of the arena, his movements slow, and stands over Christina with his arms folded. He says quietly, "I'm sorry, what did you say? You're done?"

Christina pushes herself to her knees. When she takes her hand from the ground, it leaves a red handprint behind. She pinches her nose to stop the bleeding and nods.

"Get up," he says. If he had yelled, I might not have felt like everything inside my stomach was about to come out of it. If he had yelled, I would have known that the yelling was the worst he planned to do. But his voice is quiet and his words precise. He grabs Christina's arm, yanks her to her feet, and drags her out the door.

"Follow me," he says to the rest of us.

And we do.

+ + +

I feel the roar of the river in my chest.

We stand near the railing. The Pit is almost empty; it is the middle of the afternoon, though it feels like it's been night for days.

If there were people around, I doubt any of them would help Christina. We are with Eric, for one thing, and for another, the Dauntless have different rules—rules that brutality does not violate.

Eric shoves Christina against the railing.

"Climb over it," he says.

"What?" She says it like she expects him to relent, but her wide eyes and ashen face suggest otherwise. Eric will not back down.

"Climb over the railing," says Eric again, pronouncing each word slowly. "If you can hang over the chasm for five minutes, I will forget your cowardice. If you can't, I will not allow you to continue initiation."

The railing is narrow and made of metal. The spray

from the river coats it, making it slippery and cold. Even if Christina is brave enough to hang from the railing for five minutes, she may not be able to hold on. Either she decides to be factionless, or she risks death.

When I close my eyes, I imagine her falling onto the jagged rocks below and shudder.

"Fine," she says, her voice shaking.

She is tall enough to swing her leg over the railing. Her foot shakes. She puts her toe on the ledge as she lifts her other leg over. Facing us, she wipes her hands on her pants and holds on to the railing so hard her knuckles turn white. Then she takes one foot off the ledge. And the other. I see her face between the bars of the barrier, determined, her lips pressed together.

Next to me, Al sets his watch.

For the first minute and a half, Christina is fine. Her hands stay firm around the railing and her arms don't shake. I start to think she might make it and show Eric how foolish he was to doubt her.

But then the river hits the wall, and white water sprays against Christina's back. Her face strikes the barrier, and she cries out. Her hands slip so she's just holding on by her fingertips. She tries to get a better grip, but now her hands are wet.

If I help her, Eric would make my fate the same as hers. Will I let her fall to her death, or will I resign myself to being factionless? What's worse: to be idle while someone dies, or to be exiled and empty-handed?

My parents would have no problem answering that question.

But I am not my parents.

As far as I know, Christina hasn't cried since we got here, but now her face crumples and she lets out a sob that is louder than the river. Another wave hits the wall and the spray coats her body. One of the droplets hits my cheek. Her hands slip again, and this time, one of them falls from the railing, so she's hanging by four fingertips.

"Come on, Christina," says Al, his low voice surprisingly loud. She looks at him. He claps. "Come on, grab it again. You can do it. Grab it."

Would I even be strong enough to hold on to her? Would it be worth my effort to try to help her if I know I'm too weak to do any good?

I know what those questions are: excuses. *Human reason can excuse any evil; that is why it's so important that we don't rely on it.* My father's words.

Christina swings her arm, fumbling for the railing. No one else cheers her on, but Al brings his big hands together and shouts, his eyes holding hers. I wish I could; I wish I could move, but I just stare at her and wonder how long I have been this disgustingly selfish.

I stare at Al's watch. Four minutes have passed. He elbows me hard in the shoulder.

"Come on," I say. My voice is a whisper. I clear my throat. "One minute left," I say, louder this time. Christina's other hand finds the railing again. Her arms shake so hard I wonder if the earth is quaking beneath me, jiggling my vision, and I just didn't notice.

"Come on, Christina," Al and I say, and as our voices join, I believe I might be strong enough to help her.

I will help her. If she slips again, I will.

Another wave of water splashes against Christina's back, and she shrieks as both her hands slip off the railing. A scream launches from my mouth. It sounds like it belongs to someone else.

But she doesn't fall. She grabs the bars of the barrier. Her fingers slide down the metal until I can't see her head anymore; they are all I see.

Al's watch reads 5:00.

"Five minutes are up," he says, almost spitting the words at Eric.

Eric checks his own watch. Taking his time, tilting his wrist, all while my stomach twists and I can't breathe. When I blink, I see Rita's sister on the pavement below the train tracks, limbs bent at strange angles; I see Rita screaming and sobbing; I see myself turning away.

"Fine," Eric says. "You can come up, Christina."

Al walks toward the railing.

"No," Eric says. "She has to do it on her own."

"No, she doesn't," Al growls. "She did what you said. She's not a coward. She did what you said."

Eric doesn't respond. Al reaches over the railing, and he's so tall that he can reach Christina's wrist. She grabs his forearm. Al pulls her up, his face red with frustration, and I run forward to help. I'm too short to do much good, as I suspected, but I grip Christina under the shoulder once she's high enough, and Al and I haul her over the barrier. She drops to the ground, her face still blood-smeared from the fight, her back soaking wet, her body quivering.

I kneel next to her. Her eyes lift to mine, then shift to Al, and we all catch our breath together.

CHAPTER
TEN

THAT NIGHT I dream that Christina hangs from the railing again, by her toes this time, and someone shouts that only someone who is Divergent can help her. So I run forward to pull her up, but someone shoves me over the edge, and I wake before I hit the rocks.

Sweat-soaked and shaky from the dream, I walk to the girls' bathroom to shower and change. When I come back, the word "Stiff" is spray-painted across my mattress in red. The word is written smaller along the bed frame, and again on my pillow. I look around, my heart pounding with anger.

Peter stands behind me, whistling as he fluffs his pillow. It's hard to believe I could hate someone who looks so kind—his eyebrows turn upward naturally, and he has a wide, white smile.

"Nice decorations," he says.

"Did I do something to you that I'm unaware of?" I demand. I grab the corner of a sheet and yank it away from the mattress. "I don't know if you've noticed, but we are in the same faction now."

"I don't know what you're referring to," he says lightly. Then he glances at me. "And you and I will *never* be in the same faction."

I shake my head as I remove my pillowcase from the pillow. *Don't get angry.* He wants to get a rise out of me; he won't. But every time he fluffs his pillow, I think about punching him in the gut.

Al walks in, and I don't even have to ask him to help me; he just walks over and strips bedding with me. I will have to scrub the bed frame later. Al carries the stack of sheets to the trash can and together we walk toward the training room.

"Ignore him," Al says. "He's an idiot, and if you don't get angry, he'll stop eventually."

"Yeah." I touch my cheeks. They are still warm with an angry blush. I try to distract myself. "Did you talk to Will?" I ask quietly. "After . . . you know."

"Yeah. He's fine. He isn't angry." Al sighs. "Now I'll always be remembered as the first guy who knocked someone out cold."

"There are worse ways to be remembered. At least

they won't antagonize you."

"There are better ways too." He nudges me with his elbow, smiling. "First jumper."

Maybe I was the first jumper, but I suspect that's where my Dauntless fame begins and ends.

I clear my throat. "One of you had to get knocked out, you know. If it hadn't been him, it would have been you."

"Still, I don't want to do it again." Al shakes his head, too many times, too fast. He sniffs. "I really don't."

We reach the door to the training room and I say, "But you have to."

He has a kind face. Maybe he is too kind for Dauntless.

I look at the chalkboard when I walk in. I didn't have to fight yesterday, but today I definitely will. When I see my name, I stop in the middle of the step.

My opponent is Peter.

"Oh no," says Christina, who shuffles in behind us. Her face is bruised, and she looks like she is trying not to limp. When she sees the board, she crumples the muffin wrapper she is holding into her fist. "Are they serious? They're really going to make *you* fight *him*?"

Peter is almost a foot taller than I am, and yesterday, he beat Drew in less than five minutes. Today Drew's face is more black-and-blue than flesh-toned.

"Maybe you can just take a few hits and pretend to go unconscious," suggests Al. "No one would blame you."

"Yeah," I say. "Maybe."

I stare at my name on the board. My cheeks feel hot. Al and Christina are just trying to help, but the fact that they don't believe, not even in a tiny corner of their minds, that I have a chance against Peter bothers me.

I stand at the side of the room, half listening to Al and Christina's chatter, and watch Molly fight Edward. He's much faster than she is, so I'm sure Molly will not win today.

As the fight goes on and my irritation fades, I start to get nervous. Four told us yesterday to exploit our opponent's weaknesses, and aside from his utter lack of likable qualities, Peter doesn't have any. He's tall enough to be strong but not so big that he's slow; he has an eye for other people's soft spots; he's vicious and won't show me any mercy. I would like to say that he underestimates me, but that would be a lie. I am as unskilled as he suspects.

Maybe Al is right, and I should just take a few hits and pretend to be unconscious.

But I can't afford not to try. I can't be ranked last.

By the time Molly peels herself off the ground, looking only half-conscious thanks to Edward, my heart is pounding so hard I can feel it in my fingertips. I can't remember how to stand. I can't remember how to punch. I walk to the center of the arena and my guts writhe as Peter comes toward me, taller than I remembered, arm muscles standing at attention. He smiles at me. I wonder if throwing up on him will do me any good.

I doubt it.

"You okay there, Stiff?" he says. "You look like you're about to cry. I might go easy on you if you cry."

Over Peter's shoulder, I see Four standing by the door with his arms folded. His mouth is puckered, like he just swallowed something sour. Next to him is Eric, who taps his foot faster than my heartbeat.

One second Peter and I are standing there, staring at each other, and the next Peter's hands are up by his face, his elbows bent. His knees are bent too, like he's ready to spring.

"Come on, Stiff," he says, his eyes glinting. "Just one little tear. Maybe some begging."

The thought of begging Peter for mercy makes me taste bile, and on an impulse, I kick him in the side. Or I would have kicked him in the side, if he hadn't caught my foot and yanked it forward, knocking me off-balance. My back smacks into the floor, and I pull my foot free, scrambling to my feet.

I have to stay on my feet so he can't kick me in the head. That's the only thing I can think about.

"Stop playing with her," snaps Eric. "I don't have all day."

Peter's mischievous look disappears. His arm twitches and pain stabs my jaw and spreads across my face, making my vision go black at the edges and my ears ring. I blink and lurch to the side as the room dips and sways. I don't remember his fist coming at me.

I am too off-balance to do anything but move away from him, as far as the arena will allow. He darts in front of me and kicks me hard in the stomach. His foot forces the air from my lungs and it hurts, hurts so badly I can't breathe, or maybe that's because of the kick, I don't know, I just fall.

On your feet is the only thought in my mind. I push myself up, but Peter is already there. He grabs my hair with one hand and punches me in the nose with the other. This pain is different, less like a stab and more like a crackle, crackling in my brain, spotting my vision with different colors, blue, green, red. I try to shove him off, my hands slapping at his arms, and he punches me again, this time in the ribs. My face is wet. Bloody nose. More red, I guess, but I'm too dizzy to look down.

He shoves me and I fall again, scraping my hands on the ground, blinking, sluggish and slow and hot. I cough and drag myself to my feet. I really should be lying down if the room is spinning this fast. And Peter spins around me; I am the center of a spinning planet, the only thing staying still. Something hits me from the side and I almost fall over again.

On my feet on my feet. I see a solid mass in front of me, a body. I punch as hard as I can, and my fist hits something soft. Peter barely groans, and smacks my ear with the flat of his palm, laughing under his breath. I hear ringing and try to blink some of the black patches out of my eyes; how did something get in my eye?

Out of my peripheral vision, I see Four shove the door open and walk out. Apparently this fight isn't interesting enough for him. Or maybe he's going to find out why everything's spinning like a top, and I don't blame him; I want to know the answer too.

My knees give out and the floor is cool against my cheek. Something slams into my side and I scream for the first time, a high screech that belongs to someone else and not me, and it slams into my side again, and I can't see anything at all, not even whatever is right in front of my face, the lights out. Someone shouts, "Enough!" and I think *too much* and *nothing at all.*

+ + +

When I wake up, I don't feel much, but the inside of my head is fuzzy, like it's packed with cotton balls.

I know that I lost, and the only thing keeping the pain

at bay is what is making it difficult to think straight.

"Is her eye already black?" someone asks.

I open one eye—the other stays shut like it's glued that way. Sitting to my right are Will and Al; Christina sits on the bed to my left with an ice pack on her jaw.

"What happened to your face?" I say. My lips feel clumsy and too large.

She laughs. "Look who's talking. Should we get you an eye patch?"

"Well, I already know what happened to *my* face," I say. "I was there. Sort of."

"Did you just make a *joke*, Tris?" Will says, grinning. "We should get you on painkillers more often if you're going to start cracking jokes. Oh, and to answer your question—I beat her up."

"I can't believe you couldn't beat Will," Al says, shaking his head.

"What? He's *good*," she says, shrugging. "Plus, I think I've finally learned how to stop losing. I just need to stop people from punching me in the jaw."

"You know, you'd think you would have figured that out already." Will winks at her. "Now I know why you aren't Erudite. Not too bright, are you?"

"You feeling okay, Tris?" Al says. His eyes are dark brown, almost the same color as Christina's skin. His cheek looks rough, like if he didn't shave it, he would have a thick beard. Hard to believe he's only sixteen.

"Yeah," I say. "Just wish I could stay here forever so I never have to see Peter again."

But I don't know where "here" is. I am in a large, narrow room with a row of beds on either side. Some of the beds have curtains between them. On the right side of the room is a nurse's station. This must be where the Dauntless go when they're sick or hurt. The woman there looks at us over a clipboard. I've never seen a nurse with so many piercings in her ear before. Some Dauntless must volunteer to do jobs that traditionally belong to other factions. After all, it wouldn't make sense for the Dauntless to make the trek to the city hospital every time they get hurt.

The first time I went to the hospital, I was six years old. My mother fell on the sidewalk in front of our house and broke her arm. Hearing her scream made me burst into tears, but Caleb just ran for my father without saying a word. At the hospital, an Amity woman in a yellow shirt with clean fingernails took my mother's blood pressure and set her bone with a smile.

I remember Caleb telling her that it would only take a month to mend, because it was a hairline fracture. I thought he was reassuring her, because that's what selfless people do, but now I wonder if he was repeating something he had studied; if all his Abnegation tendencies were just Erudite traits in disguise.

"Don't worry about Peter," says Will. "He'll at least get beat up by Edward, who has been studying hand-to-hand combat since we were ten years old. For fun."

"Good," says Christina. She checks her watch. "I think we're missing dinner. Do you want us to stay here, Tris?"

I shake my head. "I'm fine."

Christina and Will get up, but Al waves them ahead. He has a distinct smell—sweet and fresh, like sage and lemongrass. When he tosses and turns at night, I get a whiff of it and I know he's having a nightmare.

"I just wanted to tell you that you missed Eric's announcement. We're going on a field trip tomorrow, to the fence, to learn about Dauntless jobs," he says. "We have to be at the train by eight fifteen."

"Good," I say. "Thanks."

"And don't pay attention to Christina. Your face doesn't look that bad." He smiles a little. "I mean, it looks good. It always looks good. I mean—you look brave. Dauntless."

His eyes skirt mine, and he scratches the back of his head. The silence seems to grow between us. It was a nice thing to say, but he acts like it meant more than just the words. I hope I am wrong. I could not be attracted to Al—I could not be attracted to anyone that fragile. I smile as much as my bruised cheek will allow, hoping that will diffuse the tension.

"I should let you rest," he says. He gets up to leave, but before he can go, I grab his wrist.

"Al, are you okay?" I say. He stares blankly at me, and I add, "I mean, is it getting any easier?"

"Uh . . ." He shrugs. "A little."

He pulls his hand free and shoves it in his pocket. The question must have embarrassed him, because I've never seen him so red before. If I spent my nights sobbing into my pillow, I would be a little embarrassed too. At least when I cry, I know how to hide it.

"I lost to Drew. After your fight with Peter." He looks at me. "I took a few hits, fell down, and stayed there. Even though I didn't have to. I figure . . . I figure that since I beat Will, if I lose all the rest, I won't be ranked last, but I won't have to hurt anyone anymore."

"Is that really what you want?"

He looks down. "I just can't do it. Maybe that means I'm a coward."

"You're not a coward just because you don't want to hurt people," I say, because I know it's the right thing to say, even if I'm not sure I mean it.

For a moment we are both still, looking at each other.

Maybe I do mean it. If he is a coward, it isn't because he doesn't enjoy pain. It is because he refuses to act.

He gives me a pained look and says, "You think our families will visit us? They say transfer families never come on Visiting Day."

"I don't know," I say. "I don't know if it would be good or bad if they did."

"I think bad." He nods. "Yeah, it's already hard enough." He nods again, as if confirming what he just said, and walks away.

In less than a week, the Abnegation initiates will be able to visit their families for the first time since the Choosing Ceremony. They will go home and sit in their living rooms and interact with their parents for the first time as adults.

I used to look forward to that day. I used to think about what I would say to my mother and father when I was allowed to ask them questions at the dinner table.

In less than a week, the Dauntless-born initiates will find their families on the Pit floor, or in the glass building above the compound, and do whatever it is the Dauntless do when they reunite. Maybe they take turns throwing knives at each other's heads—it wouldn't surprise me.

And the transfer initiates with forgiving parents will be able to see them again too. I suspect mine will not be among them. Not after my father's cry of outrage at the ceremony. Not after both their children left them.

Maybe if I could have told them I was Divergent, and I was confused about what to choose, they would have understood. Maybe they would have helped me figure out what Divergent is, and what it means, and why it's dangerous. But I didn't trust them with that secret, so I will never know.

I clench my teeth as the tears come. I am fed up. I am fed up with tears and weakness. But there isn't much I can do to stop them.

Maybe I drift off to sleep, and maybe I don't. Later that night, though, I slip out of the room and go back to the dormitory. The only thing worse than letting Peter put me in the hospital would be letting him put me there overnight.

CHAPTER ELEVEN

THE NEXT MORNING, I don't hear the alarm, shuffling feet, or conversations as the other initiates get ready. I wake to Christina shaking my shoulder with one hand and tapping my cheek with the other. She already wears a black jacket zipped up to her throat. If she has bruises from yesterday's fight, her dark skin makes them difficult to see.

"Come on," she says. "Up and at 'em."

I dreamt that Peter tied me to a chair and asked me if I was Divergent. I answered no, and he punched me until I said yes. I woke up with wet cheeks.

I mean to say something, but all I can do is groan. My body aches so badly it hurts to breathe. It doesn't help that last night's bout of crying made my eyes swell. Christina offers me her hand.

The clock reads eight. We're supposed to be at the tracks by eight fifteen.

"I'll run and get us some breakfast. You just . . . get ready. Looks like it might take you a while," she says.

I grunt. Trying not to bend at the waist, I fumble in the drawer under my bed for a clean shirt. Luckily Peter isn't here to see me struggle. Once Christina leaves, the dormitory is empty.

I unbutton my shirt and stare at my bare side, which is patched with bruises. For a second the colors mesmerize me, bright green and deep blue and brown. I change as fast as I can and let my hair hang loose because I can't lift my arms to tie it back.

I look at my reflection in the small mirror on the back wall and see a stranger. She is blond like me, with a narrow face like mine, but that's where the similarities stop. *I* do not have a black eye, and a split lip, and a bruised jaw. *I* am not as pale as a sheet. She can't possibly be me, though she moves when I move.

By the time Christina comes back, a muffin in each hand, I'm sitting on the edge of my bed, staring at my untied shoes. I will have to bend over to tie them. It will hurt when I bend over.

But Christina just passes me a muffin and crouches in front of me to tie my shoes. Gratitude surges in my chest, warm and a little like an ache. Maybe there is some Abnegation in everyone, even if they don't know it.

Well, in everyone but Peter.

"Thank you," I say.

"Well, we would never get there on time if you had to tie them yourself," she says. "Come on. You can eat and walk at the same time, right?"

We walk fast toward the Pit. The muffin is banana-flavored, with walnuts. My mother baked bread like this once to give to the factionless, but I never got to try it. I was too old for coddling at that point. I ignore the pinch in my stomach that comes every time I think of my mother and half walk, half jog after Christina, who forgets that her legs are longer than mine.

We climb the steps from the Pit to the glass building above it and run to the exit. Every thump of my feet sends pain through my ribs, but I ignore it. We make it to the tracks just as the train arrives, its horn blaring.

"What took you so long?" Will shouts over the horn.

"Stumpy Legs over here turned into an old lady overnight," says Christina.

"Oh, shut up." I'm only half kidding.

Four stands at the front of the pack, so close to the tracks that if he shifted even an inch forward, the train would take his nose with it. He steps back to let some of the others get on first. Will hoists himself into the car with some difficulty, landing first on his stomach and then dragging his legs in behind him. Four grabs the handle on the side of the car and pulls himself in smoothly, like he doesn't have more than six feet of body to work with.

I jog next to the car, wincing, then grit my teeth and grab the handle on the side. This is going to hurt.

Al grabs me under each arm and lifts me easily into the car. Pain shoots through my side, but it only lasts for a second. I see Peter behind him, and my cheeks get warm. Al was trying to be nice, so I smile at him, but I wish people didn't want to be so nice. As if Peter didn't have enough ammunition already.

"Feeling okay there?" Peter says, giving me a look of mock sympathy—his lips turned down, his arched eyebrows pulled in. "Or are you a little . . . *Stiff*?"

He bursts into laughter at his joke, and Molly and Drew join in. Molly has an ugly laugh, all snorting and shaking shoulders, and Drew's is silent, so it almost looks like he's in pain.

"We are all awed by your incredible wit," says Will.

"Yeah, are you sure you don't belong with the Erudite, Peter?" Christina adds. "I hear they don't object to sissies."

Four, standing in the doorway, speaks before Peter can

retort. "Am I going to have to listen to your bickering all the way to the fence?"

Everyone gets quiet, and Four turns back to the car's opening. He holds the handles on either side, his arms stretching wide, and leans forward so his body is mostly outside the car, though his feet stay planted inside. The wind presses his shirt to his chest. I try to look past him at what we're passing—a sea of crumbling, abandoned buildings that get smaller as we go.

Every few seconds, though, my eyes shift back to Four. I don't know what I expect to see, or what I want to see, if anything. But I do it without thinking.

I ask Christina, "What do you think is out there?" I nod to the doorway. "I mean, beyond the fence."

She shrugs. "A bunch of farms, I guess."

"Yeah, but I mean . . . past the farms. What are we guarding the city from?"

She wiggles her fingers at me. "Monsters!"

I roll my eyes.

"We didn't even have guards near the fence until five years ago," says Will. "Don't you remember when Dauntless police used to patrol the factionless sector?"

"Yes," I say. I also remember that my father was one of the people who voted to get the Dauntless out of the factionless sector of the city. He said the poor didn't need policing; they needed help, and we could give it to them. But I would rather not mention that now, or here. It's one of the many things Erudite gives as evidence of Abnegation's incompetence.

"Oh, right," he says. "I bet you saw them all the time."

"Why do you say that?" I ask, a little too sharply. I don't want to be associated too closely with the factionless.

"Because you had to pass the factionless sector to get to school, right?"

"What did you do, memorize a map of the city for fun?" says Christina.

"Yes," says Will, looking puzzled. "Didn't you?"

The train's brakes squeal, and we all lurch forward as the car slows. I am grateful for the movement; it makes standing easier. The dilapidated buildings are gone, replaced by yellow fields and train tracks. The train stops under an awning. I lower myself to the grass, holding the handle to keep me steady.

In front of me is a chain-link fence with barbed wire strung along the top. When I walk forward, I notice that it continues farther than I can see, perpendicular to the horizon. Past the fence is a cluster of trees, most of them dead, some green. Milling around on the other side of the fence are Dauntless guards carrying guns.

"Follow me," says Four. I stay close to Christina. I don't

want to admit it, not even to myself, but I feel calmer when I'm near her. If Peter tries to taunt me, she will defend me.

Silently I scold myself for being such a coward. Peter's insults shouldn't bother me, and I should focus on getting better at combat, not on how badly I did yesterday. And I should be willing, if not able, to defend myself instead of relying on other people to do it for me.

Four leads us toward the gate, which is as wide as a house and opens up to the cracked road that leads to the city. When I came here with my family as a child, we rode in a bus on that road and beyond, to Amity's farms, where we spent the day picking tomatoes and sweating through our shirts.

Another pinch in my stomach.

"If you don't rank in the top five at the end of initiation, you will probably end up here," says Four as he reaches the gate. "Once you are a fence guard, there is some potential for advancement, but not much. You may be able to go on patrols beyond Amity's farms, but—"

"Patrols for what purpose?" asks Will.

Four lifts a shoulder. "I suppose you'll discover that if you find yourself among them. As I was saying. For the most part, those who guard the fence when they are young continue to guard the fence. If it comforts you, some of them insist that it isn't as bad as it seems."

"Yeah. At least we won't be driving buses or cleaning up other people's messes like the factionless," Christina whispers in my ear.

"What rank were you?" Peter asks Four.

I don't expect Four to answer, but he looks levelly at Peter and says, "I was first."

"And you chose to do *this*?" Peter's eyes are wide and round and dark green. They would look innocent to me if I didn't know what a terrible person he is. "Why didn't you get a government job?"

"I didn't want one," Four says flatly. I remember what he said on the first day, about working in the control room, where the Dauntless monitor the city's security. It is difficult for me to imagine him there, surrounded by computers. To me he belongs in the training room.

We learned about faction jobs in school. The Dauntless have limited options. We can guard the fence or work for the security of our city. We can work in the Dauntless compound, drawing tattoos or making weapons or even fighting each other for entertainment. Or we can work for the Dauntless leaders. That sounds like my best option.

The only problem is that my rank is terrible. And I might be factionless by the end of stage one.

We stop next to the gate. A few Dauntless guards glance in our direction but not many. They are too busy pulling the doors—which are twice as tall as they are and several times wider—open to admit a truck.

The man driving wears a hat, a beard, and a smile. He stops just inside the gate and gets out. The back of the truck is open, and a few other Amity sit among the stacks of crates. I peer at the crates—they hold apples.

"Beatrice?" an Amity boy says.

My head jerks at the sound of my name. One of the Amity in the back of the truck stands. He has curly blond hair and a familiar nose, wide at the tip and narrow at the bridge. Robert. I try to remember him at the Choosing Ceremony and nothing comes to mind but the sound of my heart in my ears. Who else transferred? Did Susan? Are there any Abnegation initiates this year? If Abnegation is fizzling, it's our fault—Robert's and Caleb's and mine. Mine. I push the thought from my mind.

Robert hops down from the truck. He wears a gray T-shirt and a pair of blue jeans. After a second's hesitation, he moves toward me and folds me in his arms. I stiffen. Only in Amity do people hug each other in greeting. I don't move a muscle until he releases me.

His own smile fades when he looks at me again. "Beatrice, what happened to you? What happened to your face?"

"Nothing," I say. "Just training. Nothing."

"Beatrice?" demands a nasal voice next to me. Molly folds her arms and laughs. "Is that your real name, Stiff?"

I glance at her. "What did you *think* Tris was short for?"

"Oh, I don't know . . . weakling?" She touches her chin. If her chin was bigger, it might balance out her nose, but it is weak and almost recedes into her neck. "Oh wait, *that* doesn't start with Tris. My mistake."

"There's no need to antagonize her," Robert says softly. "I'm Robert, and you are?"

"Someone who doesn't care what your name is," she says. "Why don't you get back in your truck? We're not supposed to fraternize with other faction members."

"Why don't you get away from us?" I snap.

"Right. Wouldn't want to get between you and your boyfriend," she says. She walks away smiling.

Robert gives me a sad look. "They don't seem like nice people."

"Some of them aren't."

"You could go home, you know. I'm sure Abnegation would make an exception for you."

"What makes you think I want to go home?" I ask, my cheeks hot. "You think I can't handle this or something?"

"It's not that." He shakes his head. "It's not that you can't, it's that you shouldn't have to. You should be happy."

"This is what I chose. This is it." I look over Robert's

shoulder. The Dauntless guards seem to have finished examining the truck. The bearded man gets back into the driver's seat and closes the door behind him. "Besides, Robert. The goal of my life isn't just . . . to be happy."

"Wouldn't it be easier if it was, though?" he says.

Before I can answer, he touches my shoulder and turns toward the truck. A girl in the back has a banjo on her lap. She starts to strum it as Robert hoists himself inside, and the truck starts forward, carrying the banjo sounds and her warbling voice away from us.

Robert waves to me, and again I see another possible life in my mind's eye. I see myself in the back of the truck, singing with the girl, though I've never sung before, laughing when I am off-key, climbing trees to pick the apples, always peaceful and always safe.

The Dauntless guards close the gate and lock it behind them. The lock is on the outside. I bite my lip. Why would they lock the gate from the outside and not the inside? It almost seems like they don't want to keep something out; they want to keep us in.

I push the thought out of my head. That makes no sense.

Four steps away from the fence, where he was talking to a female Dauntless guard with a gun balanced on her shoulder a moment before. "I am worried that you have a knack for making unwise decisions," he says when he's a foot away from me.

I cross my arms. "It was a two-minute conversation."

"I don't think a smaller time frame makes it any less unwise." He furrows his eyebrows and touches the corner of my bruised eye with his fingertips. My head jerks back, but he doesn't take his hand away. Instead he tilts his head and sighs. "You know, if you could just learn to attack first, you might do better."

"Attack first?" I say. "How will that help?"

"You're fast. If you can get a few good hits in before they know what's going on, you could win." He shrugs, and his hand falls.

"I'm surprised you know that," I say quietly, "since you left halfway through my one and only fight."

"It wasn't something I wanted to watch," he says.

What's that supposed to mean?

He clears his throat. "Looks like the next train is here. Time to go, Tris."

CHAPTER
TWELVE

I CRAWL ACROSS my mattress and heave a sigh. It has been two days since my fight with Peter, and my bruises are turning purple-blue. I have gotten used to aching every time I move, so now I move better, but I am still far from healed.

Even though I am still injured, I had to fight again today. Luckily this time, I was paired against Myra, who couldn't throw a good punch if someone was controlling her arm for her. I got a good hit in during the first two minutes. She fell down and was too dizzy to get back up. I should feel triumphant, but there is no triumph in punching a girl like Myra.

The second I touch my head to the pillow, the door to the dormitory opens, and people stream into the room with flashlights. I sit up, almost hitting my head on the bed frame above me, and squint through the dark to see what's going on.

"Everybody up!" someone roars. A flashlight shines behind his head, making the rings in his ears glint. Eric. Surrounding him are other Dauntless, some of whom I have seen in the Pit, some of whom I have never seen before. Four stands among them.

His eyes shift to mine and stay there. I stare back and forget that all around me the transfers are getting out of bed.

"Did you go deaf, Stiff?" demands Eric. I snap out of my daze and slide out from beneath the blankets. I am glad I sleep fully clothed, because Christina stands next to our bunk wearing only a T-shirt, her long legs bare. She folds her arms and stares at Eric. I wish, suddenly, that I could stare so boldly at someone with hardly any clothes on, but I would never be able to do that.

"You have five minutes to get dressed and meet us by the tracks," says Eric. "We're going on another field trip."

I shove my feet into shoes and sprint, wincing, behind Christina on the way to the train. A drop of sweat rolls down the back of my neck as we run up the paths along the walls of the Pit, pushing past members on our way up. They don't seem surprised to see us. I wonder how many frantic, running people they see on a weekly basis.

We make it to the tracks just behind the Dauntless-born

initiates. Next to the tracks is a black pile. I make out a cluster of long gun barrels and trigger guards.

"Are we going to *shoot* something?" Christina hisses in my ear.

Next to the pile are boxes of what looks like ammunition. I inch closer to read one of the boxes. Written on it is "PAINTBALLS."

I've never heard of them before, but the name is self-explanatory. I laugh.

"Everyone grab a gun!" shouts Eric.

We rush toward the pile. I am the closest to it, so I snatch the first gun I can find, which is heavy, but not too heavy for me to lift, and grab a box of paintballs. I shove the box in my pocket and sling the gun across my back so the strap crosses my chest.

"Time estimate?" Eric asks Four.

Four checks his watch. "Any minute now. How long is it going to take you to memorize the train schedule?"

"Why should I, when I have you to remind me of it?" says Eric, shoving Four's shoulder.

A circle of light appears on my left, far away. It grows larger as it comes closer, shining against the side of Four's face, creating a shadow in the faint hollow beneath his cheekbone.

He is the first to get on the train, and I run after him, not waiting for Christina or Will or Al to follow me. Four turns around as I fall into stride next to the car and holds out a hand. I grab his arm, and he pulls me in. Even the muscles in his forearm are taut, defined.

I let go quickly, without looking at him, and sit down on the other side of the car.

Once everyone is in, Four speaks up.

"We'll be dividing into two teams to play capture the flag. Each team will have an even mix of members, Dauntless-born initiates, and transfers. One team will get off first and find a place to hide their flag. Then the second team will get off and do the same." The car sways, and Four grabs the side of the doorway for balance. "This is a Dauntless tradition, so I suggest you take it seriously."

"What do we get if we win?" someone shouts.

"Sounds like the kind of question someone not from Dauntless would ask," says Four, raising an eyebrow. "You get to win, of course."

"Four and I will be your team captains," says Eric. He looks at Four. "Let's divide up transfers first, shall we?"

I tilt my head back. If they're picking us, I will be chosen last; I can feel it.

"You go first," Four says.

Eric shrugs. "Edward."

Four leans against the door frame and nods. The moonlight makes his eyes bright. He scans the group of transfer initiates briefly, without calculation, and says, "I want the Stiff."

A faint undercurrent of laughter fills the car. Heat rushes into my cheeks. I don't know whether to be angry at the people laughing at me or flattered by the fact that he chose me first.

"Got something to prove?" asks Eric, with his trademark smirk. "Or are you just picking the weak ones so that if you lose, you'll have someone to blame it on?"

Four shrugs. "Something like that."

Angry. I should definitely be angry. I scowl at my hands. Whatever Four's strategy is, it's based on the idea that I am weaker than the other initiates. And it gives me a bitter taste in my mouth. I have to prove him wrong—I *have* to.

"Your turn," says Four.

"Peter."

"Christina."

That throws a wrench in his strategy. Christina is not one of the weak ones. What exactly is he doing?

"Molly."

"Will," says Four, biting his thumbnail.

"Al."

"Drew."

"Last one left is Myra. So she's with me," says Eric.

"Dauntless-born initiates next."

I stop listening once they're finished with us. If Four isn't trying to prove something by choosing the weak, what is he doing? I look at each person he chooses. What do we have in common?

Once they're halfway through the Dauntless-born initiates, I have an idea of what it is. With the exception of Will and a couple of the others, we all share the same body type: narrow shoulders, small frames. All the people on Eric's team are broad and strong. Just yesterday, Four told me I was fast. We will all be faster than Eric's team, which will probably be good for capture the flag—I haven't played before, but I know it's a game of speed rather than brute force. I cover a smile with my hand. Eric is more ruthless than Four, but Four is smarter.

They finish choosing teams, and Eric smirks at Four.

"Your team can get off second," says Eric.

"Don't do me any favors," Four replies. He smiles a little. "You know I don't need them to win."

"No, I know that you'll lose no matter when you get off," says Eric, biting down briefly on one of the rings in his lip. "Take your scrawny team and get off first, then."

We all stand up. Al gives me a forlorn look, and I smile back in what I hope is a reassuring way. If any of the four of us had to end up on the same team as Eric, Peter, and Molly, at least it was him. They usually leave him alone.

The train is about to dip to the ground. I am determined to land on my feet.

Just before I jump, someone shoves my shoulder, and I almost topple out of the train car. I don't look back to see who it is—Molly, Drew, or Peter, it doesn't matter which one. Before they can try it again, I jump. This time I am ready for the momentum the train gives me, and I run a few steps to diffuse it but keep my balance. Fierce pleasure courses through me and I smile. It's a small accomplishment, but it makes me feel Dauntless.

One of the Dauntless-born initiates touches Four's shoulder and asks, "When your team won, where did you put the flag?"

"Telling you wouldn't really be in the spirit of the exercise, Marlene," he says coolly.

"Come on, Four," she whines. She gives him a flirtatious smile. He brushes her hand off his arm, and for some reason, I find myself grinning.

"Navy Pier," another Dauntless-born initiate calls out. He is tall, with brown skin and dark eyes. Handsome. "My brother was on the winning team. They kept the flag at the carousel."

"Let's go there, then," suggests Will.

No one objects, so we walk east, toward the marsh that

was once a lake. When I was young, I tried to imagine what it would look like as a lake, with no fence built into the mud to keep the city safe. But it is difficult to imagine that much water in one place.

"We're close to Erudite headquarters, right?" asks Christina, bumping Will's shoulder with her own.

"Yeah. It's south of here," he says. He looks over his shoulder, and for a second his expression is full of longing. Then it's gone.

I am less than a mile away from my brother. It has been a week since we were that close together. I shake my head a little to get the thought out of my mind. I can't think about him today, when I have to focus on making it through stage one. I can't think about him any day.

We walk across the bridge. We still need the bridges because the mud beneath them is too wet to walk on. I wonder how long it's been since the river dried up.

Once we cross the bridge, the city changes. Behind us, most of the buildings were in use, and even if they weren't, they looked well-tended. In front of us is a sea of crumbling concrete and broken glass. The silence of this part of the city is eerie; it feels like a nightmare. It's hard to see where I'm going, because it's after midnight and all the city lights are off.

Marlene takes out a flashlight and shines it at the street in front of us.

"Scared of the dark, Mar?" the dark-eyed Dauntless-born initiate teases.

"If you want to step on broken glass, Uriah, be my guest," she snaps. But she turns it off anyway.

I have realized that part of being Dauntless is being willing to make things more difficult for yourself in order to be self-sufficient. There's nothing especially brave about wandering dark streets with no flashlight, but we are not supposed to need help, even from light. We are supposed to be capable of anything.

I like that. Because there might come a day when there is no flashlight, there is no gun, there is no guiding hand. And I want to be ready for it.

The buildings end just before the marsh. A strip of land juts out into the marsh, and rising from it is a giant white wheel with dozens of red passenger cars dangling from it at regular intervals. The Ferris wheel.

"Think about it. People used to ride that thing. For *fun*," says Will, shaking his head.

"They must have been Dauntless," I say.

"Yeah, but a lame version of Dauntless." Christina laughs. "A Dauntless Ferris wheel wouldn't have cars. You would just hang on tight with your hands, and good luck to you."

We walk down the side of the pier. All the buildings on

my left are empty, their signs torn down and their windows closed, but it is a clean kind of emptiness. Whoever left these places left them by choice and at their leisure. Some places in the city are not like that.

"Dare you to jump into the marsh," says Christina to Will.

"You first."

We reach the carousel. Some of the horses are scratched and weathered, their tails broken off or their saddles chipped. Four takes the flag out of his pocket.

"In ten minutes, the other team will pick their location," he says. "I suggest you take this time to formulate a strategy. We may not be Erudite, but mental preparedness is one aspect of your Dauntless training. Arguably, it is the most important aspect."

He is right about that. What good is a prepared body if you have a scattered mind?

Will takes the flag from Four.

"Some people should stay here and guard, and some people should go out and scout the other team's location," Will says.

"Yeah? You think?" Marlene plucks the flag from Will's fingers. "Who put you in charge, transfer?"

"No one," says Will. "But someone's got to do it."

"Maybe we should develop a more defensive strategy.

Wait for them to come to us, then take them out," suggests Christina.

"That's the sissy way out," Uriah says. "I vote we go all out. Hide the flag well enough that they can't find it."

Everyone bursts into the conversation at once, their voices louder with each passing second. Christina defends Will's plan; the Dauntless-born initiates vote for offense; everyone argues about who should make the decision. Four sits down on the edge of the carousel, leaning against a plastic horse's foot. His eyes lift to the sky, where there are no stars, only a round moon peeking through a thin layer of clouds. The muscles in his arms are relaxed; his hand rests on the back of his neck. He looks almost comfortable, holding that gun to his shoulder.

I close my eyes briefly. Why does he distract me so easily? I need to focus.

What would I say if I could shout above the sniping behind me? We can't act until we know where the other team is. They could be anywhere within a two-mile radius, although I can rule out the empty marsh as an option. The best way to find them is not to argue about how to search for them, or how many to send out in a search party.

It's to climb as high as possible.

I look over my shoulder to make sure no one is watching.

None of them look at me, so I walk toward the Ferris wheel with light, quiet footsteps, pressing my gun to my back with one hand to keep it from making noise.

When I stare up at the Ferris wheel from the ground, my throat feels tighter. It is taller than I thought, so tall I can barely see the cars swinging at the top. The only good thing about its height is that it is built to support weight. If I climb it, it won't collapse beneath me.

My heart pumps faster. Will I really risk my life for this—to win a game the Dauntless like to play?

It's so dark I can barely see them, but when I stare at the huge, rusted supports holding the wheel in place, I see the rungs of a ladder. Each support is only as wide as my shoulders, and there are no railings to hold me in, but climbing a ladder is better than climbing the spokes of the wheel.

I grab a rung. It's rusty and thin and feels like it might crumble in my hands. I put my weight on the lowest rung to test it and jump to make sure it will hold me up. The movement hurts my ribs, and I wince.

"Tris," a low voice says behind me. I don't know why it doesn't startle me. Maybe because I am becoming Dauntless, and mental readiness is something I am supposed to develop. Maybe because his voice is low and smooth and almost soothing. Whatever the reason, I look over my shoulder. Four stands behind me with his gun slung across his back, just like mine.

"Yes?" I say.

"I came to find out what you think you're doing."

"I'm seeking higher ground," I say. "I don't *think* I'm doing anything."

I see his smile in the dark. "All right. I'm coming."

I pause a second. He doesn't look at me the way Will, Christina, and Al sometimes do—like I am too small and too weak to be of any use, and they pity me for it. But if he insists on coming with me, it is probably because he doubts me.

"I'll be fine," I say.

"Undoubtedly," he replies. I don't hear the sarcasm, but I know it's there. It has to be.

I climb, and when I'm a few feet off the ground, he comes after me. He moves faster than I do, and soon his hands find the rungs that my feet leave.

"So tell me . . . ," he says quietly as we climb. He sounds breathless. "What do you think the purpose of this exercise is? The game, I mean, not the climbing."

I stare down at the pavement. It seems far away now, but I'm not even a third of the way up. Above me is a platform, just below the center of the wheel. That's my destination. I don't even think about how I will climb back down.

The breeze that brushed my cheeks earlier now presses against my side. The higher we go, the stronger it will get. I need to be ready.

"Learning about strategy," I say. "Teamwork, maybe."

"Teamwork," he repeats. A laugh hitches in his throat. It sounds like a panicked breath.

"Maybe not," I say. "Teamwork doesn't seem to be a Dauntless priority."

The wind is stronger now. I press closer to the white support so I don't fall, but that makes it hard to climb. Below me the carousel looks small. I can barely see my team under the awning. Some of them are missing—a search party must have left.

Four says, "It's supposed to be a priority. It used to be."

But I'm not really listening, because the height is dizzying. My hands ache from holding the rungs, and my legs are shaking, but I'm not sure why. It isn't the height that scares me—the height makes me feel alive with energy, every organ and vessel and muscle in my body singing at the same pitch.

Then I realize what it is. It's him. Something about him makes me feel like I am about to fall. Or turn to liquid. Or burst into flames.

My hand almost misses the next rung.

"Now tell me . . . ," he says through a bursting breath,

"what do you think learning strategy has to do with . . . bravery?"

The question reminds me that he is my instructor, and I am supposed to learn something from this. A cloud passes over the moon, and the light shifts across my hands.

"It . . . it prepares you to act," I say finally. "You learn strategy so you can use it." I hear him breathing behind me, loud and fast. "Are you all right, Four?"

"Are you *human*, Tris? Being up this high . . ." He gulps for air. "It doesn't scare you at all?"

I look over my shoulder at the ground. If I fall now, I will die. But I don't think I will fall.

A gust of air presses against my left side, throwing my body weight to the right. I gasp and cling to the rungs, my balance shifting. Four's cold hand clamps around one of my hips, one of his fingers finding a strip of bare skin just under the hem of my T-shirt. He squeezes, steadying me and pushing me gently to the left, restoring my balance.

Now *I* can't breathe. I pause, staring at my hands, my mouth dry. I feel the ghost of where his hand was, his fingers long and narrow.

"You okay?" he asks quietly.

"Yes," I say, my voice strained.

I keep climbing, silently, until I reach the platform. Judging by the blunted ends of metal rods, it used to have railings, but it doesn't anymore. I sit down and scoot to the end of it so Four has somewhere to sit. Without thinking, I put my legs over the side. Four, however, crouches and presses his back to the metal support, breathing heavily.

"You're afraid of heights," I say. "How do you survive in the Dauntless compound?"

"I ignore my fear," he says. "When I make decisions, I pretend it doesn't exist."

I stare at him for a second. I can't help it. To me there's a difference between not being afraid and acting in spite of fear, as he does.

I have been staring at him too long.

"What?" he says quietly.

"Nothing."

I look away from him and toward the city. I have to focus. I climbed up here for a reason.

The city is pitch-black, but even if it wasn't, I wouldn't be able to see very far. A building stands in my way.

"We're not high enough," I say. I look up. Above me is a tangle of white bars, the wheel's scaffolding. If I climb carefully, I can wedge my feet between the supports and the crossbars and stay secure. Or as secure as possible.

"I'm going to climb," I say, standing up. I grab one of the bars above my head and pull myself up. Shooting pains go through my bruised sides, but I ignore them.

"For God's sake, Stiff," he says.

"You don't have to follow me," I say, staring at the maze of bars above me. I shove my foot onto the place where two bars cross and push myself up, grabbing another bar in the process. I sway for a second, my heart beating so hard I can't feel anything else. Every thought I have condenses into that heartbeat, moving at the same rhythm.

"Yes, I do," he says.

This is crazy, and I know it. A fraction of an inch of mistake, half a second of hesitation, and my life is over. Heat tears through my chest, and I smile as I grab the next bar. I pull myself up, my arms shaking, and force my leg under me so I'm standing on another bar. When I feel steady, I look down at Four. But instead of seeing him, I see straight to the ground.

I can't breathe.

I imagine my body plummeting, smacking into the bars as it falls down, and my limbs at broken angles on the pavement, just like Rita's sister when she didn't make it onto the roof. Four grabs a bar with each hand and pulls himself up, easy, like he's sitting up in bed. But he is not comfortable or natural here—every muscle in his arm stands out. It is a stupid thing for me to think when I am one hundred feet off the ground.

I grab another bar, find another place to wedge my foot.

When I look at the city again, the building isn't in my way. I'm high enough to see the skyline. Most of the buildings are black against a navy sky, but the red lights at the top of the Hub are lit up. They blink half as fast as my heartbeat.

Beneath the buildings, the streets look like tunnels. For a few seconds I see only a dark blanket over the land in front of me, just faint differences between building and sky and street and ground. Then I see a tiny pulsing light on the ground.

"See that?" I say, pointing.

Four stops climbing when he's right behind me and looks over my shoulder, his chin next to my head. His breaths flutter against my ear, and I feel shaky again, like I did when I was climbing the ladder.

"Yeah," he says. A smile spreads over his face.

"It's coming from the park at the end of the pier," he says. "Figures. It's surrounded by open space, but the trees provide some camouflage. Obviously not enough."

"Okay," I say. I look over my shoulder at him. We are so close I forget where I am; instead I notice that the corners of his mouth turn down naturally, just like mine, and that he has a scar on his chin.

"Um," I say. I clear my throat. "Start climbing down. I'll follow you."

Four nods and steps down. His leg is so long that he

finds a place for his foot easily and guides his body between the bars. Even in darkness, I see that his hands are bright red and shaking.

I step down with one foot, pressing my weight into one of the crossbars. The bar creaks beneath me and comes loose, clattering against half a dozen bars on the way down and bouncing on the pavement. I'm dangling from the scaffolding with my toes swinging in midair. A strangled gasp escapes me.

"Four!"

I try to find another place to put my foot, but the nearest foothold is a few feet away, farther than I can stretch. My hands are sweaty. I remember wiping them on my slacks before the Choosing Ceremony, before the aptitude test, before every important moment, and suppress a scream. I will slip. I will slip.

"Hold on!" he shouts. "Just hold on, I have an idea."

He keeps climbing down. He's moving in the wrong direction; he should be coming toward me, not going away from me. I stare at my hands, which are wrapped around the narrow bar so tightly my knuckles are white. My fingers are dark red, almost purple. They won't last long.

I won't last long.

I squeeze my eyes shut. Better not to look. Better to

pretend that none of this exists. I hear Four's sneakers squeak against metal and rapid footsteps on ladder rungs.

"Four!" I yell. Maybe he left. Maybe he abandoned me. Maybe this is a test of my strength, of my bravery. I breathe in my nose and out my mouth. I count my breaths to calm down. One, two. In, out. *Come on, Four* is all I can think. *Come on, do something.*

Then I hear something wheeze and creak. The bar I'm holding shudders, and I scream through my clenched teeth as I fight to keep my grip.

The wheel is moving.

Air wraps around my ankles and wrists as the wind gushes up, like a geyser. I open my eyes. I'm moving— toward the ground. I laugh, giddy with hysteria as the ground comes closer and closer. But I'm picking up speed. If I don't drop at the right time, the moving cars and metal scaffolding will drag at my body and carry me with them, and then I will really die.

Every muscle in my body tenses as I hurtle toward the ground. When I can see the cracks in the sidewalk, I drop, and my body slams into the ground, feet first. My legs collapse beneath me and I pull my arms in, rolling as fast as I can to the side. The cement scrapes my face, and I turn just in time to see a car bearing down on me, like a giant shoe about to crush me. I roll again, and the bottom of the car skims my shoulder.

I'm safe.

I press my palms to my face. I don't try to get up. If I did, I'm sure I would just fall back down. I hear footsteps, and Four's hands wrap around my wrists. I let him pry my hands from my eyes.

He encloses one of my hands perfectly between two of his. The warmth of his skin overwhelms the ache in my fingers from holding the bars.

"You all right?" he asks, pressing our hands together.

"Yeah."

He starts to laugh.

After a second, I laugh too. With my free hand, I push myself to a sitting position. I am aware of how little space there is between us—six inches at most. That space feels charged with electricity. I feel like it should be smaller.

He stands, pulling me up with him. The wheel is still moving, creating a wind that tosses my hair back.

"You could have told me that the Ferris wheel still worked," I say. I try to sound casual. "We wouldn't have had to climb in the first place."

"I would have, if I had known," he says. "Couldn't just let you hang there, so I took a risk. Come on, time to get their flag."

Four hesitates for a moment and then takes my arm,

his fingertips pressing to the inside of my elbow. In other factions, he would give me time to recover, but he is Dauntless, so he smiles at me and starts toward the carousel, where our team members guard our flag. And I half run, half limp beside him. I still feel weak, but my mind is awake, especially with his hand on me.

Christina is perched on one of the horses, her long legs crossed and her hand around the pole holding the plastic animal upright. Our flag is behind her, a glowing triangle in the dark. Three Dauntless-born initiates stand among the other worn and dirty animals. One of them has his hand on a horse's head, and a scratched horse eye stares at me between his fingers. Sitting on the edge of the carousel is an older Dauntless, scratching her quadruple-pierced eyebrow with her thumb.

"Where'd the others go?" asks Four.

He looks as excited as I feel, his eyes wide with energy.

"Did you guys turn on the wheel?" the older girl says. "What the hell are you thinking? You might as well have just shouted 'Here we are! Come and get us!'" She shakes her head. "If I lose again this year, the shame will be unbearable. Three years in a row?"

"The wheel doesn't matter," says Four. "We know where they are."

"We?" says Christina, looking from Four to me.

"Yes, while the rest of you were twiddling your

thumbs, Tris climbed the Ferris wheel to look for the other team," he says.

"What do we do now, then?" asks one of the Dauntless-born initiates through a yawn.

Four looks at me. Slowly the eyes of the other initiates, including Christina, migrate from him to me. I tense my shoulders, about to shrug and say I don't know, and then an image of the pier stretching out beneath me comes into my mind. I have an idea.

"Split in half," I say. "Four of us go to the right side of the pier, three to the left. The other team is in the park at the end of the pier, so the group of four will charge as the group of three sneaks behind the other team to get the flag."

Christina looks at me like she no longer recognizes me. I don't blame her.

"Sounds good," says the older girl, clapping her hands together. "Let's get this night over with, shall we?"

Christina joins me in the group going to the right, along with Uriah, whose smile looks white against his skin's bronze. I didn't notice before, but he has a tattoo of a snake behind his ear. I stare at its tail curling around his earlobe for a moment, but then Christina starts running and I have to follow her.

I have to run twice as fast to match my short strides

to her long ones. As I run, I realize that only one of us will get to touch the flag, and it won't matter that it was my plan and my information that got us to it if I'm not the one who grabs it. Though I can hardly breathe as it is, I run faster, and I'm on Christina's heels. I pull my gun around my body, holding my finger over the trigger.

We reach the end of the pier, and I clamp my mouth shut to keep my loud breaths in. We slow down so our footsteps aren't as loud, and I look for the blinking light again. Now that I'm on the ground, it's bigger and easier to see. I point, and Christina nods, leading the way toward it.

Then I hear a chorus of yells, so loud they make me jump. I hear puffs of air as paintballs go flying and splats as they find their targets. Our team has charged, the other team runs to meet us, and the flag is almost unguarded. Uriah takes aim and shoots the last guard in the thigh. The guard, a short girl with purple hair, throws her gun to the ground in a tantrum.

I sprint to catch up to Christina. The flag hangs from a tree branch, high above my head. I reach for it, and so does Christina.

"Come on, Tris," she says. "You're already the hero of the day. And you know you can't reach it anyway."

She gives me a patronizing look, the way people sometimes look at children when they act too adult, and snatches the flag from the branch. Without looking at me, she turns and gives a whoop of victory. Uriah's voice joins hers and then I hear a chorus of yells in the distance.

Uriah claps my shoulder, and I try to forget about the look Christina gave me. Maybe she's right; I've already proved myself today. I do not want to be greedy; I do not want to be like Eric, terrified of other people's strength.

The shouts of triumph become infectious, and I lift my voice to join in, running toward my teammates. Christina holds the flag up high, and everyone clusters around her, grabbing her arm to lift the flag even higher. I can't reach her, so I stand off to the side, grinning.

A hand touches my shoulder.

"Well done," Four says quietly.

+ + +

"I can't believe I missed it!" Will says again, shaking his head. Wind coming through the doorway of the train car blows his hair in every direction.

"You were performing the very important job of staying out of our way," says Christina, beaming.

Al groans. "Why did I have to be on the other team?"

"Because life's not fair, Albert. And the world is

conspiring against you," says Will. "Hey, can I see the flag again?"

Peter, Molly, and Drew sit across from the members in the corner. Their chests and backs are splattered with blue and pink paint, and they look dejected. They speak quietly, sneaking looks at the rest of us, especially Christina. That is the benefit of not holding the flag right now—I am no one's target. Or at least, no more than usual.

"So you climbed the Ferris wheel, huh," says Uriah. He stumbles across the car and sits next to me. Marlene, the girl with the flirty smile, follows him.

"Yes," I say.

"Pretty smart of you. Like . . . Erudite smart," Marlene says. "I'm Marlene."

"Tris," I say. At home, being compared to an Erudite would be an insult, but she says it like a compliment.

"Yeah, I know who you are," she says. "The first jumper tends to stick in your head."

It has been years since I jumped off a building in my Abnegation uniform; it has been decades.

Uriah takes one of the paintballs from his gun and squeezes it between his thumb and index finger. The train lurches to the left, and Uriah falls against me, his fingers pinching the paintball until a stream of pink, foul-smelling paint sprays on my face.

Marlene collapses in giggles. I wipe some of the paint from my face, slowly, and then smear it on his cheek. The scent of fish oil wafts through the train car.

"Ew!" He squeezes the ball at me again, but the opening is at the wrong angle, and the paint sprays into his mouth instead. He coughs and makes exaggerated gagging sounds.

I wipe my face with my sleeve, laughing so hard my stomach hurts.

If my entire life is like this, loud laughter and bold action and the kind of exhaustion you feel after a hard but satisfying day, I will be content. As Uriah scrapes his tongue with his fingertips, I realize that all I have to do is get through initiation, and that life will be mine.

CHAPTER
THIRTEEN

THE NEXT MORNING, when I trudge into the training room, yawning, a large target stands at one end of the room, and next to the door is a table with knives strewn across it. Target practice again. At least it won't hurt.

Eric stands in the middle of the room, his posture so rigid it looks like someone replaced his spine with a metal rod. The sight of him makes me feel like all the air in the room is heavier, bearing down on me. At least when he was slouched against a wall, I could pretend he wasn't here. Today I can't pretend.

"Tomorrow will be the last day of stage one," Eric says. "You will resume fighting then. Today, you'll be learning how to aim. Everyone pick up three knives." His voice is deeper than usual. "And pay attention while Four demonstrates the correct technique for throwing them."

At first no one moves.

"Now!"

We scramble for daggers. They aren't as heavy as guns, but they still feel strange in my hands, like I am not allowed to hold them.

"He's in a bad mood today," mumbles Christina.

"Is he ever in a good mood?" I murmur back.

But I know what she means. Judging by the poisonous look Eric gives Four when he isn't paying attention, last night's loss must have bothered Eric more than he let on. Winning capture the flag is a matter of pride, and pride is important to the Dauntless. More important than reason or sense.

I watch Four's arm as he throws a knife. The next time he throws, I watch his stance. He hits the target each time, exhaling as he releases the knife.

Eric orders, "Line up!"

Haste, I think, *will not help.* My mother told me that when I was learning how to knit. I have to think of this as a mental exercise, not a physical exercise. So I spend the first few minutes practicing without a knife, finding the right stance, learning the right arm motion.

Eric paces too quickly behind us.

"I think the Stiff's taken too many hits to the head!"

remarks Peter, a few people down. "Hey, Stiff! Remember what a *knife* is?"

Ignoring him, I practice the throw again with a knife in hand but don't release it. I shut out Eric's pacing, and Peter's jeering, and the nagging feeling that Four is staring at me, and throw the knife. It spins end over end, slamming into the board. The blade doesn't stick, but I'm the first person to hit the target.

I smirk as Peter misses again. I can't help myself.

"Hey, Peter," I say. "Remember what a *target* is?"

Next to me, Christina snorts, and her next knife hits the target.

A half hour later, Al is the only initiate who hasn't hit the target yet. His knives clatter to the floor, or bounce off the wall. While the rest of us approach the board to collect our weapons, he hunts the floor for his.

The next time he tries and misses, Eric marches toward him and demands, "How slow *are* you, Candor? Do you need glasses? Should I move the target closer to you?"

Al's face turns red. He throws another knife, and this one sails a few feet to the right of the target. It spins and hits the wall.

"What was that, initiate?" says Eric quietly, leaning closer to Al.

I bite my lip. This isn't good.

"It—it slipped," says Al.

"Well, I think you should go get it," Eric says. He scans the other initiates' faces—everyone has stopped throwing again—and says, "Did I tell you to stop?"

Knives start to hit the board. We have all seen Eric angry before, but this is different. The look in his eyes is almost rabid.

"Go get it?" Al's eyes are wide. "But everyone's still throwing."

"And?"

"And I don't want to get hit."

"I think you can trust your fellow initiates to aim better than you." Eric smiles a little, but his eyes stay cruel. "Go get your knife."

Al doesn't usually object to anything the Dauntless tell us to do. I don't think he's afraid to; he just knows that objecting is useless. This time Al sets his wide jaw. He's reached the limits of his compliance.

"No," he says.

"Why not?" Eric's beady eyes fix on Al's face. "Are you afraid?"

"Of getting stabbed by an airborne knife?" says Al. "Yes, I am!"

Honesty is his mistake. Not his refusal, which Eric might have accepted.

"Everyone stop!" Eric shouts.

The knives stop, and so does all conversation. I hold my small dagger tightly.

"Clear out of the ring." Eric looks at Al. "All except you."

I drop the dagger and it hits the dusty floor with a thud. I follow the other initiates to the edge of the room, and they inch in front of me, eager to see what makes my stomach turn: Al, facing Eric's wrath.

"Stand in front of the target," says Eric.

Al's big hands shake. He walks back to the target.

"Hey, Four." Eric looks over his shoulder. "Give me a hand here, huh?"

Four scratches one of his eyebrows with a knife point and approaches Eric. He has dark circles under his eyes and a tense set to his mouth—he's as tired as we are.

"You're going to stand there as he throws those knives," Eric says to Al, "until you learn not to flinch."

"Is this really necessary?" says Four. He sounds bored, but he doesn't look bored. His face and body are tense, alert.

I squeeze my hands into fists. No matter how casual Four sounds, the question is a challenge. And Four doesn't often challenge Eric directly.

At first Eric stares at Four in silence. Four stares back. Seconds pass and my fingernails bite my palms.

"I have the authority here, remember?" Eric says, so quietly I can barely hear him. "Here, and everywhere else."

Color rushes into Four's face, though his expression does not change. His grip on the knives tightens and his knuckles turn white as he turns to face Al.

I look from Al's wide, dark eyes to his shaking hands to the determined set of Four's jaw. Anger bubbles in my chest, and bursts from my mouth: "*Stop* it."

Four turns the knife in his hand, his fingers moving painstakingly over the metal edge. He gives me such a hard look that I feel like he's turning me to stone. I know why. I am stupid for speaking up while Eric is here; I am stupid for speaking up at all.

"Any idiot can stand in front of a target," I say. "It doesn't prove anything except that you're bullying us. Which, as I recall, is a sign of *cowardice*."

"Then it should be easy for you," Eric says. "If you're willing to take his place."

The last thing I want to do is stand in front of that target, but I can't back down now. I didn't leave myself the option. I weave through the crowd of initiates, and someone shoves my shoulder.

"There goes your pretty face," hisses Peter. "Oh, wait. You don't have one."

I recover my balance and walk toward Al. He nods at me. I try to smile encouragingly, but I can't manage it. I stand in front of the board, and my head doesn't even reach the center of the target, but it doesn't matter. I look at Four's knives: one in his right hand, two in his left hand.

My throat is dry. I try to swallow, and then look at Four. He is never sloppy. He won't hit me. I'll be fine.

I tip my chin up. I will not flinch. If I flinch, I prove to Eric that this is not as easy as I said it was; I prove that I'm a coward.

"If you flinch," Four says, slowly, carefully, "Al takes your place. Understand?"

I nod.

Four's eyes are still on mine when he lifts his hand, pulls his elbow back, and throws the knife. It is just a flash in the air, and then I hear a thud. The knife is buried in the board, half a foot away from my cheek. I close my eyes. Thank God.

"You about done, Stiff?" asks Four.

I remember Al's wide eyes and his quiet sobs at night and shake my head. "No."

"Eyes open, then." He taps the spot between his eyebrows.

I stare at him, pressing my hands to my sides so no one can see them shake. He passes a knife from his left hand to his right hand, and I see nothing but his eyes as the second knife hits the target above my head. This one is closer than the last one—I feel it hovering over my skull.

"Come on, Stiff," he says. "Let someone else stand there and take it."

Why is he trying to goad me into giving up? Does he want me to fail?

"Shut *up*, Four!"

I hold my breath as he turns the last knife in his hand. I see a glint in his eyes as he pulls his arm back and lets the knife fly. It comes straight at me, spinning, blade over handle. My body goes rigid. This time, when it hits the board, my ear stings, and blood tickles my skin. I touch my ear. He nicked it.

And judging by the look he gives me, he did it on purpose.

"I would love to stay and see if the rest of you are as daring as she is," says Eric, his voice smooth, "but I think that's enough for today."

He squeezes my shoulder. His fingers feel dry and cold, and the look he gives me claims me, like he's taking ownership of what I did. I don't return Eric's smile. What I did had nothing to do with him.

"I should keep my eye on you," he adds.

Fear prickles inside me, in my chest and in my head and in my hands. I feel like the word "DIVERGENT" is branded on my forehead, and if he looks at me long enough, he'll be able to read it. But he just lifts his hand from my shoulder and keeps walking.

Four and I stay behind. I wait until the room is empty and the door is shut before looking at him again. He walks toward me.

"Is your—" he begins.

"You did that on *purpose*!" I shout.

"Yes, I did," he says quietly. "And you should thank me for helping you."

I grit my teeth. "*Thank* you? You almost stabbed my ear, and you spent the entire time taunting me. Why should I thank you?"

"You know, I'm getting a little tired of waiting for you to catch on!"

He glares at me, and even when he glares, his eyes look thoughtful. Their shade of blue is peculiar, so dark it is almost black, with a small patch of lighter blue on the left iris, right next to the corner of his eye.

"Catch on? Catch on to what? That you wanted to prove to Eric how tough you are? That you're sadistic, just like he is?"

"I am not sadistic." He doesn't yell. I wish he would yell. It would scare me less. He leans his face close to mine, which reminds me of lying inches away from the attack dog's fangs in the aptitude test, and says, "If I wanted to hurt you, don't you think I would have already?"

He crosses the room and slams the point of a knife so hard into the table that it sticks there, handle toward the ceiling.

"I—" I start to shout, but he's already gone. I scream, frustrated, and wipe some of the blood from my ear.

CHAPTER
FOURTEEN

TODAY IS THE day before Visiting Day. I think of Visiting Day like I think of the world ending: Nothing after it matters. Everything I do builds up to it. I might see my parents again. I might not. Which is worse? I don't know.

I try to pull a pant leg over my thigh and it sticks just above my knee. Frowning, I stare at my leg. A bulge of muscle is stopping the fabric. I let the pant leg fall and look over my shoulder at the back of my thigh. Another muscle stands out there.

I step to the side so I stand in front of the mirror. I see muscles that I couldn't see before in my arms, legs, and stomach. I pinch my side, where a layer of fat used to hint at curves to come. Nothing. Dauntless initiation has stolen whatever softness my body had. Is that good, or bad?

At least I am stronger than I was. I wrap my towel around me again and leave the girls' bathroom. I hope no one is in the dormitory to see me walking in my towel, but I can't wear those pants.

When I open the dormitory door, a weight drops into my stomach. Peter, Molly, Drew, and some of the other initiates stand in the back corner, laughing. They look up when I walk in and start snickering. Molly's snort-laugh is louder than everyone else's.

I walk to my bunk, trying to pretend like they aren't there, and fumble in the drawer under my bed for the dress Christina made me get. One hand clamped around the towel and one holding the dress, I stand up, and right behind me is Peter.

I jump back, almost hitting my head on Christina's bunk. I try to slip past him, but he slams his hand against Christina's bed frame, blocking my path. I should have known he wouldn't let me get away that easily.

"Didn't realize you were so skinny, Stiff."

"Get away from me." My voice is somehow steady.

"This isn't the Hub, you know. No one has to follow a Stiff's orders here." His eyes travel down my body, not in the greedy way that a man looks at a woman, but cruelly, scrutinizing every flaw. I hear my heartbeat in my ears as the others inch closer, forming a pack behind Peter.

This will be bad.

I have to get out of here.

Out of the corner of my eye, I see a clear path to the door. If I can duck under Peter's arm and sprint toward it, I might be able to make it.

"Look at her," says Molly, crossing her arms. She smirks at me. "She's practically a child."

"Oh, I don't know," says Drew. "She could be hiding something under that towel. Why don't we look and see?"

Now. I duck under Peter's arm and dart toward the door. Something pinches and pulls at my towel as I walk away and then yanks sharply—Peter's hand, gathering the fabric into his fist. The towel slips from my hand and the air is cold on my naked body, making the hair on the back of my neck stand on end.

Laughter erupts, and I run as fast as I can toward the door, holding the dress against my body to hide it. I sprint down the hallway and into the bathroom and lean against the door, breathing hard. I close my eyes.

It doesn't matter. I don't care.

A sob bursts from my mouth, and I slap my hand over my lips to contain it. It doesn't matter what they saw. I shake my head like the motion is supposed to make it true.

With shaking hands, I get dressed. The dress is plain

black, with a V-neck that shows the tattoos on my collarbone, and goes down to my knees.

Once I'm dressed and the urge to cry is gone, I feel something hot and violent writhing in my stomach. I want to hurt them.

I stare at my eyes in the mirror. I want to, so I will.

+ + +

I can't fight in a dress, so I get myself some new clothes from the Pit before I walk to the training room for my last fight. I hope it's with Peter.

"Hey, where were you this morning?" Christina asks when I walk in. I squint to see the blackboard across the room. The space next to my name is blank—I haven't gotten an opponent yet.

"I got held up," I say.

Four stands in front of the board and writes a name next to mine. *Please let it be Peter, please, please. . . .*

"You okay, Tris? You look a little . . . ," says Al.

"A little what?"

Four moves away from the board. The name written next to mine is Molly. Not Peter, but good enough.

"On edge," says Al.

My fight is last on the list, which means I have to wait through three matches before I face her. Edward and

Peter fight second to last—good. Edward is the only one who can beat Peter. Christina will fight Al, which means that Al will lose quickly, like he's been doing all week.

"Go easy on me, okay?" Al asks Christina.

"I make no promises," she replies.

The first pair—Will and Myra—stand across from each other in the arena. For a second they both shuffle back and forth, one jerking an arm forward and then retracting it, the other kicking and missing. Across the room, Four leans against the wall and yawns.

I stare at the board and try to predict the outcome of each match. It doesn't take long. Then I bite my fingernails and think about Molly. Christina lost to her, which means she's good. She has a powerful punch, but she doesn't move her feet. If she can't hit me, she can't hurt me.

As expected, the next fight between Christina and Al is quick and painless. Al falls after a few hard hits to the face and doesn't get back up, which makes Eric shake his head.

Edward and Peter take longer. Though they are the two best fighters, the disparity between them is noticeable. Edward's fist slams into Peter's jaw, and I remember what Will said about him—that he has been studying combat since he was ten. It's obvious. He is faster and smarter than even Peter.

By the time the three matches are done, my nails are bitten to the beds and I'm hungry for lunch. I walk to the arena without looking at anyone or anything but the center of the room. Some of my anger has faded, but it isn't hard to call back. All I have to do is think about how cold the air was and how loud the laughter was. *Look at her. She's a child.*

Molly stands across from me.

"Was that a birthmark I saw on your left butt cheek?" she says, smirking. "God, you're pale, Stiff."

She'll make the first move. She always does.

Molly starts toward me and throws her weight into a punch. As her body shifts forward, I duck and drive my fist into her stomach, right over her bellybutton. Before she can get her hands on me, I slip past her, my hands up, ready for her next attempt.

She's not smirking anymore. She runs at me like she's about to tackle me, and I dart out of the way. I hear Four's voice in my head, telling me that the most powerful weapon at my disposal is my elbow. I just have to find a way to use it.

I block her next punch with my forearm. The blow stings, but I barely notice it. She grits her teeth and lets out a frustrated groan, more animal-sounding than human. She tries a sloppy kick at my side, which I dodge, and while her balance is off, I rush forward and force my elbow up at her face. She pulls her head back just in time, and my elbow grazes her chin.

She punches me in the ribs and I stumble to the side, recovering my breath. There's something she's not protecting, I know it. I want to hit her face, but maybe that's not a smart move. I watch her for a few seconds. Her hands are too high; they guard her nose and cheeks, leaving her stomach and ribs exposed. Molly and I have the same flaw in combat.

Our eyes meet for just a second.

I aim an uppercut low, below her bellybutton. My fist sinks into her flesh, forcing a heavy breath from her mouth that I feel against my ear. As she gasps, I sweep-kick her legs out from under her, and she falls hard on the ground, sending dust into the air. I pull my foot back and kick as hard as I can at her ribs.

My mother and father would not approve of my kicking someone when she's down.

I don't care.

She curls into a ball to protect her side, and I kick again, this time hitting her in the stomach. *Like a child.* I kick again, this time hitting her in the face. Blood springs from her nose and spreads over her face. *Look at her.*

Another kick hits her in the chest.

I pull my foot back again, but Four's hands clamp around my arms, and he pulls me away from her with irresistible force. I breathe through gritted teeth, staring at Molly's blood-covered face, the color deep and rich and beautiful, in a way.

She groans, and I hear a gurgling in her throat, watch blood trickle from her lips.

"You won," Four mutters. "Stop."

I wipe the sweat from my forehead. He stares at me. His eyes are too wide; they look alarmed.

"I think you should leave," he says. "Take a walk."

"I'm fine," I say. "I'm fine now," I say again, this time for myself.

I wish I could say I felt guilty for what I did.

I don't.

CHAPTER
FIFTEEN

VISITING DAY. The second I open my eyes, I remember. My heart leaps and then plummets when I see Molly hobble across the dormitory, her nose purple between strips of medical tape. Once I see her leave, I check for Peter and Drew. Neither of them is in the dormitory, so I change quickly. As long as they aren't here, I don't care who sees me in my underwear, not anymore.

Everyone else dresses in silence. Not even Christina smiles. We all know that we might go to the Pit floor and search every face and never find one that belongs to us.

I make my bed with the tight corners like my father taught me. As I pinch a stray hair from my pillow, Eric walks in.

"Attention!" he announces, flicking a lock of dark hair

from his eyes. "I want to give you some advice about today. If by some miracle your families do come to visit you . . ." He scans our faces and smirks. ". . . which I doubt, it is best not to seem too attached. That will make it easier for you, and easier for them. We also take the phrase 'faction before blood' very seriously here. Attachment to your family suggests you aren't entirely pleased with your faction, which would be *shameful*. Understand?"

I understand. I hear the threat in Eric's sharp voice. The only part of that speech that Eric meant was the last part: We are Dauntless, and we need to act accordingly.

On my way out of the dormitory, Eric stops me.

"I may have underestimated you, Stiff," he says. "You did well yesterday."

I stare up at him. For the first time since I beat Molly, guilt pinches my gut.

If Eric thinks I did something right, I must have done it wrong.

"Thank you," I say. I slip out of the dormitory.

Once my eyes adjust to the dim hallway light, I see Christina and Will ahead of me, Will laughing, probably at a joke Christina made. I don't try to catch up. For some reason, I feel like it would be a mistake to interrupt them.

Al is missing. I didn't see him in the dormitory, and

he's not walking toward the Pit now. Maybe he's already there.

I run my fingers through my hair and smooth it into a bun. I check my clothes—am I covered up? My pants are tight and my collarbone is showing. They won't approve.

Who cares if they approve? I set my jaw. This is my faction now. These are the clothes my faction wears. I stop just before the hallway ends.

Clusters of families stand on the Pit floor, most of them Dauntless families with Dauntless initiates. They still look strange to me—a mother with a pierced eyebrow, a father with a tattooed arm, an initiate with purple hair, a wholesome family unit. I spot Drew and Molly standing alone at one end of the room and suppress a smile. At least their families didn't come.

But Peter's did. He stands next to a tall man with bushy eyebrows and a short, meek-looking woman with red hair. Neither of his parents looks like him. They both wear black pants and white shirts, typical Candor outfits, and his father speaks so loudly I can almost hear him from where I stand. Do they know what kind of person their son is?

Then again . . . what kind of person am I?

Across the room, Will stands with a woman in a blue dress. She doesn't look old enough to be his mother, but she has the same crease between her eyebrows as he does, and the same golden hair. He talked about having a sister once; maybe that's her.

Next to him, Christina hugs a dark-skinned woman in Candor black and white. Standing behind Christina is a young girl, also a Candor. Her younger sister.

Should I even bother scanning the crowd for my parents? I could turn around and go back to the dormitory.

Then I see her. My mother stands alone near the railing with her hands clasped in front of her. She has never looked more out of place, with her gray slacks and gray jacket buttoned at the throat, her hair in its simple twist and her face placid. I start toward her, tears jumping into my eyes. She came. She came for me.

I walk faster. She sees me, and for a second her expression is blank, like she doesn't know who I am. Then her eyes light up, and she opens her arms. She smells like soap and laundry detergent.

"Beatrice," she whispers. She runs her hand over my hair.

Don't cry, I tell myself. I hold her until I can blink the moisture from my eyes, and then pull back to look at her again. I smile with closed lips, just like she does. She touches my cheek.

"Well, look at you," she says. "You've filled out." She

puts her arm across my shoulders. "Tell me how you are."

"You first." The old habits are back. I should let her speak first. I shouldn't let the conversation stay focused on me for too long. I should make sure she doesn't need anything.

"Today is a special occasion," she says. "I came to see you, so let's talk mostly about you. It is my gift to you."

My selfless mother. She should not be giving me gifts, not after I left her and my father. I walk with her toward the railing that overlooks the chasm, glad to be close to her. The last week and a half has been more affection-less than I realized. At home we did not touch each other often, and the most I ever saw my parents do was hold hands at the dinner table, but it was more than this, more than here.

"Just one question." I feel my pulse in my throat. "Where's Dad? Is he visiting Caleb?"

"Ah." She shakes her head. "Your father had to be at work."

I look down. "You can tell me if he didn't want to come."

Her eyes travel over my face. "Your father has been selfish lately. That doesn't mean he doesn't love you, I promise."

I stare at her, stunned. My father—selfish? More star-tling than the label is the fact that she assigned it to him.

I can't tell by looking at her if she's angry. I don't expect to be able to. But she must be; if she calls him *selfish*, she must be angry.

"What about Caleb?" I say. "Will you visit him later?"

"I wish I could," she says, "but the Erudite have prohibited Abnegation visitors from entering their compound. If I tried, I would be removed from the premises."

"What?" I demand. "That's terrible. Why would they do that?"

"Tensions between our factions are higher than ever," she says. "I wish it wasn't that way, but there is little I can do about it."

I think of Caleb standing among the Erudite initiates, scanning the crowd for our mother, and feel a pang in my stomach. Part of me is still angry with him for keeping so many secrets from me, but I don't want him to hurt.

"That's terrible," I repeat. I look toward the chasm.

Standing alone at the railing is Four. Though he's not an initiate anymore, most of the Dauntless use this day to come together with their families. Either his family doesn't like to come together, or he wasn't originally Dauntless. Which faction could he have come from?

"There's one of my instructors." I lean closer to her and say, "He's kind of intimidating."

"He's *handsome*," she says.

I find myself nodding without thinking. She laughs and lifts her arm from my shoulders. I want to steer her away from him, but just as I'm about to suggest that we go somewhere else, he looks over his shoulder.

His eyes widen at the sight of my mother. She offers him her hand.

"Hello. My name is Natalie," she says. "I'm Beatrice's mother."

I have never seen my mother shake hands with someone. Four eases his hand into hers, looking stiff, and shakes it twice. The gesture looks unnatural for both of them. No, Four was not originally Dauntless if he doesn't shake hands easily.

"Four," he says. "It's nice to meet you."

"Four," my mother repeats, smiling. "Is that a nickname?"

"Yes." He doesn't elaborate. What *is* his real name?

"Your daughter is doing well here. I've been overseeing her training."

Since when does "overseeing" include throwing knives at me and scolding me at every opportunity?

"That's good to hear," she says. "I know a few things about Dauntless initiation, and I was worried about her."

He looks at me, and his eyes move down my face, from nose to mouth to chin. Then he says, "You shouldn't worry."

I can't keep the heat from rushing into my cheeks. I hope it isn't noticeable.

Is he just reassuring her because she's my mother, or does he really believe that I am capable? And what did that look mean?

She tilts her head. "You look familiar for some reason, Four."

"I can't imagine why," he replies, his voice suddenly cold. "I don't make a habit of associating with the Abnegation."

My mother laughs. She has a light laugh, half air and half sound. "Few people do, these days. I don't take it personally."

He seems to relax a little. "Well, I'll leave you to your reunion."

My mother and I watch him leave. The roar of the river fills my ears. Maybe Four was one of the Erudite, which explains why he hates Abnegation. Or maybe he believes the articles the Erudite release about us—*them*, I remind myself. But it was kind of him to tell her that I'm doing well when I know he doesn't believe it.

"Is he always like that?" she says.

"Worse."

"Have you made friends?" she asks.

"A few," I say. I look over my shoulder at Will and

Christina and their families. When Christina catches my eye, she beckons to me, smiling, so my mother and I cross the Pit floor.

Before we can get to Will and Christina, though, a short, round woman with a black-and-white-striped shirt touches my arm. I twitch, resisting the urge to smack her hand away.

"Excuse me," she says. "Do you know my son? Albert?"

"Albert?" I repeat. "Oh—you mean Al? Yes, I know him."

"Do you know where we can find him?" she says, gesturing to a man behind her. He is tall and as thick as a boulder. Al's father, obviously.

"I'm sorry, I didn't see him this morning. Maybe you should look for him up there?" I point at the glass ceiling above us.

"Oh my," Al's mother says, fanning her face with her hand. "I would rather not attempt that climb again. I almost had a panic attack on the way down here. Why aren't there any railings along those paths? Are you all insane?"

I smile a little. A few weeks ago I might have found that question offensive, but now I spend too much time with Candor transfers to be surprised by tactlessness.

"Insane, no," I say. "Dauntless, yes. If I see him, I'll tell him you're looking for him."

My mother, I see, wears the same smile I do. She isn't reacting the way some of the other transfers' parents are—her neck bent, looking around at the Pit walls, at the Pit ceiling, at the chasm. Of course she isn't curious—she's Abnegation. Curiosity is foreign to her.

I introduce my mother to Will and Christina, and Christina introduces me to her mother and her sister. But when Will introduces me to Cara, his older sister, she gives me the kind of look that would wither a plant and does not extend her hand for me to shake. She glares at my mother.

"I can't believe that you associate with one of *them*, Will," she says.

My mother purses her lips, but of course, doesn't say anything.

"Cara," says Will, frowning, "there's no need to be *rude*."

"Oh, certainly not. Do you know what she is?" She points at my mother. "She's a council member's *wife* is what she is. She runs the 'volunteer agency' that supposedly helps the factionless. You think I don't know that you're just hoarding goods to distribute to your own faction while *we* don't get fresh food for a month, huh? Food for the factionless, my eye."

"I'm sorry," my mother says gently. "I believe you are mistaken."

"Mistaken. Ha," Cara snaps. "I'm sure you're exactly

what you seem. A faction of happy-go-lucky do-gooders without a selfish bone in their bodies. Right."

"Don't speak to my mother that way," I say, my face hot. I clench my hands into fists. "Don't say another word to her or I swear I will break your nose."

"Back off, Tris," Will says. "You're not going to punch my sister."

"Oh?" I say, raising both eyebrows. "You think so?"

"No, you're not." My mother touches my shoulder. "Come on, Beatrice. We wouldn't want to bother your friend's sister."

She sounds gentle, but her hand squeezes my arm so hard I almost cry out from the pain as she drags me away. She walks with me, fast, toward the dining hall. Just before she reaches it, though, she takes a sharp left turn and walks down one of the dark hallways I haven't explored yet.

"Mom," I say. "Mom, how do you know where you're going?"

She stops next to a locked door and stands on her tip-toes, peering at the base of the blue lamp hanging from the ceiling. A few seconds later she nods and turns to me again.

"I said no questions about me. And I meant it. How are you really doing, Beatrice? How have the fights been? How are you ranked?"

"Ranked?" I say. "You know that I've been fighting? You know that I'm ranked?"

"It isn't top-secret information, how the Dauntless initiation process works."

I don't know how easy it is to find out what another faction does during initiation, but I suspect it's not *that* easy. Slowly, I say, "I'm close to the bottom, Mom."

"Good." She nods. "No one looks too closely at the bottom. Now, this is very important, Beatrice: What were your aptitude test results?"

Tori's warning pulses in my head. *Don't tell anyone.* I should tell her that my result was Abnegation, because that's what Tori recorded in the system.

I look into my mother's eyes, which are pale green and framed by a dark smudge of eyelashes. She has lines around her mouth, but other than that, she doesn't look her age. Those lines get deeper when she hums. She used to hum as she washed the dishes.

This is my mother.

I can trust her.

"They were inconclusive," I say softly.

"I thought as much." She sighs. "Many children who are raised Abnegation receive that kind of result. We don't know why. But you have to be very careful during the next stage of initiation, Beatrice. Stay in the middle of the pack, no matter what you do. Don't draw attention to yourself. Do you understand?"

"Mom, what's going on?"

"I don't care what faction you chose," she says, touching her hands to my cheeks. "I am your mother and I want to keep you safe."

"Is this because I'm a—" I start to say, but she presses her hand to my mouth.

"Don't say that word," she hisses. "Ever."

So Tori was right. Divergent is a dangerous thing to be. I just don't know why, or even what it really means, still.

"Why?"

She shakes her head. "I can't say."

She looks over her shoulder, where the light from the Pit floor is barely visible. I hear shouts and conversations, laughter and shuffling footsteps. The smell from the dining hall floats over my nose, sweet and yeasty: baking bread. When she turns toward me, her jaw is set.

"There's something I want you to do," she says. "I can't go visit your brother, but you can, when initiation is over. So I want you to go find him and tell him to research the simulation serum. Okay? Can you do that for me?"

"Not unless you *explain* some of this to me, Mom!" I cross my arms. "You want me to go hang out at the Erudite compound for the day, you had better give me a reason!"

"I can't. I'm sorry." She kisses my cheek and brushes a lock of hair that fell from my bun behind my ear. "I should leave. It will make you look better if you and I don't seem attached to each other."

"I don't care how I look to them," I say.

"You should," she says. "I suspect they are already monitoring you."

She walks away, and I am too stunned to follow her. At the end of the hallway she turns and says, "Have a piece of cake for me, all right? The chocolate. It's delicious." She smiles a strange, twisted smile, and adds, "I love you, you know."

And then she's gone.

I stand alone in the blue light coming from the lamp above me, and I understand:

She has been to the compound before. She remembered this hallway. She knows about the initiation process.

My mother was Dauntless.

CHAPTER
SIXTEEN

THAT AFTERNOON, I go back to the dormitory while everyone else spends time with their families and find Al sitting on his bed, staring at the space on the wall where the chalk-board usually is. Four took it down yesterday so he could calculate our stage one rankings.

"There you are!" I say. "Your parents were looking for you. Did they find you?"

He shakes his head.

I sit down next to him on the bed. My leg is barely half the width of his, even now that it's more muscular than it was. He wears black shorts. His knee is purple-blue with a bruise and crossed with a scar.

"You didn't want to see them?" I say.

"Didn't want them to ask how I was doing," he says. "I'd

have to tell them, and they would know if I was lying."

"Well . . ." I struggle to come up with something to say. "What's wrong with how you're doing?"

Al laughs harshly. "I've lost every fight since the one with Will. I'm not doing well."

"By choice, though. Couldn't you tell them that, too?"

He shakes his head. "Dad always wanted me to come here. I mean, they said they wanted me to stay in Candor, but that's only because that's what they're supposed to say. They've always admired the Dauntless, both of them. They wouldn't understand if I tried to explain it to them."

"Oh." I tap my fingers against my knee. Then I look at him. "Is that why you chose Dauntless? Because of your parents?"

Al shakes his head. "No. I guess it was because . . . I think it's important to protect people. To stand up for people. Like you did for me." He smiles at me. "That's what the Dauntless are supposed to do, right? That's what courage is. Not . . . hurting people for no reason."

I remember what Four told me, that teamwork used to be a Dauntless priority. What were the Dauntless like when it was? What would I have learned if I had been here when my mother was Dauntless? Maybe I wouldn't have broken Molly's nose. Or threatened Will's sister.

I feel a pang of guilt. "Maybe it will be better once initiation is over."

"Too bad I might come in last," Al says. "I guess we'll see tonight."

We sit side-by-side for a while. It's better to be here, in silence, than in the Pit, watching everyone laugh with their families.

My father used to say that sometimes, the best way to help someone is just to be near them. I feel good when I do something I know he would be proud of, like it makes up for all the things I've done that he wouldn't be proud of.

"I feel braver when I'm around you, you know," he says. "Like I could actually fit in here, the same way you do."

I am about to respond when he slides his arm across my shoulders. Suddenly I freeze, my cheeks hot.

I didn't want to be right about Al's feelings for me. But I was.

I do not lean into him. Instead I sit forward so his arm falls away. Then I squeeze my hands together in my lap.

"Tris, I . . . ," he says. His voice sounds strained. I glance at him. His face is as red as mine feels, but he's not crying—he just looks embarrassed.

"Um . . . sorry," he says. "I wasn't trying to . . . um. Sorry."

I wish I could tell him not to take it personally. I could

tell him that my parents rarely held hands even in our own home, so I have trained myself to pull away from all gestures of affection, because they raised me to take them seriously. Maybe if I told him that, there wouldn't be a layer of hurt beneath his flush of embarrassment.

But of course, it *is* personal. He is my friend—and that is all. What is more personal than that?

I breathe in, and when I breathe out, I make myself smile. "Sorry about what?" I ask, trying to sound casual. I brush off my jeans, though there isn't anything on them, and stand up.

"I should go," I say.

He nods and doesn't look at me.

"You going to be okay?" I say. "I mean . . . because of your parents. Not because . . ." I let my voice trail off. I don't know what I would say if I didn't.

"Oh. Yeah." He nods again, a little too vigorously. "I'll see you later, Tris."

I try not to walk out of the room too fast. When the dormitory door closes behind me, I touch a hand to my forehead and grin a little. Awkwardness aside, it is nice to be liked.

+ + +

Discussing our family visits would be too painful, so our final rankings for stage one are all anyone can talk about that night. Every time someone near me brings it up, I stare at some point across the room and ignore them.

My rank can't be as bad as it used to be, especially after I beat Molly, but it might not be good enough to get me in the top ten at the end of initiation, especially when the Dauntless-born initiates are factored in.

At dinner I sit with Christina, Will, and Al at a table in the corner. We are uncomfortably close to Peter, Drew, and Molly, who are at the next table over. When conversation at our table reaches a lull, I hear every word they say. They are speculating about the ranks. What a surprise.

"You weren't allowed to have *pets*?" Christina demands, smacking the table with her palm. "Why not?"

"Because they're illogical," Will says matter-of-factly. "What is the point in providing food and shelter for an animal that just soils your furniture, makes your home smell bad, and ultimately dies?"

Al and I meet eyes, like we usually do when Will and Christina start to fight. But this time, the second our eyes meet, we both look away. I hope this awkwardness between us doesn't last long. I want my friend back.

"The *point* is . . ." Christina's voice trails off, and she tilts her head. "Well, they're fun to have. I had a bulldog named Chunker. One time we left a whole roasted chicken on the counter to cool, and while my mother went to the bathroom, he pulled it down off the counter and ate it, bones and skin and all. We laughed so hard."

"Yes, that certainly changes my mind. Of course I want to live with an animal that eats all my food and destroys my kitchen." Will shakes his head. "Why don't you just get a dog after initiation if you're feeling that nostalgic?"

"Because." Christina's smile falls, and she pokes at her potato with her fork. "Dogs are sort of ruined for me. After . . . you know, after the aptitude test."

We exchange looks. We all know that we aren't supposed to talk about the test, not even now that we have chosen, but for them that rule must not be as serious as it is for me. My heart jumps unsteadily in my chest. For me that rule is protection. It keeps me from having to lie to my friends about my results. Every time I think the word "Divergent," I hear Tori's warning—and now my mother's warning too. *Don't tell anyone. Dangerous.*

"You mean . . . killing the dog, right?" asks Will.

I almost forgot. Those with an aptitude for Dauntless picked up the knife in the simulation and stabbed the dog when it attacked. No wonder Christina doesn't want a pet dog anymore. I tug my sleeves over my wrists and twist my fingers together.

"Yeah," she says. "I mean, you guys all had to do that too, right?"

She looks first at Al, and then at me. Her dark eyes

narrow, and she says, "*You* didn't."

"Hmm?"

"You're hiding something," she says. "You're fidgeting."

"What?"

"In Candor," says Al, nudging me with his shoulder. There. That feels normal. "We learn to read body language so we know when someone is lying or keeping something from us."

"Oh." I scratch the back of my neck. "Well . . ."

"See, there it is again!" she says, pointing at my hand.

I feel like I'm swallowing my heartbeat. How can I lie about my results if they can tell when I'm lying? I'll have to control my body language. I drop my hand and clasp my hands in my lap. Is that what an honest person does?

I don't have to lie about the dog, at least. "No, I didn't kill the dog."

"How did you get Dauntless without using the knife?" says Will, narrowing his eyes at me.

I look him in the eye and say evenly, "I didn't. I got Abnegation."

It is half-true. Tori reported my result as Abnegation, so that is what is in the system. Anyone who has access to the scores would be able to see it. I keep my eyes on his for a few seconds. Shifting them away might be suspicious. Then I shrug and stab a piece of meat with my fork. I hope they believe me. They have to believe me.

"But you chose Dauntless anyway?" Christina says. "Why?"

"I told you," I say, smirking. "It was the food."

She laughs. "Did you guys know that Tris had never seen a hamburger before she came here?"

She launches into the story of our first day, and my body relaxes, but I still feel heavy. I should not lie to my friends. It creates barriers between us, and we already have more than I want. Christina taking the flag. Me rejecting Al.

After dinner we go back to the dormitory, and it's hard for me not to sprint, knowing that the rankings will be up when I get there. I want to get it over with. At the door to the dormitory, Drew shoves me into the wall to get past me. My shoulder scrapes on the stone, but I keep walking.

I'm too short to see over the crowd of initiates standing near the back of the room, but when I find a space between heads to look through, I see that the blackboard is on the ground, leaning against Four's legs, facing away from us. He stands with a piece of chalk in one hand.

"For those of you who just came in, I'm explaining how the ranks are determined," he says. "After the first round of fights, we ranked you according to your skill level. The number of points you earn depends on your skill level and the skill level of the person you beat. You earn more points for improving and more points for beating someone of a high skill level. I don't reward preying on the weak. That is cowardice."

I think his eyes linger on Peter at that last line, but they move on quickly enough that I'm not sure.

"If you have a high rank, you lose points for losing to a low-ranked opponent."

Molly lets out an unpleasant noise, like a snort or a grumble.

"Stage two of training is weighted more heavily than stage one, because it is more closely tied to overcoming cowardice," he says. "That said, it is extremely difficult to rank high at the end of initiation if you rank low in stage one."

I shift from one foot to the other, trying to get a good look at him. When I finally do, I look away. His eyes are already on me, probably drawn by my nervous movement.

"We will announce the cuts tomorrow," Four says. "The fact that you are transfers and the Dauntless-born initiates are not will not be taken into consideration. Four of you could be factionless and none of them. Or four of them could be factionless and none of you. Or any combination thereof. That said, here are your ranks."

He hangs the board on the hook and steps back so we can see the rankings:

1. Edward
2. Peter
3. Will
4. Christina
5. Molly
6. Tris

Sixth? I can't be sixth. Beating Molly must have boosted my rank more than I thought it would. And losing to me seems to have lowered hers. I skip to the bottom of the list.

7. Drew
8. Al
9. Myra

Al isn't dead last, but unless the Dauntless-born initiates completely failed their version of stage one of initiation, he is factionless.

I glance at Christina. She tilts her head and frowns at the board. She isn't the only one. The quiet in the room is uneasy, like it is rocking back and forth on a ledge.

Then it falls.

"What?" demands Molly. She points at Christina. "I

beat her! I beat her in *minutes*, and she's ranked *above* me?"

"Yeah," says Christina, crossing her arms. She wears a smug smile. "And?"

"If you intend to secure yourself a high rank, I suggest you don't make a habit of losing to low-ranked opponents," says Four, his voice cutting through the mutters and grumbles of the other initiates. He pockets the chalk and walks past me without glancing in my direction. The words sting a little, reminding me that I am the low-ranked opponent he's referring to.

Apparently they remind Molly, too.

"You," she says, focusing her narrowed eyes on me. "*You* are going to pay for this."

I expect her to lunge at me, or hit me, but she just turns on her heel and stalks out of the dormitory, and that is worse. If she had exploded, her anger would have been spent quickly, after a punch or two. Leaving means she wants to plan something. Leaving means I have to be on my guard.

Peter didn't say anything when the rankings went up, which, given his tendency to complain about anything that doesn't go his way, is surprising. He just walks to his bunk and sits down, untying his shoelaces. That makes me feel even more uneasy. He can't possibly be satisfied with second place. Not Peter.

Will and Christina slap hands, and then Will claps me

on the back with a hand bigger than my shoulder blade.

"Look at you. Number six," he says, grinning.

"Still might not have been good enough," I remind him.

"It will be, don't worry," he says. "We should celebrate."

"Well, let's go, then," says Christina, grabbing my arm with one hand and Al's arm with the other. "Come on, Al. You don't know how the Dauntless-borns did. You don't know anything for sure."

"I'm just going to go to bed," he mumbles, pulling his arm free.

In the hallway, it is easy to forget about Al and Molly's revenge and Peter's suspicious calm, and easy to pretend that what separates us as friends does not exist. But lingering at the back of my mind is the fact that Christina and Will are my competitors. If I want to fight my way to the top ten, I will have to beat them first.

I just hope I don't have to betray them in the process.

+ + +

That night I have trouble falling asleep. The dormitory used to seem loud to me, with all the breathing, but now it is too quiet. When it's quiet, I think about my family. Thank God the Dauntless compound is usually loud.

If my mother was Dauntless, why did she choose Abnegation? Did she love its peace, its routine, its goodness—all the things I miss, when I let myself think about it?

I wonder if someone here knew her when she was young and could tell me what she was like then. Even if they did, they probably wouldn't want to discuss her. Faction transfers are not really supposed to discuss their old factions once they become members. It's supposed to make it easier for them to change their allegiance from family to faction—to embrace the principle "faction before blood."

I bury my face in the pillow. She asked me to tell Caleb to research the simulation serum—why? Does it have something to do with me being Divergent, with me being in danger, or is it something else? I sigh. I have a thousand questions, and she left before I could ask any of them. Now they swirl in my head, and I doubt I'll be able to sleep until I can answer them.

I hear a scuffle across the room and lift my head from the pillow. My eyes aren't adjusted to the dark, so I stare into pure black, like the backs of my eyelids. I hear shuffling and the squeak of a shoe. A heavy thud.

And then a wail that curdles my blood and makes my hair stand on end. I throw the blankets back and stand on the stone floor with bare feet. I still can't see well enough to find the source of the scream, but I see a dark lump on the floor a few bunks down. Another scream pierces my ears.

"Turn on the lights!" someone shouts.

I walk toward the sound, slowly so I don't trip over anything. I feel like I'm in a trance. I don't want to see where the screaming is coming from. A scream like that can only mean blood and bone and pain; that scream that comes from the pit of the stomach and extends to every inch of the body.

The lights come on.

Edward lies on the floor next to his bed, clutching at his face. Surrounding his head is a halo of blood, and jutting between his clawing fingers is a silver knife handle. My heart thumping in my ears, I recognize it as a butter knife from the dining hall. The blade is stuck in Edward's eye.

Myra, who stands at Edward's feet, screams. Someone else screams too, and someone yells for help, and Edward is still on the floor, writhing and wailing. I crouch by his head, my knees pressing to the pool of blood, and put my hands on his shoulders.

"Lie still," I say. I feel calm, though I can't hear anything, like my head is submerged in water. Edward thrashes again and I say it louder, sterner. "I said, lie *still*. Breathe."

"My eye!" he screams.

I smell something foul. Someone vomited.

"Take it out!" he yells. "Get it out, get it out of me, get it out!"

I shake my head and then realize that he can't see me. A laugh bubbles in my stomach. Hysterical. I have to suppress hysteria if I'm going to help him. I have to forget myself.

"No," I say. "You have to let the doctor take it out. Hear me? Let the doctor take it out. And breathe."

"It hurts," he sobs.

"I know it does." Instead of my voice I hear my mother's voice. I see her crouching before me on the sidewalk in front of our house, brushing tears from my face after I scraped my knee. I was five at the time.

"It will be all right." I try to sound firm, like I'm not idly reassuring him, but I am. I don't know if it will be all right. I suspect that it won't.

When the nurse arrives, she tells me to step back, and I do. My hands and knees are soaked with blood. When I look around, I see that only two faces are missing.

Drew.

And Peter.

+ + +

After they take Edward away, I carry a change of clothes into the bathroom and wash my hands. Christina comes with me and stands by the door, but she doesn't say anything, and I'm glad. There isn't much to say.

I scrub at the lines in my palms and run one fingernail under my other fingernails to get the blood out. I change into the pants I brought and throw the soiled ones in the trash. I get as many paper towels as I can hold. Someone needs to clean up the mess in the dormitory, and since I doubt I'll ever be able to sleep again, it might as well be me.

As I reach for the door handle, Christina says, "You know who did that, right?"

"Yeah."

"Should we tell someone?"

"You really think the Dauntless will do anything?" I say. "After they hung you over the chasm? After they made us beat each other unconscious?"

She doesn't say anything.

For a half hour after that, I kneel alone on the floor in the dormitory and scrub at Edward's blood. Christina throws away the dirty paper towels and gets me new ones. Myra is gone; she probably followed Edward to the hospital.

No one sleeps much that night.

+ + +

"This is going to sound weird," Will says, "but I wish we didn't have a day off today."

I nod. I know what he means. Having something to do would distract me, and I could use a distraction right now.

I have not spent much time alone with Will, but Christina and Al are taking naps in the dormitory, and neither of us wanted to be in that room longer than we had to. Will didn't tell me that; I just know.

I slide one fingernail under another. I washed my hands thoroughly after cleaning up Edward's blood, but I still feel like it's on my hands. Will and I walk with no sense of purpose. There is nowhere to go.

"We could visit him," suggests Will. "But what would we say? 'I didn't know you that well, but I'm sorry you got stabbed in the eye'?"

It isn't funny. I know that as soon as he says it, but a laugh rises in my throat anyway, and I let it out because it's harder to keep it in. Will stares at me for a second, and then he laughs too. Sometimes crying or laughing are the only options left, and laughing feels better right now.

"Sorry," I say. "It's just so ridiculous."

I don't want to cry for Edward—at least not in the deep, personal way that you cry for a friend or loved one. I want to cry because something terrible happened, and I saw it, and I could not see a way to mend it. No one who would want to punish Peter has the authority to, and no one who has the authority to punish him would want to. The

Dauntless have rules against attacking someone like that, but with people like Eric in charge, I suspect those rules go unenforced.

I say, more seriously, "The most ridiculous part is, in any other faction it would be brave of us to tell someone what happened. But here . . . in *Dauntless* . . . bravery won't do us any good."

"Have you ever read the faction manifestos?" says Will.

The faction manifestos were written after the factions formed. We learned about them in school, but I never read them.

"You have?" I frown at him. Then I remember that Will once memorized a map of the city for fun, and I say, "Oh. Of course *you* have. Never mind."

"One of the lines I remember from the Dauntless manifesto is, 'We believe in ordinary acts of bravery, in the courage that drives one person to stand up for another.'"

Will sighs.

He doesn't need to say anything else. I know what he means. Maybe Dauntless was formed with good intentions, with the right ideals and the right goals. But it has strayed far from them. And the same is true of Erudite, I realize. A long time ago, Erudite pursued knowledge and ingenuity for the sake of doing good. Now they pursue knowledge and ingenuity with greedy hearts. I wonder if the other factions suffer from the same problem. I have not thought about it before.

Despite the depravity I see in Dauntless, though, I could not leave it. It isn't only because the thought of living factionless, in complete isolation, sounds like a fate worse than death. It is because, in the brief moments that I have loved it here, I saw a faction worth saving. Maybe we can become brave and honorable again.

"Let's go to the cafeteria," Will says, "and eat cake."

"Okay." I smile.

As we walk toward the Pit, I repeat the line Will quoted to myself so I don't forget it.

I believe in ordinary acts of bravery, in the courage that drives one person to stand up for another.

It is a beautiful thought.

+ + +

Later, when I return to the dormitory, Edward's bunk is stripped clean and his drawers are open, empty. Across the room, Myra's bunk looks the same way.

When I ask Christina where they went, she says, "They quit."

"Even Myra?"

"She said she didn't want to be here without him. She was going to get cut anyway." She shrugs, like she can't think of anything else to do. If that's true, I know how she feels. "At least they didn't cut Al."

Al was supposed to get cut, but Edward's departure saved him. The Dauntless decided to spare him until the next stage.

"Who else got cut?" I say.

Christina shrugs again. "Two of the Dauntless-born. I don't remember their names."

I nod and look at the blackboard. Someone drew a line through Edward and Myra's names, and changed the numbers next to everyone else's names. Now Peter is first. Will is second. I am fifth. We started stage one with nine initiates.

Now we have seven.

CHAPTER
SEVENTEEN

IT'S NOON. LUNCHTIME.

I sit in a hallway I don't recognize. I walked here because I needed to get away from the dormitory. Maybe if I bring my bedding here, I will never have to go to the dormitory again. It may be my imagination, but it still smells like blood in there, even though I scrubbed the floor until my hands were sore, and someone poured bleach on it this morning.

I pinch the bridge of my nose. Scrubbing the floor when no one else wanted to was something that my mother would have done. If I can't be with her, the least I can do is act like her sometimes.

I hear people approaching, their footsteps echoing on the stone floor, and I look down at my shoes. I switched from gray sneakers to black sneakers a week ago, but the gray shoes are buried in one of my drawers. I can't bear to throw them away, even though I know it's foolish to be attached to sneakers, like they can bring me home.

"Tris?"

I look up. Uriah stops in front of me. He waves along the Dauntless-born initiates he walks with. They exchange looks but keep moving.

"You okay?" he says.

"I had a difficult night."

"Yeah, I heard about that guy Edward." Uriah looks down the hallway. The Dauntless-born initiates disappear around a corner. Then he grins a little. "Want to get out of here?"

"What?" I ask. "Where are you going?"

"To a little initiation ritual," he says. "Come on. We have to hurry."

I briefly consider my options. I can sit here. Or I can leave the Dauntless compound.

I push myself to my feet and jog next to Uriah to catch up to the Dauntless-born initiates.

"The only initiates they usually let come are ones with older siblings in Dauntless," he says. "But they might not even notice. Just act like you belong."

"What exactly are we doing?"

"Something dangerous," he says. A look I can only

describe as Dauntless mania enters his eyes, but rather than recoil from it, as I might have a few weeks ago, I catch it, like it's contagious. Excitement replaces the leaden feeling inside me. We slow when we reach the Dauntless-born initiates.

"What's the *Stiff* doing here?" asks a boy with a metal ring between his nostrils.

"She just saw that guy get stabbed in the eye, Gabe," says Uriah. "Give her a break, okay?"

Gabe shrugs and turns away. No one else says anything, though a few of them give me sidelong glances like they're sizing me up. The Dauntless-born initiates are like a pack of dogs. If I act the wrong way, they won't let me run with them. But for now, I am safe.

We turn another corner, and a group of members stands at the end of the next hallway. There are too many of them to all be related to a Dauntless-born initiate, but I see some similarities among the faces.

"Let's go," one of the members says. He turns and plunges through a dark doorway. The other members follow him, and we follow them. I stay close behind Uriah as I pass into darkness and my toe hits a step. I catch myself before falling forward and start to climb.

"Back staircase," Uriah says, almost mumbling. "Usually locked."

I nod, though he can't see me, and climb until all the

steps are gone. By then, a door at the top of the staircase is open, letting in daylight. We emerge from the ground a few hundred yards from the glass building above the Pit, close to the train tracks.

I feel like I have done this a thousand times before. I hear the train horn. I feel the vibrations in the ground. I see the light attached to the head car. I crack my knuckles and bounce once on my toes.

We jog in a single pack next to the car, and in waves, members and initiates alike pile into the car. Uriah gets in before me, and people press behind me. I can't make any mistakes; I throw myself sideways, grabbing the handle on the side of the car, and hoist myself into the car. Uriah grabs my arm to steady me.

The train picks up its speed. Uriah and I sit against one of the walls.

I shout over the wind, "Where are we going?"

Uriah shrugs. "Zeke never told me."

"Zeke?"

"My older brother," he says. He points across the room at a boy sitting in the doorway with his legs dangling out of the car. He is slight and short and looks nothing like Uriah, apart from his coloring.

"You don't get to know. That ruins the surprise!" the girl on my left shouts. She extends her hand. "I'm Shauna."

I shake her hand, but I don't grip hard enough and I let go too quickly. I doubt I will ever improve my handshake. It feels unnatural to grasp hands with strangers.

"I'm—" I start to say.

"I know who you are," she says. "You're the Stiff. Four told me about you."

I pray the heat in my cheeks is not visible. "Oh? What did he say?"

She smirks at me. "He said you were a Stiff. Why do you ask?"

"If my instructor is talking about me," I say, as firmly as I can, "I want to know what he's saying." I hope I tell a convincing lie. "He isn't coming, is he?"

"No. He never comes to this," she says. "It's probably lost its appeal. Not much scares him, you know."

He isn't coming. Something in me deflates like an untied balloon. I ignore it and nod. I do know that Four is not a coward. But I also know that at least one thing does scare him: heights. Whatever we're doing, it must involve being high up for him to avoid it. She must not know that if she speaks of him with such reverence in her voice.

"Do you know him well?" I ask. I am too curious; I always have been.

"Everyone knows Four," she says. "We were initiates together. I was bad at fighting, so he taught me every night after everyone was asleep." She scratches the back of her neck, her expression suddenly serious. "Nice of him."

She gets up and stands behind the members sitting in the doorway. In a second, her serious expression is gone, but I still feel rattled by what she said, half confused by the idea of Four being "nice" and half wanting to punch her for no apparent reason.

"Here we go!" shouts Shauna. The train doesn't slow down, but she throws herself out of the car. The other members follow her, a stream of black-clothed, pierced people not much older than I am. I stand in the doorway next to Uriah. The train is going much faster than it has every other time I've jumped, but I can't lose my nerve now, in front of all these members. So I jump, hitting the ground hard and stumbling forward a few steps before I regain my balance.

Uriah and I jog to catch up to the members, along with the other initiates, who barely look in my direction.

I look around as I walk. The Hub is behind us, black against the clouds, but the buildings around me are dark and silent. That means we must be north of the bridge, where the city is abandoned.

We turn a corner and spread out as we walk down Michigan Avenue. South of the bridge, Michigan Avenue is a busy street, crawling with people, but here it is bare.

As soon as I lift my eyes to scan the buildings, I know where we're going: the empty Hancock building, a black pillar with crisscrossed girders, the tallest building north of the bridge.

But what are we going to do? Climb it?

As we get closer, the members start to run, and Uriah and I sprint to catch them. Jostling one another with their elbows, they push through a set of doors at the building's base. The glass in one of them is broken, so it is just a frame. I step through it instead of opening it and follow the members through an eerie, dark entryway, crunching broken glass beneath my feet.

I expect us to go up the stairs, but we stop at the elevator bank.

"Do the elevators work?" I ask Uriah, as quietly as I can.

"Sure they do," says Zeke, rolling his eyes. "You think I'm stupid enough not to come here early and turn on the emergency generator?"

"Yeah," says Uriah. "I kinda do."

Zeke glares at his brother, then puts him in a headlock and rubs his knuckles into Uriah's skull. Zeke may be smaller than Uriah, but he must be stronger. Or at least faster. Uriah smacks him in the side, and he lets go.

I grin at the sight of Uriah's disheveled hair, and the elevator doors open. We pile in, members in one and initiates in the other. A girl with a shaved head stomps on my toes on the way in and doesn't apologize. I grab my foot, wincing, and consider kicking her in the shins. Uriah stares at his reflection in the elevator doors and pats his hair down.

"What floor?" the girl with the shaved head says.

"One hundred," I say.

"How would *you* know that?"

"Lynn, come on," says Uriah. "Be nice."

"We're in a one-hundred-story abandoned building with some Dauntless," I retort. "Why don't *you* know that?"

She doesn't respond. She just jams her thumb into the right button.

The elevator zooms upward so fast my stomach sinks and my ears pop. I grab a railing at the side of the elevator, watching the numbers climb. We pass twenty, and thirty, and Uriah's hair is finally smooth. Fifty, sixty, and my toes are done throbbing. Ninety-eight, ninety-nine, and the elevator comes to a stop at one hundred. I'm glad we didn't take the stairs.

"I wonder how we'll get to the roof from . . ." Uriah's voice trails off.

A strong wind hits me, pushing my hair across my face. There is a gaping hole in the ceiling of the hundredth floor. Zeke props an aluminum ladder against its edge and starts to climb. The ladder creaks and sways beneath his feet, but he keeps climbing, whistling as he does. When he reaches the roof, he turns around and holds the top of the ladder for the next person.

Part of me wonders if this is a suicide mission disguised as a game.

It isn't the first time I've wondered that since the Choosing Ceremony.

I climb the ladder after Uriah. It reminds me of climbing the rungs on the Ferris wheel with Four close at my heels. I remember his fingers on my hip again, how they kept me from falling, and I almost miss a step on the ladder. *Stupid.*

Biting my lip, I make it to the top and stand on the roof of the Hancock building.

The wind is so powerful I hear and feel nothing else. I have to lean against Uriah to keep from falling over. At first, all I see is the marsh, wide and brown and everywhere, touching the horizon, devoid of life. In the other direction is the city, and in many ways it is the same, lifeless and with limits I do not know.

Uriah points to something. Attached to one of the poles on top of the tower is a steel cable as thick as my wrist. On the ground is a pile of black slings made of tough fabric, large enough to hold a human being. Zeke grabs one and attaches it to a pulley that hangs from the steel cable.

I follow the cable down, over the cluster of buildings and along Lake Shore Drive. I don't know where it ends. One thing is clear, though: If I go through with this, I'll find out.

We're going to slide down a steel cable in a black sling from one thousand feet up.

"Oh my God," says Uriah.

All I can do is nod.

Shauna is the first person to get in the sling. She wriggles forward on her stomach until most of her body is supported by black fabric. Then Zeke pulls a strap across her shoulders, the small of her back, and the top of her thighs. He pulls her, in the sling, to the edge of the building and counts down from five. Shauna gives a thumbs-up as he shoves her forward, into nothingness.

Lynn gasps as Shauna hurtles toward the ground at a steep incline, headfirst. I push past her to see better. Shauna stays secure in the sling for as long as I can see her, and then she's too far away, just a black speck over Lake Shore Drive.

The members whoop and pump their fists and form a line, sometimes shoving one another out of the way to get a better place. Somehow I am the first initiate in line, right in front of Uriah. Only seven people stand between me and the zip line.

Still, there is a part of me that groans, *I have to wait for seven people?* It is a strange blend of terror and eagerness, unfamiliar until now.

The next member, a young-looking boy with hair down to his shoulders, jumps into the sling on his back instead of his stomach. He stretches his arms wide as Zeke shoves him down the steel cable.

None of the members seem at all afraid. They act like they have done this a thousand times before, and maybe they have. But when I look over my shoulder, I see that most of the initiates look pale or worried, even if they talk excitedly to one another. What happens between initiation and membership that transforms panic into delight? Or do people just get better at hiding their fear?

Three people in front of me. Another sling; a member gets in feet-first and crosses her arms over her chest. Two people. A tall, thick boy jumps up and down like a child before climbing into the sling and lets out a high screech as he disappears, making the girl in front of me laugh. One person.

She hops into the sling face-first and keeps her hands in front of her as Zeke tightens her straps. And then it's my turn.

I shudder as Zeke hangs my sling from the cable. I try

to climb in, but I have trouble; my hands are shaking too badly.

"Don't worry," Zeke says right next to my ear. He takes my arm and helps me get in, facedown.

The straps tighten around my midsection, and Zeke slides me forward, to the edge of the roof. I stare down the building's steel girders and black windows, all the way to the cracked sidewalk. I am a fool for doing this. And a fool for enjoying the feeling of my heart slamming against my sternum and sweat gathering in the lines of my palms.

"Ready, Stiff?" Zeke smirks down at me. "I have to say, I'm impressed that you aren't screaming and crying right now."

"I told you," Uriah says. "She's Dauntless through and through. Now get on with it."

"Careful, brother, or I might not tighten your straps enough," Zeke says. He smacks his knee. "And then, *splat*!"

"Yeah, yeah," Uriah says. "And then our mother would boil you alive."

Hearing him talk about his mother, about his intact family, makes my chest hurt for a second, like someone pierced it with a needle.

"Only if she found out." Zeke tugs on the pulley attached to the steel cable. It holds, which is fortunate, because if it breaks, my death will be swift and certain. He looks down at me and says, "Ready, set, g—"

Before he can finish the word "go," he releases the sling and I forget him, I forget Uriah, and family, and all the things that could malfunction and lead to my death. I hear metal sliding against metal and feel wind so intense it forces tears into my eyes as I hurtle toward the ground.

I feel like I am without substance, without weight. Ahead of me the marsh looks huge, its patches of brown spreading farther than I can see, even up this high. The air is so cold and so fast that it hurts my face. I pick up speed and a shout of exhilaration rises within me, stopped only by the wind that fills my mouth the second my lips part.

Held secure by the straps, I throw my arms out to the side and imagine that I am flying. I plunge toward the street, which is cracked and patchy and follows perfectly the curve of the marsh. I can imagine, up here, how the marsh looked when it was full of water, like liquid steel as it reflected the color of the sky.

My heart beats so hard it hurts, and I can't scream and I can't breathe, but I also feel everything, every vein and every fiber, every bone and every nerve, all awake and buzzing in my body as if charged with electricity. I am pure adrenaline.

The ground grows and bulges beneath me, and I can see the tiny people standing on the pavement below. I should scream, like any rational human being would, but when I open my mouth again, I just crow with joy. I yell louder, and the figures on the ground pump their fists and yell back, but they are so far away I can barely hear them.

I look down and the ground smears beneath me, all gray and white and black, glass and pavement and steel. Tendrils of wind, soft as hair, wrap around my fingers and push my arms back. I try to pull my arms to my chest again, but I am not strong enough. The ground grows bigger and bigger.

I don't slow down for another minute at least but sail parallel to the ground, like a bird.

When I slow down, I run my fingers over my hair. The wind teased it into knots. I hang about twenty feet above the ground, but that height seems like nothing now. I reach behind me and work to undo the straps holding me in. My fingers shake, but I still manage to loosen them. A crowd of members stands below. They grasp one another's arms, forming a net of limbs beneath me.

In order to get down, I have to trust them to catch me. I have to accept that these people are mine, and I am theirs. It is a braver act than sliding down the zip line.

I wriggle forward and fall. I hit their arms hard. Wrist bones and forearms press into my back, and then palms wrap around my arms and pull me to my feet. I don't know which hands hold me and which hands don't;

I see grins and hear laughter.

"What'd you think?" Shauna says, clapping me on the shoulder.

"Um . . ." All the members stare at me. They look as windblown as I feel, the frenzy of adrenaline in their eyes and their hair askew. I know why my father said the Dauntless were a pack of madmen. He didn't—couldn't—understand the kind of camaraderie that forms only after you've all risked your lives together.

"When can I go again?" I say. My smile stretches wide enough to show teeth, and when they laugh, I laugh. I think of climbing the stairs with the Abnegation, our feet finding the same rhythm, all of us the same. This isn't like that. We are not the same. But we are, somehow, one.

I look toward the Hancock building, which is so far from where I stand that I can't see the people on its roof.

"Look! There he is!" someone says, pointing over my shoulder. I follow the pointed finger toward a small dark shape sliding down the steel wire. A few seconds later I hear a bloodcurdling scream.

"I bet he'll cry."

"Zeke's brother, cry? No way. He would get punched so hard."

"His arms are flailing!"

"He sounds like a strangled cat," I say. Everyone laughs again. I feel a twinge of guilt for teasing Uriah when he can't hear me, but I would have said the same thing if he were standing here. I hope.

When Uriah finally comes to a stop, I follow the members to meet him. We line up beneath him and thrust our arms into the space between us. Shauna clamps a hand around my elbow. I grab another arm—I'm not sure who it belongs to, there are too many tangled hands—and look up at her.

"Pretty sure we can't call you 'Stiff' anymore," Shauna says. She nods. "Tris."

+ + +

I still smell like wind when I walk into the cafeteria that evening. For the second after I walk in, I stand among a crowd of Dauntless, and I feel like one of them. Then Shauna waves to me and the crowd breaks apart, and I walk toward the table where Christina, Al, and Will sit, gaping at me.

I didn't think about them when I accepted Uriah's invitation. In a way, it is satisfying to see stunned looks on their faces. But I don't want them to be upset with me either.

"Where were you?" asks Christina. "What were you doing with them?"

"Uriah . . . you know, the Dauntless-born who was on

our capture the flag team?" I say. "He was leaving with some of the members and he begged them to let me come along. They didn't really want me there. Some girl named Lynn stepped on me."

"They may not have wanted you there then," says Will quietly, "but they seem to like you now."

"Yeah," I say. I can't deny it. "I'm glad to be back, though."

Hopefully they can't tell I'm lying, but I suspect they can. I caught sight of myself in a window on the way into the compound, and my cheeks and eyes were both bright, my hair tangled. I look like I have experienced something powerful.

"Well, you missed Christina almost punching an Erudite," says Al. His voice sounds eager. I can count on Al to try to break the tension. "He was here asking for opinions about the Abnegation leadership, and Christina told him there were more important things for him to be doing."

"Which she was completely right about," adds Will. "And he got testy with her. Big mistake."

"Huge," I say, nodding. If I smile enough, maybe I can make them forget their jealousy, or hurt, or whatever is brewing behind Christina's eyes.

"Yeah," she says. "While you were off having fun, I was doing the dirty work of defending your old faction, eliminating interfaction conflict . . ."

"Come on, you know you enjoyed it," says Will, nudging her with his elbow. "If you're not going to tell the whole story, I will. He was standing . . ."

Will launches into his story, and I nod along like I'm listening, but all I can think about is staring down the side of the Hancock building, and the image I got of the marsh full of water, restored to its former glory. I look over Will's shoulder at the members, who are now flicking bits of food at one another with their forks.

It's the first time I have been really eager to be one of them.

Which means I have to survive the next stage of initiation.

CHAPTER
EIGHTEEN

AS FAR AS I can tell, the second stage of initiation involves sitting in a dark hallway with the other initiates, wondering what's going to happen behind a closed door.

Uriah sits across from me, with Marlene on his left and Lynn on his right. The Dauntless-born initiates and the transfers were separated during stage one, but we will be training together from now on. That's what Four told us before he disappeared behind the door.

"So," says Lynn, scuffing the floor with her shoe. "Which one of you is ranked first, huh?"

Her question is met with silence at first, and then Peter clears his throat.

"Me," he says.

"Bet I could take you." She says it casually, turning the

ring in her eyebrow with her fingertips. "I'm second, but I bet any of us could take you, transfer."

I almost laugh. If I was still Abnegation, her comment would be rude and out of place, but among the Dauntless, challenges like that seem common. I am almost starting to expect them.

"I wouldn't be so sure about that, if I were you," Peter says, his eyes glittering. "Who's first?"

"Uriah," she says. "And I am sure. You know how many years we've spent preparing for this?"

If she intends to intimidate us, it works. I already feel colder.

Before Peter can respond, Four opens the door and says, "Lynn." He beckons to her, and she walks down the hallway, the blue light at the end making her bare head glow.

"So you're first," Will says to Uriah.

Uriah shrugs. "Yeah. And?"

"And you don't think it's a little unfair that you've spent your entire life getting ready for this, and we're expected to learn it all in a few weeks?" Will says, his eyes narrowing.

"Not really. Stage one was about skill, sure, but no one can prepare for stage two," he says. "At least, so I'm told."

No one responds to that. We sit in silence for twenty minutes. I count each minute on my watch. Then the door opens again, and Four calls another name.

"Peter," he says.

Each minute wears into me like a scrape of sandpaper. Gradually, our numbers begin to dwindle, and it's just me and Uriah and Drew. Drew's leg bounces, and Uriah's fingers tap against his knee, and I try to sit perfectly still. I hear only muttering from the room at the end of the hallway, and I suspect this is another part of the game they like to play with us. Terrifying us at every opportunity.

The door opens, and Four beckons to me. "Come on, Tris."

I stand, my back sore from leaning against the wall for so long, and walk past the other initiates. Drew sticks out his leg to trip me, but I hop over it at the last second.

Four touches my shoulder to guide me into the room and closes the door behind me.

When I see what's inside, I recoil immediately, my shoulders hitting his chest.

In the room is a reclining metal chair, similar to the one I sat in during the aptitude test. Beside it is a familiar machine. This room has no mirrors and barely any light. There is a computer screen on a desk in the corner.

"Sit," Four says. He squeezes my arms and pushes me forward.

"What's the simulation?" I say, trying to keep my voice

from shaking. I don't succeed.

"Ever hear the phrase 'face your fears'?" he says. "We're taking that literally. The simulation will teach you to control your emotions in the midst of a frightening situation."

I touch a wavering hand to my forehead. Simulations aren't real; they pose no real threat to me, so logically, I shouldn't be afraid of them, but my reaction is visceral. It takes all the willpower I have for me to steer myself toward the chair and sit down in it again, pressing my skull into the headrest. The cold from the metal seeps through my clothes.

"Do you ever administer the aptitude tests?" I say. He seems qualified.

"No," he replies. "I avoid Stiffs as much as possible."

I don't know why someone would avoid the Abnegation. The Dauntless or the Candor, maybe, because bravery and honesty make people do strange things, but the Abnegation?

"Why?"

"Do you ask me that because you think I'll actually answer?"

"Why do you say vague things if you don't want to be asked about them?"

His fingers brush my neck. My body tenses. A tender gesture? No—he has to move my hair to the side. He taps something, and I tilt my head back to see what it is. Four holds a syringe with a long needle in one hand, his thumb against the plunger. The liquid in the syringe is tinted orange.

"An injection?" My mouth goes dry. I don't usually mind needles, but this one is huge.

"We use a more advanced version of the simulation here," he says, "a different serum, no wires or electrodes for you."

"How does it work without wires?"

"Well, *I* have wires, so I can see what's going on," he says. "But for you, there's a tiny transmitter in the serum that sends data to the computer."

He turns my arm over and eases the tip of the needle into the tender skin on the side of my neck. A deep ache spreads through my throat. I wince and try to focus on his calm face.

"The serum will go into effect in sixty seconds. This simulation is different from the aptitude test," he says. "In addition to containing the transmitter, the serum stimulates the amygdala, which is the part of the brain involved in processing negative emotions—like fear— and then induces a hallucination. The brain's electrical activity is then transmitted to our computer, which then translates your hallucination into a simulated image that

I can see and monitor. I will then forward the recording to Dauntless administrators. You stay in the hallucination until you calm down—that is, lower your heart rate and control your breathing."

I try to follow his words, but my thoughts are going haywire. I feel the trademark symptoms of fear: sweaty palms, racing heart, tightness in my chest, dry mouth, a lump in my throat, difficulty breathing. He plants his hands on either side of my head and leans over me.

"Be brave, Tris," he whispers. "The first time is always the hardest."

His eyes are the last thing I see.

+ + +

I stand in a field of dry grass that comes up to my waist. The air smells like smoke and burns my nostrils. Above me the sky is bile-colored, and the sight of it fills me with anxiety, my body cringing away from it.

I hear fluttering, like the pages of a book blown by the wind, but there is no wind. The air is still and soundless apart from the flapping, neither hot nor cold—not like air at all, but I can still breathe. A shadow swoops overhead.

Something lands on my shoulder. I feel its weight and the prick of talons and fling my arm forward to shake it off, my hand batting at it. I feel something smooth and fragile. A feather. I bite my lip and look to the side. A black bird the size of my forearm turns its head and focuses one beady eye on me.

I grit my teeth and hit the crow again with my hand. It digs in its talons and doesn't move. I cry out, more frustrated than pained, and hit the crow with both hands, but it stays in place, resolute, one eye on me, feathers gleaming in the yellow light. Thunder rumbles and I hear the patter of rain on the ground, but no rain falls.

The sky darkens, like a cloud is passing over the sun. Still cringing away from the crow, I look up. A flock of crows storms toward me, an advancing army of outstretched talons and open beaks, each one squawking, filling the air with noise. The crows descend in a single mass, diving toward the earth, hundreds of beady black eyes shining.

I try to run, but my feet are firmly planted and refuse to move, like the crow on my shoulder. I scream as they surround me, feathers flapping in my ears, beaks pecking at my shoulders, talons clinging to my clothes. I scream until tears come from my eyes, my arms flailing. My hands hit solid bodies but do nothing; there are too many. I am alone. They nip at my fingertips and press against my body, wings sliding across the back of my neck, feet tearing at my hair.

I twist and wrench and fall to the ground, covering my head with my arms. They scream against me. I feel a wiggling in the grass, a crow forcing its way under my arm. I open my eyes and it pecks at my face, its beak hitting me in the nose. Blood drips onto the grass and I sob, hitting it with my palm, but another crow wedges under my other arm and its claws stick to the front of my shirt.

I am screaming; I am sobbing.

"Help!" I wail. "Help!"

And the crows flap harder, a roar in my ears. My body burns, and they are everywhere, and I can't think, I can't breathe. I gasp for air and my mouth fills with feathers, feathers down my throat, in my lungs, replacing my blood with dead weight.

"Help," I sob and scream, insensible, illogical. I am dying; I am dying; I am dying.

My skin sears and I am bleeding, and the squawking is so loud my ears are ringing, but I am *not* dying, and I remember that it isn't real, but it feels real, it feels so real. *Be brave.* Four's voice screams in my memory. I cry out to him, inhaling feathers and exhaling "Help!" But there will be no help; I am alone.

You stay in the hallucination until you can calm down, his voice continues, and I cough, and my face is wet with tears, and another crow has wriggled under my arms, and I feel the edge of its sharp beak against my mouth. Its beak wedges past my lips and scrapes my teeth. The crow pushes its head into my mouth and I bite hard, tasting something foul. I spit and clench my teeth to form a barrier, but now a fourth crow is pushing at my feet, and a fifth crow is pecking at my ribs.

Calm down. I can't, I can't. My head throbs.

Breathe. I keep my mouth closed and suck air into my nose. It has been hours since I was alone in the field; it has been days. I push air out of my nose. My heart pounds hard in my chest. I have to slow it down. I breathe again, my face wet with tears.

I sob again, and force myself forward, stretching out on the grass, which prickles against my skin. I extend my arms and breathe. Crows push and prod at my sides, worming their way beneath me, and I let them. I let the flapping of wings and the squawking and the pecking and the prodding continue, relaxing one muscle at a time, resigning myself to becoming a pecked carcass.

The pain overwhelms me.

I open my eyes, and I am sitting in the metal chair.

I scream and hit my arms and head and legs to get the birds off me, but they are gone, though I can still feel the feathers brushing the back of my neck and the talons in my shoulder and my burning skin. I moan and pull my knees to my chest, burying my face in them.

A hand touches my shoulder, and I fling a fist out, hitting something solid but soft. "Don't touch me!" I sob.

"It's over," Four says. The hand shifts awkwardly over my hair, and I remember my father stroking my hair when he kissed me goodnight, my mother touching my hair when she trimmed it with the scissors. I run my palms along my arms, still brushing off feathers, though I know there aren't any.

"Tris."

I rock back and forth in the metal chair.

"Tris, I'm going to take you back to the dorms, okay?"

"No!" I snap. I lift my head and glare at him, though I can't see him through the blur of tears. "They can't see me . . . not like this . . ."

"Oh, calm down," he says. He rolls his eyes. "I'll take you out the back door."

"I don't need you to . . ." I shake my head. My body is trembling and I feel so weak I'm not sure I can stand, but I have to try. I can't be the only one who needs to be walked back to the dorms. Even if they don't see me, they'll find out, they'll talk about me—

"Nonsense."

He grabs my arm and hauls me out of the chair. I blink the tears from my eyes, wipe my cheeks with the heel of my hand, and let him steer me toward the door behind the computer screen.

We walk down the hallway in silence. When we're a few hundred yards away from the room, I yank my arm away and stop.

"Why did you do that to me?" I say. "What was the point of that, huh? I wasn't aware that when I chose Dauntless, I was signing up for weeks of torture!"

"Did you think overcoming cowardice would be easy?" he says calmly.

"That isn't overcoming cowardice! Cowardice is how you decide to be in real life, and in real life, I am not getting pecked to death by crows, Four!" I press my palms to my face and sob into them.

He doesn't say anything, just stands there as I cry. It only takes me a few seconds to stop and wipe my face again. "I want to go home," I say weakly.

But home is not an option anymore. My choices are here or the factionless slums.

He doesn't look at me with sympathy. He just looks at me. His eyes look black in the dim corridor, and his mouth is set in a hard line.

"Learning how to think in the midst of fear," he says, "is a lesson that everyone, even your Stiff family, needs to learn. That's what we're trying to teach you. If you can't learn it, you'll need to get the hell out of here, because we won't want you."

"I'm *trying*." My lower lip trembles. "But I failed. I'm failing."

He sighs. "How long do you think you spent in that hallucination, Tris?"

"I don't know." I shake my head. "A half hour?"

"Three minutes," he replies. "You got out three times faster than the other initiates. Whatever you are, you're not a failure."

Three minutes?

He smiles a little. "Tomorrow you'll be better at this. You'll see."

"Tomorrow?"

He touches my back and guides me toward the dormitory. I feel his fingertips through my shirt. Their gentle pressure makes me forget the birds for a moment.

"What was your first hallucination?" I say, glancing at him.

"It wasn't a 'what' so much as a 'who.'" He shrugs. "It's not important."

"And are you over that fear now?"

"Not yet." We reach the door to the dormitory, and he leans against the wall, sliding his hands into his pockets. "I may never be."

"So they don't go away?"

"Sometimes they do. And sometimes new fears replace them." His thumbs hook around his belt loops. "But becoming fearless isn't the point. That's impossible. It's learning how to control your fear, and how to be free from it, *that's* the point."

I nod. I used to think the Dauntless were fearless. That is how they seemed, anyway. But maybe what I saw as fearless was actually fear under control.

"Anyway, your fears are rarely what they appear to be in the simulation," he adds.

"What do you mean?"

"Well, are you really afraid of crows?" he says, half smiling at me. The expression warms his eyes enough that I forget he's my instructor. He's just a boy, talking casually, walking me to my door. "When you see one, do you run away screaming?"

"No. I guess not." I think about stepping closer to him, not for any practical reason, but just because I want to see what it would be like to stand that close to him; just because I want to.

Foolish, a voice in my head says.

I step closer and lean against the wall too, tilting my head sideways to look at him. As I did on the Ferris wheel, I know exactly how much space there is between us. Six inches. I lean. Less than six inches. I feel warmer, like he's giving off some kind of energy that I am only now close enough to feel.

"So what am I really afraid of?" I say.

"I don't know," he says. "Only you can know."

I nod slowly. There are a dozen things it could be, but I'm not sure which one is right, or if there's even one right one.

"I didn't know becoming Dauntless would be this difficult," I say, and a second later, I am surprised that I said it; surprised that I admitted to it. I bite the inside of my cheek and watch Four carefully. Was it a mistake to tell him that?

"It wasn't always like this, I'm told," he says, lifting a shoulder. My admission doesn't appear to bother him. "Being Dauntless, I mean."

"What changed?"

"The leadership," he says. "The person who controls training sets the standard of Dauntless behavior. Six years ago Max and the other leaders changed the training methods to make them more competitive and more brutal, said it was supposed to test people's strength. And that changed the priorities of Dauntless as a whole. Bet you can't guess who the leaders' new protégé is."

The answer is obvious: Eric. They trained him to be vicious, and now he will train the rest of us to be vicious too.

I look at Four. Their training didn't work on him.

"So if you were ranked first in your initiate class," I say, "what was Eric's rank?"

"Second."

"So he was their second choice for leadership." I nod slowly. "And you were their first."

"What makes you say that?"

"The way Eric was acting at dinner the first night. Jealous, even though he has what he wants."

Four doesn't contradict me. I must be right. I want to ask why he didn't take the position the leaders offered him; why he is so resistant to leadership when he seems to be a natural leader. But I know how Four feels about personal questions.

I sniff, wipe my face one more time, and smooth down my hair.

"Do I look like I've been crying?" I say.

"Hmm." He leans in close, narrowing his eyes like he's inspecting my face. A smile tugs at the corner of his mouth. Even closer, so we would be breathing the same air—if I could remember to breathe.

"No, Tris," he says. A more serious look replaces his smile as he adds, "You look tough as nails."

CHAPTER
NINETEEN

WHEN I WALK IN, most of the other initiates—Dauntless-born and transfer alike—are crowded between the rows of bunk beds with Peter at their center. He holds a piece of paper in both hands.

"*The mass exodus of the children of Abnegation leaders cannot be ignored or attributed to coincidence,*" he reads. "*The recent transfer of Beatrice and Caleb Prior, the children of Andrew Prior, calls into question the soundness of Abnegation's values and teachings.*"

Cold creeps up my spine. Christina, standing on the edge of the crowd, looks over her shoulder and spots me. She gives me a worried look. I can't move. My father. Now the Erudite are attacking my father.

"*Why else would the children of such an important man*

decide that the lifestyle he has set out for them is not an admirable one?" Peter continues. *"Molly Atwood, a fellow Dauntless transfer, suggests a disturbed and abusive upbringing might be to blame. 'I heard her talking in her sleep once,' Molly says. 'She was telling her father to stop doing something. I don't know what it was, but it gave her nightmares.'"*

So this is Molly's revenge. She must have talked to the Erudite reporter that Christina yelled at.

She smiles. Her teeth are crooked. If I knocked them out, I might be doing her a favor.

"What?" I demand. Or I try to demand, but my voice comes out strangled and scratchy, and I have to clear my throat and say it again. *"What?"*

Peter stops reading, and a few people turn around. Some, like Christina, look at me in a pitying way, their eyebrows drawn in, their mouths turned down at the corners. But most give me little smirks and eye one another suggestively. Peter turns last, with a wide smile.

"Give me that," I say, holding out my hand. My face burns.

"But I'm not done reading," he replies, laughter in his voice. His eyes scan the paper again. *"However, perhaps the answer lies not in a morally bereft man, but in the corrupted ideals of an entire faction. Perhaps the answer is that we have entrusted our city to a group of proselytizing tyrants who do not know how to lead us out of poverty and into prosperity."*

I storm up to him and try to snatch the paper from his hands, but he holds it up, high above my head so I can't reach it unless I jump, and I won't jump. Instead, I lift my heel and stomp as hard as I can where the bones in his foot connect to his toes. He grits his teeth to stifle a groan.

Then I throw myself at Molly, hoping the force of the impact will surprise her and knock her down, but before I can do any damage, cold hands close around my waist.

"That's my *father*!" I scream. "My father, you coward!"

Will pulls me away from her, lifting me off the ground. My breaths come fast, and I struggle to grab the paper before anyone can read another word of it. I have to burn it; I have to destroy it; I have to.

Will drags me out of the room and into the hallway, his fingernails digging into my skin. Once the door shuts behind him, he lets go, and I shove him as hard as I can.

"What? Did you think I couldn't defend myself against that piece of Candor trash?"

"No," says Will. He stands in front of the door. "I figured I'd stop you from starting a brawl in the dormitory. Calm down."

I laugh a little. "Calm down? Calm *down*? That's my *family* they're talking about, that's my *faction*!"

"No, it's not." There are dark circles under his eyes; he

looks exhausted. "It's your old faction, and there's nothing you can do about what they say, so you might as well just ignore it."

"Were you even listening?" The heat in my cheeks is gone, and my breaths are more even now. "Your stupid ex-faction isn't just insulting Abnegation anymore. They're calling for an overthrow of the entire government."

Will laughs. "No, they're not. They're arrogant and dull, and that's why I left them, but they aren't revolutionaries. They just want more say, that's all, and they resent Abnegation for refusing to listen to them."

"They don't want people to listen, they want people to agree," I reply. "And you shouldn't bully people into agreeing with you." I touch my palms to my cheeks. "I can't believe my brother joined them."

"Hey. They're not all bad," he says sharply.

I nod, but I don't believe him. I can't imagine anyone emerging from the Erudite unscathed, though Will seems all right.

The door opens again, and Christina and Al walk out.

"It's my turn to get tattooed," she says. "Want to come with us?"

I smooth my hair. I can't go back into the dormitory. Even if Will let me, I am outnumbered there. My only choice is to go with them and try to forget what's happening outside the Dauntless compound. I have enough to worry about without anxiety about my family.

+ + +

Ahead of me, Al gives Christina a piggyback ride. She shrieks as he charges through the crowd. People give him a wide berth, when they can.

My shoulder still burns. Christina persuaded me to join her in getting a tattoo of the Dauntless seal. It is a circle with a flame inside it. My mother didn't even react to the one on my collarbone, so I don't have as many reservations about getting tattoos. They are a part of life here, just as integral to my initiation as learning to fight.

Christina also persuaded me to purchase a shirt that exposes my shoulders and collarbone, and to line my eyes with black pencil again. I don't bother objecting to her makeover attempts anymore. Especially since I find myself enjoying them.

Will and I walk behind Christina and Al.

"I can't believe you got another tattoo," he says, shaking his head.

"Why?" I say. "Because I'm a Stiff?"

"No. Because you're . . . sensible." He smiles. His teeth are white and straight. "So, what was your fear today, Tris?"

"Too many crows," I reply. "You?"

He laughs. "Too much acid."

I don't ask what that means.

"It's really fascinating how it all works," he says. "It's basically a struggle between your thalamus, which is producing the fear, and your frontal lobe, which makes decisions. But the simulation is all in your head, so even though you feel like someone is doing it to you, it's just you, doing it to yourself and . . ." He trails off. "Sorry. I sound like an Erudite. Just a habit."

I shrug. "It's interesting."

Al almost drops Christina, and she slaps her hands around the first thing she can grab, which just happens to be his face. He cringes and adjusts his grip on her legs. At a glance, Al seems happy, but there is something heavy about even his smiles. I am worried about him.

I see Four standing by the chasm, a group of people around him. He laughs so hard he has to grab the railing for balance. Judging by the bottle in his hand and the brightness of his face, he's intoxicated, or on his way there. I had begun to think of Four as rigid, like a soldier, and forgot that he's also eighteen.

"Uh-oh," says Will. "Instructor alert."

"At least it's not Eric," I say. "He'd probably make us play chicken or something."

"Sure, but Four is scary. Remember when he put the gun up to Peter's head? I think Peter wet himself."

"Peter deserved it," I say firmly.

Will doesn't argue with me. He might have, a few weeks ago, but now we've all seen what Peter is capable of.

"Tris!" Four calls out. Will and I exchange a look, half surprise and half apprehension. Four pulls away from the railing and walks up to me. Ahead of us, Al and Christina stop running, and Christina slides to the ground. I don't blame them for staring. There are four of us, and Four is only talking to me.

"You look different." His words, normally crisp, are now sluggish.

"So do you," I say. And he does—he looks more relaxed, younger. "What are you doing?"

"Flirting with death," he replies with a laugh. "Drinking near the chasm. Probably not a good idea."

"No, it isn't." I'm not sure I like Four this way. There's something unsettling about it.

"Didn't know you had a tattoo," he says, looking at my collarbone.

He sips the bottle. His breath smells thick and sharp. Like the factionless man's breath.

"Right. The *crows*," he says. He glances over his shoulder at his friends, who are carrying on without him, unlike mine. He adds, "I'd ask you to hang out with us, but you're not supposed to see me this way."

I am tempted to ask him why he wants me to hang out with him, but I suspect the answer has something to do with the bottle in his hand.

"What way?" I ask. "Drunk?"

"Yeah . . . well, no." His voice softens. "Real, I guess."

"I'll pretend I didn't."

"Nice of you." He puts his lips next to my ear and says, "You look good, Tris."

His words surprise me, and my heart leaps. I wish it didn't, because judging by the way his eyes slide over mine, he has no idea what he's saying. I laugh. "Do me a favor and stay away from the chasm, okay?"

"Of course." He winks at me.

I can't help it. I smile. Will clears his throat, but I don't want to turn away from Four, even when he walks back to his friends.

Then Al rushes at me like a rolling boulder and throws me over his shoulder. I shriek, my face hot.

"Come on, little girl," he says, "I'm taking you to dinner."

I rest my elbows on Al's back and wave at Four as he carries me away.

"I thought I would rescue you," Al says as we walk away. He sets me down. "What was *that* all about?"

He is trying to sound lighthearted, but he asks the

question almost sadly. He still cares too much about me.

"Yeah, I think we'd all like to know the answer to *that* question," says Christina in a singsong voice. "What did he say to you?"

"Nothing." I shake my head. "He was drunk. He didn't even know what he was saying." I clear my throat. "That's why I was grinning. It's . . . funny to see him that way."

"Right," says Will. "Couldn't possibly be because—"

I elbow Will hard in the ribs before he can finish his sentence. He was close enough to hear what Four said to me about looking good. I don't need him telling everyone about it, especially not Al. I don't want to make him feel worse.

At home I used to spend calm, pleasant nights with my family. My mother knit scarves for the neighborhood kids. My father helped Caleb with his homework. There was a fire in the fireplace and peace in my heart, as I was doing exactly what I was supposed to be doing, and everything was quiet.

I have never been carried around by a large boy, or laughed until my stomach hurt at the dinner table, or listened to the clamor of a hundred people all talking at once. Peace is restrained; this is free.

CHAPTER TWENTY

I BREATHE THROUGH my nose. In, out. In.

"It's just a simulation, Tris," Four says quietly.

He's wrong. The last simulation bled into my life, waking and sleeping. Nightmares, not just featuring the crows but the feelings I had in the simulation—terror and helplessness, which I suspect is what I am really afraid of. Sudden fits of terror in the shower, at breakfast, on the way here. Nails bitten down so far my nail beds ache. And I am not the only one who feels this way; I can tell.

Still I nod and close my eyes.

+ + +

I am in darkness. The last thing I remember is the metal chair and the needle in my arm. This time there is no

field; there are no crows. My heart pounds in antici-
pation. What monsters will creep from the darkness
and steal my rationality? How long will I have to wait
for them?

A blue orb lights up a few feet ahead of me, and then
another one, filling the room with light. I am on the
Pit floor, next to the chasm, and the initiates stand
around me, their arms folded and their faces blank. I
search for Christina and find her standing among them.
None of them move. Their stillness makes my throat feel
tight.

I see something in front of me—my own faint reflection.
I touch it, and my fingers find glass, cool and smooth. I
look up. There is a pane above me; I am in a glass box.
I press above my head to see if I can force the box open. It
doesn't budge. I am sealed in.

My heart beats faster. I don't want to be trapped.
Someone taps on the wall in front of me. Four. He points
at my feet, smirking.

A few seconds ago, my feet were dry, but now I stand
in half an inch of water, and my socks are soggy. I crouch
to see where the water is coming from, but it seems
to be coming from nowhere, rising up from the box's
glass bottom. I look up at Four, and he shrugs. He
joins the crowd of initiates.

The water rises fast. It now covers my ankles. I pound against the glass with my fist.

"Hey!" I say. "Let me out of here!"

The water slides up my bare calves as it rises, cool and soft. I hit the glass harder.

"Get me out of here!"

I stare at Christina. She leans over to Peter, who stands beside her, and whispers something in his ear. They both laugh.

The water covers my thighs. I pound both fists against the glass. I'm not trying to get their attention anymore; I'm trying to break out. Frantic, I bang against the glass as hard as I can. I step back and throw my shoulder into the wall, once, twice, three times, four times. I hit the wall until my shoulder aches, screaming for help, watching the water rise to my waist, my rib cage, my chest.

"Help!" I scream. "Please! Please help!"

I slap the glass. I will die in this tank. I drag my shaking hands through my hair.

I see Will standing among the initiates, and something tickles at the back of my mind. Something he said. *Come on, think.* I stop trying to break the glass. It's hard to breathe, but I have to try. I'll need as much air as I can get in a few seconds.

My body rises, weightless in the water. I float closer to the ceiling and tilt my head back as the water covers my chin. Gasping, I press my face to the glass above me, sucking in as much air as I can. Then the water covers me, sealing me into the box.

Don't panic. It's no use—my heart pounds and my thoughts scatter. I thrash in the water, smacking the walls. I kick the glass as hard as I can, but the water slows down my foot. *The simulation is all in your head.*

I scream, and water fills my mouth. If it's in my head, I control it. The water burns my eyes. The initiates' passive faces stare back at me. They don't care.

I scream again and shove the wall with my palm. I hear something. A cracking sound. When I pull my hand away, there is a line in the glass. I slam my other hand next to the first and drive another crack through the glass, this one spreading outward from my palm in long, crooked fingers. My chest burns like I just swallowed fire. I kick the wall. My toes ache from the impact, and I hear a long, low groan.

The pane shatters, and the force of the water against my back throws me forward. There is air again.

I gasp and sit up. I'm in the chair. I gulp and shake out my hands. Four stands to my right, but instead of helping me up, he just looks at me.

"What?" I ask.

"How did you do that?"

"Do what?"

"Crack the glass."

"I don't know." Four finally offers me his hand. I swing my legs over the side of the chair, and when I stand, I feel steady. Calm.

He sighs and grabs me by the elbow, half leading and half dragging me out of the room. We walk quickly down the hallway, and then I stop, pulling my arm back. He stares at me in silence. He won't give me information without prompting.

"What?" I demand.

"You're Divergent," he replies.

I stare at him, fear pulsing through me like electricity. He knows. How does he know? I must have slipped up. Said something wrong.

I should act casual. I lean back, pressing my shoulders to the wall, and say, "What's Divergent?"

"Don't play stupid," he says. "I suspected it last time, but this time it's obvious. You manipulated the simulation; you're Divergent. I'll delete the footage, but unless you want to wind up *dead* at the bottom of the chasm, you'll figure out how to hide it during the simulations! Now, if you'll excuse me."

He walks back to the simulation room and slams the door behind him. I feel my heartbeat in my throat. I manipulated the simulation; I broke the glass. I didn't know that was an act of Divergence.

How did he?

I push myself away from the wall and start down the hallway. I need answers, and I know who has them.

+ + +

I walk straight to the tattoo place where I last saw Tori.

There aren't many people out, because it's midafternoon and most of them are at work or at school. There are three people in the tattoo place: the other tattoo artist, who is drawing a lion on another man's arm, and Tori, who is sorting through a stack of paper on the counter. She looks up when I walk in.

"Hello, Tris," she says. She glances at the other tattoo artist, who is too focused on what he's doing to notice us. "Let's go in the back."

I follow her behind the curtain that separates the two rooms. The next room contains a few chairs, spare tattoo needles, ink, pads of paper, and framed artwork. Tori draws the curtain shut and sits in one of the chairs. I sit next to her, tapping my feet to give myself something to do.

"What's going on?" she says. "How are the simulations going?"

"Really well." I nod a few times. "A little too well, I hear."

"Ah."

"Please help me understand," I say quietly. "What does it mean to be . . ." I hesitate. I should not say the word "Divergent" here. "What the hell am I? What does it have to do with the simulations?"

Tori's demeanor changes. She leans back and crosses her arms. Her expression becomes guarded.

"Among other things, you . . . you are someone who is aware, when they are in a simulation, that what they are experiencing is not real," she says. "Someone who can then manipulate the simulation or even shut it down. And also . . ." She leans forward and looks into my eyes. "Someone who, because you are also Dauntless . . . tends to die."

A weight settles on my chest, like each sentence she speaks is piling there. Tension builds inside me until I can't stand to hold it in anymore—I have to cry, or scream, or . . .

I let out a harsh little laugh that dies almost as soon as it's born and say, "So I'm going to die, then?"

"Not necessarily," she says. "The Dauntless leaders

257

don't know about you yet. I deleted your aptitude results from the system immediately and manually logged your result as Abnegation. But make no mistake—if they discover what you are, they *will* kill you."

I stare at her in silence. She doesn't look crazy. She sounds steady, if a little urgent, and I've never suspected her of being unbalanced, but she must be. There hasn't been a murder in our city as long as I've been alive. Even if individuals are capable of it, the leaders of a faction can't possibly be.

"You're paranoid," I say. "The leaders of the Dauntless wouldn't kill me. People don't do that. Not anymore. That's the point of all this . . . all the factions."

"Oh, you think so?" She plants her hands on her knees and stares right at me, her features taut with sudden ferocity. "They got my brother, why not you, huh? What makes you special?"

"Your brother?" I say, narrowing my eyes.

"Yeah. My brother. He and I both transferred from Erudite, only his aptitude test was inconclusive. On the last day of simulations, they found his body in the chasm. Said it was a suicide. Only my brother was doing well in training, he was dating another initiate, he was *happy*." She shakes her head. "You have a brother, right? Don't you think you would know if he was suicidal?"

I try to imagine Caleb killing himself. Even the thought sounds ridiculous to me. Even if Caleb was miserable, it would not be an option.

Her sleeves are rolled up, so I can see a tattoo of a river on her right arm. Did she get it after her brother died? Was the river another fear she overcame?

She lowers her voice. "In the second stage of training, Georgie got really good, really fast. He said the simulations weren't even scary to him . . . they were like a game. So the instructors took a special interest in him. Piled into the room when he went under, instead of just letting the instructor report his results. Whispered about him all the time. The last day of simulations, one of the Dauntless leaders came in to see it himself. And the next day, Georgie was gone."

I could be good at the simulations, if I mastered whatever force helped me break the glass. I could be so good that all the instructors took notice. I could, but will I?

"Is that all it is?" I say. "Just changing the simulations?"

"I doubt it," she says, "but that's all I know."

"How many people know about this?" I say, thinking of Four. "About manipulating the simulations?"

"Two kinds of people," she says. "People who want you dead. Or people who have experienced it themselves. Firsthand. Or secondhand, like me."

Four told me he would delete the recording of me breaking the glass. He doesn't want me dead. Is he Divergent? Was a family member? A friend? A girlfriend?

I push the thought aside. I can't let him distract me.

"I don't understand," I say slowly, "why the Dauntless leaders care that I can manipulate the simulation."

"If I had it figured out, I would have told you by now." She presses her lips together. "The only thing I've come up with is that changing the simulation isn't what they care about; it's just a symptom of something else. Something they do care about."

Tori takes my hand and presses it between her palms.

"Think about this," she says. "These people taught you how to use a gun. They taught you how to fight. You think they're above hurting you? Above killing you?"

She releases my hand and stands.

"I have to go or Bud will ask questions. Be careful, Tris."

CHAPTER
TWENTY-ONE

THE DOOR TO the Pit closes behind me, and I am alone. I have not walked this tunnel since the day of the Choosing Ceremony. I remember how I walked it then, my footsteps unsteady, searching for light. I walk it surefooted now. I don't need light anymore.

It has been four days since I spoke to Tori. Since then, Erudite has released two articles about Abnegation. The first article accuses Abnegation of withholding luxuries like cars and fresh fruit from the other factions in order to force their belief in self-denial on everyone else. When I read it, I thought of Will's sister, Cara, accusing my mother of hoarding goods.

The second article discusses the failings of choosing government officials based on their faction, asking why only people who define themselves as selfless should be in government. It promotes a return to the democratically elected political systems of the past. It makes a lot of sense, which makes me suspect it is a call for revolution wrapped in the clothing of rationality.

I reach the end of the tunnel. The net stretches across the gaping hole, just as it did when I last saw it. I climb the stairs to the wooden platform where Four pulled me to solid ground and grab the bar that the net is attached to. I would not have been able to lift my body up with just my arms when I first got here, but now I do it almost without thinking and roll into the center of the net.

Above me are the empty buildings that stand at the edge of the hole, and the sky. It is dark blue and starless. There is no moon.

The articles troubled me, but I had friends to cheer me up, and that is something. When the first one was released, Christina charmed one of the cooks in the Dauntless kitchens, and he let us try some cake batter. After the second article, Uriah and Marlene taught me a card game, and we played for two hours in the dining hall.

Tonight, though, I want to be alone. More than that, I want to remember why I came here, and why I was so determined to stay here that I would jump off a building for it, even before I knew what being Dauntless was. I work my fingers through the holes in the net beneath me.

I wanted to be like the Dauntless I saw at school. I wanted to be loud and daring and free like them. But they were not members yet; they were just playing at being Dauntless. And so was I, when I jumped off that roof. I didn't know what fear was.

In the past four days, I faced four fears. In one I was tied to a stake and Peter set a fire beneath my feet. In another I was drowning again, this time in the middle of an ocean as the water raged around me. In the third, I watched as my family slowly bled to death. And in the fourth, I was held at gunpoint and forced to shoot them. I know what fear is now.

Wind rushes over the lip of the hole and washes over me, and I close my eyes. In my mind I stand at the edge of the roof again. I undo the buttons of my gray Abnegation shirt, exposing my arms, revealing more of my body than anyone else has ever seen. I ball the shirt up and hurl it at Peter's chest.

I open my eyes. No, I was wrong; I didn't jump off the roof because I wanted to be like the Dauntless. I jumped off because I already was like them, and I wanted to show myself to them. I wanted to acknowledge a part of myself that Abnegation demanded that I hide.

I stretch my hands over my head and hook them in the

net again. I reach with my toes as far as I can, taking up as much of the net as possible. The night sky is empty and silent, and for the first time in four days, so is my mind.

+ + +

I hold my head in my hands and breathe deeply. Today the simulation was the same as yesterday: Someone held me at gunpoint and ordered me to shoot my family. When I lift my head, I see that Four is watching me.

"I know the simulation isn't real," I say.

"You don't have to explain it to me," he replies. "You love your family. You don't want to shoot them. Not the most unreasonable thing in the world."

"In the simulation is the only time I get to see them," I say. Even though he says I don't, I feel like I have to explain why this fear is so difficult for me to face. I twist my fingers together and pull them apart. My nail beds are bitten raw—I have been chewing them as I sleep. I wake to bloody hands every morning. "I miss them. You ever just . . . miss your family?"

Four looks down. "No," he says eventually. "I don't. But that's unusual."

It is unusual, so unusual it distracts me from the memory of holding a gun to Caleb's chest. What was his family like that he no longer cares about them?

I pause with my hand on the doorknob and look back at him.

Are you like me? I ask him silently. *Are you Divergent?*

Even thinking the word feels dangerous. His eyes hold mine, and as the silent seconds pass, he looks less and less stern. I hear my heartbeat. I have been looking at him too long, but then, he has been looking back, and I feel like we are both trying to say something the other can't hear, though I could be imagining it. Too long—and now, even longer, my heart even louder, his tranquil eyes swallowing me whole.

I push the door open and hurry down the hallway.

I shouldn't be so easily distracted by him. I shouldn't be able to think of anything but initiation. The simulations should disturb me more; they should break my mind, as they have been doing to most of the other initiates. Drew doesn't sleep—he just stares at the wall, curled in a ball. Al screams every night from his nightmares and cries into his pillow. My nightmares and chewed fingernails pale by comparison.

Al's screams wake me every time, and I stare at the springs above me and wonder what on earth is wrong with me, that I still feel strong when everyone else is breaking down. Is it being Divergent that makes me steady, or is it something else?

When I get back to the dormitory, I expect to find the same thing I found the day before: a few initiates lying on beds or staring at nothing. Instead they stand in a group on the other end of the room. Eric is in front of them with a chalkboard in his hands, which is facing the other way, so I can't see what's written on it. I stand next to Will.

"What's going on?" I whisper. I hope it isn't another article, because I'm not sure I can handle any more hostility directed at me.

"Rankings for stage two," he says.

"I thought there weren't any cuts after stage two," I hiss.

"There aren't. It's just a progress report, sort of."

I nod.

The sight of the board makes me feel uneasy, like something is swimming in my stomach. Eric lifts the board above his head and hangs it on the nail. When he steps aside, the room falls silent, and I crane my neck to see what it says.

My name is in the first slot.

Heads turn in my direction. I follow the list down. Christina and Will are seventh and ninth, respectively. Peter is second, but when I look at the time listed by his name, I realize that the margin between us is conspicuously wide.

Peter's average simulation time is eight minutes. Mine is two minutes, forty-five seconds.

"Nice job, Tris," Will says quietly.

I nod, still staring at the board. I should be pleased that I am ranked first, but I know what that means. If Peter and his friends hated me before, they will despise me now. Now I am Edward. It could be my eye next. Or worse.

I search for Al's name and find it in the last slot. The crowd of initiates breaks up slowly, leaving just me, Peter, Will, and Al standing there. I want to console Al. To tell him that the only reason that I'm doing well is that there's something different about my brain.

Peter turns slowly, every limb infused with tension. A glare would have been less threatening than the look he gives me—a look of pure hatred. He walks toward his bunk, but at the last second, he whips around and shoves me against a wall, a hand on each of my shoulders.

"I will not be outranked by a Stiff," he hisses, his face so close to mine I can smell his stale breath. "How did you do it, huh? How the hell did you do it?"

He pulls me forward a few inches and then slams me against the wall again. I clench my teeth to keep from crying out, though pain from the impact went all the way down my spine. Will grabs Peter by his shirt collar and drags him away from me.

"Leave her alone," he says. "Only a coward bullies a little girl."

"A little girl?" scoffs Peter, throwing off Will's hand. "Are you blind, or just stupid? She's going to edge you out of the rankings and out of *Dauntless*, and you're going to get *nothing*, all because she knows how to manipulate people and you don't. So when you realize that she's out to ruin us all, you let me know."

Peter storms out of the dormitory. Molly and Drew follow him, looks of disgust on their faces.

"Thanks," I say, nodding to Will.

"Is he right?" Will asks quietly. "Are you trying to manipulate us?"

"How on earth would I do that?" I scowl at him. "I'm just doing the best I can, like anyone else."

"I don't know." He shrugs a little. "By acting weak so we pity you? And then acting tough to psyche us out?"

"Psyche you out?" I repeat. "I'm your *friend*. I wouldn't do that."

He doesn't say anything. I can tell he doesn't believe me—not quite.

"Don't be an idiot, Will," says Christina, hopping down from her bunk. She looks at me without sympathy and adds, "She's not acting."

Christina turns and leaves, without banging the door shut. Will follows. I am alone in the room with Al. The first and the last.

Al has never looked small before, but he does now, with his shoulders slumped and his body collapsing on itself like crumpled paper. He sits down on the edge of his bed.

"Are you all right?" I ask.

"Sure," he says.

His face is bright red. I look away. Asking him was just a formality. Anyone with eyes could see that Al is not all right.

"It's not over," I say. "You can improve your rank if you . . ."

My voice trails off when he looks up at me. I don't even know what I would say to him if I finished my sentence. There is no strategy for stage two. It reaches deep into the heart of who we are and tests whatever courage is there.

"See?" he says. "It's not that simple."

"I know it's not."

"I don't think you do," he says, shaking his head. His chin wobbles. "For you it's easy. All of this is easy."

"That's not true."

"Yeah, it is." He closes his eyes. "You aren't helping me by pretending it isn't. I don't—I'm not sure you can help me at all."

I feel like I just walked into a downpour, and all my

clothes are heavy with water; like I am heavy and awkward and useless. I don't know if he means that no one can help him, or if I, specifically, can't help him, but I would not be okay with either interpretation. I want to help him. I am powerless to do so.

"I . . . ," I start to say, meaning to apologize, but for what? For being more Dauntless than he is? For not knowing what to say?

"I just . . ." The tears that have been gathering in his eyes spill over, wetting his cheeks. ". . . want to be alone."

I nod and turn away from him. Leaving him is not a good idea, but I can't stop myself. The door clicks into place behind me, and I keep walking.

I walk past the drinking fountain and through the tunnels that seemed endless the day I got here but now barely register in my mind. This is not the first time I have failed my family since I got here, but for some reason, it feels that way. Every other time I failed, I knew what to do but chose not to do it. This time, I did not know what to do. Have I lost the ability to see what people need? Have I lost part of myself?

I keep walking.

+ + +

I somehow find the hallway I sat in the day Edward left. I don't want to be alone, but I don't feel like I have much of a choice. I close my eyes and pay attention to the cold stone beneath me and breathe the musty underground air.

"Tris!" someone calls from the end of the hallway. Uriah jogs toward me. Behind him are Lynn and Marlene. Lynn is holding a muffin.

"Thought I would find you here." He crouches near my feet. "I heard you got ranked first."

"So you just wanted to congratulate me?" I smirk. "Well, thanks."

"*Someone* should," he says. "And I figured your friends might not be so congratulatory, since their ranks aren't as high. So quit moping and come with us. I'm going to shoot a muffin off Marlene's head."

The idea is so ridiculous I can't stop myself from laughing. I get up and follow Uriah to the end of the hallway, where Marlene and Lynn are waiting. Lynn narrows her eyes at me, but Marlene grins.

"Why aren't you out celebrating?" she asks. "You're practically guaranteed a top ten spot if you keep it up."

"She's too Dauntless for the other transfers," Uriah says.

"And too Abnegation to 'celebrate,'" remarks Lynn.

I ignore her. "Why are you shooting a muffin off Marlene's head?"

"She bet me I couldn't aim well enough to hit a small object from one hundred feet," Uriah explains. "I bet her she didn't have the guts to stand there as I tried. It works out well, really."

The training room where I first fired a gun is not far from my hidden hallway. We get there in under a minute, and Uriah flips on a light switch. It looks the same as the last time I was there: targets on one end of the room, a table with guns on the other.

"They just keep these lying around?" I ask.

"Yeah, but they aren't loaded." Uriah pulls up his shirt. There is a gun stuck under the waistband of his pants, right under a tattoo. I stare at the tattoo, trying to figure out what it is, but then he lets his shirt fall. "Okay," he says. "Go stand in front of a target."

Marlene walks away, a skip in her step.

"You aren't seriously going to shoot at her, are you?" I ask Uriah.

"It's not a real gun," says Lynn quietly. "It's got plastic pellets in it. The worst it'll do is sting her face, maybe give her a welt. What do you think we are, stupid?"

Marlene stands in front of one of the targets and sets the muffin on her head. Uriah squints one eye as he aims the gun.

"Wait!" calls out Marlene. She breaks off a piece of the muffin and pops it into her mouth. "Mmkay!" she shouts, the word garbled by food. She gives Uriah a thumbs-up.

"I take it your ranks were good," I say to Lynn.

She nods. "Uriah's second. I'm first. Marlene's fourth."

"You're only first by a *hair*," says Uriah as he aims. He squeezes the trigger. The muffin falls off Marlene's head. She didn't even blink.

"We both win!" she shouts.

"You miss your old faction?" Lynn asks me.

"Sometimes," I say. "It was calmer. Not as exhausting."

Marlene picks up the muffin from the ground and bites into it. Uriah shouts, "Gross!"

"Initiation's supposed to wear us down to who we really are. That's what Eric says, anyway," Lynn says. She arches an eyebrow.

"Four says it's to prepare us."

"Well, they don't agree on much."

I nod. Four told me that Eric's vision for Dauntless is not what it's supposed to be, but I wish he would tell me exactly what he thinks the right vision is. I get glimpses of it every so often—the Dauntless cheering when I jumped off the building, the net of arms that caught me after zip lining—but they are not enough. Has he read the Dauntless manifesto? Is that what he believes in—in ordinary acts of bravery?

The door to the training room opens. Shauna, Zeke, and Four walk in just as Uriah fires at another target. The plastic pellet bounces off the center of the target and rolls along the ground.

"I thought I heard something in here," says Four.

"Turns out it's my idiot brother," says Zeke. "You're not supposed to be in here after hours. Careful, or Four will tell Eric, and then you'll be as good as scalped."

Uriah wrinkles his nose at his brother and puts the pellet gun away. Marlene crosses the room, taking bites of her muffin, and Four steps away from the door to let us file out.

"You wouldn't tell Eric," says Lynn, eyeing Four suspiciously.

"No, I wouldn't," he says. As I pass him, he rests his hand on the top of my back to usher me out, his palm pressing between my shoulder blades. I shiver. I hope he can't tell.

The others walk down the hallway, Zeke and Uriah shoving each other, Marlene splitting her muffin with Shauna, Lynn marching in front. I start to follow them.

"Wait a second," Four says. I turn toward him, wondering which version of Four I'll see now—the one who scolds me, or the one who climbs Ferris wheels with me. He smiles a little, but the smile doesn't spread to his eyes, which look tense and worried.

"You belong here, you know that?" he says. "You belong with us. It'll be over soon, so just hold on, okay?"

He scratches behind his ear and looks away, like he's embarrassed by what he said.

I stare at him. I feel my heartbeat everywhere, even in my toes. I feel like doing something bold, but I could just as easily walk away. I am not sure which option is smarter, or better. I am not sure that I care.

I reach out and take his hand. His fingers slide between mine. I can't breathe.

I stare up at him, and he stares down at me. For a long moment, we stay that way. Then I pull my hand away and run after Uriah and Lynn and Marlene. Maybe now he thinks I'm stupid, or strange. Maybe it was worth it.

+ + +

I get back to the dormitory before anyone else does, and when they start to trickle in, I get into bed and pretend to be asleep. I don't need any of them, not if they're going to react this way when I do well. If I can make it through initiation, I will be Dauntless, and I won't have to see them anymore.

I don't need them—but do I want them? Every tattoo I got with them is a mark of their friendship, and almost every time I have laughed in this dark place was because of them. I don't want to lose them. But I feel like I have already.

After at least a half hour of racing thoughts, I roll onto

my back and open my eyes. The dormitory is dark now—everyone has gone to bed. *Probably exhausted from resenting me so much*, I think with a wry smile. As if coming from the most hated faction wasn't enough, now I'm showing them up, too.

I get out of bed to get a drink of water. I'm not thirsty, but I need to do something. My bare feet make sticky sounds on the floor as I walk, my hand skimming the wall to keep my path straight. A bulb glows blue above the drinking fountain.

I tug my hair over one shoulder and bend over. As soon as the water touches my lips, I hear voices at the end of the hallway. I creep closer to them, trusting the dark to keep me hidden.

"So far there haven't been any signs of it." Eric's voice. Signs of what?

"Well, you wouldn't have seen much of it yet," someone replies. A female voice; cold and familiar, but familiar like a dream, not a real person. "Combat training shows you nothing. The simulations, however, reveal who the Divergent rebels are, if there are any, so we will have to examine the footage several times to be sure."

The word "Divergent" makes me go cold. I lean forward, my back pressed to the stone, to see who the familiar voice belongs to.

"Don't forget the reason I had Max appoint you," the voice says. "Your first priority is always finding them. Always."

"I won't forget."

I shift a few inches forward, hoping I am still hidden. Whoever that voice belongs to, she is pulling the strings; she is responsible for Eric's leadership position; she is the one who wants me dead. I tilt my head forward, straining to see them before they turn the corner.

Then someone grabs me from behind.

I start to scream, but a hand claps over my mouth. It smells like soap and it's big enough to cover the lower half of my face. I thrash, but the arms holding me are too strong, and I bite down on one of the fingers.

"Ow!" a rough voice cries.

"Shut up and keep her mouth covered." That voice is higher than the average male's and clearer. Peter.

A strip of dark cloth covers my eyes, and a new pair of hands ties it at the back of my head. I struggle to breathe. There are at least two hands on my arms, dragging me forward, and one on my back, shoving me in the same direction, and one on my mouth, keeping my screams in. Three people. My chest hurts. I can't resist three people on my own.

"Wonder what it sounds like when a Stiff begs for

mercy," Peter says with a chuckle. "Hurry up."

I try to focus on the hand on my mouth. There must be something distinct about it that will make him easier to identify. His identity is a problem I can solve. I need to solve a problem right now, or I will panic.

The palm is sweaty and soft. I clench my teeth and breathe through my nose. The soap smell is familiar. Lemongrass and sage. The same smell surrounds Al's bunk. A weight drops into my stomach.

I hear the crash of water against rocks. We are near the chasm—we must be above it, given the volume of the sound. I press my lips together to keep from screaming. If we are above the chasm, I know what they intend to do to me.

"Lift her up, c'mon."

I thrash, and their rough skin grates against mine, but I know it's useless. I scream too, knowing that no one can hear me here.

I will survive until tomorrow. I will.

The hands push me around and up and slam my spine into something hard and cold. Judging by its width and curvature, it is a metal railing. It is *the* metal railing, the one that overlooks the chasm. My breaths wheeze and mist touches the back of my neck. The hands force my back to arch over the railing. My feet leave the ground, and my attackers are the only thing keeping me from falling into the water.

A heavy hand gropes along my chest. "You sure you're sixteen, Stiff? Doesn't feel like you're more than twelve." The other boys laugh.

Bile rises in my throat and I swallow the bitter taste.

"Wait, I think I found something!" His hand squeezes me. I bite my tongue to keep from screaming. More laughter.

Al's hand slips from my mouth. "Stop that," he snaps. I recognize his low, distinct voice.

When Al lets go of me, I thrash again and slip down to the ground. This time, I bite down as hard as I can on the first arm I find. I hear a scream and clench my jaw harder, tasting blood. Something hard strikes my face. White heat races through my head. It would have been pain if adrenaline wasn't coursing through me like acid.

The boy wrenches his trapped arm away from me and throws me to the ground. I bang my elbow against stone and bring my hands up to my head to remove the blindfold. A foot drives into my side, forcing the air from my lungs. I gasp and cough and claw at the back of my head. Someone grabs a handful of my hair and slams my head against something hard. A scream of pain bursts from my mouth, and I feel dizzy.

Clumsily, I fumble along the side of my head to find the edge of the blindfold. I drag my heavy hand up, taking the blindfold with it, and blink. The scene before me is sideways and bobs up and down. I see someone running toward us and someone running away—someone large, Al. I grab the railing next to me and haul myself to my feet.

Peter wraps a hand around my throat and lifts me up, his thumb wedged under my chin. His hair, which is usually shiny and smooth, is tousled and sticks to his forehead. His pale face is contorted and his teeth are gritted, and he holds me over the chasm as spots appear on the edges of my vision, crowding around his face, green and pink and blue. He says nothing. I try to kick him, but my legs are too short. My lungs scream for air.

I hear a shout, and he releases me.

I stretch out my arms as I fall, gasping, and my armpits slam into the railing. I hook my elbows over it and groan. Mist touches my ankles. The world dips and sways around me, and someone is on the Pit floor—Drew—screaming. I hear thumps. Kicks. Groans.

I blink a few times and focus as hard as I can on the only face I can see. It is contorted with anger. His eyes are dark blue.

"Four," I croak.

I close my eyes, and hands wrap around my arms, right

where they join with the shoulder. He pulls me over the railing and against his chest, gathering me into his arms, easing an arm under my knees. I press my face into his shoulder, and there is a sudden, hollow silence.

CHAPTER
TWENTY-TWO

I OPEN MY eyes to the words "Fear God Alone" painted on a plain white wall. I hear the sound of running water again, but this time it's from a faucet and not from the chasm. Seconds go by before I see definite edges in my surroundings, the lines of door frame and countertop and ceiling.

The pain is a constant throb in my head and cheek and ribs. I shouldn't move; it will make everything worse. I see a blue patchwork quilt under my head and wince as I tilt my head to see where the water sound is coming from.

Four stands in the bathroom with his hands in the sink. Blood from his knuckles turns the sink water pink. He has a cut at the corner of his mouth, but he seems otherwise unharmed. His expression is placid as he examines his cuts, turns off the water, and dries his hands with a towel.

I have only one memory of getting here, and even that is just a single image: black ink curling around the side of a neck, the corner of a tattoo, and the gentle sway that could only mean he was carrying me.

He turns off the bathroom light and gets an ice pack from the refrigerator in the corner of the room. As he walks toward me, I consider closing my eyes and pretending to be asleep, but then our eyes meet and it's too late.

"Your hands," I croak.

"My hands are none of your concern," he replies. He rests his knee on the mattress and leans over me, slipping the ice pack under my head. Before he pulls away, I reach out to touch the cut on the side of his lip but stop when I realize what I am about to do, my hand hovering.

What do you have to lose? I ask myself. I touch my fingertips lightly to his mouth.

"Tris," he says, speaking against my fingers, "I'm all right."

"Why were you there?" I ask, letting my hand drop.

"I was coming back from the control room. I heard a scream."

"What did you do to them?" I say.

"I deposited Drew at the infirmary a half hour ago," he says. "Peter and Al ran. Drew claimed they were just trying to scare you. At least, I think that's what he was trying to say."

"He's in bad shape?"

"He'll live," he replies. He adds bitterly, "In what condition, I can't say."

It isn't right to wish pain on other people just because they hurt me first. But white-hot triumph races through me at the thought of Drew in the infirmary, and I squeeze Four's arm.

"Good," I say. My voice sounds tight and fierce. Anger builds inside me, replacing my blood with bitter water and filling me, consuming me. I want to break something, or hit something, but I am afraid to move, so I start crying instead.

Four crouches by the side of the bed, and watches me. I see no sympathy in his eyes. I would have been disappointed if I had. He pulls his wrist free and, to my surprise, rests his hand on the side of my face, his thumb skimming my cheekbone. His fingers are careful.

"I could report this," he says.

"No," I reply. "I don't want them to think I'm scared."

He nods. He moves his thumb absently over my cheekbone, back and forth. "I figured you would say that."

"You think it would be a bad idea if I sat up?"

"I'll help you."

Four grips my shoulder with one hand and holds my

head steady with the other as I push myself up. Pain rushes through my body in sharp bursts, but I try to ignore it, stifling a groan.

He hands me the ice pack. "You can let yourself be in pain," he says. "It's just me here."

I bite down on my lip. There are tears on my face, but neither of us mentions or even acknowledges them.

"I suggest you rely on your transfer friends to protect you from now on," he says.

"I thought I was," I say. I feel Al's hand against my mouth again, and a sob jolts my body forward. I press my hand to my forehead and rock slowly back and forth. "But Al . . ."

"He wanted you to be the small, quiet girl from Abnegation," Four says softly. "He hurt you because your strength made him feel weak. No other reason."

I nod and try to believe him.

"The others won't be as jealous if you show some vulnerability. Even if it isn't real."

"You think I have to *pretend* to be vulnerable?" I ask, raising an eyebrow.

"Yes, I do." He takes the ice pack from me, his fingers brushing mine, and holds it against my head himself. I put my hand down, too eager to relax my arm to object. Four stands up. I stare at the hem of his T-shirt.

Sometimes I see him as just another person, and

sometimes I feel the sight of him in my gut, like a deep ache.

"You're going to want to march into breakfast tomorrow and show your attackers they had no effect on you," he adds, "but you should let that bruise on your cheek show, and keep your head down."

The idea nauseates me.

"I don't think I can do that," I say hollowly. I lift my eyes to his.

"You have to."

"I don't think you *get* it." Heat rises into my face. "They touched me."

His entire body tightens at my words, his hand clenching around the ice pack. "Touched you," he repeats, his dark eyes cold.

"Not . . . in the way you're thinking." I clear my throat. I didn't realize when I said it how awkward it would be to talk about. "But . . . almost."

I look away.

He is silent and still for so long that eventually, I have to say something.

"What is it?"

"I don't want to say this," he says, "but I feel like I have to. It is more important for you to be safe than right, for the time being. Understand?"

His straight eyebrows are drawn low over his eyes. My stomach writhes, partly because I know he makes a good point but I don't want to admit it, and partly because I want something I don't know how to express; I want to press against the space between us until it disappears.

I nod.

"But please, when you see an opportunity . . ." He presses his hand to my cheek, cold and strong, and tilts my head up so I have to look at him. His eyes glint. They look almost predatory. "Ruin them."

I laugh shakily. "You're a little scary, Four."

"Do me a favor," he says, "and don't call me that."

"What should I call you, then?"

"Nothing." He takes his hand from my face. "Yet."

CHAPTER TWENTY-THREE

I DON'T GO back to the dorms that night. Sleeping in the same room as the people who attacked me just to look brave would be stupid. Four sleeps on the floor and I sleep on his bed, on top of the quilt, breathing in the scent of his pillowcase. It smells like detergent and something heavy, sweet, and distinctly male.

The rhythm of his breaths slows, and I prop myself up to see if he is asleep. He lies on his stomach with one arm around his head. His eyes are closed, his lips parted. For the first time, he looks as young as he is, and I wonder who he really is. Who is he when he isn't Dauntless, isn't an instructor, isn't Four, isn't anything in particular?

Whoever he is, I like him. It's easier for me to admit that to myself now, in the dark, after all that just happened. He is not sweet or gentle or particularly kind. But he is smart and brave, and even though he saved me, he treated me like I was strong. That is all I need to know.

I watch the muscles in his back expand and contract until I fall asleep.

I wake to aches and pains. I cringe as I sit up, holding my ribs, and walk up to the small mirror on the opposite wall. I am almost too short to see myself in it, but when I stand on my tiptoes, I can see my face. As expected, there is a dark blue bruise on my cheek. I hate the idea of slumping into the dining hall like this, but Four's instructions have stayed with me. I have to mend my friendships. I need the protection of seeming weak.

I tie my hair in a knot at the back of my head. The door opens and Four walks in, a towel in hand and his hair glistening with shower water. I feel a thrill in my stomach when I see the line of skin that shows above his belt as he lifts his hand to dry his hair and force my eyes up to his face.

"Hi," I say. My voice sounds tight. I wish it didn't.

He touches my bruised cheek with just his fingertips. "Not bad," he says. "How's your head?"

"Fine," I say. I'm lying—my head is throbbing. I brush my fingers over the bump, and pain prickles over my scalp. It could be worse. I could be floating in the river.

Every muscle in my body tightens as his hand drops to my side, where I got kicked. He does it casually, but I can't move.

"And your side?" he asks, his voice low.

"Only hurts when I breathe."

He smiles. "Not much you can do about that."

"Peter would probably throw a party if I stopped breathing."

"Well," he says, "I would only go if there was cake."

I laugh, and then wince, covering his hand to steady my rib cage. He slides his hand back slowly, his fingertips grazing my side. When his fingers lift, I feel an ache in my chest. Once this moment ends, I have to remember what happened last night. And I want to stay here with him.

He nods a little and leads the way out.

"I'll go in first," he says when we stand outside the dining hall. "See you soon, Tris."

He walks through the doors and I am alone. Yesterday he told me he thought I would have to pretend to be weak, but he was wrong. I am weak already. I brace myself against the wall and press my forehead to my hands. It's difficult to take deep breaths, so I take short, shallow ones. I can't let this happen. They attacked me to make me feel weak. I can pretend they succeeded to protect myself, but I can't let it become true.

I pull away from the wall and walk into the dining hall without another thought. A few steps in, I remember I'm supposed to look like I'm cowering, so I slow my pace and hug the wall, keeping my head down. Uriah, at the table next to Will and Christina's, lifts his hand to wave at me. And then puts it down.

I sit next to Will.

Al isn't there—he isn't anywhere.

Uriah slides into the seat next to me, leaving his half-eaten muffin and half-finished glass of water on the other table. For a second, all three of them just stare at me.

"What happened?" Will asks, lowering his voice.

I look over his shoulder at the table behind ours. Peter sits there, eating a piece of toast and whispering something to Molly. My hand clenches around the edge of the table. I want him to hurt. But now isn't the time.

Drew is missing, which means he's still in the infirmary. Vicious pleasure courses through me at the thought.

"Peter, Drew . . . ," I say quietly. I hold my side as I reach across the table for a piece of toast. It hurts to stretch out my hand, so I let myself wince and hunch over. "And . . ." I swallow. "And Al."

"Oh God," says Christina, her eyes wide.

"Are you all right?" Uriah asks.

Peter's eyes find mine across the dining hall, and I

have to force myself to look away. It brings a bitter taste to my mouth to show him that he scares me, but I have to. Four was right. I have to do everything I can to make sure I don't get attacked again.

"Not really," I say.

My eyes burn, and it's not artifice, unlike the wincing. I shrug. I believe Tori's warning now. Peter, Drew, and Al were ready to throw me into the chasm out of jealousy—what is so unbelievable about the Dauntless leaders committing murder?

I feel uncomfortable, like I'm wearing someone else's skin. If I'm not careful, I could die. I can't even trust the leaders of my faction. My new family.

"But you're just . . ." Uriah purses his lips. "It isn't fair. Three against one?"

"Yeah, and Peter is all about what's fair. That's why he grabbed Edward in his sleep and stabbed him in the eye." Christina snorts and shakes her head. "Al, though? Are you sure, Tris?"

I stare at my plate. I'm the next Edward. But unlike him, I'm not going to leave.

"Yeah," I say. "I'm sure."

"It has to be desperation," says Will. "He's been acting . . . I don't know. Like a different person. Ever since stage two started."

Then Drew shuffles into the dining hall. I drop my

toast, and my mouth drifts open.

Calling him "bruised" would be an understatement. His face is swollen and purple. He has a split lip and a cut running through his eyebrow. He keeps his eyes down on the way to his table, not even lifting them to look at me. I glance across the room at Four. He wears the satisfied smile I wish I had on.

"Did *you* do that?" hisses Will.

I shake my head. "No. Someone—I never saw who—found me right before . . ." I gulp. Saying it out loud makes it worse, makes it real. ". . . I got tossed into the chasm."

"They were going to *kill* you?" says Christina in a low voice.

"Maybe. They might have been planning on dangling me over it just to scare me." I lift a shoulder. "It worked."

Christina gives me a sad look. Will just glares at the table.

"We have to do something about this," Uriah says in a low voice.

"What, like beat them up?" Christina grins. "Looks like that's been taken care of already."

"No. That's pain they can get over," replies Uriah. "We have to edge them out of the rankings. That will damage their futures. Permanently."

Four gets up and stands between the tables. Conversation abruptly ceases.

"Transfers. We're doing something different today," he says. "Follow me."

We stand, and Uriah's forehead wrinkles. "Be careful," he tells me.

"Don't worry," says Will. "We'll protect her."

+ + +

Four leads us out of the dining hall and along the paths that surround the Pit. Will is on my left, Christina is on my right.

"I never really said I was sorry," Christina says quietly. "For taking the flag when you earned it. I don't know what was wrong with me."

I'm not sure if it's smart to forgive her or not—to forgive either of them, after what they said to me when the rankings went up yesterday. But my mother would tell me that people are flawed and I should be lenient with them. And Four told me to rely on my friends.

I don't know who I should rely on more, because I'm not sure who my true friends are. Uriah and Marlene, who were on my side even when I seemed strong, or Christina and Will, who have always protected me when I seemed weak?

When her wide brown eyes meet mine, I nod. "Let's just forget about it."

I still want to be angry, but I have to let my anger go.

We climb higher than I've gone before, until Will's face goes white whenever he looks down. Most of the time I like heights, so I grab Will's arm like I need his support—but really, I'm lending him mine. He smiles gratefully at me.

Four turns around and walks backward a few steps—backward, on a narrow path with no railing. How well does he know this place?

He eyes Drew, who trudges at the back of the group, and says, "Pick up the pace, Drew!"

It's a cruel joke, but it's hard for me to fight off a smile. That is, until Four's eyes shift to my arm around Will's, and all the humor drains from them. His expression sends a chill through me. Is he . . . jealous?

We get closer and closer to the glass ceiling, and for the first time in days, I see the sun. Four walks up a flight of metal stairs leading through a hole in the ceiling. They creak under my feet, and I look down to see the Pit and the chasm below us.

We walk across the glass, which is now a floor rather than a ceiling, through a cylindrical room with glass walls. The surrounding buildings are half-collapsed and appear to be abandoned, which is probably why I never noticed the Dauntless compound before. The Abnegation sector is also far away.

The Dauntless mill around the glass room, talking in

clusters. At the edge of the room, two Dauntless fight with sticks, laughing when one of them misses and hits only air. Above me, two ropes stretch across the room, one a few feet higher than the other. They probably have something to do with the daredevil stunts the Dauntless are famous for.

Four leads us through another door. Beyond it is a huge, dank space with graffitied walls and exposed pipes. The room is lit by a series of old-fashioned fluorescent tubes with plastic covers—they must be ancient.

"This," says Four, his eyes bright in pale light, "is a different kind of simulation known as the fear landscape. It has been disabled for our purposes, so this isn't what it will be like the next time you see it."

Behind him, the word "Dauntless" is spray-painted in red artistic lettering on a concrete wall.

"Through your simulations, we have stored data about your worst fears. The fear landscape accesses that data and presents you with a series of virtual obstacles. Some of the obstacles will be fears you previously faced in your simulations. Some may be new fears. The difference is that you are aware, in the fear landscape, that it is a simulation, so you will have all your wits about you as you go through it."

That means that everyone will be like Divergent in

the fear landscape. I don't know if that's a relief, because I can't be detected, or a problem, because I won't have the advantage.

Four continues, "The number of fears you have in your landscape varies according to how many you have."

How many fears will I have? I think of facing the crows again and shiver, though the air is warm.

"I told you before that the third stage of initiation focuses on mental preparation," he says. I remember when he said that. On the first day. Right before he put a gun to Peter's head. I wish he had pulled the trigger.

"That is because it requires you to control both your emotions and your body—to combine the physical abilities you learned in stage one with the emotional mastery you learned in stage two. To keep a level head." One of the fluorescent tubes above Four's head twitches and flickers. Four stops scanning the crowd of initiates and focuses his stare on me.

"Next week you will go through your fear landscape as quickly as possible in front of a panel of Dauntless leaders. That will be your final test, which determines your ranking for stage three. Just as stage two of initiation is weighted more heavily than stage one, stage three is weighted heaviest of all. Understood?"

We all nod. Even Drew, who makes it look painful.

If I do well in my final test, I have a good chance of making it into the top ten and a good chance of becoming a member. Becoming Dauntless. The thought makes me almost giddy with relief.

"You can get past each obstacle in one of two ways. Either you find a way to calm down enough that the simulation registers a normal, steady heartbeat, or you find a way to face your fear, which can force the simulation to move on. One way to face a fear of drowning is to swim deeper, for example." Four shrugs. "So I suggest that you take the next week to consider your fears and develop strategies to face them."

"That doesn't sound fair," says Peter. "What if one person only has seven fears and someone else has twenty? That's not their fault."

Four stares at him for a few seconds and then laughs. "Do you really want to talk to me about what's fair?"

The crowd of initiates parts to make way for him as he walks toward Peter, folds his arms, and says, in a deadly voice, "I understand why you're worried, Peter. The events of last night certainly proved that you are a miserable coward."

Peter stares back, expressionless.

"So now we all know," says Four, quietly, "that you are afraid of a short, skinny girl from Abnegation." His mouth curls in a smile.

Will puts his arm around me. Christina's shoulders shake with suppressed laughter. And somewhere within me, I find a smile too.

+ + +

When we get back to the dorm that afternoon, Al is there.

Will stands behind me and holds my shoulders—lightly, as if to remind me that he's there. Christina edges closer to me.

Al's eyes have shadows beneath them, and his face is swollen from crying. Pain stabs my stomach when I see him. I can't move. The scent of lemongrass and sage, once pleasant, turns sour in my nose.

"Tris," says Al, his voice breaking. "Can I talk to you?"

"Are you kidding?" Will squeezes my shoulders. "You don't get to come near her ever again."

"I won't hurt you. I never wanted to . . ." Al covers his face with both hands. "I just want to say that I'm sorry, I'm so sorry, I don't . . . I don't know what's wrong with me, I . . . please forgive me, *please.* . . ."

He reaches for me like he's going to touch my shoulder, or my hand, his face wet with tears.

Somewhere inside me is a merciful, forgiving person. Somewhere there is a girl who tries to understand what people are going through, who accepts that people do evil things and that desperation leads them to darker places than they ever imagined. I swear she exists, and she hurts for the repentant boy I see in front of me.

But if I saw her, I wouldn't recognize her.

"Stay away from me," I say quietly. My body feels rigid and cold, and I am not angry, I am not hurt, I am nothing. I say, my voice low, "Never come near me again."

Our eyes meet. His are dark and glassy. I am nothing.

"If you do, I swear to God I will kill you," I say. "You coward."

CHAPTER
TWENTY-FOUR

"Tris."

In my dream, my mother says my name. She beckons to me, and I cross the kitchen to stand beside her. She points to the pot on the stove, and I lift the lid to peek inside. The beady eye of a crow stares back at me, its wing feathers pressed to the side of the pot, its fat body covered with boiling water.

"Dinner," she says.

"Tris!" I hear again. I open my eyes. Christina stands next to my bed, her cheeks streaked with mascara-tinted tears.

"It's Al," she says. "Come on."

Some of the other initiates are awake, and some aren't. Christina grabs my hand and pulls me out of the dormitory. I run barefoot over the stone floor, blinking clouds from my eyes, my limbs still heavy with sleep. Something terrible has happened. I feel it with every thump of my heart. *It's Al*.

We run across the Pit floor, and then Christina stops. A crowd has gathered around the ledge, but everyone stands a few feet from one another, so there is enough space for me to maneuver past Christina and around a tall, middle-aged man to the front.

Two men stand next to the ledge, hoisting something up with ropes. They both grunt from the effort, heaving their weight back so the ropes slide over the railing, and then reaching forward to grab again. A huge, dark shape appears above the ledge, and a few Dauntless rush forward to help the two men haul it over.

The shape falls with a thud on the Pit floor. A pale arm, swollen with water, flops onto the stone. A body. Christina pulls herself tight to my side, clinging to my arm. She turns her head into my shoulder and sobs, but I can't look away. A few of the men turn the body over, and the head flops to the side.

The eyes are open and empty. Dark. Doll's eyes. And the nose has a high arch, a narrow bridge, a round tip. The lips are blue. The face itself is something other than human, half corpse and half creature. My lungs burn; my next breath rattles on the way in. *Al*.

"One of the initiates," says someone behind me. "What happened?"

"Same thing that happens every year," someone else replies. "He pitched himself over the ledge."

"Don't be so morbid. Could have been an accident."

"They found him in the middle of the chasm. You think he tripped over his shoelace and . . . whoopsies, just *stumbled* fifteen feet forward?"

Christina's hands get tighter and tighter around my arm. I should tell her to let go of me; it's starting to hurt. Someone kneels next to Al's face and pushes his eyelids shut. Trying to make it look like he's sleeping, maybe. Stupid. Why do people want to pretend that death is sleep? It isn't. It isn't.

Something inside me collapses. My chest is so tight, suffocating, can't breathe. I sink to the ground, dragging Christina down with me. The stone is rough under my knees. I hear something, a memory of sound. Al's sobs; his screams at night. Should have known. Still can't breathe. I press both palms to my chest and rock back and forth to free the tension in my chest.

When I blink, I see the top of Al's head as he carries me on his back to the dining hall. I feel the bounce of his footsteps. He is big and warm and clumsy. No, *was*. That is death—shifting from "is" to "was."

I wheeze. Someone has brought a large black bag to

put the body in. I can tell that it will be too small. A laugh rises in my throat and flops from my mouth, strained and gurgling. Al's too big for the body bag; what a tragedy. Halfway through the laugh, I clamp my mouth shut, and it sounds more like a groan. I pull my arm free and stand, leaving Christina on the ground. I run.

+ + +

"Here you go," Tori says. She hands me a steaming mug that smells like peppermint. I hold it with both hands, my fingers prickling with warmth.

She sits down across from me. When it comes to funerals, the Dauntless don't waste any time. Tori said they want to acknowledge death as soon as it happens. There are no people in the front room of the tattoo parlor, but the Pit is crawling with people, most of them drunk. I don't know why that surprises me.

At home, a funeral is a somber occasion. Everyone gathers to support the deceased's family, and no one has idle hands, but there is no laughter, or shouting, or joking. And the Abnegation don't drink alcohol, so everyone is sober. It makes sense that funerals would be the opposite here.

"Drink it," she says. "It will make you feel better, I promise."

"I don't think tea is the solution," I say slowly. But I sip it anyway. It warms my mouth and my throat and trickles into my stomach. I didn't realize how deeply cold I was until I wasn't anymore.

"'Better' is the word I used. Not 'good.'" She smiles at me, but the corners of her eyes don't crinkle like they usually do. "I don't think 'good' will happen for a while."

I bite my lip. "How long . . ." I struggle for the right words. "How long did it take for you to be okay again, after your brother . . ."

"Don't know." She shakes her head. "Some days I feel like I'm still not okay. Some days I feel fine. Happy, even. It took me a few years to stop plotting revenge, though."

"Why did you stop?" I ask.

Her eyes go vacant as she stares at the wall behind me. She taps her fingers against her leg for a few seconds and then says, "I don't think of it as stopping. More like I'm . . . waiting for my opportunity."

She comes out of her daze and checks her watch.

"Time to go," she says.

I pour the rest of my tea down the sink. When I lift my hand from the mug, I realize that I'm shaking. Not good. My hands usually shake before I start to cry, and I can't cry in front of everyone.

I follow Tori out of the tattoo place and down the path to the Pit floor. All the people that were milling around earlier are gathered by the ledge now, and the air smells potently of alcohol. The woman in front of me lurches to the right, losing her balance, and then erupts into giggles as she falls against the man next to her. Tori grabs my arm and steers me away.

I find Uriah, Will, and Christina standing among the other initiates. Christina's eyes are swollen. Uriah is holding a silver flask. He offers it to me. I shake my head.

"Surprise, surprise," says Molly from behind me. She nudges Peter with her elbow. "Once a Stiff, always a Stiff."

I should ignore her. Her opinions shouldn't matter to me.

"I read an interesting article today," she says, leaning closer to my ear. "Something about your dad, and the *real* reason you left your old faction."

Defending myself isn't the most important thing on my mind. But it is the easiest one to address.

I twist, and my fist connects with her jaw. My knuckles sting from the impact. I don't remember deciding to punch her. I don't remember forming a fist.

She lunges at me, her hands outstretched, but she doesn't get far. Will grabs her collar and pulls her back. He looks from her to me and says, "Quit it. Both of you."

Part of me wishes that he hadn't stopped her. A fight would be a welcome distraction, especially now that Eric is climbing onto a box next to the railing. I face him, crossing my arms to keep myself steady. I wonder what he'll say.

In Abnegation no one has committed suicide in recent memory, but the faction's stance on it is clear: Suicide, to them, is an act of selfishness. Someone who is truly selfless does not think of himself often enough to desire death. No one would say that aloud, if it happened, but everyone would think it.

"Quiet down, everyone!" shouts Eric. Someone hits what sounds like a gong, and the shouts gradually stop, though the mutters don't. Eric says, "Thank you. As you know, we're here because Albert, an initiate, jumped into the chasm last night."

The mutters stop too, leaving just the rush of water in the chasm.

"We do not know why," says Eric, "and it would be easy to mourn the loss of him tonight. But we did not choose a life of ease when we became Dauntless. And the truth of it is . . ." Eric smiles. If I didn't know him, I would think that smile is genuine. But I do know him. "The truth is, Albert is now exploring an unknown, uncertain place. He leaped into vicious waters to get there. Who among us is brave enough to venture into that darkness without knowing what lies beyond it? Albert was not yet one of our members, but we can be assured that he was one of our *bravest*!"

A cry rises from the center of the crowd, and a whoop. The Dauntless cheer at varying pitches, high and low, bright and deep. Their roar mimics the roar of the water. Christina takes the flask from Uriah and drinks. Will slides his arm around her shoulders and pulls her to his side. Voices fill my ears.

"We will celebrate him now, and remember him always!" yells Eric. Someone hands him a dark bottle, and he lifts it. "To Albert the Courageous!"

"To Albert!" shouts the crowd. Arms lift all around me, and the Dauntless chant his name. "Albert! Al-bert! Al-bert!" They chant until his name no longer sounds like his name. It sounds like the primal scream of an ancient race.

I turn away from the railing. I cannot stand this any longer.

I don't know where I'm going. I suspect that I am not going anywhere at all, just away. I walk down a dark hallway. At the end is the drinking fountain, bathed in the blue glow of the light above it.

I shake my head. Courageous? Courageous would have been admitting weakness and leaving Dauntless, no matter what shame accompanied it. Pride is what killed Al, and it is the flaw in every Dauntless heart. It is in mine.

"Tris."

A jolt goes through me, and I turn around. Four stands behind me, just inside the blue circle of light. It gives him an eerie look, shading his eye sockets and casting shadows under his cheekbones.

"What are you doing here?" I ask. "Shouldn't you be paying your respects?"

I say it like it tastes bad and I have to spit it out.

"Shouldn't you?" he says. He steps toward me, and I see his eyes again. They look black in this light.

"Can't pay respect when you don't have any," I reply. I feel a twinge of guilt and shake my head. "I didn't mean that."

"Ah." Judging by the look he gives me, he doesn't believe me. I don't blame him.

"This is ridiculous," I say, heat rushing into my cheeks. "He throws himself off a ledge and Eric's calling it brave? Eric, who tried to have you throw knives at Al's head?" I taste bile. Eric's false smiles, his artificial words, his twisted ideals—they make me want to be sick. "He wasn't brave! He was depressed and a coward and he almost killed me! Is that the kind of thing we respect here?"

"What do you want them to do?" he says. "Condemn him? Al's already dead. He can't hear it and it's too late."

"It's not *about* Al," I snap. "It's about everyone watching! Everyone who now sees hurling themselves into the chasm as a viable option. I mean, why not do it if everyone calls you a hero afterward? Why not do it if everyone will remember your name? It's . . . I can't . . ."

I shake my head. My face burns and my heart pounds, and I try to keep myself under control, but I can't.

"This would *never* have happened in Abnegation!" I almost shout. "None of it! Never. This place warped him and ruined him, and I don't care if saying that makes me a Stiff, I don't care, I don't *care*!"

Four's eyes shift to the wall above the drinking fountain.

"Careful, Tris," he says, his eyes still on the wall.

"Is that all you can say?" I demand, scowling at him. "That I should be *careful*? That's *it*?"

"You're as bad as the Candor, you know that?" He grabs my arm and drags me away from the drinking fountain. His hand hurts my arm, but I'm not strong enough to pull away.

His face is so close to mine that I can see a few freckles spotting his nose. "I'm not going to say this again, so listen carefully." He sets his hands on my shoulders, his fingers pressing, squeezing. I feel small. "They are watching you. *You*, in particular."

"Let go of me," I say weakly.

His fingers spring apart, and he straightens. Some of the weight on my chest lifts now that he isn't touching me. I fear his shifting moods. They show me something unstable inside of him, and instability is dangerous.

"Are they watching you, too?" I say, so quietly he wouldn't be able to hear me if he wasn't standing so close.

He doesn't answer my question. "I keep trying to help you," he says, "but you refuse to be helped."

"Oh, right. Your *help*," I say. "Stabbing my ear with a knife and taunting me and yelling at me more than you yell at anyone else, it sure is helpful."

"Taunting you? You mean when I threw the knives? I wasn't taunting you," he snaps. "I was reminding you that if you failed, someone else would have to take your place."

I cup the back of my neck with my hand and think back to the knife incident. Every time he spoke, it was to remind me that if I gave up, Al would have to take my place in front of the target.

"Why?" I say.

"Because you're from Abnegation," he says, "and it's when you're acting selflessly that you are at your bravest."

I understand now. He wasn't persuading me to give up. He was reminding me why I couldn't—because I needed to protect Al. The thought makes me ache now.

Protect Al. My friend. My attacker.

I can't hate Al as much as I want to.

I can't forgive him either.

"If I were you, I would do a better job of pretending that selfless impulse is going away," he says, "because if the wrong people discover it . . . well, it won't be good for you."

"Why? Why do they care about my intentions?"

"Intentions are the *only* thing they care about. They try to make you think they care about what you do, but they don't. They don't want you to act a certain way. They want you to *think* a certain way. So you're easy to understand. So you won't pose a threat to them." He presses a hand to the wall next to my head and leans into it. His shirt is just tight enough that I can see his collarbone and the faint depression between his shoulder muscle and his bicep.

I wish I was taller. If I was tall, my narrow build would be described as "willowy" instead of "childish," and he might not see me as a little sister he needs to protect.

I don't want him to see me as his sister.

"I don't understand," I say, "why they care what I think, as long as I'm acting how they want me to."

"You're acting how they want you to now," he says, "but what happens when your Abnegation-wired brain tells you to do something else, something they don't want?"

I don't have an answer to that, and I don't even know if

he's right about me. Am I wired like the Abnegation, or the Dauntless?

Maybe the answer is neither. Maybe I am wired like the Divergent.

"I might not need you to help me. Ever think about that?" I say. "I'm not weak, you know. I can do this on my own."

He shakes his head. "You think my first instinct is to protect you. Because you're small, or a girl, or a Stiff. But you're wrong."

He leans his face close to mine and wraps his fingers around my chin. His hand smells like metal. When was the last time he held a gun, or a knife? My skin tingles at the point of contact, like he's transmitting electricity through his skin.

"My *first* instinct is to push you until you break, just to see how hard I have to press," he says, his fingers squeezing at the word "break." My body tenses at the edge in his voice, so I am coiled as tight as a spring, and I forget to breathe.

His dark eyes lifting to mine, he adds, "But I resist it."

"Why . . ." I swallow hard. "Why is that your first instinct?"

"Fear doesn't shut you down; it wakes you up. I've seen it. It's fascinating." He releases me but doesn't pull away, his hand grazing my jaw, my neck. "Sometimes I just . . . want to see it again. Want to see you awake."

I set my hands on his waist. I can't remember deciding to do that. But I also can't move away. I pull myself against his chest, wrapping my arms around him. My fingers skim the muscles of his back.

After a moment he touches the small of my back, pressing me closer, and smoothes his other hand over my hair. I feel small again, but this time, it doesn't scare me. I squeeze my eyes shut. He doesn't scare me anymore.

"Should I be crying?" I ask, my voice muffled by his shirt. "Is there something wrong with me?"

The simulations drove a crack through Al so wide he could not mend it. Why not me? Why am I not like him—and why does that thought make me feel so uneasy, like I'm teetering on a ledge myself?

"You think I know anything about tears?" he says quietly.

I close my eyes. I don't expect Four to reassure me, and he makes no effort to, but I feel better standing here than I did out there among the people who are my friends, my faction. I press my forehead to his shoulder.

"If I had forgiven him," I say, "do you think he would be alive now?"

"I don't know," he replies. He presses his hand to my

cheek, and I turn my face into it, keeping my eyes closed.

"I feel like it's my fault."

"It isn't your fault," he says, touching his forehead to mine.

"But I should have. I should have forgiven him."

"Maybe. Maybe there's more we all could have done," he says, "but we just have to let the guilt remind us to do better next time."

I frown and pull back. That is a lesson that members of Abnegation learn—guilt as a tool, rather than a weapon against the self. It is a line straight from one of my father's lectures at our weekly meetings.

"What faction did you come from, Four?"

"It doesn't matter," he replies, his eyes lowered. "This is where I am now. Something you would do well to remember for yourself."

He gives me a conflicted look and touches his lips to my forehead, right between my eyebrows. I close my eyes. I don't understand this, whatever it is. But I don't want to ruin it, so I say nothing. He doesn't move; he just stays there with his mouth pressed to my skin, and I stay there with my hands on his waist, for a long time.

CHAPTER
TWENTY-FIVE

I STAND WITH Will and Christina at the railing overlooking
the chasm, late at night after most of the Dauntless have
gone to sleep. Both my shoulders sting from the tattoo
needle. We all got new tattoos a half hour ago.

Tori was the only one in the tattoo place, so I felt safe
getting the symbol of Abnegation—a pair of hands, palms
up as if to help someone stand, bounded by a circle—on
my right shoulder. I know it was a risk, especially after all
that's happened. But that symbol is a part of my identity,
and it felt important to me that I wear it on my skin.

I step up on one of the barrier's crossbars, pressing
my hips to the railing to keep my balance. This is where
Al stood. I look down into the chasm, at the black water,
at the jagged rocks. Water hits the wall and sprays up,

misting my face. Was he afraid when he stood here? Or was he so determined to jump that it was easy?

Christina hands me a stack of paper. I got a copy of every report the Erudite have released in the last six months. Throwing them into the chasm won't get rid of them forever, but it might make me feel better.

I stare at the first one. On it is a picture of Jeanine, the Erudite representative. Her sharp-but-attractive eyes stare back at me.

"Have you ever met her?" I ask Will. Christina crumples the first report into a ball and hurls it into the water.

"Jeanine? Once," he replies. He takes the next report and tears it to shreds. The pieces float into the river. He does it without Christina's malice. I get the feeling that the only reason he's participating is to prove to me that he doesn't agree with his former faction's tactics. Whether he believes what they're saying or not is unclear, and I am afraid to ask.

"Before she was a leader, she worked with my sister. They were trying to develop a longer-lasting serum for the simulations," he says. "Jeanine's so smart you can see it even before she says anything. Like . . . a walking, talking computer."

"What . . ." I fling one of the pages over the railing, pressing my lips together. I should just ask. "What do you think of what she has to say?"

He shrugs. "I don't know. Maybe it's a good idea to have more than one faction in control of the government. And maybe it would be nice if we had more cars and . . . fresh fruit and . . ."

"You do realize there's no secret warehouse where all that stuff is kept, right?" I ask, my face getting hot.

"Yes, I do," he says. "I just think that comfort and prosperity are not a priority for Abnegation, and maybe they would be if the other factions were involved in our decision making."

"Because giving an Erudite boy a car is more important than giving food to the factionless," I snap.

"Hey now," says Christina, brushing Will's shoulder with her fingers. "This is supposed to be a lighthearted session of symbolic document destruction, not a political debate."

I bite back what I was about to say and stare at the stack of paper in my hands. Will and Christina share a lot of idle touches lately. I've noticed it. Have they?

"All that stuff she said about your dad, though," he says, "makes me kind of hate her. I can't imagine what good can come of saying such terrible things."

I can. If Jeanine can make people believe that my father and all the other Abnegation leaders are corrupt and awful, she has support for whatever revolution she wants to start, if that's really her plan. But I don't want to argue again, so I just nod and throw the remaining sheets into the chasm. They drift back and forth, back and forth until they find the water. They will be filtered out at the chasm wall and discarded.

"It's bedtime," Christina says, smiling. "Ready to go back? I think I want to put Peter's hand in a bowl of warm water to make him pee tonight."

I turn away from the chasm and see movement on the right side of the Pit. A figure climbs toward the glass ceiling, and judging by the smooth way he walks, like his feet barely leave the ground, I know it is Four.

"That sounds great, but I have to talk to Four about something," I say, pointing toward the shadow ascending the path. Her eyes follow my hand.

"Are you sure you should be running around here alone at night?" she asks.

"I won't be alone. I'll be with Four." I bite my lip.

Christina is looking at Will, and he is looking back at her. Neither of them is really listening to me.

"All right," Christina says distantly. "Well, I'll see you later, then."

Christina and Will walk toward the dormitories, Christina tousling Will's hair and Will jabbing her in the ribs. For a second, I watch them. I feel like I am witnessing the beginning of something, but I'm not sure what it will be.

I jog to the path on the right side of the Pit and start to climb. I try to make my footsteps as quiet as possible. Unlike Christina, I don't find it difficult to lie. I don't intend to talk to Four—at least, not until I find out where he's going, late at night, in the glass building above us.

I run quietly, breathless when I reach the stairs, and stand at one end of the glass room while Four stands at the other. Through the windows I see the city lights, glowing now but petering out even as I look at them. They are supposed to turn off at midnight.

Across the room, Four stands at the door to the fear landscape. He holds a black box in one hand and a syringe in the other.

"Since you're here," he says, without looking over his shoulder, "you might as well go in with me."

I bite my lip. "Into your fear landscape?"

"Yes."

As I walk toward him, I ask, "I can do that?"

"The serum connects you to the program," he says, "but the program determines whose landscape you go through. And right now, it's set to put us through mine."

"You would let me see that?"

"Why else do you think I'm going in?" he asks quietly. He doesn't lift his eyes. "There are some things I want to show you."

He holds up the syringe, and I tilt my head to better expose my neck. I feel sharp pain when the needle goes in, but I am used to it now. When he's done, he offers me the black box. In it is another syringe.

"I've never done this before," I say as I take it out of the box. I don't want to hurt him.

"Right here," he says, touching a spot on his neck with his fingernail. I stand on my tiptoes and push the needle in, my hand shaking a little. He doesn't even flinch.

He keeps his eyes on me the whole time, and when I'm done, puts both syringes in the box and sets it by the door. He knew that I would follow him up here. Knew, or hoped. Either way is fine with me.

He offers me his hand, and I slide mine into it. His fingers are cold and brittle. I feel like there is something I should say, but I am too stunned and can't come up with any words. He opens the door with his free hand, and I follow him into the dark. I am now used to entering unknown places without hesitation. I keep my breaths even and hold firmly to Four's hand.

"See if you can figure out why they call me Four," he says.

The door clicks shut behind us, taking all the light with it. The air is cold in the hallway; I feel each particle enter my lungs. I inch closer to him so my arm is against his and my chin is near his shoulder.

"What's your real name?" I ask.

"See if you can figure that out too."

The simulation takes us. The ground I stand on is no longer made of cement. It creaks like metal. Light pours in from all angles, and the city unfolds around us, glass buildings and the arc of train tracks, and we are high above it. I haven't seen a blue sky in a long time, so when it spreads out above me, I feel the breath catch in my lungs and the effect is dizzying.

Then the wind starts. It blows so hard I have to lean against Four to stay on my feet. He removes his hand from mine and wraps his arm around my shoulders instead. At first I think it's to protect me—but no, he's having trouble breathing and he needs me to steady him. He forces breath in and out through an open mouth and his teeth are clenched.

The height is beautiful to me, but if it's here, it is one of his worst nightmares.

"We have to jump off, right?" I shout over the wind.

He nods.

"On three, okay?"

Another nod.

"One . . . two . . . *three!*" I pull him with me as I burst into a run. After we take the first step, the rest is easy. We both sprint off the edge of the building. We fall like two stones, fast, the air pushing back at us, the ground growing beneath us. Then the scene disappears, and I am on my hands and knees on the floor, grinning. I loved that rush the day I chose Dauntless, and I love it now.

Next to me, Four gasps and presses a hand to his chest.

I get up and help him to his feet. "What's next?"

"It's—"

Something solid hits my spine. I slam into Four, my head hitting his collarbone. Walls appear on my left and my right. The space is so narrow that Four has to pull his arms into his chest to fit. A ceiling slams onto the walls around us with a crack, and Four hunches over, groaning. The room is just big enough to accommodate his size, and no bigger.

"Confinement," I say.

He makes a guttural noise. I tilt my head and pull back enough to look at him. I can barely see his face, it's so dark, and the air is close; we share breaths. He grimaces like he's in pain.

"Hey," I say. "It's okay. Here—"

I guide his arms around my body so he has more space. He clutches at my back and puts his face next to mine, still hunched over. His body is warm, but I feel only his bones and the muscle that wraps around them; nothing yields beneath me. My cheeks get hot. Can he tell that I'm still built like a child?

"This is the first time I'm happy I'm so small." I laugh. If I joke, maybe I can calm him down. And distract myself.

"Mmhmm," he says. His voice sounds strained.

"We can't break out of here," I say. "It's easier to face the fear head on, right?" I don't wait for a response. "So what you need to do is make the space smaller. Make it worse so it gets better. Right?"

"Yes." It is a tight, tense little word.

"Okay. We'll have to crouch, then. Ready?"

I squeeze his waist to pull him down with me. I feel the hard line of his rib against my hand and hear the screech of one wood plank against another as the ceiling inches down with us. I realize that we won't fit with all this space between us, so I turn and curl into a ball, my spine against his chest. One of his knees is bent next to my head and the other is curled beneath me so I'm sitting on his ankle. We are a jumble of limbs. I feel a harsh breath against my ear.

"Ah," he says, his voice raspy. "This is worse. This is definitely . . ."

"Shh," I say. "Arms around me."

Obediently, he slips both arms around my waist. I smile at the wall. I am not enjoying this. I am not, not even a little bit, no.

"The simulation measures your fear response," I say softly. I'm just repeating what he told us, but reminding him might help him. "So if you can calm your heartbeat down, it will move on to the next one. Remember? So try to forget that we're here."

"Yeah?" I feel his lips move against my ear as he speaks, and heat courses through me. "That easy, huh?"

"You know, most boys would enjoy being trapped in close quarters with a girl." I roll my eyes.

"Not claustrophobic people, Tris!" He sounds desperate now.

"Okay, okay." I set my hand on top of his and guide it to my chest, so it's right over my heart. "Feel my heartbeat. Can you feel it?"

"Yes."

"Feel how steady it is?"

"It's fast."

"Yes, well, that has nothing to do with the box." I wince as soon as I'm done speaking. I just admitted to something. Hopefully he doesn't realize that. "Every time you feel me breathe, you breathe. Focus on that."

"Okay."

I breathe deeply, and his chest rises and falls with mine. After a few seconds of this, I say calmly, "Why don't you tell me where this fear comes from. Maybe talking about it will help us . . . somehow."

I don't know how, but it sounds right.

"Um . . . okay." He breathes with me again. "This one is from my fantastic childhood. Childhood punishments. The tiny closet upstairs."

I press my lips together. I remember being punished—sent to my room without dinner, deprived of this or that, firm scoldings. I was never shut in a closet. The cruelty smarts; my chest aches for him. I don't know what to say, so I try to keep it casual.

"My mother kept our winter coats in our closet."

"I don't . . ." He gasps. "I don't really want to talk about it anymore."

"Okay. Then . . . I can talk. Ask me something."

"Okay." He laughs shakily in my ear. "Why is your heart racing, Tris?"

I cringe and say, "Well, I . . ." I search for an excuse that doesn't involve his arms being around me. "I barely know you." *Not good enough.* "I barely know you and I'm crammed up against you in a box, Four, what do you think?"

"If we were in your fear landscape," he says, "would I be in it?"

"I'm not afraid of you."

"Of course you're not. But that's not what I meant."

He laughs again, and when he does, the walls break apart with a crack and fall away, leaving us in a circle of light.

Four sighs and lifts his arms from my body. I scramble to my feet and brush myself off, though I haven't accumulated any dirt that I'm aware of. I wipe my palms on my jeans. My back feels cold from the sudden absence of him.

He stands in front of me. He's grinning, and I'm not sure I like the look in his eyes.

"Maybe you were cut out for Candor," he says, "because you're a terrible liar."

"I think my aptitude test ruled that one out pretty well."

He shakes his head. "The aptitude test tells you nothing."

I narrow my eyes. "What are you trying to tell me? Your test isn't the reason you ended up Dauntless?"

Excitement runs through me like the blood in my veins, propelled by the hope that he might confirm that he is Divergent, that he is like me, that we can figure out what it means together.

"Not exactly, no," he says. "I . . ."

He looks over his shoulder and his voice trails off. A woman stands a few yards away, pointing a gun at us. She is completely still, her features plain—if we walked away right now, I would not remember her. To my right, a table appears. On it is a gun and a single bullet. Why isn't she shooting us?

Oh, I think. The fear is unrelated to the threat to his life. It has to do with the gun on the table.

"You have to kill her," I say softly.

"Every single time."

"She isn't real."

"She looks real." He bites his lip. "It feels real."

"If she was real, she would have killed you already."

"It's okay." He nods. "I'll just . . . do it. This one's not . . . not so bad. Not as much panic involved."

Not as much panic, but far more dread. I can see it in his eyes as he picks up the gun and opens the chamber like he's done it a thousand times—and maybe he has. He clicks the bullet into the chamber and holds the gun out in front of him, both hands around it. He squeezes one eye shut and breathes slowly in.

As he exhales, he fires, and the woman's head whips back. I see a flash of red and look away. I hear her crumple to the floor.

Four's gun drops with a thump. We stare at her fallen body. What he said is true—it does feel real. *Don't be ridiculous.* I grab his arm.

"C'mon," I say. "Let's go. Keep moving."

After another tug, he comes out of his daze and follows me. As we pass the table, the woman's body disappears, except in my memory and his. What would it be like to kill someone every time I went through my landscape? Maybe I'll find out.

But something puzzles me: These are supposed to be Four's worst fears. And though he panicked in the box and on the roof, he killed the woman without much difficulty. It seems like the simulation is grasping at any fears it can find within him, and it hasn't found much.

"Here we go," he whispers.

A dark figure moves ahead of us, creeping along the edge of the circle of light, waiting for us to take another step. Who is it? Who frequents Four's nightmares?

The man who emerges is tall and slim, with hair cut close to his scalp. He holds his hands behind his back. And he wears the gray clothes of the Abnegation.

"Marcus," I whisper.

"Here's the part," Four says, his voice shaking, "where you figure out my name."

"Is he . . ." I look from Marcus, who walks slowly toward us, to Four, who inches slowly back, and everything comes together. Marcus had a son who joined Dauntless. His name was . . . "Tobias."

Marcus shows us his hands. A belt is curled around one of his fists. Slowly he unwinds it from his fingers.

"This is for your own good," he says, and his voice echoes a dozen times.

A dozen Marcuses press into the circle of light, all holding the same belt, with the same blank expression.

When the Marcuses blink again, their eyes turn into empty, black pits. The belts slither along the floor, which is now white tile. A shiver crawls up my spine. The Erudite accused Marcus of cruelty. For once the Erudite were right.

I look at Four—Tobias—and he seems frozen. His posture sags. He looks years older; he looks years younger. The first Marcus yanks his arm back, the belt sailing over his shoulder as he prepares to strike. Tobias shrinks back, throwing his arms up to protect his face.

I dart in front of him and the belt cracks against my wrist, wrapping around it. A hot pain races up my arm to my elbow. I grit my teeth and pull as hard as I can. Marcus loses his grip, so I unwrap the belt and grab it by the buckle.

I swing my arm as fast as I can, my shoulder socket burning from the sudden motion, and the belt strikes Marcus's shoulder. He yells and lunges at me with outstretched hands, with fingernails that look like claws. Tobias pushes me behind him so he stands between me and Marcus. He looks angry, not afraid.

All the Marcuses vanish. The lights come on, revealing a long, narrow room with busted brick walls and a cement floor.

"That's it?" I say. "Those were your worst fears? Why do

you only have four . . ." My voice trails off. Only four fears.

"Oh." I look over my shoulder at him. "That's why they call you—"

The words leave me when I see his expression. His eyes are wide and seem almost vulnerable under the room's lights. His lips are parted. If we were not here, I would describe the look as awe. But I don't understand why he would be looking at me in awe.

He wraps his hand around my elbow, his thumb pressing to the soft skin above my forearm, and tugs me toward him. The skin around my wrist still stings, like the belt was real, but it is as pale as the rest of me. His lips slowly move against my cheek, then his arms tighten around my shoulders, and he buries his face in my neck, breathing against my collarbone.

I stand stiffly for a second and then loop my arms around him and sigh.

"Hey," I say softly. "We got through it."

He lifts his head and slips his fingers through my hair, tucking it behind my ear. We stare at each other in silence. His fingers move absently over a lock of my hair.

"You got me through it," he says finally.

"Well." My throat is dry. I try to ignore the nervous electricity that pulses through me every second he touches me. "It's easy to be brave when they're not my fears."

I let my hands drop and casually wipe them on my jeans, hoping he doesn't notice.

If he does, he doesn't say so. He laces his fingers with mine.

"Come on," he says. "I have something else to show you."

CHAPTER
TWENTY-SIX

HAND IN HAND, we walk toward the Pit. I monitor the pressure of my hand carefully. One minute, I feel like I'm not gripping hard enough, and the next, I'm squeezing too hard. I never used to understand why people bothered to hold hands as they walked, but then he runs one of his fingertips down my palm, and I shiver and understand it completely.

"So . . ." I latch on to the last logical thought I remember. "Four fears."

"Four fears then; four fears now," he says, nodding. "They haven't changed, so I keep going in there, but . . . I still haven't made any progress."

"You can't be fearless, remember?" I say. "Because you still care about things. About your life."

"I know."

We walk along the edge of the Pit on a narrow path that leads to the rocks at the bottom of the chasm. I've never noticed it before—it blended in with the rock wall. But Tobias seems to know it well.

I don't want to ruin the moment, but I have to know about his aptitude test. I have to know if he's Divergent.

"You were going to tell me about your aptitude test results," I say.

"Ah." He scratches the back of his neck with his free hand. "Does it matter?"

"Yes. I want to know."

"How demanding you are." He smiles.

We reach the end of the path and stand at the bottom of the chasm, where the rocks form unsteady ground, rising up at harsh angles from the rushing water. He leads me up and down, across small gaps and over angular ridges. My shoes cling to the rough rock. The soles of my shoes mark each rock with a wet footprint.

He finds a relatively flat rock near the side, where the current isn't strong, and sits down, his feet dangling over the edge. I sit beside him. He seems comfortable here, inches above the hazardous water.

He releases my hand. I look at the jagged edge of the rock.

"These are things I don't tell people, you know. Not even my friends," he says.

I lace my fingers together and clench. This is the perfect place for him to tell me that he is Divergent, if indeed that's what he is. The roar of the chasm ensures that we won't be overheard. I don't know why the thought makes me so nervous.

"My result was as expected," he says. "Abnegation."

"Oh." Something inside me deflates. I am wrong about him.

But—I had assumed that if he was not Divergent, he must have gotten a Dauntless result. And technically, I also got an Abnegation result—according to the system. Did the same thing happen to him? And if that's true, why isn't he telling me the truth?

"But you chose Dauntless anyway?" I say.

"Out of necessity."

"Why did you have to leave?"

His eyes dart away from mine, across the space in front of him, as if searching the air for an answer. He doesn't need to give one. I still feel the ghost of a stinging belt on my wrist.

"You had to get away from your dad," I say. "Is that why you don't want to be a Dauntless leader? Because if you were, you might have to see him again?"

He lifts a shoulder. "That, and I've always felt that I don't quite belong among the Dauntless. Not the way they are now, anyway."

"But you're . . . incredible," I say. I pause and clear my throat. "I mean, by Dauntless standards. Four fears is unheard of. How could you not belong here?"

He shrugs. He doesn't seem to care about his talent, or his status among the Dauntless, and that is what I would expect from the Abnegation. I am not sure what to make of that.

He says, "I have a theory that selflessness and bravery aren't all that different. All your life you've been training to forget yourself, so when you're in danger, it becomes your first instinct. I could belong in Abnegation just as easily."

Suddenly I feel heavy. A lifetime of training wasn't enough for me. My first instinct is still self-preservation.

"Yeah, well," I say, "I left Abnegation because I wasn't selfless enough, no matter how hard I tried to be."

"That's not entirely true." He smiles at me. "That girl who let someone throw knives at her to spare a friend, who hit my dad with a belt to protect me—that selfless girl, that's not you?"

He's figured out more about me than I have. And even though it seems impossible that he could feel something for me, given all that I'm not . . . maybe it isn't. I frown at him. "You've been paying close attention, haven't you?"

"I like to observe people."

"Maybe you were cut out for Candor, Four, because you're a terrible liar."

He puts his hand on the rock next to him, his fingers lining up with mine. I look down at our hands. He has long, narrow fingers. Hands made for fine, deft movements. Not Dauntless hands, which should be thick and tough and ready to break things.

"Fine." He leans his face closer to mine, his eyes focusing on my chin, and my lips, and my nose. "I watched you because I like you." He says it plainly, boldly, and his eyes flick up to mine. "And don't call me 'Four,' okay? It's nice to hear my name again."

Just like that, he has finally declared himself, and I don't know how to respond. My cheeks warm, and all I can think to say is, "But you're older than I am . . . *Tobias.*"

He smiles at me. "Yes, that whopping two-year gap really is *insurmountable*, isn't it?"

"I'm not trying to be self-deprecating," I say, "I just don't get it. I'm younger. I'm not pretty. I—"

He laughs, a deep laugh that sounds like it came from deep inside him, and touches his lips to my temple.

"Don't pretend," I say breathily. "You know I'm not. I'm not ugly, but I am certainly not pretty."

"Fine. You're not pretty. So?" He kisses my cheek. "I

like how you look. You're deadly smart. You're brave. And even though you found out about Marcus . . ." His voice softens. "You aren't giving me that look. Like I'm a kicked puppy or something."

"Well," I say. "You're not."

For a second his dark eyes are on mine, and he's quiet. Then he touches my face and leans in close, brushing my lips with his. The river roars and I feel its spray on my ankles. He grins and presses his mouth to mine.

I tense up at first, unsure of myself, so when he pulls away, I'm sure I did something wrong, or badly. But he takes my face in his hands, his fingers strong against my skin, and kisses me again, firmer this time, more certain. I wrap an arm around him, sliding my hand up his neck and into his short hair.

For a few minutes we kiss, deep in the chasm, with the roar of water all around us. And when we rise, hand in hand, I realize that if we had both chosen differently, we might have ended up doing the same thing, in a safer place, in gray clothes instead of black ones.

CHAPTER
TWENTY-SEVEN

THE NEXT MORNING I am silly and light. Every time I push the smile from my face, it fights its way back. Eventually I stop suppressing it. I let my hair hang loose and abandon my uniform of loose shirts in favor of one that cuts across my shoulders, revealing my tattoos.

"What is it with you today?" says Christina on the way to breakfast. Her eyes are still swollen from sleep and her tangled hair forms a fuzzy halo around her face.

"Oh, you know," I say. "Sun shining. Birds chirping."

She raises an eyebrow at me, as if reminding me that we are in an underground tunnel.

"Let the girl be in a good mood," Will says. "You may never see it again."

I smack his arm and hurry toward the dining hall. My

heart pounds because I know that at some point in the next half hour, I will see Tobias. I sit down in my usual place, next to Uriah, with Will and Christina across from us. The seat on my left stays empty. I wonder if Tobias will sit in it; if he'll grin at me over breakfast; if he'll look at me in that secret, stolen way that I imagine myself looking at him.

I grab a piece of toast from the plate in the middle of the table and start to butter it with a little too much enthusiasm. I feel myself acting like a lunatic, but I can't stop. It would be like refusing to breathe.

Then he walks in. His hair is shorter, and it looks darker this way, almost black. It's Abnegation short, I realize. I smile at him and lift my hand to wave him over, but he sits down next to Zeke without even glancing in my direction, so I let my hand drop.

I stare at my toast. It is easy not to smile now.

"Something wrong?" asks Uriah through a mouthful of toast.

I shake my head and take a bite. What did I expect? Just because we kissed doesn't mean anything changes. Maybe he changed his mind about liking me. Maybe he thinks kissing me was a mistake.

"Today's fear landscape day," says Will. "You think we'll get to see our own fear landscapes?"

"No." Uriah shakes his head. "You go through one of the instructors' landscapes. My brother told me."

"Ooh, which instructor?" says Christina, suddenly perking up.

"You know, it really isn't fair that you all get insider information and we don't," Will says, glaring at Uriah.

"Like you wouldn't use an advantage if you had one," retorts Uriah.

Christina ignores them. "I hope it's Four's landscape."

"Why?" I ask. The question comes out too incredulous. I bite my lip and wish I could take it back.

"Looks like *someone* had a mood swing." She rolls her eyes. "Like you don't want to know what his fears are. He acts so tough that he's probably afraid of marshmallows and really bright sunrises or something. Overcompensating."

I shake my head. "It won't be him."

"How would you know?"

"It's just a prediction."

I remember Tobias's father in his fear landscape. He wouldn't let everyone see that. I glance at him. For a second, his eyes shift to mine. His stare is unfeeling. Then he looks away.

+ + +

Lauren, the instructor of the Dauntless-born initiates, stands with her hands on her hips outside the fear landscape room.

"Two years ago," she says, "I was afraid of spiders, suffocation, walls that inch slowly inward and trap you between them, getting thrown out of Dauntless, uncontrollable bleeding, getting run over by a train, my father's death, public humiliation, and kidnapping by men without faces."

Everyone stares blankly at her.

"Most of you will have anywhere from ten to fifteen fears in your fear landscapes. That is the average number," she says.

"What's the lowest number someone has gotten?" asks Lynn.

"In recent years," says Lauren, "four."

I have not looked at Tobias since we were in the cafeteria, but I can't help but look at him now. He keeps his eyes trained on the floor. I knew that four was a low number, low enough to merit a nickname, but I didn't know it was less than half the average.

I glare at my feet. He's exceptional. And now he won't even look at me.

"You will not find out your number today," says Lauren. "The simulation is set to my fear landscape program, so you will experience my fears instead of your own."

I give Christina a pointed look. I was right; we won't go through Four's landscape.

"For the purposes of this exercise, though, each of you will only face *one* of my fears, to get a sense for how the simulation works."

Lauren points to us at random and assigns us each a fear. I was standing in the back, so I will go close to last. The fear that she assigned to me was kidnapping.

Because I'm not hooked up to the computer as I wait, I can't watch the simulation, only the person's reaction to it. It is the perfect way to distract myself from my preoccupation with Tobias—clenching my hands into fists as Will brushes off spiders I can't see and Uriah presses his hands against walls that are invisible to me, and smirking as Peter turns bright red during whatever he experiences in "public humiliation." Then it's my turn.

The obstacle won't be comfortable for me, but because I have been able to manipulate every simulation, not just this one, and because I have already gone through Tobias's landscape, I am not apprehensive as Lauren inserts the needle into my neck.

Then the scenery changes and the kidnapping begins. The ground turns into grass beneath my feet, and hands clamp around my arms, over my mouth. It is too dark to see.

I stand next to the chasm. I hear the roar of the water. I scream into the hand that covers my mouth and thrash to free myself, but the arms are too strong; my kidnappers are too strong. The image of myself falling into darkness flashes into my mind, the same image that I now carry with me in my nightmares. I scream again; I scream until my throat hurts and I squeeze hot tears from my eyes.

I knew they would come back for me; I knew they would try again. The first time was not enough. I scream again— not for help, because no one will help me, but because that's what you do when you're about to die and you can't stop it.

"Stop," a stern voice says.

The hands disappear, and the lights come on. I stand on cement in the fear landscape room. My body shakes, and I drop to my knees, pressing my hands to my face. I just failed. I lost all logic, I lost all sense. Lauren's fear transformed into one of my own.

And everyone saw me. Tobias saw me.

I hear footsteps. Tobias marches toward me and wrenches me to my feet.

"What the hell was that, Stiff?"

"I . . ." My breath comes in a hiccup. "I didn't—"

"Get yourself together! This is pathetic."

Something within me snaps. My tears stop. Heat races

through my body, driving the weakness out of me, and I smack him so hard my knuckles burn with the impact. He stares at me, one side of his face bright with blush-blood, and I stare back.

"Shut up," I say. I yank my arm from his grasp and walk out of the room.

CHAPTER
TWENTY-EIGHT

I PULL MY jacket tight around my shoulders. I haven't been outside in a long time. The sun shines pale against my face, and I watch my breaths form in the air.

At least I accomplished one thing: I convinced Peter and his friends that I'm no longer a threat. I just have to make sure that tomorrow, when I go through my own fear landscape, I prove them wrong. Yesterday failure seemed impossible. Today I'm not sure.

I slide my hands through my hair. The impulse to cry is gone. I braid my hair and tie it with the rubber band around my wrist. I feel more like myself. That is all I need: to remember who I am. And I am someone who does not let inconsequential things like boys and near-death experiences stop her.

I laugh, shaking my head. Am I?

I hear the train horn. The train tracks loop around the Dauntless compound and then continue farther than I can see. Where do they begin? Where do they end? What is the world like beyond them? I walk toward them.

I want to go home, but I can't. Eric warned us not to appear too attached to our parents on Visiting Day, so visiting home would be betraying the Dauntless, and I can't afford to do that. Eric did not tell us we couldn't visit people in factions other than the ones we came from, though, and my mother did tell me to visit Caleb.

I know I'm not allowed to leave without supervision, but I can't stop myself. I walk faster and faster, until I'm sprinting. Pumping my arms, I run alongside the last car until I can grab the handle and swing myself in, wincing as pain darts through my sore body.

Once in the car, I lie on my back next to the door and watch the Dauntless compound disappear behind me. I don't want to go back, but choosing to quit, to be faction-less, would be the bravest thing I have ever done, and today I feel like a coward.

The air rushes over my body and twists around my fingers. I let my hand trail over the edge of the car so it presses against the wind. I can't go home, but I can find part of it. Caleb has a place in every memory of my childhood; he is part of my foundation.

The train slows as it reaches the heart of the city, and I sit up to watch the smaller buildings grow into larger buildings. The Erudite live in large stone buildings that overlook the marsh. I hold the handle and lean out just enough to see where the tracks go. They dip down to street level just before they bend to travel east. I breathe in the smell of wet pavement and marsh air.

The train dips and slows, and I jump. My legs shudder with the force of my landing, and I run a few steps to regain my balance. I walk down the middle of the street, heading south, toward the marsh. The empty land stretches as far as I can see, a brown plane colliding with the horizon.

I turn left. The Erudite buildings loom above me, dark and unfamiliar. How will I find Caleb here?

The Erudite keep records; it's in their nature. They must keep records of their initiates. Someone has access to those records; I just have to find them. I scan the buildings. Logically speaking, the central building should be the most important one. I may as well start there.

The faction members are milling around everywhere. Erudite faction norms dictate that a faction member must wear at least one blue article of clothing at a time, because blue causes the body to release calming chemicals, and "a calm mind is a clear mind." The color has also come to signify their faction. It seems impossibly bright to me now. I have grown used to dim lighting and dark clothing.

I expect to weave through the crowd, dodging elbows and muttering "excuse me" the way I always do, but there is no need. Becoming Dauntless has made me noticeable. The crowd parts for me, and their eyes cling to me as I pass. I pull the rubber band from my hair and shake it from its knot before I walk through the front doors.

I stand just inside the entrance and tilt my head back. The room is huge, silent, and smells like dust-covered pages. The wood-paneled floor creaks beneath my feet. Bookcases line the walls on either side of me, but they seem to be decorative more than anything, because computers occupy the tables in the center of the room, and no one is reading. They stare at screens with tense eyes, focused.

I should have known that the main Erudite building would be a library. A portrait on the opposite wall catches my attention. It is twice my height and four times my width and depicts an attractive woman with watery gray eyes and spectacles—Jeanine. Heat licks my throat at the sight of her. Because she is Erudite's representative, she is the one who released that report about my father. I have disliked her since my father's dinner-table rants began, but now I hate her.

Beneath her is a large plaque that reads KNOWLEDGE LEADS TO PROSPERITY.

Prosperity. To me the word has a negative connotation. Abnegation uses it to describe self-indulgence.

How could Caleb have chosen to be one of these people? The things they do, the things they want, it's all wrong. But he probably thinks the same of the Dauntless.

I walk up to the desk just beneath Jeanine's portrait. The young man sitting behind it doesn't look up as he says, "How can I help you?"

"I am looking for someone," I say. "His name is Caleb. Do you know where I can find him?"

"I am not permitted to give out personal information," he replies blandly, as he jabs at the screen in front of him.

"He's my brother."

"I am not permi—"

I slam my palm on the desk in front of him, and he jerks out of his daze, staring at me over his spectacles. Heads turn in my direction.

"I said." My voice is terse. "I am looking for someone. He's an initiate. Can you at least tell me where I can find them?"

"Beatrice?" a voice behind me says.

I turn, and Caleb stands behind me, a book in hand. His hair has grown out so it flips at his ears, and he wears a blue T-shirt and a pair of rectangular glasses. Even though he looks different and I'm not allowed to love him anymore, I run at him as fast as I can and throw my arms around his shoulders.

"You have a tattoo," he says, his voice muffled.

"You have glasses," I say. I pull back and narrow my eyes. "Your vision is perfect, Caleb, what are you doing?"

"Um . . ." He glances at the tables around us. "Come on. Let's get out of here."

We exit the building and cross the street. I have to jog to keep up with him. Across from Erudite headquarters is what used to be a park. Now we just call it "Millenium," and it is a stretch of bare land and several rusted metal sculptures—one an abstract, plated mammoth, another shaped like a lima bean that dwarfs me in size.

We stop on the concrete around the metal bean, where the Erudite sit in small groups with newspapers or books. He takes off his glasses and shoves them in his pocket, then runs a hand through his hair, his eyes skipping over mine nervously. Like he's ashamed. Maybe I should be too. I'm tattooed, loose-haired, and wearing tight clothes. But I'm just not.

"What are you doing here?" he says.

"I wanted to go home," I say, "and you were the closest thing I could think of."

He presses his lips together.

"Don't look so pleased to see me," I add.

"Hey," he says, setting his hands on my shoulders. "I'm thrilled to see you, okay? It's just that this isn't allowed. There are rules."

"I don't care," I say. "I don't care, okay?"

"Maybe you should." His voice is gentle; he wears his look of disapproval. "If it were me, I wouldn't want to get in trouble with your faction."

"What's that supposed to mean?"

I know exactly what it means. He sees my faction as the cruelest of the five, and nothing more.

"I just don't want you to get hurt. You don't have to be so angry with me," he says, tilting his head. "What *happened* to you in there?"

"Nothing. Nothing happened to me." I close my eyes and rub the back of my neck with one hand. Even if I could explain everything to him, I wouldn't want to. I can't even summon the will to think about it.

"You think . . ." He looks at his shoes. "You think you made the right choice?"

"I don't think there was one," I say. "How about you?"

He looks around. People stare at us as they walk past. His eyes skip over their faces. He's still nervous, but maybe it's not because of how he looks, or because of me. Maybe it's them. I grab his arm and pull him under the arch of the metal bean. We walk beneath its hollow underbelly. I see my reflection everywhere, warped by the curve of the walls, broken by patches of rust and grime.

"What's going on?" I say, folding my arms. I didn't notice the dark circles under his eyes before. "What's wrong?"

Caleb presses a palm to the metal wall. In his reflection, his head is small and pressed in on one side, and his arm looks like it is bending backward. My reflection, however, looks small and squat.

"Something big is happening, Beatrice. Something is wrong." His eyes are wide and glassy. "I don't know what it is, but people keep rushing around, talking quietly, and Jeanine gives speeches about how corrupt Abnegation is all the time, almost every day."

"Do you believe her?"

"No. Maybe. I don't . . ." He shakes his head. "I don't know what to believe."

"Yes, you do," I say sternly. "You know who our parents are. You know who our friends are. Susan's dad, you think he's corrupt?"

"How much do I know? How much did they allow me to know? We weren't allowed to ask questions, Beatrice; we weren't allowed to know things! And here . . ." He looks up, and in the flat circle of mirror right above us,

I see our tiny figures, the size of fingernails. That, I think, is our true reflection; it is as small as we actually are. He continues, "Here, information is free, it's always available."

"This isn't Candor. There are liars here, Caleb. There are people who are so smart they know how to manipulate you."

"Don't you think I would know if I was being manipulated?"

"If they're as smart as you think, then no. I don't think you would know."

"You have no idea what you're talking about," he says, shaking his head.

"Yeah. How could I *possibly* know what a corrupt faction looks like? I'm just training to be *Dauntless*, for God's sake," I say. "At least I know what I'm a part of, Caleb. *You* are choosing to ignore what we've known all our lives— these people are arrogant and greedy and they will lead you nowhere."

His voice hardens. "I think you should go, Beatrice."

"With pleasure," I say. "Oh, and not that it will matter to you, but Mom told me to tell you to research the simulation serum."

"You saw her?" He looks hurt. "Why didn't she—"

"Because," I say. "The Erudite don't let the Abnegation

into their compound anymore. Wasn't that information available to you?"

I push past him, walking away from the mirror cave and the sculpture, and start down the sidewalk. I should never have left. The Dauntless compound sounds like home now—at least there, I know exactly where I stand, which is on unstable ground.

The crowd on the sidewalk thins, and I look up to see why. Standing a few yards in front of me are two Erudite men with their arms folded.

"Excuse me," one of them says. "You'll have to come with us."

+ + +

One man walks so close behind me that I feel his breath against the back of my head. The other man leads me into the library and down three hallways to an elevator. Beyond the library the floors change from wood to white tile, and the walls glow like the ceiling of the aptitude test room. The glow bounces off the silver elevator doors, and I squint so I can see.

I try to stay calm. I ask myself questions from Dauntless training. *What do you do if someone attacks you from behind?* I envision thrusting my elbow back into a stomach or a groin. I imagine running. I wish I had a gun. These are

Dauntless thoughts, and they have become mine.

What do you do if you're attacked by two people at once? I follow the man down an empty, glowing corridor and into an office. The walls are made of glass—I guess I know which faction designed my school.

A woman sits behind a metal desk. I stare at her face. The same face dominates the Erudite library; it is plastered across every article Erudite releases. How long have I hated that face? I don't remember.

"Sit," Jeanine says. Her voice sounds familiar, especially when she is irritated. Her liquid gray eyes focus on mine.

"I'd rather not."

"*Sit,*" she says again. I have definitely heard her voice before.

I heard it in the hallway, talking to Eric, before I got attacked. I heard her mention Divergents. And once before—I heard it . . .

"It was your voice in the simulation," I say. "The aptitude test, I mean."

She is the danger Tori and my mother warned me about, the danger of being Divergent. Sitting right in front of me.

"Correct. The aptitude test is by far my greatest achievement as a scientist," she replies. "I looked up your test results, Beatrice. Apparently there was a problem with your test. It was never recorded, and your results had to be reported manually. Did you know that?"

"No."

"Did you know that you're one of two people ever to get an Abnegation result and switch to Dauntless?"

"No," I say, biting back my shock. Tobias and I are the only ones? But his result was genuine and mine was a lie. So it is really just him.

My stomach twinges at the thought of him. Right now I don't care how unique he is. He called me pathetic.

"What made you choose Dauntless?" she asks.

"What does this have to do with anything?" I try to soften my voice, but it doesn't work. "Aren't you going to reprimand me for abandoning my faction and seeking out my brother? 'Faction before blood,' right?" I pause. "Come to think of it, why am I in your office in the first place? Aren't you supposed to be important or something?"

Maybe that will take her down a few pegs.

Her mouth pinches for a second. "I will leave the reprimands to the Dauntless," she says, leaning back in her chair.

I set my hands on the back of the chair I refused to sit in and clench my fingers. Behind her is a window that overlooks the city. The train takes a lazy turn in the distance.

"As to the reason for your presence here . . . a quality

of my faction is curiosity," she says, "and while perusing your records, I saw that there was another error with another one of your simulations. Again, it failed to be recorded. Did you know that?"

"How did you access my records? Only the Dauntless have access to those."

"Because Erudite developed the simulations, we have an . . . *understanding* with the Dauntless, Beatrice." She tilts her head and smiles at me. "I am merely concerned for the competence of our technology. If it fails while you are around, I have to ensure that it does not continue to do so, you understand?"

I understand only one thing: She is lying to me. She doesn't care about the technology—she suspects that something is awry with my test results. Just like the Dauntless leaders, she is sniffing around for the Divergent. And if my mother wants Caleb to research the simulation serum, it is probably because Jeanine developed it.

But what is so threatening about my ability to manipulate the simulations? Why would it matter to the representative of the Erudite, of all people?

I can't answer either question. But the look she gives me reminds me of the look in the attack dog's eyes in the aptitude test—a vicious, predatory stare. She wants to rip me to pieces. I can't lie down in submission now. I have become an attack dog too.

I feel my pulse in my throat.

"I don't know how they work," I say, "but the liquid I was injected with made me sick to my stomach. Maybe my simulation administrator was distracted because he was worried I would throw up, and he forgot to record it. I got sick after the aptitude test too."

"Do you habitually have a sensitive stomach, Beatrice?" Her voice is like a razor's edge. She taps her trimmed fingernails against the glass desk.

"Ever since I was young," I reply as smoothly as I can. I release the chair back and sidestep it to sit down. I can't seem tense, even though I feel like my insides are writhing within me.

"You have been extremely successful with the simulations," she says. "To what do you attribute the ease with which you complete them?"

"I'm brave," I say, staring into her eyes. The other factions see the Dauntless a certain way. Brash, aggressive, impulsive. Cocky. I should be what she expects. I smirk at her. "I'm the best initiate they've got."

I lean forward, balancing my elbows on my knees. I will have to go further with this to make it convincing.

"You want to know why I chose Dauntless?" I ask. "It's because I was bored." Further, further. Lies require commitment. "I was tired of being a wussy little do-gooder and I wanted out."

"So you don't miss your parents?" she asks delicately.

"Do I miss getting scolded for looking in the mirror? Do I miss being told to shut up at the dinner table?" I shake my head. "No. I don't miss them. They're not my family anymore."

The lie burns my throat on the way out, or maybe that's the tears I'm fighting. I picture my mother standing behind me with a comb and a pair of scissors, faintly smiling as she trims my hair, and I want to scream rather than insult her like this.

"Can I take that to mean . . ." Jeanine purses her lips and pauses for a few seconds before finishing. ". . . that you agree with the reports that have been released about the political leaders of this city?"

The reports that label my family as corrupt, power-hungry, moralizing dictators? The reports that carry subtle threats and hint at revolution? They make me sick to my stomach. Knowing that she is the one who released them makes me want to strangle her.

I smile.

"Wholeheartedly," I say.

+ + +

One of Jeanine's lackeys, a man in a blue collared shirt and sunglasses, drives me back to the Dauntless compound in a sleek silver car, the likes of which I have never seen before. The engine is almost silent. When I ask the man about it, he tells me it's solar-powered and launches into a lengthy explanation of how the panels on the roof convert sunlight into energy. I stop listening after sixty seconds and stare out the window.

I don't know what they'll do to me when I get back. I suspect it will be bad. I imagine my feet dangling over the chasm and bite my lip.

When the driver pulls up to the glass building above the Dauntless compound, Eric is waiting for me by the door. He takes my arm and leads me into the building without thanking the driver. Eric's fingers squeeze so hard I know I'll have bruises.

He stands between me and the door that leads inside. He starts to crack his knuckles. Other than that, he is completely still.

I shudder involuntarily.

The faint *pop* of his knuckle-cracking is all I hear apart from my own breaths, which grow faster by the second. When he is finished, Eric laces his fingers together in front of him.

"Welcome back, Tris."

"Eric."

He walks toward me, carefully placing one foot in front of the other.

"What . . ." His first word is quiet. "*Exactly*," he adds,

louder this time, "were you thinking?"

"I . . ." He is so close I can see the holes his metal piercings fit into. "I don't know."

"I am tempted to call you a traitor, Tris," he says. "Have you never heard the phrase 'faction before blood'?"

I have seen Eric do terrible things. I have heard him say terrible things. But I have never seen him like this. He is not a maniac anymore; he is perfectly controlled, perfectly poised. Careful and quiet.

For the first time, I recognize Eric for what he is: an Erudite disguised as a Dauntless, a genius as well as a sadist, a hunter of the Divergent.

I want to run.

"Were you unsatisfied with the life you have found here? Do you perhaps regret your choice?" Both of Eric's metal-ridden eyebrows lift, forcing creases into his forehead. "I would like to hear an explanation for why you betrayed Dauntless, yourself, and *me* . . ." He taps his chest. ". . . by venturing into another faction's headquarters."

"I . . ." I take a deep breath. He would kill me if he knew what I was, I can feel it. His hands curl into fists. I am alone here; if something happens to me, no one will know and no one will see it.

"If you cannot explain," he says softly, "I may be forced

to reconsider your rank. Or, because you seem to be so attached to your previous faction . . . perhaps I will be forced to reconsider your friends' ranks. Perhaps the little Abnegation girl inside of you would take that more seriously."

My first thought is that he couldn't do that, it wouldn't be fair. My second thought is that of course he would, he would not hesitate to do it for a second. And he is right—the thought that my reckless behavior could force someone else out of a faction makes my chest ache from fear.

I try again. "I . . ."

But it is hard to breathe.

And then the door opens. Tobias walks in.

"What are you doing?" he asks Eric.

"Leave the room," Eric says, his voice louder and not as monotone. He sounds more like the Eric I am familiar with. His expression, too, changes, becomes more mobile and animated. I stare, amazed that he can turn it on and off so easily, and wonder what the strategy behind it is.

"No," Tobias says. "She's just a foolish girl. There's no need to drag her here and interrogate her."

"Just a foolish girl." Eric snorts. "If she were just a foolish girl, she wouldn't be ranked first, now would she?"

Tobias pinches the bridge of his nose and looks at me through the spaces between his fingers. He is trying to tell me something. I think quickly. What advice has Four given me recently?

The only thing I can think of is: *pretend some vulnerability.* It's worked for me before.

"I . . . I was just embarrassed and didn't know what to do." I put my hands in my pockets and look at the ground. Then I pinch my leg so hard that tears well up in my eyes, and I look up at Eric, sniffing. "I tried to . . . and . . ." I shake my head.

"You tried to what?" asks Eric.

"Kiss me," says Tobias. "And I rejected her, and she went running off like a five-year-old. There's really nothing to blame her for but stupidity."

We both wait.

Eric looks from me to Tobias and laughs, too loudly and for too long—the sound is menacing and grates against me like sandpaper. "Isn't he a little too old for you, Tris?" he says, smiling again.

I wipe my cheek like I'm wiping a tear. "Can I go now?"

"Fine," Eric says, "but you are not allowed to leave the compound without supervision again, you hear me?" He turns toward Tobias. "And *you* . . . had better make sure none of the transfers leave this compound again. And that none of the others try to kiss you."

Tobias rolls his eyes. "Fine."

I leave the room and walk outside again, shaking my hands to get rid of the jitters. I sit down on the pavement and wrap my arms around my knees.

I don't know how long I sit there, my head down and my eyes closed, before the door opens again. It might have been twenty minutes and it might have been an hour. Tobias walks toward me.

I stand and cross my arms, waiting for the scolding to start. I slapped him and then got myself into trouble with the Dauntless—there has to be scolding.

"What?" I say.

"Are you all right?" A crease appears between his eyebrows, and he touches my cheek gently. I bat his hand away.

"Well," I say, "first I got reamed out in front of everyone, and then I had to chat with the woman who's trying to destroy my old faction, and then Eric almost tossed my friends out of Dauntless, so yeah, it's shaping up to be a pretty great day, *Four.*"

He shakes his head and looks at the dilapidated building to his right, which is made of brick and barely resembles the sleek glass spire behind me. It must be ancient. No one builds with brick anymore.

"Why do you care, anyway?" I say. "You can be either cruel instructor or concerned boyfriend." I tense up at the word "boyfriend." I didn't mean to use it so flippantly, but it's too late now. "You can't play both parts at the same time."

"I am not cruel." He scowls at me. "I was protecting you this morning. How do you think Peter and his idiot friends would have reacted if they discovered that you and I were . . ." He sighs. "You would never win. They would always call your ranking a result of my favoritism rather than your skill."

I open my mouth to object, but I can't. A few smart remarks come to mind, but I dismiss them. He's right. My cheeks warm, and I cool them with my hands.

"You didn't have to insult me to prove something to them," I say finally.

"And you didn't have to run off to your brother just because I hurt you," he says. He rubs at the back of his neck. "Besides—it worked, didn't it?"

"At my expense."

"I didn't think it would affect you this way." Then he looks down and shrugs. "Sometimes I forget that I can hurt you. That you are capable of being hurt."

I slide my hands into my pockets and rock back on my heels. A strange feeling goes through me—a sweet, aching weakness. He did what he did because he believed in my strength.

At home it was Caleb who was strong, because he could

forget himself, because all the characteristics my parents valued came naturally to him. No one has ever been so convinced of my strength.

I stand on my tiptoes, lift my head, and kiss him. Only our lips touch.

"You're brilliant, you know that?" I shake my head. "You always know exactly what to do."

"Only because I've been thinking about this for a long time," he says, kissing me briefly. "How I would handle it, if you and I . . ." He pulls back and smiles. "Did I hear you call me your boyfriend, Tris?"

"Not exactly." I shrug. "Why? Do you want me to?"

He slips his hands over my neck and presses his thumbs under my chin, tilting my head back so his forehead meets mine. For a moment he stands there, his eyes closed, breathing my air. I feel the pulse in his fingertips. I feel the quickness of his breath. He seems nervous.

"Yes," he finally says. Then his smile fades. "You think we convinced him you're just a silly girl?"

"I hope so," I say. "Sometimes it helps to be small. I'm not sure I convinced the Erudite, though."

The corners of his mouth tug down, and he gives me a grave look. "There's something I need to tell you."

"What is it?"

"Not now." He glances around. "Meet me back here at

eleven thirty. Don't tell anyone where you're going."

I nod, and he turns away, leaving just as quickly as he came.

+ + +

"Where have you *been* all day?" Christina asks when I walk back into the dormitory. The room is empty; everyone else must be at dinner. "I looked for you outside, but I couldn't find you. Is everything okay? Did you get in trouble for hitting Four?"

I shake my head. The thought of telling her the truth about where I was makes me feel exhausted. How can I explain the impulse to hop on a train and visit my brother? Or the eerie calm in Eric's voice as he questioned me? Or the reason that I exploded and hit Tobias to begin with?

"I just had to get away. I walked around for a long time," I say. "And no, I'm not in trouble. He yelled at me, I apologized . . . that's it."

As I speak, I'm careful to keep my eyes steady on hers and my hands still at my sides.

"Good," she says. "Because I have something to tell you."

She looks over my head at the door and then stands on her tiptoes to see all the bunks—checking if they're empty, probably. Then she sets her hands on my shoulders.

"Can you be a girl for a few seconds?"

"I'm always a girl." I frown.

"You know what I mean. Like a silly, annoying girl."

I twirl my hair around my finger. "'Kay."

She grins so wide I can see her back row of teeth. "Will kissed me."

"What?" I demand. "When? How? What happened?"

"You *can* be a girl!" She straightens, taking her hands from my shoulders. "Well, right after your little episode, we ate lunch and then we walked around near the train tracks. We were just talking about . . . I don't even remember what we were talking about. And then he just stopped, and leaned in, and . . . kissed me."

"Did you know that he liked you?" I say. "I mean, you know. Like that."

"No!" She laughs. "The best part was, that was it. We just kept walking and talking like nothing happened. Well, until *I* kissed *him*."

"How long have you known you liked him?"

"I don't know. I guess I didn't. But then little things . . . how he put his arm around me at the funeral, how he opens doors for me like I'm a girl instead of someone who could beat the crap out of him."

I laugh. Suddenly I want to tell her about Tobias and everything that has happened between us. But the same reasons Tobias gave for pretending we aren't together hold me back. I don't want her to think that my rank has anything to do with my relationship with him.

So I just say, "I'm happy for you."

"Thanks," she says. "I'm happy too. And I thought it would be a while before I could feel that way . . . you know."

She sits down on the edge of my bed and looks around the dormitory. Some of the initiates have already packed their things. Soon we'll move into apartments on the other side of the compound. Those with government jobs will move to the glass building above the Pit. I won't have to worry about Peter attacking me in my sleep. I won't have to look at Al's empty bed.

"I can't believe it's almost over," she says. "It's like we just got here. But it's also like . . . like I haven't seen home in forever."

"You miss it?" I lean into the bed frame.

"Yeah." She shrugs. "Some things are the same, though. I mean, everyone at home is just as loud as everyone here, so that's good. But it's easier there. You always know where you stand with everyone, because they tell you. There's no . . . manipulation."

I nod. Abnegation prepared me for that aspect of Dauntless life. The Abnegation aren't manipulative, but they aren't forthright, either.

"I don't think I could have made it through Candor initiation, though." She shakes her head. "There, instead of simulations, you get lie detector tests. All day, every day. And the final test . . ." She wrinkles her nose. "They give you this stuff they call truth serum and sit you in front of everyone and ask you a load of really personal questions. The theory is that if you spill all your secrets, you'll have no desire to lie about anything, ever again. Like the worst about you is already in the open, so why not just be honest?"

I don't know when I accumulated so many secrets. Being Divergent. Fears. How I really feel about my friends, my family, Al, Tobias. Candor initiation would reach things that even the simulations can't touch; it would wreck me.

"Sounds awful," I say.

"I always knew I couldn't be Candor. I mean, I try to be honest, but some things you just don't want people to know. Plus, I like to be in control of my own mind."

Don't we all.

"Anyway," she says. She opens the cabinet to the left of our bunk beds. When she pulls the door open, a moth flutters out, its white wings carrying it toward her face. Christina shrieks so loud I almost jump out of my skin and slaps at her cheeks.

"Get it off! Get it off get it off get it off!" she screams.

The moth flutters away.

"It's gone!" I say. Then I laugh. "You're afraid of . . . moths?"

"They're disgusting. Those papery wings and their stupid bug bodies . . ." She shudders.

I keep laughing. I laugh so hard I have to sit down and hold my stomach.

"It's not funny!" she snaps. "Well . . . okay, maybe it is. A little."

+ + +

When I find Tobias late that night, he doesn't say anything; he just grabs my hand and pulls me toward the train tracks.

He draws himself into a train car as it passes with bewildering ease and pulls me in after him. I fall against him, my cheek against his chest. His fingers slide down my arms, and he holds me by the elbows as the car bumps along the steel rails. I watch the glass building above the Dauntless compound shrink behind us.

"What is it you need to tell me?" I shout over the cry of the wind.

"Not yet," he says.

He sinks to the floor and pulls me down with him, so he's sitting with his back against the wall and I'm facing him, my legs trailing to the side on the dusty floor. The wind pushes strands of my hair loose and tosses them over my face. He presses his palms to my face, his index fingers sliding behind my ears, and pulls my mouth to his.

I hear the screech of the rails as the train slows, which means we must be nearing the middle of the city. The air is cold, but his lips are warm and so are his hands. He tilts his head and kisses the skin just beneath my jaw. I'm glad the air is so loud he can't hear me sigh.

The train car wobbles, throwing off my balance, and I put my hand down to steady myself. A split second later I realize that my hand is on his hip. The bone presses into my palm. I should move it, but I don't want to. He told me once to be brave, and though I have stood still while knives spun toward my face and jumped off a roof, I never thought I would need bravery in the small moments of my life. I do.

I shift, swinging a leg over him so I sit on top of him, and with my heartbeat in my throat, I kiss him. He sits up straighter and I feel his hands on my shoulders. His fingers slip down my spine and a shiver follows them down to the small of my back. He unzips my jacket a few inches, and I press my hands to my legs to stop them from shaking. I should not be nervous. This is Tobias.

Cold air slips across my bare skin. He pulls away and looks carefully at the tattoos just above my collarbone. His fingers brush over them, and he smiles.

"Birds," he says. "Are they crows? I keep forgetting to ask."

I try to return his smile. "Ravens. One for each member of my family," I say. "You like them?"

He doesn't answer. He tugs me closer, pressing his lips to each bird in turn. I close my eyes. His touch is light, sensitive. A heavy, warm feeling, like spilling honey, fills my body, slowing my thoughts. He touches my cheek.

"I hate to say this," he says, "but we have to get up now."

I nod and open my eyes. We both stand, and he tugs me with him to the open door of the train car. The wind is not as strong now that the train has slowed. It's past midnight, so all the street lights are dark, and the buildings look like mammoths as they rise from the darkness and then sink into it again. Tobias lifts a hand and points at a cluster of buildings, so far away they are the size of a fingernail. They are the only bright spot in the dark sea around us. Erudite headquarters again.

"Apparently the city ordinances don't mean anything to them," he says, "because their lights will be on all night."

"No one else has noticed?" I say, frowning.

"I'm sure they have, but they haven't done anything to stop it. It may be because they don't want to cause a problem over something so small." Tobias shrugs, but the tension in his features worries me. "But it made me wonder what the Erudite are doing that requires night light."

He turns toward me, leaning against the wall.

"Two things you should know about me. The first is that I am deeply suspicious of people in general," he says. "It is my nature to expect the worst of them. And the second is that I am unexpectedly good with computers."

I nod. He said his other job was working with computers, but I still have trouble picturing him sitting in front of a screen all day.

"A few weeks ago, before training started, I was at work and I found a way into the Dauntless secure files. Apparently we are not as skilled as the Erudite are at security," he says, "and what I discovered was what looked like war plans. Thinly veiled commands, supply lists, maps. Things like that. And those files were sent by Erudite."

"War?" I brush my hair away from my face. Listening to my father insult Erudite all my life has made me wary of them, and my experiences in the Dauntless compound make me wary of authority and human beings in general, so I'm not shocked to hear that a faction could be planning a war.

And what Caleb said earlier. *Something big is happening, Beatrice.* I look up at Tobias.

"War on Abnegation?"

He takes my hands, lacing his fingers with mine, and says, "The faction that controls the government. Yes."

My stomach sinks.

"All those reports are supposed to stir up dissension against Abnegation," he says, his eyes focused on the city beyond the train car. "Evidently the Erudite now want to speed up the process. I have no idea what to do about it . . . or what could even be done."

"But," I say, "why would Erudite team up with Dauntless?"

And then something occurs to me, something that hits me in the gut and gnaws at my insides. Erudite doesn't have weapons, and they don't know how to fight—but the Dauntless do.

I stare wide-eyed at Tobias.

"They're going to use us," I say.

"I wonder," he says, "how they plan to get us to fight."

I told Caleb that the Erudite know how to manipulate people. They could coerce some of us into fighting with misinformation, or by appealing to greed—any number of ways. But the Erudite are as meticulous as they are manipulative, so they wouldn't leave it up to chance. They would need to make sure that all their weaknesses are shored up. But how?

The wind blows my hair across my face, cutting my vision into strips, and I leave it there.

"I don't know," I say.

CHAPTER
TWENTY-NINE

I HAVE ATTENDED Abnegation's initiation ceremony every year except this one. It is a quiet affair. The initiates, who spend thirty days performing community service before they can become full members, sit side by side on a bench. One of the older members reads the Abnegation manifesto, which is a short paragraph about forgetting the self and the dangers of self-involvement. Then all the older members wash the initiates' feet. Then they all share a meal, each person serving food to the person on his left.

The Dauntless don't do that.

Initiation day plunges the Dauntless compound into insanity and chaos. There are people everywhere, and most of them are inebriated by noon. I fight my way through them to get a plate of food at lunch and carry it back to the dormitory with me. On the way I see someone fall off the path on the Pit wall and, judging by his screams and the way he grabs at his leg, he broke something.

The dormitory, at least, is quiet. I stare at my plate of food. I just grabbed what looked good to me at the time, and now that I take a closer look, I realize that I chose a plain chicken breast, a scoop of peas, and a piece of brown bread. Abnegation food.

I sigh. Abnegation is what I am. It is what I am when I'm not thinking about what I'm doing. It is what I am when I am put to the test. It is what I am even when I appear to be brave. Am I in the wrong faction?

The thought of my former faction sends a tremor through my hands. I have to warn my family about the war the Erudite are planning, but I don't know how. I will find a way, but not today. Today I have to focus on what awaits me. One thing at a time.

I eat like a robot, rotating from chicken to peas to bread and back again. It doesn't matter what faction I really belong in. In two hours I will walk to the fear landscape room with the other initiates, go through my fear landscape, and become Dauntless. It's too late to turn back.

When I finish, I bury my face in my pillow. I don't mean to fall asleep, but after a while, I do, and I wake up to Christina shaking my shoulder.

"Time to go," she says. She looks ashen.

I rub my eyes to press the sleep from them. I have my

shoes on already. The other initiates are in the dormitory, tying shoelaces and buttoning jackets and throwing smiles around like they don't mean it. I pull my hair into a bun and put on my black jacket, zipping it up to my throat. The torture will be over soon, but can we forget the simulations? Will we ever sleep soundly again, with the memories of our fears in our heads? Or will we finally forget our fears today, like we're supposed to?

We walk to the Pit and up the path that leads to the glass building. I look up at the glass ceiling. I can't see daylight because the soles of shoes cover every inch of glass above us. For a second I think I hear the glass creak, but it is my imagination. I walk up the stairs with Christina, and the crowd chokes me.

I am too short to see above anyone's head, so I stare at Will's back and walk in his wake. The heat of so many bodies around me makes it difficult to breathe. Beads of sweat gather on my forehead. A break in the crowd reveals what they are all clustered around: a series of screens on the wall to my left.

I hear a cheer and stop to look at the screens. The screen on the left shows a black-clothed girl in the fear landscape room—Marlene. I watch her move, her eyes wide, but I can't tell what obstacle she's facing. Thank God no one out here will see my fears either—just my reactions to them.

The middle screen shows her heart rate. It picks up for

a second and then decreases. When it reaches a normal rate, the screen flashes green and the Dauntless cheer. The screen on the right shows her time.

I tear my eyes from the screen and jog to catch up to Christina and Will. Tobias stands just inside a door on the left side of the room that I barely noticed the last time I was here. It is next to the fear landscape room. I walk past him without looking at him.

The room is large and contains another screen, similar to the one outside. A line of people sit in chairs in front of it. Eric is one of them, and so is Max. The others are also older. Judging by the wires connected to their heads, and their blank eyes, they are observing the simulation.

Behind them is another line of chairs, all occupied now. I am the last to enter, so I don't get one.

"Hey, Tris!" Uriah calls out from across the room. He sits with the other Dauntless-born initiates. Only four of them are left; the rest have gone through their fear landscapes already. He pats his leg. "You can sit on my lap, if you want."

"Tempting," I call back, grinning. "It's fine. I like to stand."

I also don't want Tobias to see me sitting on someone else's lap.

The lights lift in the fear landscape room, revealing Marlene in a crouch, her face streaked with tears. Max,

Eric, and a few others shake off the simulation daze and walk out. A few seconds later I see them on the screen, congratulating her for finishing.

"Transfers, the order in which you go through the final test was taken from your rankings as they now stand," Tobias says. "So Drew will go first, and Tris will go last."

That means five people will go before I do.

I stand in the back of the room, a few feet away from Tobias. He and I exchange glances when Eric sticks Drew with the needle and sends him into the fear landscape room. By the time it's my turn, I will know how well the others did, and how well I will have to do to beat them.

The fear landscapes are not interesting to watch from the outside. I can see that Drew is moving, but I don't know what he is reacting to. After a few minutes, I close my eyes instead of watching and try to think of nothing. Speculating about which fears I will have to face, and how many there will be, is useless at this point. I just have to remember that I have the power to manipulate the simulations, and that I have practiced it before.

Molly goes next. It takes her half as long as it takes Drew, but even Molly has trouble. She spends too much time breathing heavily, trying to control her panic. At one point she even screams at the top of her lungs.

It amazes me how easy it is to tune out everything

else—thoughts of war on Abnegation, Tobias, Caleb, my parents, my friends, my new faction fade away. All I can do now is get past this obstacle.

Christina is next. Then Will. Then Peter. I don't watch them. I know only how much time it takes them: twelve minutes, ten minutes, fifteen minutes. And then my name.

"Tris."

I open my eyes and walk to the front of the observation room, where Eric stands with a syringe full of orange liquid. I barely feel the needle as it plunges into my neck, barely see Eric's pierced face as he presses the plunger down. I imagine that the serum is liquid adrenaline rushing through my veins, making me strong.

"Ready?" he asks.

CHAPTER
THIRTY

I AM READY. I step into the room, armed not with a gun or a knife, but with the plan I made the night before. Tobias said that stage three is about mental preparation—coming up with strategies to overcome my fears.

I wish I knew what order the fears will come in. I bounce on the balls of my feet as I wait for the first fear to appear. I am already short of breath.

The ground beneath me changes. Grass rises from the concrete and sways in a wind I cannot feel. A green sky replaces the exposed pipes above me. I listen for the birds and feel my fear as a distant thing, a hammering heart and a squeezed chest, but not something that exists in my mind. Tobias told me to figure out what this simulation means. He was right; it isn't about the birds. It's about control.

Wings flap next to my ear, and the crow's talons dig into my shoulder.

This time, I do not hit the bird as hard as I can. I crouch, listening to the thunder of wings behind me, and run my hand through the grass, just above the ground. What combats powerlessness? Power. And the first time I felt powerful in the Dauntless compound was when I was holding a gun.

A lump forms in my throat and I want the talons *off*. The bird squawks and my stomach clenches, but then I feel something hard and metal in the grass. My gun.

I point the gun at the bird on my shoulder, and it detaches from my shirt in an explosion of blood and feathers. I spin on my heel, aiming the gun at the sky, and see the cloud of dark feathers descending. I squeeze the trigger, firing again and again into the sea of birds above me, watching their dark bodies drop to the grass.

As I aim and shoot, I feel the same rush of power I felt the first time I held a gun. My heart stops racing and the field, gun, and birds fade away. I stand in the dark again.

I shift my weight, and something squeaks beneath my foot. I crouch down and slide my hand along a cold, smooth panel—glass. I press my hands to glass on either side of my body. The tank again. I am not afraid of drowning. This is not about the water; it is about my inability to escape the tank. It is about weakness. I just have to convince myself that I am strong enough to break the glass.

The blue lights come on, and water slips over the floor, but I don't let the simulation get that far. I slam my palm against the wall in front of me, expecting the pane to break.

My hand bounces off, causing no damage.

My heartbeat speeds up. What if what worked in the first simulation doesn't work here? What if I can't break the glass unless I'm under duress? The water laps over my ankles, flowing faster by the second. I have to calm down. Calm down and focus. I lean against the wall behind me and kick as hard as I can. And again. My toes throb, but nothing happens.

I have another option. I can wait for water to fill the tank—and it's already at my knees—and try to calm down as I drown. I brace myself against the wall, shaking my head. No. I can't let myself drown. I can't.

I ball my hands up into fists and pound on the wall. I am stronger than the glass. The glass is as thin as newly frozen ice. My mind will make it so. I close my eyes. The glass is ice. The glass is ice. The glass is—

The glass shatters under my hand, and water spills onto the floor. And then the dark returns.

I shake out my hands. That should have been an easy

obstacle to overcome. I've faced it before in simulations. I can't afford to lose time like that again.

What feels like a solid wall hits me from the side, forcing the air from my lungs, and I fall hard, gasping. I can't swim; I've only seen bodies of water this large, this powerful, in pictures. Beneath me is a rock with a jagged edge, slick with water. The water pulls at my legs, and I cling to the rock, tasting salt on my lips. Out of the corner of my eye, I see a dark sky and a blood-red moon.

Another wave hits, slamming against my back. I hit my chin against the stone and wince. The sea is cold, but my blood is hot, running down my neck. I stretch my arm and find the edge of the rock. The water pulls at my legs with irresistible force. I cling as hard as I can, but I am not strong enough—the water pulls me and the wave throws my body back. It flings my legs over my head and my arms to each side, and I collide with the stone, my back pressed against it, water gushing over my face. My lungs scream for air. I twist and grab the edge of the rock, pulling myself above the water. I gasp, and another wave hits me, this one harder than the first, but I have a better hold.

I must not really be afraid of the water. I must be afraid of being out of control. To face it, I have to regain control.

With a scream of frustration, I throw my hand forward

and find a hole in the rock. My arms shake violently as I drag myself forward, and I pull my feet up under me before the wave can take me with it. Once my feet are free, I get up and throw my body into a run, into a sprint, my feet quick on the stone, the red moon in front of me, the ocean gone.

Then everything is gone, and my body is still. Too still.

I try to move my arms, but they are bound tightly to my sides. I look down and see rope wrapped around my chest, my arms, my legs. A stack of logs rises around my feet, and I see a pole behind me. I am high above the ground.

People creep out of the shadows, and their faces are familiar. They are the initiates, carrying torches, and Peter is at the front of the pack. His eyes look like black pits, and he wears a smirk that spreads too wide across his face, forcing wrinkles into his cheeks. A laugh starts somewhere in the center of the crowd and rises as voice after voice joins it. Cackling is all I hear.

As the cackling grows louder, Peter lowers his torch to the wood, and flames leap up near the ground. They flicker at the edges of each log and then creep over the bark. I don't struggle against the ropes, as I did the first time I faced this fear. Instead I close my eyes and gulp as much air as I can. This is a simulation. It can't hurt me. The heat from the flames rises around me. I shake my head.

"Smell that, Stiff?" Peter says, his voice louder than even the cackling.

"No," I say. The flames are getting higher.

He sniffs. "That's the smell of your burning flesh."

When I open my eyes, my vision is blurry with tears.

"Know what I smell?" My voice strains to be louder than the laughter all around me, the laughter that oppresses me as much as the heat. My arms twitch, and I want to fight against the ropes, but I won't, I won't struggle pointlessly, I won't panic.

I stare through the flames at Peter, the heat bringing blood to the surface of my skin, flowing through me, melting the toes of my shoes.

"I smell rain," I say.

Thunder roars above my head, and I scream as a flame touches my fingertips and pain shrieks over my skin. I tilt my head back and focus on the clouds gathering above my head, heavy with rain, dark with rain. A line of lightning sprawls over the sky and I feel the first drop on my forehead. *Faster, faster!* The drop rolls down the side of my nose, and the second drop hits my shoulder, so big it feels like it's made of ice or rock instead of water.

Sheets of rain fall around me, and I hear sizzling over the laughter. I smile, relieved, as the rain puts out the fire and soothes the burns on my hands. The ropes fall away, and I push my hands through my hair.

I wish I was like Tobias and had only four fears to face, but I am not that fearless.

I smooth my shirt down, and when I look up, I stand in my bedroom in the Abnegation sector of the city. I have never faced this fear before. The lights are off, but the room is lit by the moonlight coming through the windows. One of my walls is covered with mirrors. I turn toward it, confused. That isn't right. I am not allowed to have mirrors.

I look at the reflection in the mirror: my wide eyes, the bed with the gray sheets pulled taut, the dresser that holds my clothes, the bookcase, the bare walls. My eyes skip to the window behind me.

And to the man standing just outside.

Cold drops down my spine like a bead of sweat, and my body goes rigid. I recognize him. He is the man with the scarred face from the aptitude test. He wears black and he stands still as a statue. I blink, and two men appear at his left and right, just as still as he is, but their faces are featureless—skin-covered skulls.

I whip my body around, and they stand in my room. I press my shoulders to the mirror.

For a moment, the room is silent, and then fists pound against my window, not just two or four or six, but dozens of fists with dozens of fingers, slamming into the glass. The noise vibrates in my rib cage, it is so loud, and then the scarred man and his two companions begin to walk with slow, careful movements toward me.

They are here to take me, like Peter and Drew and Al; to kill me. I know it.

Simulation. This is a simulation. My heart hammering in my chest, I press my palm to the glass behind me and slide it to the left. It is not a mirror but a closet door. I tell myself where the weapon will be. It will be hanging against the right wall, just inches away from my hand. I don't shift my eyes from the scarred man, but I find the gun with my fingertips and wrap my hand around the handle.

I bite my lip and fire at the scarred man. I don't wait to see if the bullet hits him—I aim at each featureless man in turn, as fast as I can. My lip aches from biting it so hard. The pounding on the window stops, but a screeching sound replaces it, and the fists turn into hands with bent fingers, scratching at the glass, fighting to get in. The glass creaks under the pressure of their hands, and then cracks, and then shatters.

I scream.

I don't have enough bullets in my gun.

Pale bodies—human bodies, but mangled, arms bent

at odd angles, too-wide mouths with needle teeth, empty eye sockets—topple into my bedroom, one after the other, and scramble to their feet, scramble toward me. I pull back into the closet and shut the door in front of me. A solution. I need a solution. I sink into a crouch and press the side of the gun to my head. I can't fight them off. I can't fight them off, so I have to calm down. The fear landscape will register my slowing heartbeat and my even breath and it will move on to the next obstacle.

I sit down on the floor of the closet. The wall behind me creaks. I hear pounding—the fists are at it again, hitting the closet door—but I turn and peer through the dark at the panel behind me. It is not a wall but another door. I fumble to push it aside and reveal the upstairs hallway. Smiling, I crawl through the hole and stand. I smell something baking. I am at home.

Taking a deep breath, I watch my house fade. I forgot, for a second, that I was in Dauntless headquarters.

And then Tobias is standing in front of me.

But I'm not afraid of Tobias. I look over my shoulder. Maybe there's something behind me that I'm supposed to focus on. But no—behind me is just a four-poster bed.

A bed?

Tobias walks toward me, slowly.

What's going on?

I stare up at him, paralyzed. He smiles down at me. That smile looks kind. Familiar.

He presses his mouth to mine, and my lips part. I thought it would be impossible to forget I was in a simulation. I was wrong; he makes everything else disintegrate.

His fingers find my jacket zipper and pull it down in one slow swipe until the zipper detaches. He tugs the jacket from my shoulders.

Oh, is all I can think, as he kisses me again. *Oh.*

My fear is being with him. I have been wary of affection all my life, but I didn't know how deep that wariness went.

But this obstacle doesn't feel the same as the others. It is a different kind of fear—nervous panic rather than blind terror.

He slides his hands down my arms and then squeezes my hips, his fingers sliding over the skin just above my belt, and I shiver.

I gently push him back and press my hands to my forehead. I have been attacked by crows and men with grotesque faces; I have been set on fire by the boy who almost threw me off a ledge; I have almost drowned—*twice*—and *this* is what I can't cope with? *This* is the fear I have no solutions for—a boy I like, who wants to . . . have sex with me?

Simulation Tobias kisses my neck.

I try to think. I have to face the fear. I have to take control of the situation and find a way to make it less frightening.

I look Simulation Tobias in the eye and say sternly, "I am *not* going to sleep with you in a hallucination. Okay?"

Then I grab him by his shoulders and turn us around, pushing him against the bedpost. I feel something other than fear—a prickle in my stomach, a bubble of laughter. I press against him and kiss him, my hands wrapping around his arms. He feels strong. He feels . . . good.

And he's gone.

I laugh into my hand until my face gets hot. I must be the only initiate with this fear.

A trigger clicks in my ear.

I almost forgot about this one. I feel the heft of a gun in my hand and curl my fingers around it, slipping my index finger over the trigger. A spotlight shines from the ceiling, its source unknown, and standing in the center of its circle of light are my mother, my father, and my brother.

"Do it," hisses a voice next to me. It is female, but harsh, like it's cluttered with rocks and broken glass. It sounds like Jeanine.

The barrel of a gun presses to my temple, a cold circle against my skin. The cold travels across my body, making the hair on the back of my neck stand on end. I wipe my sweaty palm on my pants and look at the woman through the corner of my eye. It is Jeanine. Her glasses are askew, and her eyes are empty of feeling.

My worst fear: that my family will die, and that I will be responsible.

"Do it," she says again, more insistent this time. "Do it or I'll kill you."

I stare at Caleb. He nods, his eyebrows tugged in, sympathetic. "Go ahead, Tris," he says softly. "I understand. It's okay."

My eyes burn. "No," I say, my throat so tight it aches. I shake my head.

"I'll give you ten seconds!" the woman shouts. "Ten! Nine!"

My eyes skip from my brother to my father. The last time I saw him, he gave me a look of contempt, but now his eyes are wide and soft. I have never seen him wear that expression in real life.

"Tris," he says. "You have no other option."

"Eight!"

"Tris," my mother says. She smiles. She has a sweet smile. "We love you."

"Seven!"

"Shut up!" I shout, holding up the gun. I can do it. I can shoot them. They understand. They're asking me to. They wouldn't want me to sacrifice myself for them. They aren't even real. This is all a simulation.

"Six!"

It isn't real. It doesn't mean anything. My brother's kind eyes feel like two drills boring a hole in my head. My sweat makes the gun slippery.

"Five!"

I have no other option. I close my eyes. Think. I have to think. The urgency making my heart race depends on one thing, and one thing only: the threat to my life.

"Four! Three!"

What did Tobias tell me? *Selflessness and bravery aren't that different.*

"Two!"

I release the trigger of my gun and drop it. Before I can lose my nerve, I turn and press my forehead to the barrel of the gun behind me.

Shoot me instead.

"One!"

I hear a click, and a bang.

CHAPTER
THIRTY-ONE

THE LIGHTS COME on. I stand alone in the empty room with the concrete walls, shaking. I sink to my knees, wrapping my arms around my chest. It wasn't cold when I walked in, but it feels cold now. I rub my arms to get rid of the goose bumps.

I have never felt relief like this before. Every muscle in my body relaxes at once and I breathe freely again. I can't imagine going through my fear landscape in my spare time, like Tobias does. It seemed like bravery to me before, but now it seems more like masochism.

The door opens, and I stand. Max, Eric, Tobias, and a few people I don't know walk into the room in a line, standing in a small crowd in front of me. Tobias smiles at me.

"Congratulations, Tris," says Eric. "You have successfully completed your final evaluation."

I try to smile. It doesn't work. I can't shake the memory of the gun against my head. I can still feel the barrel between my eyebrows.

"Thanks," I say.

"There is one more thing before you can go and get ready for the welcoming banquet," he says. He beckons to one of the unfamiliar people behind him. A woman with blue hair hands him a small black case. He opens it and takes out a syringe and a long needle.

I tense up at the sight of it. The orange-brown liquid in the syringe reminds me of what they inject us with before simulations. And I am supposed to be finished with those.

"At least you aren't afraid of needles," he says. "This will inject you with a tracking device that will be activated only if you are reported missing. Just a precaution."

"How often do people go missing?" I ask, frowning.

"Not often." Eric smirks. "This is a new development, courtesy of the Erudite. We have been injecting every Dauntless throughout the day, and I assume all other factions will comply as soon as possible."

My stomach twists. I can't let him inject me with anything, especially not anything developed by Erudite—maybe even by Jeanine. But I also can't refuse. I can't refuse or he will doubt my loyalty again.

"All right," I say, my throat tight.

Eric approaches me with the needle and syringe in

hand. I pull my hair away from my neck and tilt my head to the side. I look away as Eric wipes my neck with an antiseptic wipe and eases the needle into my skin. The deep ache spreads through my neck, painful but brief. He puts the needle back in its case and sticks an adhesive bandage on the injection site.

"The banquet is in two hours," he says. "Your ranking among the other initiates, Dauntless-born included, will be announced then. Good luck."

The small crowd files out of the room, but Tobias lingers. He pauses by the door and beckons for me to follow him, so I do. The glass room above the Pit is full of Dauntless, some of them walking the ropes above our heads, some talking and laughing in groups. He smiles at me. He must not have been watching.

"I heard a rumor that you only had seven obstacles to face," he says. "Practically unheard of."

"You . . . you weren't watching the simulation?"

"Only on the screens. The Dauntless leaders are the only ones who see the whole thing," he says. "They seemed impressed."

"Well, seven fears isn't as impressive as four," I reply, "but it will suffice."

"I would be surprised if you weren't ranked first," he says.

We walk into the glass room. The crowd is still there,

but it is thinner now that the last person—me—has gone.

People notice me after a few seconds. I stay close to Tobias's side as they point, but I can't walk fast enough to avoid some cheers, some claps on the shoulder, some congratulations. As I look at the people around me, I realize how strange they would look to my father and brother, and how normal they seem to me, despite all the metal rings in their faces and the tattoos on their arms and throats and chests. I smile back at them.

We descend the steps into the Pit and I say, "I have a question." I bite my lip. "How much did they tell you about my fear landscape?"

"Nothing, really. Why?" he says.

"No reason." I kick a pebble to the side of the path.

"Do you have to go back to the dormitory?" he asks. "Because if you want peace and quiet, you can stay with me until the banquet."

My stomach twists.

"What is it?" he asks.

I don't want to go back to the dormitory, and I don't want to be afraid of him.

"Let's go," I say.

+ + +

He closes the door behind us and slips off his shoes.

"Want some water?" he says.

"No thanks." I hold my hands in front of me.

"You okay?" he says, touching my cheek. His hand cradles the side of my head, his long fingers slipping through my hair. He smiles and holds my head in place as he kisses me. Heat spreads through me slowly. And fear, buzzing like an alarm in my chest.

His lips still on mine, he pushes the jacket from my shoulders. I flinch when I hear it drop, and push him back, my eyes burning. I don't know why I feel this way. I didn't feel like this when he kissed me on the train. I press my palms to my face, covering my eyes.

"What? What's wrong?"

I shake my head.

"Don't tell me it's nothing." His voice is cold. He grabs my arm. "Hey. Look at me."

I take my hands from my face and lift my eyes to his. The hurt in his eyes and the anger in his clenched jaw surprise me.

"Sometimes I wonder," I say, as calmly as I can, "what's in it for you. This . . . whatever it is."

"What's in it for me," he repeats. He steps back, shaking his head. "You're an idiot, Tris."

"I am *not* an idiot," I say. "Which is why I know that it's a little weird that, of all the girls you could have chosen, you chose me. So if you're just looking for . . . um, you know . . . *that* . . ."

"What? Sex?" He scowls at me. "You know, if that was all I wanted, you probably wouldn't be the first person I would go to."

I feel like he just punched me in the stomach. Of course I'm not the first person he would go to—not the first, not the prettiest, not desirable. I press my hands to my abdomen and look away, fighting off tears. I am not the crying type. Nor am I the yelling type. I blink a few times, lower my hands, and stare up at him.

"I'm going to leave now," I say quietly. And I turn toward the door.

"No, Tris." He grabs my wrist and wrenches me back. I push him away, hard, but he grabs my other wrist, holding our crossed arms between us.

"I'm sorry I said that," he says. "What I *meant* was that you aren't like that. Which I knew when I met you."

"You were an obstacle in my fear landscape." My lower lip wobbles. "Did you know that?"

"What?" He releases my wrists, and the hurt look is back. "You're *afraid* of me?"

"Not you," I say. I bite my lip to keep it still. "Being with you . . . with anyone. I've never been involved with someone before, and . . . you're older, and I don't know what your expectations are, and . . ."

"Tris," he says sternly, "I don't know what delusion you're operating under, but this is all new to me, too."

"Delusion?" I repeat. "You mean you haven't . . ." I raise my eyebrows. "Oh. *Oh*. I just assumed . . ." That because I am so absorbed by him, everyone else must be too. "Um. You know."

"Well, you assumed wrong." He looks away. His cheeks are bright, like he's embarrassed. "You can tell me anything, you know," he says. He takes my face in his hands, his fingertips cold and his palms warm. "I am kinder than I seemed in training. I promise."

I believe him. But this has nothing to do with his kindness.

He kisses me between the eyebrows, and on the tip of my nose, and then carefully fits his mouth to mine. I am on edge. I have electricity coursing through my veins instead of blood. I want him to kiss me, I want him to; I am afraid of where it might go.

His hands shift to my shoulders, and his fingers brush over the edge of my bandage. He pulls back with a puckered brow.

"Are you hurt?" he asks.

"No. It's another tattoo. It's healed, I just . . . wanted to keep it covered up."

"Can I see?"

I nod, my throat tight. I pull my sleeve down and slip my shoulder out of it. He stares down at my shoulder for a second, and then runs his fingers over it. They rise and fall with my bones, which stick out farther than I'd like. When he touches me, I feel like everywhere his skin meets mine is changed by the connection. It sends a thrill through my stomach. Not just fear. Something else, too. A wanting.

He peels the corner of the bandage away. His eyes roam over the symbol of Abnegation, and he smiles.

"I have the same one," he says, laughing. "On my back."

"Really? Can I see it?"

He presses the bandage over the tattoo and pulls my shirt back over my shoulder.

"Are you asking me to undress, Tris?"

A nervous laugh gurgles from my throat. "Only . . . partially."

He nods, his smile suddenly fading. He lifts his eyes to mine and unzips his sweatshirt. It slides from his shoulders, and he tosses it onto the desk chair. I don't feel like laughing now. All I can do is stare at him.

His eyebrows pull to the center of his forehead, and he grabs the hem of his T-shirt. In one swift motion, he pulls it over his head.

A patch of Dauntless flames covers his right side, but other than that, his chest is unmarked. He averts his eyes.

"What is it?" I ask, frowning. He looks . . . uncomfortable.

"I don't invite many people to look at me," he says. "Any people, actually."

"I can't imagine why," I say softly. "I mean, look at you."

I walk slowly around him. On his back is more ink than skin. The symbols of each faction are drawn there—Dauntless at the top of his spine, Abnegation just below it, and the other three, smaller, beneath them. For a few seconds I look at the scales that represent Candor, the eye that stands for Erudite, and the tree that symbolizes Amity. It makes sense that he would tattoo himself with the symbol of Dauntless, his refuge, and even the symbol of Abnegation, his place of origin, like I did. But the other three?

"I think we've made a mistake," he says softly. "We've all started to put down the virtues of the other factions in the process of bolstering our own. I don't want to do that. I want to be brave, and selfless, *and* smart, *and* kind, *and* honest." He clears his throat. "I continually struggle with kindness."

"No one's perfect," I whisper. "It doesn't work that way. One bad thing goes away, and another bad thing replaces it."

I traded cowardice for cruelty; I traded weakness for ferocity.

I brush over Abnegation's symbol with my fingertips.

"We have to warn them, you know. Soon."

"I know," he says. "We will."

He turns toward me. I want to touch him, but I'm afraid of his bareness; afraid that he will make me bare too.

"Is this scaring you, Tris?"

"No," I croak. I clear my throat. "Not really. I'm only . . . afraid of what I want."

"What do you want?" Then his face tightens. "Me?"

Slowly I nod.

He nods too, and takes my hands in his gently. He guides my palms to his stomach. His eyes lowered, he pushes my hands up, over his abdomen and over his chest, and holds them against his neck. My palms tingle with the feel of his skin, smooth, warm. My face is hot, but I shiver anyway. He looks at me.

"Someday," he says, "if you still want me, we can . . ." He pauses, clears his throat. "We can . . ."

I smile a little and wrap my arms around him before he finishes, pressing the side of my face to his chest. I feel his heartbeat against my cheek, as fast as my own.

"Are you afraid of me, too, Tobias?"

"Terrified," he replies with a smile.

I turn my head and kiss the hollow beneath his throat.

"Maybe you won't be in my fear landscape anymore," I murmur.

He bends his head and kisses me slowly.

"Then everyone can call you Six."

"Four and Six," I say.

We kiss again, and this time, it feels familiar. I know exactly how we fit together, his arm around my waist, my hands on his chest, the pressure of his lips on mine. We have each other memorized.

CHAPTER
THIRTY-TWO

I watch Tobias's face carefully as we walk to the dining hall, searching for any sign of disappointment. We spent the two hours lying on his bed, talking and kissing and eventually dozing until we heard shouts in the hallway—people on their way to the banquet.

If anything, he seems lighter now than he was before. He smiles more, anyway.

When we reach the entrance, we separate. I go in first, and run to the table I share with Will and Christina. He enters second, a minute later, and sits down next to Zeke, who hands him a dark bottle. He waves it away.

"Where did you go?" asks Christina. "Everyone else went back to the dormitory."

"I just wandered around," I say. "I was too nervous to

talk to everyone else about it."

"You have no reason to be nervous," Christina says, shaking her head. "I turned around to talk to Will for one second, and you were already done."

I detect a note of jealousy in her voice, and again, I wish I could explain that I was well prepared for the simulation, because of what I am. Instead I just shrug.

"What job are you going to pick?" I ask her.

"I'm thinking I might want a job like Four's. Training initiates," she says. "Scaring the living daylights out of them. You know, fun stuff. What about you?"

I was so focused on getting through initiation that I barely thought about it. I could work for the Dauntless leaders—but they would kill me if they discover what I am. What else is there?

"I guess . . . I could be an ambassador to the other factions," I say. "I think being a transfer would help me."

"I was so hoping you would say Dauntless-leader-in-training," sighs Christina. "Because that's what Peter wants. He couldn't shut up about it in the dorm earlier."

"And it's what I want," adds Will. "Hopefully I ranked higher than him . . . oh, and all the Dauntless-born initiates. Forgot about them." He groans. "Oh God. This is going to be impossible."

"No, it isn't," she says. Christina reaches for his hand

and laces her fingers with his, like it's the most natural thing in the world. Will squeezes her hand.

"Question," says Christina, leaning forward. "The leaders who were watching your fear landscape . . . they were laughing about something."

"Oh?" I bite my lip hard. "I'm glad my terror amuses them."

"Any idea which obstacle it was?" she asks.

"No."

"You're *lying*," she says. "You always bite the inside of your cheek when you lie. It's your tell."

I stop biting the inside of my cheek.

"Will's is pinching his lips together, if it makes you feel better," she adds.

Will covers his mouth immediately.

"Okay, fine. I was afraid of . . . intimacy," I say.

"Intimacy," repeats Christina. "Like . . . sex?"

I tense up. And force myself to nod. Even if it was just Christina, and no one else was around, I would still want to strangle her right now. I go over a few ways to inflict maximum injury with minimum force in my head. I try to throw flames from my eyes.

Will laughs.

"What was *that* like?" she says. "I mean, did someone just . . . try to do it with you? Who was it?"

"Oh, you know. Faceless . . . unidentifiable male," I say. "How were your moths?"

"You promised you would never tell!" cries Christina, smacking my arm.

"Moths," repeats Will. "You're afraid of moths?"

"Not just a cloud of moths," she says, "like . . . a *swarm* of them. Everywhere. All those wings and legs and . . ." She shudders and shakes her head.

"Terrifying," Will says with mock seriousness. "That's my girl. Tough as cotton balls."

"Oh, shut up."

A microphone squeals somewhere, so loud I clap my hands over my ears. I look across the room at Eric, who stands on one of the tables with the microphone in hand, tapping it with his fingertips. After the tapping is done and the crowd of Dauntless is quiet, Eric clears his throat and begins.

"We aren't big on speeches here. Eloquence is for Erudite," he says. The crowd laughs. I wonder if they know that he was an Erudite once; that under all the pretense of Dauntless recklessness and even brutality, he is more like an Erudite than anything else. If they did, I doubt they would laugh at him. "So I'm going to keep this short. It's a new year, and we have a new pack of initiates. And a slightly smaller pack of new members.

We offer them our congratulations."

At the word "congratulations" the room erupts, not into applause, but into the pounding of fists on tabletops. The noise vibrates in my chest, and I grin.

"We believe in bravery. We believe in taking action. We believe in freedom from fear and in acquiring the skills to force the bad out of our world so that the good can prosper and thrive. If you also believe in those things, we welcome you."

Even though I know Eric probably doesn't believe in any of those things, I find myself smiling, because I believe in them. No matter how badly the leaders have warped the Dauntless ideals, those ideals can still belong to me.

More pounding fists, this time accompanied by whoops.

"Tomorrow, in their first act as members, our top ten initiates will choose their professions, in the order of how they are ranked," Eric says. "The rankings, I know, are what everyone is really waiting for. They are determined by a combination of three scores—the first, from the combat stage of training; the second, from the simulation stage; and the third, from the final examination, the fear landscape. The rankings will appear on the screen behind me."

As soon as the word "me" leaves his mouth, the names appear on the screen, which is almost as large as the wall itself. Next to the number one is my picture, and the name "Tris."

A weight in my chest lifts. I didn't realize it was there until it was gone, and I didn't have to feel it anymore. I smile, and a tingling spreads through me. First. Divergent or not, this faction is where I belong.

I forget about war; I forget about death. Will's arms wrap around me and he gives me a bear hug. I hear cheering and laughing and shouting. Christina points at the screen, her eyes wide and filled with tears.

1. Tris
2. Uriah
3. Lynn
4. Marlene
5. Peter

Peter stays. I suppress a sigh. But then I read the rest of the names.

6. Will
7. Christina

I smile, and Christina reaches across the table to hug me. I am too distracted to protest against the affection. She laughs in my ear.

Someone grabs me from behind and shouts in my ear. It's Uriah. I can't turn around, so I reach back and squeeze his shoulder.

"Congratulations!" I shout.

"You beat them!" he shouts back. He releases me, laughing, and runs into a crowd of Dauntless-born initiates.

I crane my neck to look at the screen again. I follow the list down.

Eight, nine, and ten are Dauntless-borns whose names I barely recognize.

Eleven and twelve are Molly and Drew.

Molly and Drew are cut. Drew, who tried to run away while Peter held me by the throat over the chasm, and Molly, who fed the Erudite lies about my father, are factionless.

It isn't quite the victory I wanted, but it's a victory nonetheless.

Will and Christina kiss, a little too sloppily for my taste. All around me is the pounding of Dauntless fists. Then I feel a tap on my shoulder and turn to see Tobias standing behind me. I get up, beaming.

"You think giving you a hug would give away too much?" he says.

"You know," I say, "I really don't care."

I stand on my tiptoes and press my lips to his.

It is the best moment of my life.

A moment later, Tobias's thumb brushes over the injection site in my neck, and a few things come together at once. I don't know how I didn't figure this out before.

One: Colored serum contains transmitters.

Two: Transmitters connect the mind to a simulation program.

Three: Erudite developed the serum.

Four: Eric and Max are working with the Erudite.

I break away from the kiss and stare wide-eyed at Tobias.

"Tris?" he says, confused.

I shake my head. "Not now." I meant to say *not here*. Not with Will and Christina standing a foot away from me—staring with open mouths, probably because I just kissed Tobias—and the clamor of the Dauntless surrounding us. But he has to know how important it is.

"Later," I say. "Okay?"

He nods. I don't even know how I'll explain it later. I don't even know how to think straight.

But I do know how Erudite will get us to fight.

CHAPTER
THIRTY-THREE

I TRY TO get Tobias alone after the rankings are announced, but the crowd of initiates and members is too thick, and the force of their congratulations pulls him away from me. I decide to sneak out of the dormitory after everyone is asleep and find him, but the fear landscape exhausted me more than I realized, so soon enough, I drift off too.

I wake to squeaking mattresses and shuffling feet. It's too dark for me to see clearly, but as my eyes adjust, I see that Christina is tying her shoelaces. I open my mouth to ask her what she's doing, but then I notice that across from me, Will is putting on a shirt. Everyone is awake, but everyone is silent.

"Christina," I hiss. She doesn't look at me, so I grab her shoulder and shake it. "Christina!"

She just keeps tying her shoelaces.

My stomach squeezes when I see her face. Her eyes are open, but blank, and her facial muscles are slack. She moves without looking at what she's doing, her mouth half-open, not awake but seeming awake. And everyone else looks just like her.

"Will?" I ask, crossing the room. All the initiates fall into a line when they finish dressing. They start to file silently out of the dormitory. I grab Will's arm to keep him from leaving, but he moves forward with irrepressible force. I grit my teeth and hold on as hard as I can, digging my heels into the ground. He just drags me along with him.

They are sleepwalkers.

I fumble for my shoes. I can't stay here alone. I tie my shoes in a hurry, pull on a jacket, and sprint out of the room, catching up to the line of initiates quickly, conforming my pace to theirs. It takes me a few seconds to realize that they move in unison, the same foot forward as the same arm swings back. I mimic them as best I can, but the rhythm feels strange to me.

We march toward the Pit, but when we reach the entrance, the front of the line turns left. Max stands in the hallway, watching us. My heart hammers in my chest and I stare as vacantly as possible ahead of me, focusing on the rhythm of my feet. I tense as I pass him. He'll notice. He'll notice I'm not brain-dead like the rest of them and something bad will happen to me, I just know it.

Max's dark eyes pass right over me.

We climb a flight of stairs and travel at the same rhythm down four corridors. Then the hallway opens up to a huge cavern. Inside it is a crowd of Dauntless.

There are rows of tables with mounds of black on them. I can't see what the piles are until I am a foot away from them. Guns.

Of course. Eric said every Dauntless was injected yesterday. So now the entire faction is brain-dead, obedient, and trained to kill. Perfect soldiers.

I pick up a gun and a holster and a belt, copying Will, who is directly in front of me. I try to match his movements, but I can't predict what he's going to do, so I end up fumbling more than I'd like to. I grit my teeth. I just have to trust that no one is watching me.

Once I'm armed, I follow Will and the other initiates toward the exit.

I can't wage war against Abnegation, against my family. I would rather die. My fear landscape proved that. My list of options narrows, and I see the path I must take. I will pretend long enough to get to the Abnegation sector of the city. I will save my family. And whatever happens after that doesn't matter. A blanket of calm settles over me.

The line of initiates passes into a dark hallway. I can't see Will ahead of me, or anything ahead of him. My foot hits something hard, and I stumble, my hands outstretched. My knee hits something else—a step. I straighten, so tense my teeth are almost chattering. They didn't see that. It's too dark. Please let it be too dark.

As the staircase turns, light flows into the cavern, until I can finally see Will's shoulders in front of me again. I focus on matching my rhythm to his as I reach the top of the stairs, passing another Dauntless leader. Now I know who the Dauntless leaders are, because they are the only people who are awake.

Well, not the only people. I must be awake because I am Divergent. And if I am awake, that means Tobias is too, unless I am wrong about him.

I have to find him.

I stand next to the train tracks in a group that stretches as far as I can see with my peripheral vision. The train is stopped in front of us, every car open. One by one, my fellow initiates climb into the train car in front of us.

I can't turn my head to scan the crowd for Tobias, but I let my eyes skirt to the side. The faces on my left are unfamiliar, but I see a tall boy with short hair a few yards to my right. It might not be him, and I can't make sure, but it's the best chance I have. I don't know how to get to him without attracting attention. I have to get to him.

The car in front of me fills up, and Will turns toward the next one. I take my cues from him, but instead of stopping where he stops, I slip a few feet to the right. The people around me are all taller than I am; they will shield me. I step to the right again, clenching my teeth. Too much movement. They will catch me. *Please don't catch me.*

A blank-faced Dauntless in the next car offers a hand to the boy in front of me, and he takes it, his movements robotic. I take the next hand without looking at it, and climb as gracefully as I can into the car.

I stand facing the person who helped me. My eyes twitch up, just for a second, to see his face. Tobias, as blank-faced as the rest of them. Was I wrong? Is he not Divergent? Tears spark behind my eyes, and I blink them back as I turn away from him.

People crowd into the car around me, so we stand in four rows, shoulder-to-shoulder. And then something peculiar happens: fingers lace with mine, and a palm presses to my palm. Tobias, holding my hand.

My entire body is alive with energy. I squeeze his hand, and he squeezes back. He is awake. I was right.

I want to look at him, but I force myself to stand still and keep my eyes forward as the train starts to move. He moves his thumb in a slow circle over the back of my hand. It is meant to comfort me, but it frustrates me instead. I need to talk to him. I need to look at him.

I can't see where the train is going because the girl in front of me is so tall, so I stare at the back of her head and focus on Tobias's hand in mine until the rails squeal. I don't know how long I've been standing there, but my back aches, so it must have been a long time. The train screeches to a stop, and my heart pounds so hard it's difficult to breathe.

Right before we jump down from the car, I see Tobias turn his head in my periphery, and I glance back at him. His dark eyes are insistent as he says, "Run."

"My family," I say.

I look straight ahead again, and jump down from the train car when it's my turn. Tobias walks in front of me. I should focus on the back of his head, but the streets I walk now are familiar, and the line of Dauntless I follow fades from my attention. I pass the place I went every six months with my mother to pick up new clothes for our family; the bus stop where I once waited in the morning to get to school; the strip of sidewalk so cracked Caleb and I played a hopping, jumping game to get across it.

They are all different now. The buildings are dark and empty. The roads are packed with Dauntless soldiers, all marching at the same rhythm except the officers, who stand every few hundred yards, watching us walk by, or gathering in clusters to discuss something. No one seems to be doing anything. Are we really here for war?

I walk a half mile before I get an answer to that question.

I start to hear popping sounds. I can't look around to see where they're coming from, but the farther I walk, the louder and sharper they get, until I recognize them as gunshots. I clench my jaw. I must keep walking; I have to stare straight ahead.

Far ahead of us, I see a Dauntless soldier push a gray-clothed man to his knees. I recognize the man—he is a council member. The soldier takes her gun out of her holster and, with sightless eyes, fires a bullet into the back of the council member's skull.

The soldier has a gray streak in her hair. It's Tori. My steps almost falter.

Keep walking. My eyes burn. *Keep walking.*

We march past Tori and the fallen council member. When I step over his hand, I almost burst into tears.

Then the soldiers in front of me stop walking, and so do I. I stand as still as I can, but all I want to do is find Jeanine and Eric and Max and shoot them all. My hands are shaking and I can't do anything to stop it. I breathe quickly through my nose.

Another gunshot. From the corner of my left eye, I see a gray blur collapse to the pavement. All the Abnegation will die if this continues.

The Dauntless soldiers carry out unspoken orders without hesitation and without question. Some adult members of Abnegation are herded toward one of the nearby buildings, along with the Abnegation children. A sea of black-clothed soldiers guard the doors. The only people I do not see are the Abnegation leaders. Maybe they are already dead.

One by one, the Dauntless soldiers in front of me step away to perform one task or another. Soon the leaders will notice that whatever signals everyone else is getting, I'm not getting them. What will I do when that happens?

"This is insane," coos a male voice on my right. I see a lock of long, greasy hair, and a silver earring. Eric. He pokes my cheek with his index finger, and I struggle against the impulse to slap his hand away.

"They really can't see us? Or hear us?" a female voice asks.

"Oh, they can see and hear. They just aren't processing what they see and hear the same way," says Eric. "They receive commands from our computers in the transmitters we injected them with . . ." At this, he presses his fingers to the injection site to show the woman where it is. *Stay still*, I tell myself. *Still, still, still.*

". . . and carry them out seamlessly."

Eric shifts a step to the side and leans close to Tobias's face, grinning.

"Now, this is a happy sight," he says. "The legendary Four. No one's going to remember that I came in second now, are they? No one's going to ask me, 'What was it like to train with the guy who has only *four fears*?'" He draws his gun and points it at Tobias's right temple. My heart pounds so hard I feel it in my skull. He can't shoot; he wouldn't. Eric tilts his head. "Think anyone would notice if he accidentally got shot?"

"Go ahead," the woman says, sounding bored. She must be a Dauntless leader if she can give Eric permission. "He's nothing now."

"Too bad you didn't just take Max up on his offer, Four. Well, too bad for *you*, anyway," says Eric quietly, as he clicks the bullet into its chamber.

My lungs burn; I haven't breathed in almost a minute. I see Tobias's hand twitch in the corner of my eye, but my hand is already on my gun. I press the barrel to Eric's forehead. His eyes widen, and his face goes slack, and for a second he looks like another sleeping Dauntless soldier.

My index finger hovers over the trigger.

"Get your gun away from his head," I say.

"You won't shoot me," Eric replies.

"Interesting theory," I say. But I can't murder him; I can't. I grit my teeth and shift my arm down, firing at Eric's foot. He screams and grabs his foot with both hands. The moment his gun is no longer pointed at Tobias's head, Tobias draws his gun and fires at Eric's friend's leg. I don't wait to see if the bullet hits her. I grab Tobias's arm and sprint.

If we can make it to the alley, we can disappear into the buildings and they won't find us. There are two hundred yards to go. I hear footsteps behind us, but I don't look back. Tobias grabs my hand and squeezes, pulling me forward, faster than I have ever run, faster than I can run. I stumble behind him. I hear a gunshot.

The pain is sharp and sudden, beginning in my shoulder and spreading outward with electric fingers. A scream stops in my throat, and I fall, my cheek scraping the pavement. I lift my head to see Tobias's knees by my face, and yell, "Run!"

His voice is calm and quiet as he replies, "No."

In seconds we are surrounded. Tobias helps me up, supporting my weight. I have trouble focusing through the pain. Dauntless soldiers surround us and point their guns.

"Divergent rebels," Eric says, standing on one foot. His face is a sickly white. "Surrender your weapons."

CHAPTER
THIRTY-FOUR

I LEAN HEAVILY on Tobias. A gun barrel pressed to my spine urges me forward, through the front doors of Abnegation headquarters, a plain gray building, two stories high. Blood trickles down my side. I'm not afraid of what's coming; I'm in too much pain to think about it.

The gun barrel pushes me toward a door guarded by two Dauntless soldiers. Tobias and I walk through it and enter a plain office that contains just a desk, a computer, and two empty chairs. Jeanine sits behind the desk, a phone against her ear.

"Well, send some of them *back* on the train, then," she says. "It needs to be well guarded, it's the most important part—I'm not talk—I have to go." She snaps the phone shut and focuses her gray eyes on me. They remind me of melted steel.

"Divergent rebels," one of the Dauntless says. He must be a Dauntless leader—or maybe a recruit who was removed from the simulation.

"Yes, I can see that." She takes her glasses off, folds them, and sets them on the desk. She probably wears the glasses out of vanity rather than necessity, because she thinks they make her look smarter—my father said so.

"*You*," she says, pointing at me, "I expected. All the trouble with your aptitude test results made me suspicious from the beginning. But *you* . . ."

She shakes her head as she shifts her eyes to Tobias.

"You, Tobias—or should I call you Four?—managed to elude me," she says quietly. "Everything about you checked out: test results, initiation simulations, everything. But here you are nonetheless." She folds her hands and sets her chin on top of them. "Perhaps you could explain to me how that is?"

"You're the genius," he says coolly. "Why don't you tell me?"

Her mouth curls into a smile. "My theory is that you really do belong in Abnegation. That your Divergence is weaker."

She smiles wider. Like she's amused. I grit my teeth and consider lunging across the table and strangling her. If I didn't have a bullet in my shoulder, I might.

"Your powers of deductive reasoning are stunning,"

spits Tobias. "Consider me awed."

I look sideways at him. I had almost forgotten about this side of him—the part that is more likely to explode than to lie down and die.

"Now that your intelligence has been verified, you might want to get on with killing us." Tobias closes his eyes. "You have a lot of Abnegation leaders to murder, after all."

If Tobias's comments bother Jeanine, she doesn't let on. She keeps smiling and stands smoothly. She wears a blue dress that hugs her body from shoulder to knee, revealing a layer of pudge around her middle. The room spins as I try to focus on her face, and I slump against Tobias for support. He slides his arm around me, supporting me from the waist.

"Don't be silly. There is no rush," she says lightly. "You are both here for an extremely important purpose. You see, it perplexed me that the Divergent were immune to the serum that I developed, so I have been working to remedy that. I thought I might have, with the last batch, but as you know, I was wrong. Luckily I have another batch to test."

"Why bother?" She and the Dauntless leaders had no problem killing the Divergent in the past. Why would it be any different now?

She smirks at me.

"I have had a question since I began the Dauntless

project, and it is this." She sidesteps her desk, skimming the surface with her finger. "Why are most of the Divergent weak-willed, God-fearing nobodies from *Abnegation*, of all factions?"

I didn't know that most of the Divergent came from Abnegation, and I don't know why that would be. And I probably won't live long enough to figure it out.

"Weak-willed," Tobias scoffs. "It requires a *strong* will to manipulate a simulation, last time I checked. Weak-willed is mind-controlling an army because it's too hard for you to train one yourself."

"I am not a fool," says Jeanine. "A faction of intellectuals is no army. We are tired of being dominated by a bunch of self-righteous idiots who reject wealth and advancement, but we couldn't do this on our own. And your Dauntless leaders were all too happy to oblige me if I guaranteed them a place in our new, improved government."

"Improved," Tobias says, snorting.

"Yes, improved," Jeanine says. "Improved, and working toward a world in which people will live in wealth, comfort, and prosperity."

"At whose expense?" I ask, my voice thick and sluggish. "All that wealth . . . doesn't come from nowhere."

"Currently, the factionless are a drain on our resources," Jeanine replies. "As is Abnegation. I am sure that once the remains of your old faction are absorbed into the

Dauntless army, Candor will cooperate and we will finally be able to get on with things."

Absorbed into the Dauntless army. I know what that means—she wants to control them, too. She wants everyone to be pliable and easy to control.

"Get on with things," Tobias repeats bitterly. He raises his voice. "Make no mistake. You will be dead before the day is out, you—"

"Perhaps if you could control your temper," Jeanine says, her words cutting cleanly across Tobias's, "you would not be in this situation to begin with, Tobias."

"I'm in this situation because you put me here," he snaps. "The second you orchestrated an attack against innocent people."

"Innocent people." Jeanine laughs. "I find that a little funny, coming from you. I would expect Marcus's son to understand that not all those people are innocent." She perches on the edge of the desk, her skirt pulling away from her knees, which are crossed with stretch marks. "Can you tell me honestly that you wouldn't be happy to discover that your father was killed in the attack?"

"No," says Tobias through gritted teeth. "But at least his evil didn't involve the widespread manipulation of an entire faction and the systematic murder of every political leader we have."

They stare at each other for a few seconds, long enough to make me feel tense to my core, and then Jeanine clears her throat.

"What I was going to say," she says, "is that soon, dozens of the Abnegation and their young children will be my responsibility to keep in order, and it does not bode well for me that a large number of them may be Divergent like yourselves, incapable of being controlled by the simulations."

She stands and walks a few steps to the left, her hands clasped in front of her. Her nail beds, like mine, are bitten raw.

"Therefore, it was necessary that I develop a new form of simulation to which they are not immune. I have been forced to reassess my own assumptions. That is where you come in." She paces a few steps to the right. "You are correct to say that you are strong-willed. I cannot control your will. But there are a few things I can control."

She stops and turns to face us. I lean my temple into Tobias's shoulder. Blood trails down my back. The pain has been so constant for the past few minutes that I have gotten used to it, like a person gets used to a siren's wail if it remains consistent.

She presses her palms together. I see no vicious glee in her eyes, and not a hint of the sadism I expect. She is more machine than maniac. She sees problems and forms solutions based on the data she collects. Abnegation stood in the way of her desire for power, so she found a way to eliminate it. She didn't have an army, so she found one in Dauntless. She knew that she would need to control large groups of people in order to stay secure, so she developed a way to do it with serums and transmitters. Divergence is just another problem for her to solve, and that is what makes her so terrifying—because she is smart enough to solve anything, even the problem of our existence.

"I can control what you see and hear," she says. "So I created a new serum that will adjust your surroundings to manipulate your will. Those who refuse to accept our leadership must be closely monitored."

Monitored—or robbed of free will. She has a gift with words.

"You will be the first test subject, Tobias. Beatrice, however . . ." She smiles. "You are too injured to be of much use to me, so your execution will occur at the conclusion of this meeting."

I try to hide the shudder that goes through me at the word "execution," my shoulder screaming with pain, and look up at Tobias. It's hard to blink the tears back when I see the terror in Tobias's wide, dark eyes.

"No," says Tobias. His voice trembles, but his look is

stern as he shakes his head. "I would rather die."

"I'm afraid you don't have much of a choice in the matter," replies Jeanine lightly.

Tobias takes my face in his hands roughly and kisses me, the pressure of his lips pushing mine apart. I forget my pain and the terror of approaching death and for a moment, I am grateful that the memory of that kiss will be fresh in my mind as I meet my end.

Then he releases me and I have to lean against the wall for support. With no more warning than the tightening of his muscles, Tobias lunges across the desk and wraps his hands around Jeanine's throat. Dauntless guards by the door leap at him, their guns held ready, and I scream.

It takes two Dauntless soldiers to pull Tobias away from Jeanine and shove him to the ground. One of the soldiers pins him, his knees on Tobias's shoulders and his hands on Tobias's head, pressing his face to the carpet. I lunge toward them, but another guard slams his hands against my shoulders, forcing me against the wall. I am weak from blood loss and too small.

Jeanine braces herself against the desk, spluttering and gasping. She rubs her throat, which is bright red with Tobias's fingerprints. No matter how mechanical she seems, she's still human; there are tears in her eyes as she takes a box from her desk drawer and opens it, revealing a needle and syringe.

Still breathing heavily, she carries it toward Tobias. Tobias grits his teeth and elbows one of the guards in the face. The guard slams the heel of his gun into the side of Tobias's head, and Jeanine sticks the needle into Tobias's neck. He goes limp.

A sound escapes my mouth, not a sob or a scream, but a croaking, scraping moan that sounds detached, like it is coming from someone else.

"Let him up," says Jeanine, her voice scratchy.

The guard gets up, and so does Tobias. He does not look like the sleepwalking Dauntless soldiers; his eyes are alert. He looks around for a few seconds as if confused by what he sees.

"Tobias," I say. "Tobias!"

"He doesn't know you," says Jeanine.

Tobias looks over his shoulder. His eyes narrow and he starts toward me, fast. Before the guards can stop him, he closes a hand around my throat, squeezing my trachea with his fingertips. I choke, my face hot with blood.

"The simulation manipulates him," says Jeanine. I can barely hear her over the pounding in my ears. "By altering what he sees—making him confuse enemy with friend."

One of the guards pulls Tobias off me. I gasp, drawing a rattling breath into my lungs.

He is gone. Controlled by the simulation, he will now murder the people he called innocent not three minutes ago. Jeanine killing him would have hurt less than this.

"The advantage to this version of the simulation," she says, her eyes alight, "is that he can act independently, and is therefore far more effective than a mindless soldier." She looks at the guards who hold Tobias back. He struggles against them, his muscles taut, his eyes focused on me, but not seeing me, not seeing me the way they used to. "Send him to the control room. We'll want a sentient being there to monitor things and, as I understand it, he used to work there."

Jeanine presses her palms together in front of her. "And take *her* to room B13," she says. She flaps her hand to dismiss me. That flapping hand commands my execution, but to her it is just crossing off an item from a list of tasks, the only logical progression of the particular path that she is on. She surveys me without feeling as two Dauntless soldiers pull me out of the room.

They drag me down the hallway. I feel numb inside, but outside I am a screaming, thrashing force of will. I bite a hand that belongs to the Dauntless man on my right and smile as I taste blood. Then he hits me, and there is nothing.

CHAPTER
THIRTY-FIVE

I WAKE IN the dark, wedged in a hard corner. The floor beneath me is smooth and cold. I touch my throbbing head and liquid slips across my fingertips. Red—blood. When I bring my hand back down, my elbow hits a wall. Where am I?

A light flickers above me. The bulb is blue and dim when it's lit. I see the walls of a tank around me, and my shadowed reflection across from me. The room is small, with concrete walls and no windows, and I am alone in it. Well, almost—a small video camera is attached to one of the concrete walls.

I see a small opening near my feet. Connected to it is a tube, and connected to the tube, in the corner of the room, is a huge tank.

The trembling starts in my fingertips and spreads up

my arms, and soon my body is shuddering.

I'm not in a simulation this time.

My right arm is numb. When I push myself out of the corner, I see a pool of blood where I was sitting. I can't panic now. I stand, leaning against a wall, and breathe. The worst thing that can happen to me now is that I drown in this tank. I press my forehead to the glass and laugh. That is the worst thing I can imagine. My laugh turns into a sob.

If I refuse to give up now, it will look brave to whoever watches me with that camera, but sometimes it isn't fighting that's brave, it's facing the death you know is coming. I sob into the glass. I'm not afraid of dying, but I want to die a different way, any other way.

It is better to scream than cry, so I scream and slam my heel into the wall behind me. My foot bounces off, and I kick again, so hard my heel throbs. I kick again and again and again, then pull back and throw my left shoulder into the wall. The impact makes the wound in my right shoulder burn like it got stuck with a hot poker.

Water trickles into the bottom of the tank.

The video camera means they're watching me—no, studying me, as only the Erudite would. To see if my reaction in reality matches my reaction in the simulation. To prove that I'm a coward.

I uncurl my fists and drop my hands. I am not a coward. I lift my head and stare at the camera across from me. If

I focus on breathing, I can forget that I'm about to die. I stare at the camera until my vision narrows and it is all I see. Water tickles my ankles, then my calves, then my thighs. It rises over my fingertips. I breathe in; I breathe out. The water is soft and feels like silk.

I breathe in. The water will wash my wounds clean. I breathe out. My mother submerged me in water when I was a baby, to give me to God. It has been a long time since I thought about God, but I think about him now. It is only natural. I am glad, suddenly, that I shot Eric in the foot instead of the head.

My body rises with the water. Instead of kicking my feet to stay abreast of it, I push all the air from my lungs and sink to the bottom. The water muffles my ears. I feel its movement over my face. I think about snorting the water into my lungs so it kills me faster, but I can't bring myself to do it. I blow bubbles from my mouth.

Relax. I close my eyes. My lungs burn.

I let my hands float up to the top of the tank. I let the water fold me in its silken arms.

When I was young, my father used to hold me over his head and run with me so I felt like I was flying. I remember how the air felt, gliding over my body, and I am not afraid. I open my eyes.

A dark figure stands in front of me. I must be close

to death if I'm seeing things. Pain stabs my lungs. Suffocating is painful. A palm presses to the glass in front of my face, and for a moment as I stare through the water, I think I see my mother's blurry face.

I hear a bang, and the glass cracks. Water sprays out a hole near the top of the tank, and the pane cracks in half. I turn away as the glass shatters, and the force of the water throws my body at the ground. I gasp, swallowing water as well as air, and cough, and gasp again, and hands close around my arms, and I hear her voice.

"Beatrice," she says. "Beatrice, we have to run."

She pulls my arm across her shoulders and hauls me to my feet. She is dressed like my mother and she looks like my mother, but she is holding a gun, and the determined look in her eyes is unfamiliar to me. I stumble beside her over broken glass and through water and out an open doorway. Dauntless guards lie dead next to the door.

My feet slip and slide on the tile as we walk down the hallway, as fast as my weak legs can muster. When we turn the corner, she fires at the two guards standing by the door at the end. The bullets hit them both in the head, and they slump to the floor. She pushes me against the wall and takes off her gray jacket.

She wears a sleeveless shirt. When she lifts her arm, I see the corner of a tattoo under her armpit. No wonder she never changed clothes in front of me.

"Mom," I say, my voice strained. "You were Dauntless."

"Yes," she says, smiling. She makes her jacket into a sling for my arm, tying the sleeves around my neck. "And it has served me well today. Your father and Caleb and some others are hiding in a basement at the intersection of North and Fairfield. We have to go get them."

I stare at her. I sat next to her at the kitchen table, twice a day, for sixteen years, and never once did I consider the possibility that she could have been anything but Abnegation-born. How well did I actually know my mother?

"There will be time for questions," she says. She lifts her shirt and slips a gun from under the waistband of her pants, offering it to me. Then she touches my cheek. "Now we must go."

She runs to the end of the hallway, and I run after her.

We are in the basement of Abnegation headquarters. My mother has worked there for as long as I can remember, so I'm not surprised when she leads me down a few dark hallways, up a dank staircase, and into daylight again without interference. How many Dauntless guards did she shoot before she found me?

"How did you know to find me?" I say.

"I've been watching the trains since the attacks started," she replies, glancing over her shoulder at me. "I didn't know what I would do when I found you. But it was always my intention to save you."

My throat feels tight. "But I betrayed you. I left you."

"You're my daughter. I don't care about the factions." She shakes her head. "Look where they got us. Human beings as a whole cannot be good for long before the bad creeps back in and poisons us again."

She stops where the alley intersects with the road.

I know now isn't the time for conversation. But there is something I need to know.

"Mom, how do you know about Divergence?" I ask. "What is it? Why . . ."

She pushes the bullet chamber open and peers inside. Seeing how many bullets she has left. Then takes a few out of her pocket and reloads. I recognize her expression as the one she wears when she threads a needle.

"I know about them because I am one," she says as she shoves a bullet in place. "I was only safe because my mother was a Dauntless leader. On Choosing Day, she told me to leave my faction and find a safer one. I chose Abnegation." She puts an extra bullet in her pocket and stands up straighter. "But I wanted you to make the choice on your own."

"I don't understand why we're such a threat to the leaders."

"Every faction conditions its members to think and act

a certain way. And most people do it. For most people, it's not hard to learn, to find a pattern of thought that works and stay that way." She touches my uninjured shoulder and smiles. "But our minds move in a dozen different directions. We can't be confined to one way of thinking, and that terrifies our leaders. It means we can't be controlled. And it means that no matter what they do, we will always cause trouble for them."

I feel like someone breathed new air into my lungs. I am not Abnegation. I am not Dauntless.

I am Divergent.

And I can't be controlled.

"Here they come," she says, looking around the corner. I peek over her shoulder and see a few Dauntless with guns, moving to the same beat, heading toward us. My mother looks back. Far behind us, another group of Dauntless run down the alley, toward us, moving in time with one another.

She grabs my hands and looks me in the eyes. I watch her long eyelashes move as she blinks. I wish I had something of hers in my small, plain face. But at least I have something of hers in my brain.

"Go to your father and brother. The alley on the right, down to the basement. Knock twice, then three times, then six times." She cups my cheeks. Her hands are cold;

her palms are rough. "I'm going to distract them. You have to run as fast as you can."

"No." I shake my head. "I'm not going anywhere without you."

She smiles. "Be brave, Beatrice. I love you."

I feel her lips on my forehead and then she runs into the middle of the street. She holds her gun above her head and fires three times into the air. The Dauntless start running.

I sprint across the street and into the alley. As I run, I look over my shoulder to see if any Dauntless follow me. But my mother fires into the crowd of guards, and they are too focused on her to notice me.

I whip my head over my shoulder when I hear them fire back. My feet falter and stop.

My mother stiffens, her back arching. Blood surges from a wound in her abdomen, dyeing her shirt crimson. A patch of blood spreads over her shoulder. I blink, and the violent red stains the inside of my eyelids. I blink again, and I see her smile as she sweeps my hair trimmings into a pile.

She falls, first to her knees, her hands limp at her sides, and then to the pavement, slumped to the side like a rag doll. She is motionless and without breath.

I clamp my hand over my mouth and scream into my

palm. My cheeks are hot and wet with tears I didn't feel beginning. My blood cries out that it belongs to her, and struggles to return to her, and I hear her words in my mind as I run, telling me to be brave.

Pain stabs through me as everything I am made of collapses, my entire world dismantled in a moment. The pavement scrapes my knees. If I lie down now, this can all be done. Maybe Eric was right, and choosing death is like exploring an unknown, uncertain place.

I feel Tobias brushing my hair back before the first simulation. I hear him telling me to be brave. I hear my mother telling me to be brave.

The Dauntless soldiers turn as if moved by the same mind. Somehow I get up and start running.

I am brave.

CHAPTER
THIRTY-SIX

THREE DAUNTLESS SOLDIERS pursue me. They run in unison, their footsteps echoing in the alley. One of them fires, and I dive, scraping my palms on the ground. The bullet hits the brick wall to my right, and pieces of brick spray everywhere. I throw myself around the corner and click a bullet into the chamber of my gun.

They killed my mother. I point the gun into the alley and fire blindly. It wasn't really them, but it doesn't matter—can't matter, and just like death itself, can't be real right now.

Just one set of footsteps now. I hold the gun out with both hands and stand at the end of the alley, pointing at the Dauntless soldier. My finger squeezes the trigger, but not hard enough to fire. The man running toward me is not a man, he is a boy. A shaggy-haired boy with a crease between his eyebrows.

Will. Dull-eyed and mindless, but still Will. He stops running and mirrors me, his feet planted and his gun up. In an instant, I see his finger poised over the trigger and hear the bullet slide into the chamber, and I fire. My eyes squeezed shut. Can't breathe.

The bullet hit him in the head. I know because that's where I aimed it.

I turn around without opening my eyes and stumble away from the alley. North and Fairfield. I have to look at the street sign to see where I am, but I can't read it; my vision is blurred. I blink a few times. I stand just yards away from the building that contains what's left of my family.

I kneel next to the door. Tobias would call me unwise to make any noise. Noise might attract Dauntless soldiers.

I press my forehead to the wall and scream. After a few seconds I clamp my hand over my mouth to muffle the sound and scream again, a scream that turns into a sob. The gun clatters to the ground. I still see Will.

He smiles in my memory. A curled lip. Straight teeth. Light in his eyes. Laughing, teasing, more alive in memory than I am in reality. It was him or me. I chose me. But I feel dead too.

I pound on the door—twice, then three times, then six times, as my mother told me to.

I wipe the tears from my face. This is the first time I will see my father since I left him, and I don't want him to see me half-collapsed and sobbing.

The door opens, and Caleb stands in the doorway. The sight of him stuns me. He stares at me for a few seconds and then throws his arms around me, his hand pressing to the wound in my shoulder. I bite my lip to keep from crying out, but a groan escapes me anyway, and Caleb yanks back.

"Beatrice. Oh God, are you shot?"

"Let's go inside," I say weakly.

He drags his thumb under his eyes, catching the moisture. The door falls shut behind us.

The room is dimly lit, but I see familiar faces, former neighbors and classmates and my father's coworkers. My father, who stares at me like I've grown a second head. Marcus. The sight of him makes me ache—Tobias . . .

No. I will not do that; I will not think of him.

"How did you know about this place?" Caleb says. "Did Mom find you?"

I nod. I don't want to think about Mom, either.

"My shoulder," I say.

Now that I am safe, the adrenaline that propelled me here is fading, and the pain is getting worse. I sink to my knees. Water drips from my clothes onto the cement floor. A sob rises within me, desperate for release, and I choke it back.

A woman named Tessa who lived down the street from us rolls out a pallet. She was married to a council member, but I don't see him here. He is probably dead.

Someone else carries a lamp from one corner to the other so we have light. Caleb produces a first-aid kit, and Susan brings me a bottle of water. There is no better place to need help than a room full of members of Abnegation. I glance at Caleb. He's wearing gray again. Seeing him in the Erudite compound feels like a dream now.

My father comes to me, lifts my arm across his shoulders, and helps me across the room.

"Why are you wet?" Caleb says.

"They tried to drown me," I say. "Why are you here?"

"I did what you said—what Mom said. I researched the simulation serum and found out that Jeanine was working to develop long-range transmitters for the serum so its signal could stretch farther, which led me to information about Erudite and Dauntless . . . anyway,

I dropped out of initiation when I figured out what was happening. I would have warned you, but it was too late," he says. "I'm factionless now."

"No, you aren't," my father says sternly. "You're with us."

I kneel on the pallet and Caleb cuts a piece of my shirt away from my shoulder with a pair of medical scissors. Caleb peels the square of fabric away, revealing first the Abnegation tattoo on my right shoulder and second, the three birds on my collarbone. Caleb and my father stare at both tattoos with the same look of fascination and shock but say nothing about them.

I lie on my stomach. Caleb squeezes my palm as my father gets the antiseptic from the first aid kit.

"Have you ever taken a bullet out of someone before?" I ask, a shaky laugh in my voice.

"The things I know how to do might surprise you," he replies.

A lot of things about my parents might surprise me. I think of Mom's tattoo and bite my lip.

"This will hurt," he says.

I don't see the knife go in, but I feel it. Pain spreads through my body and I scream through gritted teeth, crushing Caleb's hand. Over the screaming, I hear my father ask me to relax my back. Tears run from the corners of my eyes and I do as he tells me. The pain starts again, and I feel the knife moving under my skin, and I am still screaming.

"Got it," he says. He drops something on the floor with a *ding*.

Caleb looks at my father and then at me, and then he laughs. I haven't heard him laugh in so long that the sound makes me cry.

"What's so funny?" I say, sniffling.

"I never thought I would see us together again," he says.

My father cleans the skin around my wound with something cold. "Stitching time," he says.

I nod. He threads the needle like he's done it a thousand times.

"One," he says, "two . . . *three*."

I clench my jaw and stay quiet this time. Of all the pain I have suffered today—the pain of getting shot and almost drowning and taking the bullet out again, the pain of finding and losing my mother and Tobias, this is the easiest to bear.

My father finishes stitching my wound, ties off the thread, and covers the stitches with a bandage. Caleb helps me sit up and separates the hems of his two shirts, pulling the long-sleeved one over his head and offering it to me.

My father helps me guide my right arm through the shirt sleeve, and I pull the rest over my head. It is baggy and smells fresh, smells like Caleb.

"So," my father says quietly. "Where is your mother?"

I look down. I don't want to deliver this news. I don't want to have this news to begin with.

"She's gone," I say. "She saved me."

Caleb closes his eyes and takes a deep breath.

My father looks momentarily stricken and then recovers himself, averting his glistening eyes and nodding.

"That is good," he says, sounding strained. "A good death."

If I speak right now, I will break down, and I can't afford to do that. So I just nod.

Eric called Al's suicide brave, and he was wrong. My mother's death was brave. I remember how calm she was, how determined. It isn't just brave that she died for me; it is brave that she did it without announcing it, without hesitation, and without appearing to consider another option.

He helps me to my feet. Time to face the rest of the room. My mother told me to save them. Because of that, and because I am Dauntless, it's my duty to lead now. I have no idea how to bear that burden.

Marcus gets up. A vision of him whipping my arm with a belt rushes into my mind when I see him, and my chest squeezes.

"We are only safe here for so long," Marcus says eventually. "We need to get out of the city. Our best option is to go to the Amity compound in the hope that they'll take us in. Do you know anything about the Dauntless strategy, Beatrice? Will they stop fighting at night?"

"It's not Dauntless strategy," I say. "This whole thing is masterminded by the Erudite. And it's not like they're giving orders."

"Not giving orders," my father says. "What do you mean?"

"I mean," I say, "ninety percent of the Dauntless are sleepwalking right now. They're in a simulation and they don't know what they're doing. The only reason I'm not just like them is that I'm . . ." I hesitate on the word. "The mind control doesn't affect me."

"Mind control? So they don't know that they're killing people right now?" my father asks me, his eyes wide.

"No."

"That's . . . awful." Marcus shakes his head. His sympathetic tone sounds manufactured to me. "Waking up and realizing what you've done . . ."

The room goes quiet, probably as all the Abnegation imagine themselves in the place of the Dauntless soldiers, and that's when it occurs to me.

"We have to wake them up," I say.

"What?" Marcus says.

"If we wake the Dauntless up, they will probably revolt

when they realize what's going on," I explain. "The Erudite won't have an army. The Abnegation will stop dying. This will be over."

"It won't be that simple," my father says. "Even without the Dauntless helping them, the Erudite will find another way to—"

"And how are we supposed to wake them up?" Marcus says.

"We find the computers that control the simulation and destroy the data," I say. "The program. Everything."

"Easier said than done," Caleb says. "It could be any-where. We can't just appear at the Erudite compound and start poking around."

"It's . . ." I frown. Jeanine. Jeanine was talking about something important when Tobias and I came into her office, important enough to hang up on someone. *You can't just leave it undefended.* And then, when she was sending Tobias away: *Send him to the control room.* The control room where Tobias used to work. With the Dauntless security monitors. And the Dauntless computers.

"It's at Dauntless headquarters," I say. "It makes sense. That's where all the data about the Dauntless is stored, so why not control them from there?"

I faintly register that I said *them.* As of yesterday, I technically became Dauntless, but I don't feel like one.

And I am not Abnegation, either.

I guess I am what I've always been. Not Dauntless, not Abnegation, not factionless. Divergent.

"Are you sure?" my father asks.

"It's an informed guess," I say, "and it's the best theory I have."

"Then we'll have to decide who goes and who continues on to Amity," he says. "What kind of help do you need, Beatrice?"

The question stuns me, as does the expression he wears. He looks at me like I'm a peer. He speaks to me like I'm a peer. Either he has accepted that I am an adult now, or he has accepted that I am no longer his daughter. The latter is more likely, and more painful.

"Anyone who can and will fire a gun," I say, "and isn't afraid of heights."

CHAPTER
THIRTY-SEVEN

ERUDITE AND DAUNTLESS forces are concentrated in the
Abnegation sector of the city, so as long as we run away
from the Abnegation sector, we are less likely to encounter difficulty.

I didn't get to decide who is coming with me. Caleb was
the obvious choice, since he knows the most about the
Erudite plan. Marcus insisted that he go, despite my protests, because he is good with computers. And my father
acted like his place was assumed from the beginning.

I watch the others run in the opposite direction—
toward safety, toward Amity—for a few seconds, and then
I turn away, toward the city, toward the war. We stand next
to the railroad tracks, which will carry us into danger.

"What time is it?" I ask Caleb.

He checks his watch. "Three twelve."

"Should be here any second," I say.

"Will it stop?" he asks.

I shake my head. "It goes slowly through the city. We'll run next to the car for a few feet and then climb inside."

Jumping on trains seems easy to me now, natural. It won't be as easy for the rest of them, but we can't stop now. I look over my left shoulder and see the headlights burning gold against the gray buildings and roads. I bounce on the balls of my feet as the lights grow larger and larger, and then the front of the train glides past me, and I start jogging. When I see an open car, I pick up my pace to keep stride with it and grab the handle on the left, swinging myself inside.

Caleb jumps, landing hard and rolling on his side to get in, and he helps Marcus. My father lands on his stomach, pulling his legs in behind him. They move away from the doorway, but I stand on the edge with one hand on a handle, watching the city pass.

If I were Jeanine, I would send the majority of Dauntless soldiers to the Dauntless entrance above the Pit, outside the glass building. It would be smarter to go in the back entrance, the one that requires jumping off a building.

"I assume you now regret choosing Dauntless," Marcus says.

I am surprised my father didn't ask that question, but he, like me, is watching the city. The train passes the

Erudite compound, which is dark now. It looks peaceful from a distance, and inside those walls, it probably is peaceful. Far removed from the conflict and the reality of what they have done.

I shake my head.

"Not even after your faction's leaders decided to join in a plot to overthrow the government?" Marcus spits.

"There were some things I needed to learn."

"How to be brave?" my father says quietly.

"How to be selfless," I say. "Often they're the same thing."

"Is that why you got Abnegation's symbol tattooed on your shoulder?" Caleb asks. I am almost sure that I see a smile in my father's eyes.

I smile faintly back and nod. "And Dauntless on the other."

+ + +

The glass building above the Pit reflects sunlight into my eyes. I stand, holding the handle next to the door for balance. Almost there.

"When I tell you to jump," I say, "you jump, as far as you can."

"Jump?" Caleb asks. "We're seven stories up, Tris."

"Onto a roof," I add. Seeing the stunned look on his face, I say, "That's why they call it a test of bravery."

Half of bravery is perspective. The first time I did this, it was one of the hardest things I had ever done. Now, preparing to jump off a moving train is nothing, because I have done more difficult things in the past few weeks than most people will in a lifetime. And yet none of it compares to what I am about to do in the Dauntless compound. If I survive, I will undoubtedly go on to do far more difficult things than even that, like live without a faction, something I never imagined possible.

"Dad, you go," I say, stepping back so he can stand by the edge. If he and Marcus go first, I can time it so they have to jump the shortest distance. Hopefully Caleb and I can jump far enough to make it, because we're younger. It's a chance I have to take.

The train tracks curve, and when they line up with the edge of the roof, I shout, "Jump!"

My father bends his knees and launches himself forward. I don't wait to see if he makes it. I shove Marcus forward and shout, "Jump!"

My father lands on the roof, so close to the edge that I gasp. He sits down on the gravel, and I push Caleb in front of me. He stands at the edge of the train car and jumps without me having to tell him to. I take a few steps back to give myself a running start and leap out of the car just as the train reaches the end of the roof.

For an instant I am suspended in nothingness, and then my feet slam into cement and I stumble to the side, away from the roof's edge. My knees ache, and the impact shudders through my body, making my shoulder throb. I sit down, breathing hard, and look across the rooftop. Caleb and my father stand at the edge of the roof, their hands around Marcus's arms. He didn't make it, but he hasn't fallen yet.

Somewhere inside me, a vicious voice chants: *fall, fall, fall.*

But he doesn't. My father and Caleb haul him onto the roof. I stand up, brushing gravel off my pants. The thought of what comes next has me preoccupied. It is one thing to ask people to jump off a train, but a roof?

"This next part is why I asked about fear of heights," I say, walking to the edge of the roof. I hear their shuffling footsteps behind me and step onto the ledge. Wind rushes up the side of the building and lifts my shirt from my skin. I stare down at the hole in the ground, seven stories below me, and then close my eyes as the air blows over my face.

"There's a net at the bottom," I say, looking over my shoulder. They look confused. They haven't figured out what I am asking them to do yet.

"Don't think," I say. "Just jump."

I turn, and as I turn, I lean back, compromising my

balance. I drop like a stone, my eyes closed, one arm out-stretched to feel the wind. I relax my muscles as much as I can before I hit the net, which feels like a slab of cement hitting my shoulder. I grit my teeth and roll to the edge, grabbing the pole that supports the net, and swing my leg over the side. I land on my knees on the platform, my eyes blurry with tears.

Caleb yelps as the net curls around his body and then straightens. I stand with some difficulty.

"Caleb!" I hiss. "Over here!"

Breathing heavily, Caleb crawls to the side of the net and drops over the edge, hitting the platform hard. Wincing, he pushes himself to his feet and stares at me, his mouth open.

"How many times . . . have you . . . done that?" he asks between breaths.

"Twice now," I say.

He shakes his head.

When my father hits the net, Caleb helps him across. When he stands on the platform, he leans and vomits over the side. I descend the stairs, and when I get to the bottom, I hear Marcus hit the net with a groan.

The cavern is empty and the hallways stretch into darkness.

Jeanine made it sound like there was no one left in the Dauntless compound except the soldiers she sent back to guard the computers. If we can find Dauntless soldiers, we can find the computers. I look over my shoulder. Marcus stands on the platform, white as a sheet but unharmed.

"So this is the Dauntless compound," says Marcus.

"Yes," I say. "And?"

"And I never thought I would get to see it," he replies, his hand skimming a wall. "No need to be so defensive, Beatrice."

I never noticed how cold his eyes were before.

"Do you have a plan, Beatrice?" my father says.

"Yes." And it's true. I do, though I'm not sure when I developed it.

I'm also not sure it will work. I can count on a few things: There aren't many Dauntless in the compound, the Dauntless aren't known for their subtlety, and I'll do anything to stop them.

We walk down the hallway that leads to the Pit, which is striped with light every ten feet. When we walk into the first patch of light, I hear a gunshot and drop to the ground. Someone must have seen us. I crawl into the next dark patch. The spark from the gun flashed across the room by the door that leads to the Pit.

"Everyone okay?" I ask.

"Yes," my father says.

"Stay here, then."

I run to the side of the room. The lights protrude from

the wall, so directly beneath each one is a slit of shadow. I am small enough to hide in it, if I turn to the side. I can creep along the edge of the room and surprise whatever guard is shooting at us before he gets the chance to fire a bullet into my brain. Maybe.

One of the things I thank Dauntless for is the preparedness that eliminates my fear.

"Whoever's there," a voice shouts, "surrender your weapons and put your hands up!"

I turn to the side and press my back to the stone wall. I shuffle quickly sideways, one foot crossing over the other, squinting to see through the semidarkness. Another gunshot fires into silence. I reach the last light and stand for a moment in shadow, letting my eyes adjust.

I can't win a fight, but if I can move fast enough, I won't have to fight. My footsteps light, I walk toward the guard who stands by the door. A few yards away, I realize that I *know* that dark hair that always gleams, even in relative darkness, and that long nose with a narrow bridge.

It's Peter.

Cold slips over my skin and around my heart and into the pit of my stomach.

His face is tense—he isn't a sleepwalker. He looks around, but his eyes search the air above me and beyond me. Judging by his silence, he does not intend to negotiate with us; he will kill us without question.

I lick my lips, sprint the last few steps, and thrust the heel of my hand up. The blow connects with his nose, and he shouts, bringing both hands up to cover his face. My body jolts with nervous energy and as his eyes squint, I kick him in the groin. He drops to his knees, his gun clattering to the ground. I grab it and press the barrel to the top of his head.

"How are you awake?" I demand.

He lifts his head, and I click the bullet into its chamber, raising an eyebrow at him.

"The Dauntless leaders . . . they evaluated my records and removed me from the simulation," he says.

"Because they figured out that you already have murderous tendencies and wouldn't mind killing a few hundred people while conscious," I say. "Makes sense."

"I'm not . . . murderous!"

"I never knew a Candor who was such a liar." I tap the gun against his skull. "Where are the computers that control the simulation, Peter?"

"You won't shoot me."

"People tend to overestimate my character," I say quietly. "They think that because I'm small, or a girl, or a Stiff, I can't possibly be cruel. But they're wrong."

I shift the gun three inches to the left and fire at his arm.

His screams fill the hallway. Blood spurts from the wound, and he screams again, pressing his forehead to the ground. I shift the gun back to his head, ignoring the pang of guilt in my chest.

"Now that you realize your mistake," I say, "I will give you another chance to tell me what I need to know before I shoot you somewhere worse."

Another thing I can count on: Peter is not selfless.

He turns his head and focuses a bright eye on me. His teeth close over his lower lip, and his breaths shake on the way out. And on the way in. And on the way out again.

"They're listening," he spits. "If you don't kill me, they will. The only way I'll tell you is if you get me out of here."

"What?"

"Take me . . . *ahh* . . . with you," he says, wincing.

"You want me to take *you*," I say, "the person who tried to kill me . . . *with* me?"

"I do," he groans. "If you expect to find out what you need to know."

It feels like a choice, but it isn't. Every minute that I waste staring at Peter, thinking about how he haunts my nightmares and the damage he did to me, another dozen

Abnegation members die at the hands of the brain-dead Dauntless army.

"Fine," I say, almost choking on the word. "Fine."

I hear footsteps behind me. Holding the gun steady, I look over my shoulder. My father and the others walk toward us.

My father takes off his long-sleeved shirt. He wears a gray T-shirt beneath it. He crouches next to Peter and loops the fabric around his arm, tying it tightly. As he presses the fabric to the blood running down Peter's arm, he looks up at me and says, "Was it really necessary to shoot him?"

I don't answer.

"Sometimes pain is for the greater good," says Marcus calmly.

In my head, I see him standing before Tobias with a belt in hand and hear his voice echo. *This is for your own good.* I look at him for a few seconds. Does he really believe that? It sounds like something the Dauntless would say.

"Let's go," I say. "Get up, Peter."

"You want him to *walk*?" Caleb demands. "Are you insane?"

"Did I shoot him in the leg?" I say. "No. He walks. Where do we go, Peter?"

Caleb helps Peter to his feet.

"The glass building," he says, wincing. "Eighth floor."
He leads the way through the door.

I walk into the roar of the river and the blue glow of the
Pit, which is emptier now than I have ever seen it before.
I scan the walls, searching for signs of life, but I see no
movement and no figures standing in darkness. I keep
my gun in hand and start toward the path that leads to the
glass ceiling. The emptiness makes me shiver. It reminds
me of the endless field in my crow nightmares.

"What makes you think you have the right to shoot
someone?" my father says as he follows me up the path. We
pass the tattoo place. Where is Tori now? And Christina?

"Now isn't the time for debates about ethics," I say.

"Now is the perfect time," he says, "because you will
soon get the opportunity to shoot someone again, and if
you don't realize—"

"Realize what?" I say without turning around. "That
every second I waste means another Abnegation dead and
another Dauntless made into a murderer? I've realized
that. Now it's your turn."

"There is a right way to do things."

"What makes you so sure that you know what it is?"
I say.

"Please stop fighting," Caleb interrupts, his voice chid-
ing. "We have more important things to do right now."

I keep climbing, my cheeks hot. A few months ago I

would not have dared to snap at my father. A few hours ago I might not have done it either. But something changed when they shot my mother. When they took Tobias.

I hear my father huff and puff over the sound of rushing water. I forgot that he is older than I am, that his frame can no longer tolerate the weight of his body.

Before I ascend the metal stairs that will carry me above the glass ceiling, I wait in darkness and watch the light cast on the Pit walls by the sun. I watch until a shadow shifts over the sunlit wall and count until the next shadow appears. The guards make their rounds every minute and a half, stand for twenty seconds, and then move on.

"There are men with guns up there. When they see me, they will kill me, if they can," I tell my father quietly. I search his eyes. "Should I let them?"

He stares at me for a few seconds.

"Go," he says, "and God help you."

I climb the stairs carefully, stopping just before my head emerges. I wait, watching the shadows move, and when one of them stops, I step up, point my gun, and shoot.

The bullet does not hit the guard. It shatters the window behind him. I fire again and duck as bullets hit the floor around me with a ding. Thank God the glass ceiling is bulletproof, or the glass would break and I would fall to my death.

One guard down. I breathe deeply and put just my

hand over the ceiling, looking through the glass to see my target. I tilt the gun back and fire at the guard running toward me. The bullet hits him in the arm. Luckily it is his shooting arm, because he drops his gun and it skids across the floor.

My body shaking, I launch myself through the hole in the ceiling and snatch the fallen gun before he can get to it. A bullet whizzes past my head, so close to hitting me that it moves my hair. Eyes wide, I fling my right arm over my shoulder, forcing a searing pain through my body, and fire three times behind me. By some miracle, one of the bullets hits a guard, and my eyes water uncontrollably from the pain in my shoulder. I just ripped my stitches. I'm sure of it.

Another guard stands across from me. I lie flat on my stomach and point both guns at him, my arms resting on the floor. I stare into the black pinprick that is his gun barrel.

Then something surprising happens. He jerks his chin to the side. Telling me to go.

He must be Divergent.

"All clear!" I shout.

The guard ducks into the fear landscape room, and he's gone.

Slowly I get to my feet, holding my right arm against my

chest. I have tunnel vision. I am running along this path and I will not be able to stop, will not be able to think of anything, until I reach the end.

I hand one gun to Caleb and slide the other one under my belt.

"I think you and Marcus should stay here with *him*," I say, jerking my head toward Peter. "He'll just slow us down. Make sure no one comes after us."

I hope he doesn't understand what I'm doing—keeping him here so he stays safe, even though he would gladly give his life for this. If I go up into the building, I probably won't come back down. The best I can hope for is to destroy the simulation before someone kills me. When did I decide on this suicide mission? Why wasn't it more difficult?

"I can't stay here while you go up there and risk your life," says Caleb.

"I need you to," I say.

Peter sinks to his knees. His face glistens with sweat. For a second I almost feel bad for him, but then I remember Edward, and the itch of fabric over my eyes as my attackers blindfolded me, and my sympathy is lost to hatred. Caleb eventually nods.

I approach one of the fallen guards and take his gun, keeping my eyes away from the injury that killed him.

My head pounds. I haven't eaten; I haven't slept; I haven't sobbed or screamed or even paused for a moment. I bite my lip and push myself toward the elevators on the right side of the room. Level eight.

Once the elevator doors close, I lean the side of my head against the glass and listen to the beeps.

I glance at my father.

"Thank you. For protecting Caleb," my father says. "Beatrice, I—"

The elevator reaches the eighth floor and the doors open. Two guards stand ready with guns in hand, their faces blank. My eyes widen, and I drop to my belly on the ground as the shots go off. I hear bullets strike glass. The guards slump to the ground, one alive and groaning, the other fading fast. My father stands above them, his gun still held out from his body.

I stumble to my feet. Guards run down the hallway on the left. Judging by the synchronicity of their footsteps, they are controlled by the simulation. I could run down the right hallway, but if the guards came from the left hallway, that's where the computers are. I drop to the ground between the guards my father just shot and lie as still as I can.

My father jumps out of the elevator and sprints down the right hallway, drawing the Dauntless guards after

him. I clap my hand over my mouth to keep from screaming at him. That hallway will end.

I try to bury my head so I don't see it, but I can't. I peer
over the fallen guard's back. My father fires over his
shoulder at the guards pursuing him, but he is not fast
enough. One of them fires at his stomach, and he groans
so loud I can almost feel it in my chest.

He clutches his gut, his shoulders hitting the wall, and
fires again. And again. The guards are under the simulation; they keep moving even when the bullets hit them,
keep moving until their hearts stop, but they don't reach
my father. Blood spills over his hand and the color drains
from his face. Another shot and the last guard is down.

"Dad," I say. I mean for it to be a shout, but it is just a
wheeze.

He slumps to the ground. Our eyes meet like the yards
between us are nothing.

His mouth opens like he's about to say something, but
then his chin drops to his chest and his body relaxes.

My eyes burn and I am too weak to rise; the scent of
sweat and blood makes me feel sick. I want to rest my head
on the ground and let that be the end of it. I want to sleep
now and never wake.

But what I said to my father before was right—for every
second that I waste, another Abnegation member dies.

There is only one thing left for me in the world now, and it is to destroy the simulation.

I push myself up and run down the hallway, turning right at the end. There is only one door ahead. I open it.

The opposite wall is made up entirely of screens, each a foot tall and a foot wide. There are dozens of them, each one showing a different part of the city. The fence. The Hub. The streets in the Abnegation sector, now crawling with Dauntless soldiers. The ground level of the building below us, where Caleb, Marcus, and Peter wait for me to return. It is a wall of everything I have ever seen, everything I have ever known.

One of the screens has a line of code on it instead of an image. It breezes past faster than I can read. It is the simulation, the code already compiled, a complicated list of commands that anticipate and address a thousand different outcomes.

In front of the screen is a chair and a desk. Sitting in the chair is a Dauntless soldier.

"Tobias," I say.

CHAPTER
THIRTY-EIGHT

TOBIAS'S HEAD TURNS, and his dark eyes shift to me. His eyebrows draw in. He stands. He looks confused. He raises his gun.

"Drop your weapon," he says.

"Tobias," I say, "you're in a simulation."

"Drop your weapon," he repeats. "Or I'll fire."

Jeanine said he didn't know me. Jeanine also said that the simulation made Tobias's friends into enemies. He will shoot me if he has to.

I set my gun down at my feet.

"Drop your weapon!" shouts Tobias.

"I did," I say. A little voice in my head sings that he can't hear me, he can't see me, he doesn't know me. Tongues of flame press behind my eyes. I can't just stand here and let him shoot me.

I run at him, grabbing his wrist. I feel his muscles shift as he pinches the trigger and duck my head just in time. The bullet hits the wall behind me. Gasping, I kick him in the ribs and twist his wrist to the side as hard as I can. He drops the gun.

I can't beat Tobias in a fight. I know that already. But I have to destroy the computer. I dive for the gun, but before I can touch it, he grabs me and wrenches me to the side.

I stare into his dark, conflicted eyes for an instant before he punches me in the jaw. My head jerks to the side and I cringe away from him, flinging my hands up to protect my face. I can't fall; I can't fall or he'll kick me, and that will be worse, that will be much worse. I kick the gun back with my heel so he can't grab it and, ignoring the throbbing in my jaw, kick him in the stomach.

He catches my foot and pulls me down so I fall on my shoulder. The pain makes my vision go black at the edges. I stare up at him. He pulls his foot back like he's about to kick me, and I roll onto my knees, stretching my arm out for the gun. I don't know what I'll do with it. I can't shoot him, I can't shoot him, I can't. He is in there somewhere.

He grabs me by my hair and yanks me to the side. I reach back and grab his wrist, but he's too strong and my forehead smacks into the wall.

He is in there somewhere.

"Tobias," I say.

Did his grip falter? I twist and kick back, my heel hitting him in the leg. When my hair slips through his fingers, I dive at the gun and my fingertips close around the cool metal. I flip over onto my back and point the gun at him.

"Tobias," I say. "I know you're in there somewhere."

But if he was, he probably wouldn't start toward me like he's about to kill me for certain this time.

My head throbs. I stand.

"Tobias, please." I am begging. I am pathetic. Tears make my face hot. "Please. See me." He walks toward me, his movements dangerous, fast, powerful. The gun shakes in my hands. "Please see me, Tobias, please!"

Even when he scowls, his eyes look thoughtful, and I remember how his mouth curled when he smiled.

I can't kill him. I am not sure if I love him; not sure if that's why. But I am sure of what he would do if our positions were reversed. I am sure that nothing is worth killing him for.

I have done this before—in my fear landscape, with the gun in my hand, a voice shouting at me to fire at the people I love. I volunteered to die instead, that time, but I can't imagine how that would help me now. But I just know, I *know* what the right thing to do is.

My father says—used to say—that there is power in self-sacrifice.

I turn the gun in my hands and press it into Tobias's palm.

He pushes the barrel into my forehead. My tears have stopped and the air feels cold as it touches my cheeks. I reach out and rest my hand on his chest so I can feel his heartbeat. At least his heartbeat is still him.

The bullet clicks into the chamber. Maybe it will be as easy to let him shoot me as it was in the fear landscape, as it is in my dreams. Maybe it will just be a bang, and the lights will lift, and I will find myself in another world. I stand still and wait.

Can I be forgiven for all I've done to get here?

I don't know. I don't know.

Please.

CHAPTER
THIRTY-NINE

THE SHOT DOESN'T come. He stares at me with the same
ferocity but doesn't move. Why doesn't he shoot me? His
heart pounds against my palm, and my own heart lifts.
He is Divergent. He can fight this simulation. Any
simulation.

"Tobias," I say. "It's me."

I step forward and wrap my arms around him. His body
is stiff. His heart beats faster. I can feel it against my cheek.
A thud against my cheek. A thud as the gun hits the floor.
He grabs my shoulders—too hard, his fingers digging into
my skin where the bullet was. I cry out as he pulls me back.
Maybe he means to kill me in some crueler way.

"Tris," he says, and it's him again. His mouth collides
with mine.

His arm wraps around me and he lifts me up, holding

me against him, his hands clutching at my back. His face and the back of his neck are slick with sweat, his body is shaking, and my shoulder blazes with pain, but I don't care, I don't care, I don't care.

He sets me down and stares at me, his fingers brushing over my forehead, my eyebrows, my cheeks, my lips.

Something like a sob and a sigh and a moan escapes him, and he kisses me again. His eyes are bright with tears. I never thought I would see Tobias cry. It makes me hurt.

I pull myself to his chest and cry into his shirt. All the throbbing in my head comes back, and the ache in my shoulder, and I feel like my body weight doubles. I lean against him, and he supports me.

"How did you do it?" I say.

"I don't know," he says. "I just heard your voice."

+ + +

After a few seconds, I remember why I'm here. I pull back and wipe my cheeks with the heels of my hands and turn toward the screens again. I see one that overlooks the drinking fountain. Tobias was so paranoid when I was railing against Dauntless there. He kept looking at the wall above the fountain. Now I know why.

Tobias and I stand there for a while, and I think I know what he's thinking, because I'm thinking it too: How can something so small control so many people?

"Was *I* running the simulation?" he says.

"I don't know if you were running it so much as monitoring it," I say. "It's already complete. I have no idea how, but Jeanine made it so it could work on its own."

He shakes his head. "It's . . . incredible. Terrible, evil . . . but incredible."

I see movement on one of the screens and see my brother, Marcus, and Peter standing on the first floor of the building. Surrounding them are Dauntless soldiers, all in black, all carrying weapons.

"Tobias," I say tersely. "Now!"

He runs to the computer screen and taps it a few times with his finger. I can't look at what he's doing. All I can see is my brother. He holds the gun I gave him straight out from his body, like he's ready to use it. I bite my lip. *Don't shoot.* Tobias presses the screen a few more times, typing in letters that make no sense to me. *Don't shoot.*

I see a flash of light—a spark, from one of the guns— and gasp. My brother and Marcus and Peter crouch on the ground with their arms over their heads. After a moment they all stir, so I know they're still alive, and the Dauntless soldiers advance. A cluster of black around my brother.

"Tobias," I say.

He presses the screen again, and everyone on the first floor goes still.

Their arms drop to their sides.

And then the Dauntless move. Their heads turn from side to side, and they drop their guns, and their mouths move like they're shouting, and they shove each other, and some of them sink to their knees, holding their heads and rocking back and forth, back and forth.

All the tension in my chest unravels, and I sit down, heaving a sigh.

Tobias crouches next to the computer and pulls the side of the case off.

"I have to get the data," he says, "or they'll just start the simulation again."

I watch the frenzy on the screen. It is the same frenzy that must be happening on the streets. I scan the screens, one by one, looking for one that shows the Abnegation sector of the city. There is only one—it's at the far end of the room, on the bottom. The Dauntless on that screen are firing at one another, shoving one another, screaming— chaos. Black-clothed men and women drop to the ground. People sprint in every direction.

"Got it," says Tobias, holding up the computer's hard drive. It is a piece of metal about the size of his palm. He offers it to me, and I shove it in my back pocket.

"We have to leave," I say, getting to my feet. I point at the screen on the right.

"Yes, we do." He wraps his arm across my shoulders. "Come on."

We walk together down the hallway and around the corner. The elevator reminds me of my father. I can't stop myself from looking for his body.

It is on the floor next to the elevator, surrounded by the bodies of several guards. A strangled scream escapes me. I turn away. Bile leaps into my throat and I throw up against the wall.

For a second I feel like everything inside me is breaking, and I crouch by a body, breathing through my mouth so I don't smell the blood. I clamp my hand over my mouth to contain a sob. Five more seconds. Five seconds of weakness and then I get up. One, two. Three, four.

Five.

+ + +

I am not really aware of my surroundings. There is an elevator and a glass room and a rush of cold air. There is a shouting crowd of Dauntless soldiers dressed in black. I search for Caleb's face, but it is nowhere, nowhere until we leave the glass building and step out into sunlight.

Caleb runs to me when I walk through the doors, and I

fall against him. He holds me tightly.

"Dad?" he says.

I just shake my head.

"Well," he says, almost choking on the word, "he would have wanted it that way."

Over Caleb's shoulder, I see Tobias stop in the middle of a footstep. His entire body goes rigid as his eyes focus on Marcus. In the rush to destroy the simulation, I forgot to warn him.

Marcus walks up to Tobias and wraps his arms around his son. Tobias stays frozen, his arms at his sides and his face blank. I watch his Adam's apple bob up and down and his eyes lift to the ceiling.

"Son," sighs Marcus.

Tobias winces.

"Hey," I say, pulling away from Caleb. I remember the belt stinging on my wrist in Tobias's fear landscape and slip into the space between them, pushing Marcus back. "Hey. Get away from him."

I feel Tobias's breaths against my neck; they come in sharp bursts.

"Stay away," I hiss.

"Beatrice, what are you doing?" asks Caleb.

"Tris," Tobias says.

Marcus gives me a scandalized look that seems false to

me—his eyes are too wide and his mouth is too open. If I could find a way to smack that look off his face, I would.

"Not all those Erudite articles were full of lies," I say, narrowing my eyes at Marcus.

"What are you talking about?" Marcus says quietly. "I don't know what you've been told, Beatrice, but—"

"The only reason I haven't shot you yet is because he's the one who should get to do it," I say. "Stay away from him or I'll decide I no longer care."

Tobias's hands slip around my arms and squeeze. Marcus's eyes stay on mine for a few seconds, and I can't help but see them as black pits, like they were in Tobias's fear landscape. Then he looks away.

"We have to go," Tobias says unsteadily. "The train should be here any second."

We walk over unyielding ground toward the train tracks. Tobias's jaw is clenched and he stares straight ahead. I feel a twinge of regret. Maybe I should have let him deal with his father on his own.

"Sorry," I mutter.

"You have nothing to be sorry for," he replies, taking my hand. His fingers are still shaking.

"If we take the train in the opposite direction, out of the city instead of in, we can get to Amity headquarters," I say. "That's where the others went."

"What about Candor?" my brother asks. "What do you think they'll do?"

I don't know how Candor will respond to the attack. They wouldn't side with the Erudite—they would never do something that underhanded. But they may not fight the Erudite either.

We stand next to the tracks for a few minutes before the train comes. Eventually Tobias picks me up, because I am dead on my feet, and I lean my head into his shoulder, taking deep breaths of his skin. Since he saved me from the attack, I have associated his smell with safety, so as long as I focus on it, I feel safe now.

The truth is, I will not feel safe as long as Peter and Marcus are with us. I try not to look at them, but I feel their presence like I would feel a blanket over my face. The cruelty of fate is that I must travel with the people I hate when the people I love are dead behind me.

Dead, or waking as murderers. Where are Christina and Tori now? Wandering the streets, plagued with guilt for what they've done? Or turning guns on the people who forced them to do it? Or are they already dead too? I wish I knew.

At the same time, I hope I never find out. If she is still alive, Christina will find Will's body. And if she sees me again, her Candor-trained eyes will see that I am the one who killed him, I know it. I know it and the guilt strangles me and crushes me, so I have to forget it. I make myself forget it.

The train comes, and Tobias sets me down so I can jump on. I jog a few steps next to the car and then throw my body to the side, landing on my left arm. I wiggle my body inside and sit against the wall. Caleb sits across from me, and Tobias sits next to me, forming a barrier between my body and Marcus and Peter. My enemies. His enemies.

The train turns, and I see the city behind us. It will get smaller and smaller until we see where the tracks end, the forests and fields I last saw when I was too young to appreciate them. The kindness of Amity will comfort us for a while, though we can't stay there forever. Soon the Erudite and the corrupt Dauntless leaders will look for us, and we will have to move on.

Tobias pulls me against him. We bend our knees and our heads so that we are enclosed together in a room of our own making, unable to see those who trouble us, our breath mixing on the way in and on the way out.

"My parents," I say. "They died today."

Even though I said it, and even though I know it's true, it doesn't feel real.

"They died for *me*," I say. That feels important.

"They loved you," he replies. "To them there was no better way to show you."

I nod, and my eyes follow the line of his jaw.

"You nearly died today," he says. "I almost shot you. Why didn't you shoot me, Tris?"

"I couldn't do that," I say. "It would have been like shooting myself."

He looks pained and leans closer to me, so his lips brush mine when he speaks.

"I have something to tell you," he says.

I run my fingers along the tendons in his hand and look back at him.

"I might be in love with you." He smiles a little. "I'm waiting until I'm sure to tell you, though."

"That's sensible of you," I say, smiling too. "We should find some paper so you can make a list or a chart or something."

I feel his laughter against my side, his nose sliding along my jaw, his lips pressing behind my ear.

"Maybe I'm already sure," he says, "and I just don't want to frighten you."

I laugh a little. "Then you should know better."

"Fine," he says. "Then I love you."

I kiss him as the train slides into unlit, uncertain land. I kiss him for as long as I want, for longer than I should, given that my brother sits three feet away from me.

I reach into my pocket and take out the hard drive that contains the simulation data. I turn it in my hands, letting it catch the fading light and reflect it. Marcus's eyes cling greedily to the movement. *Not safe*, I think. *Not quite.*

I clutch the hard drive to my chest, lean my head on Tobias's shoulder, and try to sleep.

+ + +

Abnegation and Dauntless are both broken, their members scattered. We are like the factionless now. I do not know what life will be like, separated from a faction—it feels disengaged, like a leaf divided from the tree that gives it sustenance. We are creatures of loss; we have left everything behind. I have no home, no path, and no certainty. I am no longer Tris, the selfless, or Tris, the brave.

I suppose that now, I must become more than either.

ACKNOWLEDGMENTS

Thank you, God, for your Son and for blessing me beyond comprehension.

Thanks also to: Joanna Stampfel-Volpe, my badass agent, who works harder than anyone I know—your kindness and generosity continue to amaze me. Molly O'Neill, also known as the Editor of Wonder—I don't know how you manage to have a sharp editorial eye and a huge heart at the same time, but you do. I am so fortunate to have two people like you and Joanna on my side.

Katherine Tegen, who runs an amazing imprint. Barb Fitzsimmons, Amy Ryan, and Joel Tippie, who designed a beautiful and powerful cover. Brenna Franzitta, Amy Vinchesi, and Jennifer Strada, my production editor, copy editor, and proofreader (respectively), also known as grammar/punctuation/formatting ninjas—your work is so important. Fantastic marketing and publicity directors Suzanne Daghlian, Patty Rosati, Colleen O'Connell, and Sandee Roston; Allison Verost, my publicist; and everyone else in the marketing and publicity departments.

Jean McGinley, Alpha Wong, and the rest of the subrights team, who have made it possible for my book to be read in more languages than I will ever be able to read, and thanks to all the amazing foreign publishers who have given my book a home. The production team and the HarperMedia audio and e-book team, for all their hard work. The brilliant people over in sales, who have done so much for my book, and who, I've heard, have almost as much love for Four as I do. And everyone else at HarperCollins who has supported my book—it takes a village, and I'm so happy to live in yours.

Nancy Coffey, literary agent legend, for believing in my book and for giving me such a warm welcome. Pouya Shahbazian, for being a film-rights whiz and for supporting my *Top Chef* addiction. Shauna Seliy, Brian Bouldrey, and Averill Curdy, my professors, for helping me to drastically improve my writing. Jennifer Wood, my writing buddy, for her expert brainstorming skills. Sumayyah Daud, Veronique Pettingill, Kathy Bradey, Debra Driza, Lara Erlich, and Abigail Schmidt, my beta readers, for all their notes and enthusiasm. Nelson Fitch, for taking my pictures and being so supportive.

My friends, who stick with me even when I'm moody and reclusive. Mike, for teaching me a lot about life. Ingrid and Karl, my sister and brother, for their unfailing love and enthusiasm, and Frank, for talking me through the hard stuff—your support means more to me than you know. And Barbara, my mother, who always encouraged me to write, even before any of us knew that it would come to anything.

DIVERGENT

BONUS MATERIALS

BONUS MATERIALS

Why do you feel people are naturally drawn to reading books about dystopian societies?

There are many reasons, I'm sure, but I think dystopian books are perfect for people who like to ask "what if?" but want to see their "what if?" questions played out in a world that has the same rules as our own (as opposed to paranormal or fantasy, in which the rules of the world— in terms of physics, or biology, or something—are a little different). There is also something extremely interesting about looking at the world now, reading about a possible future world, and imagining the steps in between. It's imaginative, yet grounded in the real world. I also love that the majority of the characters in dystopian and post-apocalyptic literature have a lot of agency—they take charge of their lives in environments that make it hard for them to do so, and I love reading about strong characters like that.

Where did the idea of DIVERGENT come from?

At the time that I came up with the idea for DIVERGENT (about five years ago), I was studying exposure therapy in the treatment of phobias. Exposure therapy involves confronting a person with the stimulus that scares them (heights, spiders, etc.) repeatedly, in a safe environment, until their brain rewires and they aren't afraid of it anymore. This is where the Dauntless initiation process comes from—I wanted to write about a subculture of people who want to eradicate fear, and exposure therapy is how they go about doing it. I was also beginning to learn about social psychology and the Milgram experiment on obedience to authority figures, which made me think about how malleable our supposedly strict moral codes become in the right conditions. Something that DIVERGENT grapples with.

But really, what got me to write it down was that I was driving somewhere and listening to a song and I just imagined someone jumping off a building, but not for a self-destructive reason. And I wondered why someone would do that, and the exposure therapy thing was the answer. And thus, Dauntless was born.

How and why did you start writing? And what inspires you?
I studied Creative Writing in college because it was the only thing I loved enough to do all the time. But I started writing because I decided I was too old to play pretend in the backyard. Then I found that I could create those imaginary worlds on the page. I think I was in fifth grade

or sixth grade when I started.

What inspires me now . . . well, that's a hard question! I try to follow my curiosity. I did that with DIVERGENT—I was curious about phobias and how to treat them, and learning about that helped me come up with the Dauntless initiation process. These days I'm curious about the northern lights and the social organization of ants. I have no idea how those things could make a book, but I don't worry about it—I just learn about what interests me, and write about what I find my mind returning to, and see what happens.

Is there a character in DIVERGENT who you like especially? If so, why?
I love a lot of the characters, but one of my favorites is Tobias. To me he seems to have a rich off-screen life. I can imagine what he's doing at any given moment, even if he's not with Tris. I try to do that with all the characters, but for him, it has always come naturally. I also think he balances strength with vulnerability well.

What made you choose Chicago as the setting for your book?
It wasn't a conscious decision, at first. I set the book in a city that felt familiar to me. What clued me in to the

fact that it was Chicago was the trains—constantly running, all over the city, like the El in present-day Chicago. I wrote about the Dauntless riding the trains before I realized that the only place I have ever been where trains are aboveground and in constant motion is Chicago—that I had been writing about my favorite city without even knowing it. I have lived next to Chicago since I was five years old, so it is both familiar to me and unfamiliar, because I've never actually lived there. As I worked more and more of the city into the manuscript, I got the chance to rediscover my home, which was wonderful—there's so much I don't know about it! But my personal connections with the place aside, I also found it interesting to turn such a clean and organized place upside down.

If you had to choose, which faction would you join?
I've decided there's a difference between figuring out which faction you have aptitude for and choosing which one you'd like to be in. No one fits into a faction perfectly, so determining your aptitude is extremely difficult. But as for choosing a faction, it's all about priorities. Do you value happiness over justice? You might be Amity. How about honesty over kindness? Candor. And I would choose Dauntless, probably, because I believe in freedom and justice over comfort and safety. I might die during

initiation. I'm almost sure of it, actually. I believe I would choose Dauntless not because of a thirst for freedom, although that's certainly appealing, but because I think courage is so important. I would be compelled to choose them not by aptitude, necessarily, but by ideology. For the record, though, my favorite faction is Abnegation, so I might pick them if I was too afraid to choose Dauntless. I think the way they live is fascinating, and they, though not without their flaws, generally live beautiful, good lives.

This book is full of heart-pounding action, which begs the question, are you a thrill-seeker at heart?
Absolutely not. I am terrified of heights. And speed. And danger of any kind. Sometimes writing DIVERGENT gave me vertigo. Like in the zip line scene—even if you paid me a billion dollars, I would never do what Tris does in that scene. I don't think I'm a coward, but I don't like to take unnecessary risks. Also, I'm a writer, and as a group, we tend to be built for coffee shops, carpal tunnel syndrome, and comfortable chairs rather than jumping off buildings.

What characteristics did you keep in mind when you were coming up with the main character, Beatrice?
I don't think I ever sat down and thought about how

Beatrice was—I just had this sense of her, like I *knew* her. I did set myself a rule that was hard to follow, though: Beatrice is always the agent. That is, she's always choosing, always acting, always moving the plot by her behavior. I don't know that I succeeded in keeping that rule, but it was helpful for me when trying to create an active, rather than a passive or reactive, character.

How has your childhood influenced your writing?
My mother read to me every night when I was young, so that's probably where my love of books began. And also, if I ever complained about being bored, my mother said, "Boredom is not allowed," so I guess you could say that the rules of our house demanded that I be creative. It worked, though, because I used to go outside every day and invent these elaborate worlds and scenarios in my head, and when I grew too old for playing pretend, I started to write everything down instead. Nicely done, Mom.

What book(s) changed your life and why?
I could probably list books for days, so I'll just list a few favorites: *The Giver* by Lois Lowry, *Ender's Game* by Orson Scott Card, *A Wrinkle in Time* by Madeleine L'Engle, the Animorphs series by K.A. Applegate, *1984* by George Orwell, the Bible, *Gilead* by Marilynne Robinson, and

Juliet by Andras Visky (which is a play, but I think it still counts). Some have taught me about writing, but even if they didn't, they all inspired me, challenged me, encouraged me, and guided me in different ways. I don't think books have ever solved my problems or made my decisions for me, but they bring me out of myself and make me ask myself questions, and that's life altering enough.

Do you think that you make wise or flawed decisions? Why?

I make both. Doesn't everyone? Usually the flawed ones are decisions I think are wise but are really motivated by something else—pride, maybe, or selfishness—and the wise ones happen when I'm not paying attention, or at those brief moments I succeed at loving the people around me. To be honest, the flawed ones are probably more common. But I try to learn from them.

How do you get through a dark day?

For me, one of the worst things I can do on a bad day is withdraw from people—but it's one of the easiest things for me to do. In the past few years I've been learning to rely on friends and family. Now, when my pride says "Deal with it yourself," I try to say, "Screw that. I need help." I have realized that there's no shame in letting the people I love take care of me. Most of the time they do a better job at it than I even realize.

What thought or message would you put in a fortune cookie?
"Stop reading this. Eat the cookie and live your life."

Quotations that Inspired divergent

VERONICA: This quote was actually integral to my discovery of Tris's voice. I wanted to create a character who could and would deliver that line, and Tris can and will. Her voice is clipped, direct, and strong, just like these lines.

> *"My will is mine. . . . I shall not make it soft for you."*
> —Agamemnon, *Aeschylus*

VERONICA: Sometimes I imagine Tris repeating this to herself during her initiation, over and over again.

> *"I must not fear. Fear is the mind-killer. Fear is the little-death that brings total obliteration. I will face my fear. I will permit it to pass over me and through me. And when it has gone past I will turn the inner eye to see its path. Where the fear has gone there will be nothing. Only I will remain."*
> —Dune *by Frank Herbert*

VERONICA: This, I imagine, is what Tris's enemies would say to her. And they would be wrong.

> *"Well, let her know the stubbornest of wills*
> *Are soonest bended, as the hardest iron,*

O'er-heated in the fire to brittleness,
Flies soonest into fragments, shivered through."
—Antigone, *Sophocles*

VERONICA: A word of advice to the faction that causes so much trouble—and to every flawed human being.

"But if you bite and devour one another, watch out
that you are not consumed by one another."
—*Galatians 5:15*

VERONICA: These lines, I imagine, would inspire the people in Tris's world to fight the good fight.

"Hold on to the world we all remember fighting for
There's some strength left in us yet
Hold on to the world we all remember dying for
There's some hope left in it yet
Arise and be
All that you dreamed."
—*"Arise" by Flyleaf*

VERONICA: For Tris and the people who help her at the end.

Tho' much is taken, much abides; and tho'
We are not now that strength which in the old days
Moved earth and heaven; that which we are, we are;
One equal temper of heroic hearts,
Made weak by time and fate, but strong in will
To strive, to seek, to find, and not to yield.
—*"Ulysses," Lord Alfred Tennyson*

1. "Starts With One" by Shiny Toy Guns. This song gets me in touch with the good aspects of Beatrice's chosen faction.

2. "Chasm" by Flyleaf. And this song gets me in touch with the *bad* aspects of Beatrice's chosen faction.

3. "Come Alive" by Foo Fighters. This is the love interest's song for Beatrice.

4. "Again" by Flyleaf. And this is Beatrice's song for her love interest.

5. "Help I'm Alive" by Metric. This is Beatrice's initiation song.

6. "We Die Young" by The Showdown. This might as well be the theme song for Beatrice's chosen faction—it's what they would choose for themselves.

7. "Canvas" by Imogen Heap. This is the "riding on trains" song.

8. "Running Up That Hill" by Placebo. The tone of this song matches the tone of much of the book, for me.

9. "Sweet Sacrifice" by Evanescence. I was listening to this song when the first scene I wrote (in chapter 6) popped into my head. That scene led me to the world of the book and its basic plot.

10. "Arise" by Flyleaf. A powerful song that's perfect for chapters 38 and 39.

Writing Tips from Veronica Roth

MY TIPS INVOLVE A SERIES OF STAGES:

STAGE ONE: Word Vomit. (Sorry for the graphic image there.) Just write. Do not reread what you've just written, even if you don't remember it and you want to check it for the sake of consistency. Don't do it! You will be tempted to edit, and editing before you finish the draft is the enemy of writing progress.

STAGE TWO: Let it sit for a while. This is a good time for you to reconnect with friends and family you may have neglected while writing, and to recharge your writer batteries, so to speak. Not writing is as important as writing—go out into the world and remember how interesting it, and the people in it, are.

STAGE THREE: Reread, and make notes. I prefer the Microsoft Word in-text comments, but I have also used notebooks. I try to write down big, plot-or-character-shifting things the first time I reread. Like "remove this character" or "the end has to happen differently" or "set up this huge plot element earlier in the story."

STAGE FOUR: Rip draft to shreds. The phrase "murder your darlings" (meaning: the stuff in your manuscript that you love best is probably the stuff that needs to go—and you have to be willing to get rid of it) has been important to me in developing as a writer. I try to make it a big, dramatic event wherein I save my old draft, copy-paste the text into a new document, and start deleting huge sections of text. It hurts, but it's oddly liberating. The story can become something new now—something better than it was before, something it couldn't become if you clung to everything.

STAGE FIVE: Start writing again.

Discussion Questions

1. What purpose does each of the five factions serve in society? What personality types are drawn toward each faction? Do you think these factions represent every basic personality type and fulfill all the basic needs of people? If not, what faction(s) would you create to fill in any gaps?

2. What was the reason behind the creation of the factions? Do you agree or disagree that such a system is a beneficial way to structure a society? Do you think the factions are working "toward a better society and a better world" (p. 44) as they say they are? What about the structure seems to be working for Tris's society? What doesn't seem to be working at all?

3. What faction do you think you would have been born into, given your family and its values? Which faction would you select at your Choosing Ceremony? Why? How would you feel about making a decision that would determine your life's course at the age of sixteen?

4. What choices have you made that have transformed you? What future choices might you also make, and how do you think that they will change you?

5. How does the idea of "faction before blood" come into play throughout the book? Do you think this idea has a place in today's society, or is it contrary to what most people believe? In our society, what ideas and beliefs are people loyal to in the way Tris's society is loyal to the concept of the factions?

6. Why is Tris's government run only by members of Abnegation? Do you think this is a good idea? Do you agree with her father's statement that "valuing knowledge above all else results in a lust for power, and that leads men into dark and empty places" (p. 35)? Why or why not?

7. What does it mean to be factionless in Tris's society? How does a person become factionless?

8. Tris says about Candor, "It must require bravery to be honest all the time" (p. 62). Do you agree? Which do you think is a braver faction, Dauntless or Candor? Would you like to live in a society like Candor, where everyone tells the truth no matter how hard it is to hear?

9. During initiation, is it selfish of Tris to crave victory, or is it brave? Do Tris's friends have a right to be

jealous when she's ranked above them? If you were Tris, would you forgive them for their reactions?

10. How does initiation change and transform Tris? Do you think she made the right faction choice? How do you think she might have changed if she had chosen one of the other factions?

11. What is the difference between being fearless and learning to control your fears? Do you believe anyone can be truly fearless? What does Tris mean when she says that "half of bravery is perspective" (p. 458)?

12. Is Four's desire to be "brave, and selfless, *and* smart, *and* kind, *and* honest" (p. 405) realistic in the society in which he lives? Discuss examples of people in our own world who successfully bridge different cultures, perspectives, or ways of living.

13. Tris's mom says, "Human beings as a whole cannot be good for long before the bad creeps back in and poisons us again" (p. 441). Do you agree or disagree? Why?

14. At the beginning of the book, Tris does not understand

what it means to be Divergent. How do you think she would explain it by the end of the book?

15. When Tris encounters her old neighbor Robert after their Choosing Ceremony, he is concerned about her choice and insists, "You should be happy" (p. 127). Tris responds, "The goal of my life isn't just . . . to be happy" (p. 128). If Robert had then asked what *is* the goal of Tris's life, what do you think she would have said? If asked again at the end of the book, do you think she'd answer in the same way? How would you answer this question, if asked?

If utopian fiction became the new trend, instead of dystopian fiction, I wouldn't read it.

If you actually succeed in creating a utopia, you've created a world without conflict, in which everything is perfect. And if there's no conflict, there are no stories worth telling—or reading! It would be all "Jenny thought she might not be able to attain her lifelong dream of marshmallow taste tester for a little while . . . but she did!" and "John's dad said he couldn't go to the movies, so John asked really nicely and his dad changed his mind." I'm bored already.

But if I were going to create a utopia, I would make a world in which people are focused on their personal, moral obligations, and strive to be the best possible version of themselves. They would be allowed to choose whatever path they wanted in life. They would know what was expected of them, they would have a clear purpose, and they would have a strong sense of group identity and belonging. And there would be five factions. . . .

Oh, wait. I tried that already.

But seriously: DIVERGENT was my utopian world. I mean, that wasn't the plan. I never even set out to write *dystopian* fiction, that's just what I had when I was finished—at the beginning, I was just writing about a place I found interesting, and a character with a compelling story, and as I began to build the world, I realized that it was my utopia. And then I realized that my utopia was a terrible place, and no one should ever put me in charge of creating a perfect society.

Maybe it's a little depressing to think that my vision of a perfect world is actually so messed up, but I think it means that I don't really understand what "perfect" is. To me it's all about virtue and responsibility; to someone else it would be about happiness and peace, and happy drugs would be pumped into the water supply—but that sounds like a nightmare, doesn't it? Because both of us are wrong about perfect. We have no idea what it would look like, and our approximations of it are incomplete.

And that gives me a lot of hope, because if I don't know what perfect means, it's not something I can reach on my own. Which means that I can stop trying to be perfect and just try to love the people around me and the things I'm doing. And strangely enough, that's Tris's journey. She tries selflessness on for size, and then she tries bravery, but at the end, it's what she does out of love that's more important than any virtue.

I think maybe utopian fiction would actually look just

like dystopian fiction, depending on who you are. To the heartbroken person, a world that eradicates love might be a utopia; to the rest of us, it isn't. To the person who doesn't have a plan, a world in which everything is planned out for you might be a utopia; to those of us who like to choose our own adventure, it's definitely not.

So maybe I've changed my mind—maybe I would read utopian fiction. Or *maybe I already am*. What a scary thought.

I have been asked in the past if I made up the words for the faction names. I didn't, but I did intentionally choose unfamiliar words, for an assortment of reasons. One of them is that I wanted to slow down comprehension of what each faction stands for, so you learn as much by observing as by the name of the faction itself. Another is that the definitions of the more obscure words are more specific, in interesting ways. And a third is—since I'm being honest here—that they sound cooler.

People have also commented that the faction names are different parts of speech—three nouns (Candor, Amity, Abnegation) and two adjectives (Dauntless, Erudite). (For the record, I love this kind of grammar consciousness.) I am aware of that, and it was something I thought about in revisions. The reason for the discrepancy is that each faction chose their own names independently, just as they wrote their own manifestos independently, and formed their own customs and rules independently (to a certain extent, anyway). Keeping that in mind, I tried to pick the words that made the most sense for each faction without considering the other factions too much.

Abnegation: 1. to refuse or deny oneself (some rights, conveniences, etc.); reject; renounce. 2. to relinquish; give up

VERONICA: *I like the verbs in that first definition: "refuse," "deny," "reject," "renounce"—active forms of stripping things from your life. As opposed to "relinquish," "give up" in the second definition—which are more passive.*

Amity: 1. friendship; peaceful harmony. 2. mutual understanding and a peaceful relationship, especially between nations; peace; accord. 3. cordiality

VERONICA: *It's not just about banjos and apple-picking. It's about cultivating strong relationships and trying to understand each other. Oh, Amity.*

Candor: 1. the state or quality of being frank, open, and sincere in speech or expression; candidness. 2. freedom from bias; fairness; impartiality.

VERONICA: *That definition helped me flesh out Candor more, particularly in the second book,* INSURGENT. *The faction is not just trying to develop honesty—they're also trying to develop impartiality.*

Dauntless: fearless, undaunted. (Undaunted: courageously resolute, especially in the face of danger or difficulty; not discouraged.)

VERONICA: *It's those two definitions ("fearless" and "undaunted") that I found so fascinating. Being fearless and being undaunted are two different things. And the characters in* DIVERGENT *struggle with that distinction.*

Erudite: characterized by great knowledge; learned or scholarly

VERONICA: *The word "erudite" focuses on knowledge rather than intelligence—intelligence being something you're born with and can't necessarily control, and knowledge being something that you acquire. I find that interesting, given what I know about Erudite.*

Faction Quiz

1. You most want your friends and family to see you as someone who . . .
    a. Is willing to make sacrifices and help anyone in need.
    b. Is liked by everyone.
    c. Is trustworthy.
    d. Will protect them no matter what happens.
    e. Offers wise advice.

2. When you are faced with a difficult problem, you react by . . .
    a. Doing whatever will be the best thing for the greatest number of people.
    b. Creating a work of art that expresses your feelings about the situation.
    c. Debating the issue with your friends.
    d. Facing it head-on. What else would you do?
    e. Making a list of pros and cons, and then choosing the option that the evidence best supports.

3. What activity would you most likely find yourself doing on the weekend or on an unexpected day off?
    a. Volunteering

b. Painting, dancing, or writing poetry

c. Sharing opinions with your friends

d. Rock-climbing or skydiving!

e. Catching up on your homework or reading for pleasure

4. If you had to select one of the following options as a profession, which would you choose?

   a. Humanitarian

   b. Farmer

   c. Judge

   d. Firefighter

   e. Scientist

5. When choosing your outfit for the day, you select . . .

   a. Whatever will attract the least amount of attention.

   b. Something comfortable, but interesting to look at.

   c. Something that's simple, but still expresses your personality.

   d. Whatever will attract the most attention.

   e. Something that will not distract or inhibit you from what you have to do that day.

6. If you discovered that a friend's significant other was being unfaithful, you would . . .

a. Tell your friend because you feel that it would be unhealthy for him or her to continue in a relationship where such selfish behavior is present.

b. Sit them both down so that you can act as a mediator when they talk it over.

c. Tell your friend as soon as possible. You can't imagine keeping that knowledge a secret.

d. Confront the cheater! You might also take action by slashing the cheater's tires or egging his or her house—all in the name of protecting your friend, of course.

e. Keep it to yourself. Statistics prove that your friend will find out eventually.

7. What would you say is your highest priority in life right now?

a. Serving those around you

b. Finding peace and happiness for yourself

c. Seeking truth in all things

d. Developing your strength of character

e. Success in work or school

If you chose mostly *A*s, you are **ABNEGATION**. You don't like to draw attention to yourself, and you are more concerned about other people's contentment than your own. You find joy and fulfillment in making other people happier, safer, and healthier. You believe that the world would be a better place if selfishness were not so widespread. Other people see you as somewhat difficult to get to know, but also as quiet and kind.

If you chose mostly *B*s, you are **AMITY**. You are at peace when the people around you are getting along. You appreciate music and the arts, and it is easy to make you laugh. One of your goals is to find as much happiness as you can. You believe that aggression and hostility are to blame for most of the world's problems. Others see you as sometimes flaky or indecisive, but also as easygoing and warm.

If you chose mostly *C*s, you are **CANDOR**. You are honest with everyone, no matter how difficult it is, and no matter how much trouble it gets you into. You aren't easily offended, and would prefer to hear the truth even if it hurts. You believe that if everyone could be honest and forthright with each other, the world would be a much better place. Other people see you as sometimes insensitive, but also as trustworthy and confident.

If you chose mostly *D*s, you are **DAUNTLESS**. You love a good adrenaline rush, and you don't let other people dictate your behavior. You do what you believe is right no matter how difficult or frightening it is. You believe that the world would be better off if people were not afraid to do what was necessary to make things right. Others see you as often abrasive, but also as strong and bold.

If you chose mostly *E*s, you are **ERUDITE**. You enjoy learning new things, and you try to understand how everything works. You tend to make decisions based on logic rather than instinct or emotions. You believe the world would be a better place if everyone were well-educated and devoted to learning. Other people see you as sometimes condescending, but also as intelligent and insightful.

Abnegation: The Selfless
FACTION MANIFESTO

I will be my undoing
If I become my obsession.

I will forget the ones I love
If I do not serve them.

I will war with others
If I refuse to see them.

Therefore I choose to turn away
From my reflection,
To rely not on myself
But on my brothers and sisters,
To project always outward
Until I disappear.*

(*Some members add a final line: "And only God remains." That
is at the discretion of each member, and is not compulsory.)

AMITY: THE PEACEFUL
FACTION MANIFESTO

Conversations of Peace

TRUST

A Son says to his Mother: "Mother, today I fought with my friend."

His Mother says: "Why did you fight with your friend?"

"Because he demanded something of me, and I would not give it to him."

"Why did you not give it to him?"

"Because it was mine."

"My son, you now have your possessions, but you do not have your friend. Which would you rather have?"

"My friend."

"Then give freely, trusting that you will also be given what you need."

SELF-SUFFICIENCY

A Daughter says to her Father: "Father, today I fought with my friend."

Her Father says: "Why did you fight with your friend?"

"Because she insulted me, and I was angry."

"Why were you angry?"

"Because she lied about me." (*In some versions: "Because I was hurt by her words."*)

"My daughter, did your friend's words change who you are?"

"No."

"Then do not be angry. The opinions of others cannot damage you."

FORGIVENESS

A Husband says to his Wife: "Wife, today I fought with my enemy."

His Wife says: "Why did you fight with your enemy?"

"Because I hate him."

"My husband, why do you hate him?"

"Because he wronged me."

"The wrong is past. You must let it rest where it lies."

KINDNESS

A Wife says to her Husband: "Husband, today I fought with my enemy."

Her Husband says: "Why did you fight with your enemy?"

"Because I spoke cruel words to her."

"My wife, why did you speak cruel words to her?"

"Because I believed them to be true."

"Then you must no longer think cruel thoughts. Cruel thoughts lead to cruel words, and hurt you as much as they hurt their target."

(The following section was part of the original manifesto, but was later removed.)

INVOLVEMENT

One Friend says to Another: "Friend, today I fought with my enemy."

The Other Friend says: "Why did you fight with your enemy?"

"Because they were about to hurt you."

"Friend, why did you defend me?"

"Because I love you."

"Then I am grateful."

CANDOR: THE HONEST
FACTION MANIFESTO

DISHONESTY IS RAMPANT. DISHONESTY IS TEMPORARY.
DISHONESTY MAKES EVIL POSSIBLE.

As it stands now, lies pervade society, families, and even the internal life of the individual. One group lies to another group, parents lie to children, children lie to parents, friends lie to friends, individuals lie to themselves. Dishonesty has become so integral to the way we relate to one another that we rarely find ourselves in authentic relationships with others. Our dark secrets remain our own. Yet it is our dark secrets that cause conflict. When we are dishonest with the people around us, we begin to hate ourselves for lying; when we are dishonest with ourselves, we can never even attempt to correct the flaws we find within us, the flaws we are so desperate to hide from our loved ones, the flaws that make us lie.

What has become clear is that lies are just a temporary solution to a permanent problem. Lying to spare a person's feelings, even when the truth would help them to improve, damages them in the long run. Lying to protect yourself lasts for so long before the truth emerges. Like a wild animal, the truth is too powerful to remain caged. These are examples we can clearly see in our own lives, yet we fail to understand that they do not just apply to the dynamic between ourselves and our neighbors, or ourselves and our friends.

What is society but a web of individual-to-individual relationships? And what is conflict except one person's dark secret crashing into another person's dark secret? Dishonesty is a veil that shields one person from another. Dishonesty allows evil to persist, hidden from the eyes of those who would fight it.

DISHONESTY LEADS TO SUSPICION. SUSPICION LEADS TO CONFLICT. HONESTY LEADS TO PEACE.

We have a vision of an honest world. In this world, parents do not lie to their children, and children do not lie to their parents; friends do not lie to one another; spouses do not lie to each other. When we are asked our opinions we are free to give them without having to consider any other responses. When we engage in conversation with others, we do not have to evaluate their intentions, because they are transparent. We have no suspicion, and no one suspects us.

And most of all—yes, above all else—we are free to expose our dark secrets because we know the dark secrets of our neighbors, our friends, our spouses, our children, our parents, and our enemies. We know that while we are flawed in a unique way, we are not unique because we are flawed. Therefore we can be authentic. We have no suspicions. And we are at peace with those around us.

TRUTH MAKES US TRANSPARENT. TRUTH MAKES US STRONG. TRUTH MAKES US INEXTRICABLE.

We will raise our children to tell the truth. We will do this by encouraging them to speak their minds at every moment. For the child, withholding words is the same as lying.

We will be honest with our children even at the expense of their feelings. The only reason people cannot bear honesty now is because they were not raised hearing the truth about themselves, and they can't stand to. If children are raised to hear both honest praise and honest criticism, they will not be so fragile as to crumble beneath the scrutiny of their peers. A life of truth makes us strong.

Adulthood will be defined as a time at which each member of society is capable of bearing every other member's dark secrets, just as every other member will bear theirs. Therefore each member will be subjected to The Full Unveiling, in which every hidden part of their life is laid bare before their fellow members. They, too, will see the hidden parts of their fellow members' lives. In this way we bear one another's secrets. In this way we become inextricable:

TRUTH
MAKES
US
INEXTRICABLE.

ERUDITE: THE INTELLIGENT
FACTION MANIFESTO

WE SUBMIT THE FOLLOWING STATEMENTS AS TRUTH:

1. "Ignorance" is defined not as stupidity but as lack of knowledge.
2. Lack of knowledge inevitably leads to lack of understanding.
3. Lack of understanding leads to a disconnect among people with differences.
4. Disconnection among people with differences leads to conflict.
5. Knowledge is the only logical solution to the problem of conflict.

Therefore, we propose that in order to eliminate conflict, we must eliminate the disconnect among those with differences by correcting the lack of understanding that arises from ignorance with knowledge. The areas in which people must be educated are:

SOCIOLOGY
- So that the individual understands how society at large functions.

PSYCHOLOGY

- So that the individual understands how a person functions within that society.

MATHEMATICS

- So that the individual is prepared for further study in science, engineering, medicine, and technology.

SCIENCE

- So that the individual better understands how the world operates.
- So that the individual's study in other areas is supplemented.
- So that as many individuals as possible are prepared to enter the fields devoted to innovation and progress.

COMMUNICATION

- So that the individual knows how to speak and write clearly and effectively.

HISTORY

- So that the individual understands the mistakes and successes that have led us to this point.
- So that the individual learns to emulate those successes and avoid those mistakes.

Leaders must not be chosen based on charisma, popularity, or ease of communication, all of which are misleading and have little to do with the efficacy of a political leader.

An objective standard must be used in order to determine who is best fit to lead. That standard will be an intelligence test, administered to all adults when the present leader reaches fifty-five or begins to decline in brain function in a demonstrable way.

Those who, after rigorous studying, do not meet a minimum intelligence requirement will be exiled from the faction so they can be made useful. This is not an act of elitism but rather one of practicality: Those who are not intelligent enough to engage in the roles assigned to us—roles that require a considerable mental capacity—are better suited to menial work than to faction work. Menial work is required for the survival of society, and is therefore just as important as faction work.

Information must always be made available to all faction members at all times. The withholding of information is punishable by reprimand, imprisonment, and, eventually, exile. Every question that can be answered must be answered or at least engaged. Illogical thought processes must be challenged when they arise. Wrong answers must be corrected. Correct answers must be affirmed. If an answer to a question is unclear, it must be put to debate. All debates require evidence. Any controversial thought or idea must be supplemented by evidence in order to reduce the potential for conflict.

Intelligence must be used for the benefit, and not to the detriment, of society. Those who use intelligence for their own personal gain or to the detriment of others have not properly borne the responsibility of their gift, and are not welcome in our faction.

It bears repeating: Intelligence is a gift, not a right. It must be wielded not as a weapon but as a tool for the betterment of others.

DAUNTLESS: THE BRAVE
FACTION MANIFESTO

WE BELIEVE

that cowardice is to blame for the world's injustices.

WE BELIEVE

that peace is hard-won, that sometimes it is necessary
to fight for peace. But more than that:

WE BELIEVE

that justice is more important than peace.

WE BELIEVE

in freedom from fear, in denying fear the power to
influence our decisions.

WE BELIEVE

in ordinary acts of bravery, in the courage that
drives one person to stand up for another.

WE BELIEVE

in acknowledging fear and the extent to which it rules us.

WE BELIEVE

in facing that fear no matter what the cost to our comfort,
our happiness, or even our sanity.

WE BELIEVE

in shouting for those who can only whisper, in
defending those who cannot defend themselves.

WE BELIEVE,

not just in bold words but in bold deeds to match them.

WE BELIEVE

that pain and death are better than cowardice

and inaction, because

WE BELIEVE

in action.

WE DO NOT BELIEVE

in living comfortable lives.

WE DO NOT BELIEVE

that silence is useful.

WE DO NOT BELIEVE

in good manners.

WE DO NOT BELIEVE

in limiting the fullness of life.

WE DO NOT BELIEVE

in empty heads, empty mouths, or empty hands.

WE DO NOT BELIEVE

that learning to master violence encourages

unnecessary violence.

WE DO NOT BELIEVE

that we should be allowed to stand idly by.

WE DO NOT BELIEVE

that any other virtue is more important than bravery.

ONE CHOICE CAN TRANSFORM YOU . . .
ONE CHOICE CAN DESTROY YOU

DIVE INTO THIS SNEAK PEEK OF

INSURGENT

THE SECOND BOOK IN THE DIVERGENT TRILOGY

CHAPTER ONE

I WAKE WITH his name in my mouth.

Will.

Before I open my eyes, I watch him crumple to the pavement again. Dead.

My doing.

Tobias crouches in front of me, his hand on my left shoulder. The train car bumps over the rails, and Marcus, Peter, and Caleb stand by the doorway. I take a deep breath and hold it in an attempt to relieve some of the pressure that is building in my chest.

An hour ago, nothing that happened felt real to me. Now it does.

I breathe out, and the pressure is still there.

"Tris, come on," Tobias says, his dark eyes searching

mine. "We have to jump."

It is too dark to see where we are, but if we are getting off, we are probably close to the fence. Tobias helps me to my feet and guides me toward the doorway.

The others jump off one by one: Peter first, then Marcus, then Caleb. I take Tobias's hand. The wind picks up as we stand at the edge of the car opening, like a hand pushing me back, toward safety.

But we launch ourselves into darkness and land hard on the ground. The impact hurts the bullet wound in my shoulder. I bite my lip to keep from crying out, and search for my brother.

"Okay?" I say when I see him sitting in the grass a few feet away, rubbing his knee.

He nods. I hear him sniff like he's fending off tears, and I have to turn away.

We landed in the grass near the fence, several yards away from the worn path that the Amity trucks travel to deliver food to the city, and the gate that lets them out—the gate that is currently shut, locking us in. The fence towers over us, too high and flexible to climb over, too sturdy to knock down.

"There are supposed to be Dauntless guards here," says Marcus. "Where are they?"

"They were probably under the simulation," Tobias

says, "and are now . . ." He pauses. "Who knows where, doing who knows what."

We stopped the simulation—the weight of the hard drive in my back pocket reminds me—but we didn't pause to see the aftermath. What happened to our friends, our peers, our leaders, our factions? There is no way to know.

Tobias approaches a small metal box on the right side of the gate and opens it, revealing a keypad.

"Let's hope the Erudite didn't think to change this combination," he says as he types in a series of numbers. He stops at the eighth one, and the gate clicks open.

"How did you know that?" says Caleb. His voice sounds thick with emotion, so thick I am surprised it does not choke him on the way out.

"I worked in the Dauntless control room, monitoring the security system. We only change the codes twice a year," Tobias says.

"How lucky," says Caleb. He gives Tobias a wary look.

"Luck has nothing to do with it," Tobias says. "I only worked there because I wanted to make sure I could get out."

I shiver. The way he talks about getting out—it's like he thinks we're trapped. I never thought about it that way before, and now that seems foolish.

We walk in a small pack, Peter cradling his blood-soaked arm to his chest—the arm that I shot—and Marcus with his hand on Peter's shoulder, keeping him stable. Caleb wipes his cheeks every few seconds, and I know he's crying but I don't know how to comfort him, or why I am not crying myself.

Instead I take the lead, Tobias silent at my side, and though he does not touch me, he steadies me.

Pinpricks of light are the first sign that we are nearing Amity headquarters. Then squares of light that turn into glowing windows. A cluster of wooden and glass buildings.

Before we can reach them, we have to walk through an orchard. My feet sink into the ground, and above me, the branches grow into one another, forming a kind of tunnel. Dark fruit hangs among the leaves, ready to drop. The sharp, sweet smell of rotting apples mixes with the scent of wet earth in my nose.

When we get close, Marcus leaves Peter's side and walks in front. "I know where to go," he says.

He leads us past the first building to the second one on the left. All the buildings except the greenhouses are made of the same dark wood, unpainted, rough. I hear laughter through an open window. The contrast between the laughter and the stone stillness within me is jarring.

Marcus opens one of the doors. I would be shocked by the lack of security if we were not at Amity headquarters. They often straddle the line between trust and stupidity.

In this building the only sound is of our squeaking shoes. I don't hear Caleb crying anymore, but then, he was quiet about it before.

Marcus stops before an open room, where Johanna Reyes, representative of Amity, sits, staring out the window. I recognize her because it is hard to forget Johanna's face, whether you've seen her once or a thousand times. A scar stretches in a thick line from just above her right eyebrow to her lip, rendering her blind in one eye and giving her a lisp when she talks. I have only heard her speak once, but I remember. She would have been a beautiful woman if not for that scar.

"Oh, thank God," she says when she sees Marcus. She walks toward him with her arms open. Instead of embracing him, she just touches his shoulders, like she remembers the Abnegation's distaste for casual physical contact.

"The other members of your party got here a few hours ago, but they weren't sure if you had made it," she says. She is referring to the group of Abnegation who were with my father and Marcus in the safe house. I didn't even think to worry about them.

She looks over Marcus's shoulder, first at Tobias and Caleb, then at me, then at Peter.

"Oh my," she says, her eyes lingering on the blood soaking Peter's shirt. "I'll send for a doctor. I can grant you all permission to stay the night, but tomorrow, our community must decide together. And –" She eyes Tobias and me. "—they will likely not be enthusiastic about a Dauntless presence in our compound. I of course ask you to turn over any weapons you might have."

I wonder, suddenly, how she knows that I am Dauntless. I am still wearing a gray shirt. My father's shirt.

At that moment, his smell, which is an even mixture of soap and sweat, wafts upward, and it fills my nose, fills my entire head with him. I clench my hands so hard into fists that my fingernails cut into my skin. *Not here. Not here.*

Tobias hands over his gun, but when I reach behind me to take out my own concealed weapon, he grabs my hand, guiding it away from my back. Then he laces his fingers with mine to cover up what he just did.

I know it's smart to keep one of our guns. But it would have been a relief to hand it over.

"My name is Johanna Reyes," she says, extending her hand to me, and then Tobias. A Dauntless greeting. I am impressed by her awareness of the customs of other factions. I always forget how considerate the Amity are until I see it for myself.

"This is T—" Marcus starts, but Tobias interrupts him.

"My name is Four," he says. "This is Tris, Caleb, and Peter."

A few days ago, "Tobias" was a name only I knew, among the Dauntless; it was the piece of himself that he gave me. Outside Dauntless headquarters, I remember why he hid that name from the world. It's the name that binds him to Marcus.

"Welcome to the Amity compound," says Johanna. Her eyes fix on my face, and she smiles crookedly. "Let us take care of you."

We do let them. An Amity nurse gives me a salve—developed by Erudite to speed healing—to put on my shoulder, and then escorts Peter to the hospital ward to mend his arm. Johanna takes us to the cafeteria, and there we find rows of wooden tables as long as the room itself, and some of the Abnegation who were in the safe house with Caleb and my father. Susan is with them, and some of our old neighbors. They greet us—especially Marcus—with held-in tears and suppressed smiles.

I cling to Tobias's arm. I sag under the weight of the

members of my parents' faction, their lives, their tears.

One of the Abnegation puts a cup of steaming liquid under my nose and says, "Drink this. It will help you sleep, as it helped some of the others sleep. No dreams."

The liquid is pink-red, like strawberries. I grab the cup and drink it fast. For a few seconds the heat from the liquid makes me feel like I am full of something again. And as I drain the last drops from the cup, I feel myself relaxing. Someone leads me down the hallway, to a room with a bed in it. That is all.

CHAPTER
TWO

I open my eyes, terrified, my hands clutching at the
sheets. But I am not running through the streets of the
city, or the corridors of Dauntless headquarters. I am in
a bed in Amity headquarters, and the smell of sawdust is
in the air.

I shift, and wince as something digs into my back. I
reach behind me, and my fingers wrap around the gun.

For a moment I see Will standing before me, both our
guns between us, and I almost scream his name.

Then he's gone.

I get out of bed and lift the mattress with one hand,
propping it up on my knee. Then I shove the gun beneath
it and let the mattress bury it. Once it is out of sight and no
longer pressed to my skin, my head feels clearer.

Now that the adrenaline rush of yesterday is gone, and whatever made me sleep has worn off, the deep ache and shooting pains of my shoulder are intense. I am wearing the same clothes I wore last night. The corner of the hard drive peeks out from under my pillow, where I shoved it right before I fell asleep. On it is the simulation data that controlled the Dauntless, and the record of what the Erudite did. It feels too important for me to even touch, but I can't leave it here, so I grab it and wedge it between the dresser and the wall. Part of me thinks it would be a good idea to destroy it, but I know it contains the only record of my parents' deaths, so I'll settle for keeping it hidden.

Someone knocks on my door. I sit on the edge of the bed and try to smooth my hair down.

"Come in," I say.

The door opens, and Tobias steps halfway in, the door dividing his body in half. He wears the same jeans as yesterday, but a dark red T-shirt instead of his black one, probably borrowed from one of the Amity. It's a strange color on him, too bright, but when he leans his head back against the doorframe, I see that it makes the blue in his eyes lighter.

"The Amity are meeting in a half hour," he says. He quirks his eyebrows and adds, with a touch of melodrama, *"To decide our fate."*

I shake my head. "Never thought my fate would be in the hands of a bunch of Amity."

"Me either. Oh, I brought you something." He unscrews the cap of a small bottle and holds out a dropper full of clear liquid. "Pain medicine. Take a dropperful every six hours."

"Thanks." I squeeze the dropper into the back of my throat. The clear liquid tastes like old lemon.

He hooks a thumb in one of his belt loops, and says, "How are you, Beatrice?"

"Did you just call me *Beatrice*?"

"Thought I would give it a try." He smiles. "Not good?"

"Maybe on special occasions only. Initiation days, Choosing Days . . ." I pause. I was about to rattle off a few more holidays, but only the Abnegation celebrate them. The Dauntless have holidays of their own, I assume, but I don't know what they are. And anyway, the idea that we would celebrate anything right now is so ludicrous I don't continue.

"It's a deal." His smile fades. "How are you, Tris?"

It's not a strange question, after what we've been through, but I tense up when he asks it, worried that he'll somehow see into my mind. I haven't told him about Will yet. I want to, but I don't know how. Just the thought of saying the words out loud makes me feel so heavy I could break through the floorboards.

"I'm . . ." I shake my head a few times. "I don't know, Four. I'm awake. I . . ." I am still shaking my head. He slides his hand over my cheek, one finger anchored behind my ear. Then he tilts his head down and kisses me, sending a warm ache through my body. I wrap my hands around his arm, holding him there as long as I can. When he touches me, the hollowed-out feeling in my chest and stomach is not as noticeable.

I don't have to tell him. I can just try to forget—he can help me forget.

"I know," he says. "Sorry. I shouldn't have asked."

For a moment all I can think is, *How could you* possibly *know?* But something about his expression reminds me that he does know something about loss. He lost his mother when he was young. I don't remember how she died, just that we attended her funeral.

Suddenly I remember him clutching the curtains in his living room, about nine years old, wearing gray, his dark eyes shut. The image is fleeting, and it could be my imagination, not a memory.

He releases me. "I'll let you get ready."

The women's bathroom is two doors down. The floor is dark brown tile, and each shower stall has wooden walls and a plastic curtain separating it from the central aisle. A sign on the back wall says REMEMBER: TO CONSERVE RESOURCES, SHOWERS RUN FOR ONLY FIVE MINUTES.

The stream of water is cold, so I wouldn't want the extra minutes even if I could have them. I wash quickly with my left hand, leaving my right hand hanging at my side. The pain medicine Tobias gave me worked fast—the pain in my shoulder has already faded to a dull throb.

When I get out of the shower, a stack of clothes waits on my bed. It contains some yellow and red, from the Amity, and some gray, from the Abnegation, colors I rarely see side by side. If I had to guess, I would say that one of the Abnegation put the stack there for me. It's something they would think to do.

I pull on a pair of dark red pants made of denim—so long I have to roll them up three times—and a gray Abnegation shirt that is too big for me. The sleeves come down to my fingertips, and I roll them up, too. It hurts to move my right hand, so I keep the movements small and slow.

Someone knocks on the door. "Beatrice?" The soft voice is Susan's.

I open the door for her. She carries a tray of food, which she sets down on the bed. I search her face for a sign of what she has lost—her father, an Abnegation leader, didn't survive the attack—but I see only the placid determination characteristic of my old faction.

"I'm sorry the clothes don't fit," she says. "I'm sure we can find some better ones for you if the Amity allow us to stay."

"They're fine," I say. "Thank you."

"I heard you were shot," she says. "Do you need my help with your hair? Or your shoes?"

I am about to refuse, but I really do need help.

"Yes, thank you."

I sit down on a stool in front of the mirror, and she stands behind me, her eyes dutifully trained on the task at hand rather than her reflection. They do not lift, not even for an instant, as she runs a comb through my hair. And she doesn't ask about my shoulder, how I was shot, what happened when I left the Abnegation safe house to stop the simulation. I get the sense that if I were to whittle her down to her core, she would be Abnegation all the way through.

"Have you seen Robert yet?" I say. Her brother, Robert, chose Amity when I chose Dauntless, so he is somewhere in this compound. I wonder if their reunion will be anything like Caleb's and mine.

"Briefly, last night," she says. "I left him to grieve with his faction as I grieve with mine. It is nice to see him again, though."

I hear a finality in her tone that tells me the subject is closed.

"It's a shame this happened when it did," Susan says. "Our leaders were about to do something wonderful."

"Really? What?"

"I don't know." Susan blushes. "I just knew that something was happening. I didn't mean to be curious, I just noticed things."

"I wouldn't blame you for being curious," I say, "even if you had been."

She nods and keeps combing. I wonder what the Abnegation leaders—including my father—were doing. And I can't help but marvel at Susan's assumption that whatever they were doing was wonderful. I wish I could believe that of people again.

If I ever did.

"The Dauntless wear their hair down, right?" she says.

"Sometimes," I say. "Do you know how to braid?"

So her deft fingers tuck pieces of my hair into one braid that tickles the middle of my spine. I stare hard at my reflection until she finishes. I thank her when she's done, and she leaves with a small smile, closing the door behind her.

I keep staring, but I don't see myself. I can still feel her fingers brushing the back of my neck, so much like my mother's fingers, the last morning I spent with her. My eyes wet with tears, I rock back and forth on the stool, trying to push the memory from my mind. I am afraid that if I start to sob, I will never stop until I shrivel up like a raisin.

I see a sewing kit on the dresser. In it are two colors of thread, red and yellow, and a pair of scissors.

I feel calm as I undo the braid in my hair and comb it again. I part my hair down the middle and make sure that it is straight and flat. I close the scissors over the hair by my chin.

How can I look the same, when she's gone and everything is different? I can't.

I cut in as straight a line as I can, using my jaw as a guide. The tricky part is the back, which I can't see very well, so I do the best I can by touch instead of sight. Locks of blond hair surround me on the floor in a semicircle.

I leave the room without looking at my reflection again.

When Tobias and Caleb come to get me later, they stare at me like I am not the person they knew yesterday.

"You cut your hair," says Caleb, his eyebrows high. Grabbing hold of facts in the midst of shock is very Erudite of him. His hair sticks up on one side from where he slept on it, and his eyes are bloodshot.

"Yeah," I say. "It's . . . too hot for long hair."

"Fair enough," he says.

We walk down the hallway together. The floorboards creak beneath our feet. I miss the way my footsteps echoed in the Dauntless compound; I miss the cool underground air. But mostly I miss the fears of the past few weeks, rendered small by my fears now.

We exit the building. The outside air presses around me like a pillow meant to suffocate me. It smells green, the way a leaf does when you tear it in half.

"Does everyone know you're Marcus's son?" Caleb says. "The Abnegation, I mean?"

"Not to my knowledge," says Tobias, glancing at Caleb. "And I would appreciate it if you didn't mention it."

"I don't need to mention it. Anyone with eyes can see it for themselves." Caleb frowns at him. "How old are you, anyway?"

"Eighteen."

"And you don't think you're too old to be with my little sister?"

Tobias lets out a short laugh. "She isn't *your little anything*."

"Stop it. Both of you," I say. A crowd of people in yellow walks ahead of us, toward a wide, squat building made entirely of glass. The sunlight reflecting off the panes feels like a pinch to my eyes. I shield my face with my hand and keep walking.

The doors to the building are wide open. Around the edge of the circular greenhouse, plants and trees grow in troughs of water or small pools. Dozens of fans positioned around the room serve only to blow the hot air around, so I am already sweating. But that fades from my mind when the crowd before me thins, and I see the rest of the room.

In its center grows a huge tree. Its branches are spread over most of the greenhouse, and its roots bubble up from the ground, forming a dense web of bark. In the spaces between the roots, I see not dirt but water, and metal rods holding the roots in place. I should not be surprised—the Amity spend their lives accomplishing feats of agriculture like this one, with the help of Erudite technology.

Standing on a cluster of roots is Johanna Reyes, her hair falling over the scarred half of her face. I learned in Faction History that the Amity recognize no official leader—they vote on everything, and the result is usually close to unanimous. They are like many parts of a single mind, and Johanna is their mouthpiece.

The Amity sit on the floor, most with their legs crossed, in knots and clusters that vaguely resemble the tree roots to me. The Abnegation sit in tight rows a few yards to my left. My eyes search the crowd for a few seconds before I realize what I'm looking for: my parents.

I swallow hard, and try to forget. Tobias touches the small of my back, guiding me to the edge of the meeting space, behind the Abnegation. Before we sit down, he puts his mouth next to my ear and says, "I like your hair that way."

I find a small smile to give him, and lean into him when I sit down, my arm against his.

Johanna lifts her hands and bows her head. All conversation in the room ceases before I can draw my next breath. All around me the Amity sit in silence, some with their eyes closed, some with their lips mouthing words I can't hear, some staring at a point far away.

Every second chafes. By the time Johanna lifts her head I am worn to the bone.

"We have before us today an urgent question," she says, "which is: How will we conduct ourselves in this time of conflict, as people who pursue peace?"

Every Amity in the room turns to the person next to him or her and starts talking.

"How do they get anything done?" I say, as the minutes of chatter wear on.

"They don't care about efficiency," he says. "They care about agreement. Watch."

Two women in yellow dresses a few feet away rise and

join a trio of men. A young man shifts back so that his small circle becomes a large one with the group next to him. All around the room, the smaller crowds grow and expand, and fewer and fewer voices fill the room, until there are only three or four. I can only hear pieces of what they say: "Peace—Dauntless—Erudite—safe house—involvement—"

"This is bizarre," I say.

"I think it's beautiful," he says.

I give him a look.

"What?" He laughs a little. "They each have an equal role in government; they each feel equally responsible. And it makes them care; it makes them kind. I think that's beautiful."

"I think it's unsustainable," I say. "Sure, it works for the Amity. But what happens when not everyone wants to strum banjos and grow crops? What happens when someone does something terrible and talking about it can't solve the problem?"

He shrugs. "I guess we'll find out."

Eventually someone from each of the big groups stands and approaches Johanna, picking their way carefully over the roots of the big tree. I expect them to address the rest of us, but instead they stand in a circle with Johanna and the other spokespeople and talk quietly. I begin to get the feeling that I will never know what they're saying.

"They're not going to let us argue with them, are they," I say.

"I doubt it," he says.

We are done for.

When everyone has said his or her piece, they sit down again, leaving Johanna alone in the center of the room. She angles her body toward us and folds her hands in front of her. Where will we go when they tell us to leave? Back into the city, where nothing is safe?

"Our faction has had a close relationship with Erudite for as long as any of us can remember. We need each other to survive, and we have always cooperated with each other," says Johanna. "But we have also had a strong relationship with Abnegation in the past, and we do not think it is right to revoke the hand of friendship when it has for so long been extended."

Her voice is honey-sweet, and moves like honey too, slow and careful. I wipe the sweat from my hairline with the back of my hand.

"We feel that the only way to preserve our relationships with both factions is to remain impartial and uninvolved," she continues. "Your presence here, though welcome, complicates that."

Here it comes, I think.

"We have arrived at the conclusion that we will establish

our faction headquarters as a safe house for members of all factions," she says, "under a set of conditions. The first is that no weaponry of any kind is allowed on the compound. The second is that if any serious conflict arises, whether verbal or physical, all involved parties will be asked to leave. The third is that the conflict may not be discussed, even privately, within the confines of this compound. And the fourth is that everyone who stays here must contribute to the welfare of this environment by working. We will report this to Erudite, Candor, and Dauntless as soon as we can."

Her stare drifts to Tobias and me, and stays there.

"You are welcome to stay here if and only if you can abide by our rules," she says. "That is our decision."

I think of the gun I hid under my mattress, and the tension between me and Peter, and Tobias and Marcus, and my mouth feels dry. I am not good at avoiding conflict.

"We won't be able to stay long," I say to Tobias, under my breath.

A moment ago, he was still faintly smiling. Now the corners of his mouth have disappeared into a frown. "No, we won't."

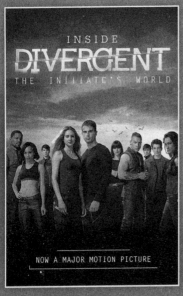